Courtroom Drama

Courtroom Drama

A Novel

Neely Tubati Alexander

THORNDIKE PRESS
A part of Gale, a Cengage Company

GALE
A Cengage Company

GALE
A Cengage Company

Thorndike Press, a part of Gale, a Cengage Company.

Thorndike Press® Large Print Diverse Voices.
The text of this Large Print edition is unabridged.
Other aspects of the book may vary from the original edition.
Set in 16 pt. Plantin.

**LIBRARY OF CONGRESS CIP DATA ON FILE.
CATALOGUING IN PUBLICATION FOR THIS BOOK
IS AVAILABLE FROM THE LIBRARY OF CONGRESS.**

ISBN-13: 978-1-4205-3036-0 (hardcover alk. paper)

Published in 2025 by arrangement with Harper Perennial, an imprint of HarperCollins Publishers.

Print Number: 1 Print Year: 2026
Printed in Mexico

For my fellow Bravoholics

Prejudice always obscures the truth.

— Henry Fonda as Juror #8,
Twelve Angry Men

Prologue

I'm sitting in traffic when I get the call.

Mel and I inch along the 101, just two miles from our Los Feliz exit, windows down to add a touch of pleasure to the forty-five minutes it's taken to creep six miles.

Despite the notorious L.A. gridlock, our daily commute is a highlight for me. My roommate, Mel, a watercolorist, has a studio just three blocks from my arbitration office. So, we commute together, in the carpool lane (shaving exactly four minutes from our drive time), while tuning in to our Rush Hour Rhythms playlist.

I glance at Mel, who's singing along to the SZA song pulsing from my car's speakers. The mere sight of her — eyes closed, head tilted back, body mid-sway — brings me a rush of amused comfort. With her extreme bohemian vibe (less Coachella, more full-on eccentric non-conformist), people sometimes write her off at first glance. But Mel is absolutely brilliant; her artistic specialty is melding intricate landscapes with dynamic animal silhouettes. My favorite hangs in our living room — a lush green forest of evergreens on the left side of the canvas that seamlessly melts into the outline of a resplendent brown stallion by the time your eyes adjust to the right edge. That piece reminds me of summer rides at horse camp as a kid, thus my insistence that we hang it prominently in our apartment. Despite her brilliance, Mel is still very much a starving artist, though we often refer to her as on the cusp of being "discovered."

"What do you think it'll be today?" Mel says, pointing to the digital roadway sign that's still several yards ahead, straining to register the words. Usually there's some clever pun that makes me smile. HANDS ON YOUR WHEEL, NOT YOUR MEAL last week. In the thick of summer, when the city held one collective scowl under triple-digit heat: THAT'S THE TEMPERATURE, NOT THE SPEED LIMIT.

"Maybe a Halloween pun?" I offer. "Something about 'don't become a ghost, wear your seat belt'?"

Mel snorts. It's one of her many endearing qualities — that she actually snorts when she laughs. It's this vibrating, piglike grunt that causes anyone in her vicinity to be instantly charmed. "That's horrible," she says when she's calmed.

We inch closer, Mel squinting to see. As the passenger, she usually deciphers the script before I can. " 'Texting while driving, oh cell no,' " she reads with delight when the words come into view.

I huff a laugh. She snorts.

It's funny, how something as negligible as a digital roadway sign pun can inject a micro-burst of happiness straight into my veins.

"I needed that," I say, releasing a breath and twisting a bit of tension from my neck.

"Rough day?" Mel asks, though I know she'd rather do most anything else than discuss the details of my job.

It *was* a particularly challenging day at work. A mediation between CEO and CFO cofounders of a late-stage fintech start-up. They had been a husband-and-wife team but are now going through a spiteful divorce and disputing ownership of shares as the company prepares for its highly anticipated IPO. Things got especially ugly this afternoon, the two of them at each other's throats, the line between business and personal so blurred it was difficult to keep negotiations on track.

"*He* thinks he deserves the majority of shares because she spent more time with her personal trainer than at work or with him. *She* thinks she deserves more because he spent nearly sixty thousand company dollars last year on an executive coach, which was really just a way for him to receive 'free therapy that didn't work,' " I recap.

"Yikes," Mel says, her standard response to any details of the mediations I handle at work. Anytime I regale her with stories from my day, it serves as a stark reminder to us both that she has positioned herself as far away from the corporate world as possible.

The truth is the whole situation today left me profoundly uneasy.

It's not the first time there have been heated arguments in my office; as a corporate mediator, it's to be expected. But this was the first time I've had to navigate the dissolution of both a business relationship *and* a marriage.

The scene today made me think of my parents, of the anxiety that still bubbles in me at the mere recall of their once marriage. It takes a lot to get me back to that place, but thinking of it all now causes a quake of unease at my core. I angle my head out the window to breathe in something fresh.

"At least it's Friday," Mel reminds me. She and I have big plans for the weekend. We've stocked the apartment with our favorite snacks — white cheddar Popchips, peanut butter pretzel bites, and two bags of those frozen chocolate-covered strawberries from Costco that I think about far too often. We plan to spend the entire weekend on the couch (save for the two hours on Saturday afternoon when Mel is teaching a watercolor class at the senior center up the road), re-watching as many seasons as possible of our favorite reality show before the start of what the media has dubbed the "Trial of the Malibu Menace."

When Margot Kitsch, an OG cast member of the hit reality show *Authentic Moms of Malibu,* was arrested for the murder of her husband, Joe, there was an immediate, unrelenting firestorm of public attention. It's to be expected, as Margot Kitsch is undeniably the most famous (or infamous, depending on who you ask) of all the Authentic Moms.

The trial is set to start a week from Monday.

Just as I'm daydreaming about being nestled on my couch beside Mel, a frozen chocolate-covered strawberry thawing in my mouth with season one of *AMOM* streaming, my phone rings.

Mel promptly lifts my phone from the cupholder between us, rakes her eyes over the screen, and then turns it to me. "Do you think it's them?"

I nod, anticipation tightening my sternum. I purposely memorized the number — *this* number — so I would not overlook the call I've been hoping for over the last several days.

"Syd! Answer it!" Mel demands, turning down the volume on the ominous Billie Eilish song now playing.

I take the phone from Mel and, still at a complete stop in traffic, answer on speaker. Mel and I stare at each other as the prerecorded message plays: "You have been selected . . . high-profile trial . . . jury sequestration . . . email with instructions . . ."

The high-pitched squeal Mel releases causes the driver beside me (his windows also down) to look over, irritated. I give him an apologetic wave/shrug combo and then hang up when the recording has ended.

Even through jury selection earlier this week, even as others were dismissed and I remained, I thought it a long shot.

"I've never been as thrilled to be your friend as I am in this moment," Mel says, squeezing me to her as tightly as the confines of the car will allow.

I can't help the smile that lifts the corners of my mouth.

Not only do I want this, but I feel like I *need* it. It's perhaps an odd thing to admit, I realize, that I might view serving on a sequestered jury in a high-profile murder trial as a welcome "break." But I do. The mounting pressure of monotony has been weighing on me as of late. I've worked so hard to get where I am. To be self-sufficient. Independent. I've been practically militant in my pursuit of success and autonomy, having spent the last ten years proving to myself that I don't need to rely on anyone for anything and never will again.

My *one* guilty pleasure is reality TV. And now, I'll have a direct influence on the most significant thing to ever happen in Margot Kitsch's life. And, perhaps, my own.

1.

High-Profile Case (phrase)

1. a case that attracts enough media or public attention that the court should make significant alterations to ordinary court procedures to manage it
2. the secret lives of celebrities

Ten Days Later

I'm buzzing with anticipation as I pull into the underground garage of the Los Angeles County Superior Court. I check the instructions on my phone again before exiting my car.

> If driving, park in the reserved spots on sublevel two past the boom barrier. Take the east elevator to the fourth floor, where a bailiff will meet you.

Your discretion is of the utmost importance.

The dramatics of the instructions only add to my anticipation.

I have to force away a grin as I step onto the cracked concrete, the click of my black suede heels rocketing from corner to corner of the synthetically lit space. I gather my roller bag from the trunk of my car, the chalk-white paint growing brittle at the trunk handle. The flickering light strip overhead hums and crackles ominously, emphasizing my aloneness. The garage is quiet and surprisingly clean, and I wonder for a moment if I have arrived at the right place and at the correct time, though there is no need to check. I've committed the instructions to memory. Despite this, I silently replay the five-page list of directives in my head as I enter the garage elevator, roller bag in tow, faux leather tote straps over my blazer-covered shoulder.

Don't enter or exit the main courtroom doors. Don't speak to those not directly involved in the case, including small talk.

Be aware of your surroundings.

Be wary of people who approach you.

My grin wins over.

It's perhaps unlikely that an *Authentic Moms of Malibu* fan would be chosen for the Margot Kitsch jury. During selection, nearly two weeks ago now, neither Margot nor *AMOM* was ever explicitly mentioned or asked about. I suppose the attorneys had given up on finding jurors who didn't know anything about the franchise; comments they made during the selection process made me believe it had been arduous and they'd already weeded through several jury pools. Because of this, there was little need to downplay my knowledge of her or the franchise (of which there are six different city casts — and I watch them all).

And while many people would have too much going on in their real lives to be sequestered for an indeterminate number of days, I only have work. No husband or kids for whom I am the sole caretaker (both reasons I heard during selection that allowed potential jurors to be excused). Work did take some finagling, as I've barely missed any days in my four years with my firm. No vacations and copious amounts of overtime have made them come to rely on and heavily benefit from my workaholic tendencies. I told them I tried every excuse I could to get myself out of this. It was a lie, of course.

In the Margot Kitsch case, because of the highly public nature of both victim and accused, and the rumors of attempted bribes to influence jury selection, sequestration was deemed not only appropriate but necessary by the presiding judge. This decision served to further captivate the public, as the last jury sequestered in California was seven years ago in the case of the L.A. Rams quarterback who ran over his offensive lineman with his custom-painted rose-gold Bugatti for missing a block. Allegedly.

Despite the public's immediate and swarming rush to the side of salaciousness and, thus, Margot's guilt, it's unfathomable to me that she could have killed Joe. They were married for twenty-four years. They have two young children together. She was utterly devoted, speaking often on the show about how much she not only loved him but *liked* him, which, from my experience, is perhaps the far greater accomplishment of the two.

As fans of the show, Mel and I have faithfully watched *AMOM* for all seven years it has been on air. In fact, *Authentic Moms of*

Malibu is the reason we met. Deep into an *AMOM* Reddit thread during the season four reunion, Mel (username AMOMsupportgrp) took on the many Margot haters and defended her decision to uninvite fellow Authentic Mom Tenley Storms from her birthday trip to Anguilla because she didn't want to be seen with someone who "wore fur to the Met Gala" and, equally disturbing, donned "so many god-awful statement necklaces."

There is NO excuse for Tenley wearing real fur, Mel had written. Not to mention, Tenley getting invited to the Met over Margot is a CRIME. Mel and I ended up live chatting during the next season's episodes. Six months later, when we both had leases expiring with unideal roommates (mine, found on Craigslist, used to lick bowls clean after use, then place them back into the cabinet), we moved in together, and our chats became side-by-side commentary on our Los Feliz couch. Having spent the last ten years of my life without many friends, no close ones at least, *AMOM* somehow became a lifeline to a real-life relationship. My most important one at that.

Interestingly, Margot would not be the first Authentic Mom to serve jail time. Harley Barlow from the Scottsdale franchise was pinned four years ago on tax fraud, and Nashville Authentic Mom Suzette Mortimer served two weeks for a DUI after careening her Range Rover into a neighbor's front gate. Needless to say, neither received a fraction of this case's attention.

In the elevator, I press the button for the fourth floor, per the instructions, though I'm rerouted to the main lobby, which I quickly realize is so I can be put through the security protocol of metal detectors and a bag search.

Here, I get my first tangible taste of the magnitude of the situation. Across the lobby, through the oversized tinted bay windows, is a horde of onlookers. The walkway and its grass-rimmed edges overflow with people, all attempting to glimpse the action. Reporters, paparazzi, fans, gawkers. I even catch sight of a few signs — homemade with markers on glossy white posterboard as if it were a Harry Styles concert. FREE MARGOT! one sign reads. WOMEN WHO WEAR CHANEL DON'T POISON THEIR HUSBANDS, reads another. And yet another, etched in messy bloodred spray paint: HANG THE MALIBU MENACE!

Aggressive.

I turn my attention to the sidewalk, where a guy sporting spiky hair with '90s-reminiscent frosted blond tips sells Margot Kitsch merch: hats, buttons, tees. One of the T-shirts facing my direction reads STYLE AND GRACE, BUT I'LL STILL SLAP YOU IN THE FACE — her *Authentic Moms* tagline.

I take in the red and brown leaves covering the ground in no discernible pattern, trampled by spectators, and the tree limbs that hang bare. I can practically hear the crisp, satisfying crunch of autumn leaves under their boots and sneakers as the shoes owners vie for better viewing placement like they're waiting for the headliner to take the main stage at a music festival.

Mel would die *if she saw this,* I think as I behold the spectacle, already anticipating the hours-long recap I'll owe her when this is over.

My eyes then catch on another of the signs held by an onlooker, causing my heart to knock firmly against my rib cage: JUSTICE FOR JOE. It's a tragedy that Joe is gone, that Margot lost her husband and their young kids lost their father. He does deserve justice, and that's why I want to ensure the correct verdict is reached — and Margot, vindicated.

My security check complete, I retreat into the elevator, but I can't unsee the circus.

My life is willfully small — just work and

Mel (and our reality shows) in an unwaning circle. I'm basically Elsa in the first half of "Let It Go" before she, you know, lets it go.

But all of this . . . this is something else entirely.

Before I can fully contemplate exactly what I've gotten myself into, the elevator door opens again on the fourth floor, which is thankfully a much quieter scene than the main lobby. I join six others with luggage, all standing avoidantly in separate sectors of the hallway. Even though we aren't yet twelve (technically, there will be fifteen of us, including three alternates), it's evident we, the jury, are a diverse group.

There's a guy leaning against the far wall with his black sweatshirt's hood over his sandy-blond hair, which pokes out in all directions, and a black backpack slung over one shoulder. He looks barely old enough to drive, let alone serve on a jury. Closest to him, a black woman in what I believe would be defined as a floral muumuu who looks to be in her early sixties. I recognize her from jury selection. She appears particularly pensive, her black eyes downturned, arms wrapped around herself protectively.

Soon, a new addition steps off the elevator, a handsome black man. His head is bald and so shiny it holds no remnants of once-there hair. With his Hawaiian shirt, flip-flops, and board shorts, it looks like he's just stepped off the red-eye from Honolulu.

I take them all in, wondering who might believe what about the case and about Margot Kitsch. At minimum, they've heard her name. In all likelihood, they have an opinion already formed about her, conscious or otherwise. I'm already eager for deliberations.

Hawaiian Shirt doesn't hesitate. Before the elevator door has closed, he approaches the woman in the muumuu, holding out his hand. "Xavier," he says as she slides her hand tentatively into his. Her eyes dart around the hallway, looking for a guard or camera, I presume, as if Hawaiian Shirt Xavier is some sort of plant, here to administer a first-day test of the rules. "Tamra," she returns, though barely audible.

"Tamra, nice to meet you," Xavier says. He then approaches the one I'm sure is a tween.

"Hey, man, Xavier." They exchange names, though from the opposite end of the hall I don't catch the younger one's.

Xavier circles back in my direction, reaching the man standing opposite Tamra. He's wearing a gray suit and has gray hair to match, with a perfectly round bald spot at his crown. With his large, almost obscene gold watch and intensely shiny shoes, he gives off a particularly rich scent. Xavier holds out his hand in greeting. Gray Man looks down at Xavier's hand, then at the wall. A clear rejection.

"No worries," Xavier says merrily, moving on to the next juror without hesitation.

I take note that Xavier would appear to be my early competition for the role of foreperson.

Busy observing Xavier's cordiality and debating whether I should jump in with my own impactful introductions, I don't immediately notice the next person stepping off the elevator. That is, until I feel his gaze. I see it in my peripheral, the exact moment it happens. He takes a few steps, then, when his eyes land on me, halts as if he's run into an invisible wall — a firm one with jagged edges and maybe some spikes. One glance in his direction is all it takes for recognition to strike, though my body might argue it knew before my eyes could verify.

Damon.

My insides flare and entangle, a muscle memory of a specific pain that only *this man* has ever been able to cause me. Our eyes catch, and for the briefest moment, his face explores a cascade of emotion. I see his recognition, surprise, discomfort — all of which surely match my own expression.

I tighten my grip on my roller bag, attempting to circumvent the free fall happening in my stomach, as though an elevator cord has been cut and we are careening to the bottom of the shaft.

He steps beside me.

"Sydney?" he says, continuing to stare, and it comes out as both a statement and a question. At my lack of immediate response, he runs his palm against the back of his neck. The act causes a needle prick of irritation in my chest. It's what he does when he's uncomfortable.

I observe with macabre amusement which memories resurface at the sight of him.

The gentle wrap of his arm from behind me, forearm curling against my neck in a gesture of warmth.

The antique shop on Chester Avenue back in Bakersfield where I held a peacock feather up to the side of his face to find his eyes a satisfying shade match to the outer green rim but also, somehow, equally paired to the bluer inner sphere.

Summer rain. Blades of grass stuck to the sides of our bare feet. His hair mopping his forehead in an adorable cling.

The memory of the last time I saw him

stampedes through my brain last, as if waiting to ensure its impact be felt most. Us at sixteen. His hair falling over his right eyebrow, shading his eye. Those blue-green eyes, more oval than almond. His jaw tight, muscle bulging across his right jawline, just as it is now. His entire body rigid, as if he had to clench every inch of himself to avoid collapsing in a pile onto his parents' driveway before me. "I don't know what to say," he had offered. "I wish I could do something to fix this."

There was nothing to do. We both knew it.

So he left.

And as a result, I buried him in my internal graveyard, where the stone reads THINGS I REFUSE TO LET DEFINE ME.

Now, on the first day of jury duty for the Margot Kitsch trial, which I must be sequestered with the other jurors for, by my side in the courthouse hallway is *Damon fucking Bradburn.* The boy — man, now — who I once thought of as my everything.

2.

Jury (n.)

1. body of people (typically twelve in number) sworn to give a verdict in a legal case on the basis of evidence submitted to them in court
2. allies or adversaries, TBD

"Damon," I say flatly.

I stare, with no attempt at hiding it, still working to take in this new version of him. He's as different as he is the same. His masculine, outdoorsy smell reminds me of Sagawa Horse Camp. He used to smell of lemongrass soap and that tobacco-y deodorant he'd started wearing at twelve. Still tall and broad, but far more expansive now. More muscular. His arms are veinier, hairier. I almost laugh at this observation, unsure what else to do with it. His shirtsleeves are rolled to just under the elbow, and I eye the length of tattoos on both forearms, wondering if they go all the way up to his shoulders, down his torso. He didn't have a single one the last time I saw him. For the briefest of moments, I mourn the loss of his bare teenage skin.

My eyes dart around the hallway, suddenly very aware that my first interaction with Damon Bradburn in ten years has an audience. Luckily, no one is paying much attention. On the surface, we must look like two jurors making indistinct introductions.

If they only knew.

I wanted to be on this trial for a reprieve from my years of grinding at work and to feed the gnawing, mounting desire for something different. But this is not what I signed up for. It occurs to me that I never saw him during jury selection. I probably came across most of the other final jurors at some point during the process, but he must have been chosen from a separate pool, or perhaps he was a last-minute addition. There's a slew of possibilities for why I haven't seen him before, though none particularly matter now.

The instructions explicitly stated not to speak to anyone. I was fully prepared to do that, assuming, as one would, that everyone I came across as part of this trial would be a stranger.

I cannot get kicked off this case. Not before being feet away from *the* Margot Kitsch in this uber-prominent trial. Not before I help save her from what feels like a witch hunt in the press. And certainly not because of Damon Bradburn.

"Hi," he says, his voice gruffer but possessing the same hypnotic, echoey quality I used to find soothing. Maybe I imagine it, but I can almost hear a sadness or perhaps reminiscence in his tone. His voice — his whole presence, even — is somehow less full than before. Like a pumpkin scooped hollow. It's quite remarkable how much I hear, real or imagined, in that one word. Resentfully, I hear the good parts of my early teen years. I hear laughter. I hear warmth. But I also hear the change in him. The formality of his goodbye.

A juror squeezes by him, and he moves closer, his arm grazing mine. I recoil at his touch.

"The rules specifically state not to speak to anyone. For all I know, you could be an undercover reporter or a brute hired to intimidate the jury," I say. I tuck my hair behind my ear, which is hot to the touch, likely crimson. I hope he doesn't notice. I don't want him to know the reaction he's causing in me.

Indifference.

I must display indifference.

He gives me an indiscernible look. His bright blue-green eyes appear more green than blue, contrasting against his blue shirt. Like a mood ring, they always did seem to adapt to his temperament.

His dark brown hair is neatly coiffed — a clean-cut fade — and he has a dimple at the base of his chin that looks like a little black hole that could lead anywhere, including another dimension. It seems even more profound than it did back then.

He's wearing a dress shirt — navy blue with thin white (or perhaps light blue) vertical stripes — and dark jeans. I can see the outline of his biceps, snug inside the sleeves. He's long and wide and could most certainly serve as a brute. A well-dressed, well-groomed, particularly handsome brute, but still — potential brute.

He scrunches his eyes, and I answer his unspoken question. "I haven't seen you in ten years. I don't know what you've gotten into since then. You could very well have taken up a life of crime."

I look down at his exposed forearms to see if any of his tattoos might be used to back up my theory. Perhaps there's a severed head or body bag tat. My eyes catch on a pair of angel wings on his right forearm and then an intricate owl extending up the other, its head disappearing under his rolled sleeve.

His eyebrows twitch together briefly, the remainder of his face unchanged. "Do people actually say 'brute'?"

I open my mouth. Nothing comes out.

"What if I was one? A hired brute, that is," he returns, narrowing his eyes at me.

I sigh at the absurdity of *this* being my first line of discussion with Damon Bradburn in ten years, yes, but also at the overwhelm of how many varied possibilities there are for how his life has turned out.

He continues, "What if, after everything that happened when we were kids, I turned to a life of brute-dom to avoid my pain?"

I lean more firmly into the hallway wall, shoved into it by the cavalier way he mentions our past. Damon is a reminder of both the best and worst times of my life — a reminder I don't want or need.

"Relax. I'm a juror. Same as you," he says at my continued silence. He clenches his jaw, and somehow, the movement expands the dimple in his chin. Then he hangs his head, shakes it gently. "Sydney Parks," he muses, as if he still can't believe it.

Neither can I, I think as I stare at his profile.

I glance down at myself, wondering what reconciliations he might be making about this new version of *me.* I'm about fifteen pounds heavier than in high school, all of which went to my hips. The scar he knew me to have along the upper right corner of my forehead from being thrown from one of the horses at Sagawa has evolved into a slight circular indent the diameter of a pencil eraser. I'm certain he's never seen me in a blazer. I don't typically wear much makeup but wore none back then, and today in particular I added what I consider a full face — foundation, mascara, a swipe of coral-colored lip gloss that gives the impression of an even deeper bronze to my already tanned skin. Overall, I'm far more put together than when he knew me. I wonder what he makes of these details, if he's noticed them, then curse myself for even slightly caring what he might think of me.

After all the times I've fantasized about running into him again — an actual run-in on the street or a glance over in a restaurant to see him seated at a table beside me where I could lay into him about how shitty he was — I never pictured it being with a group of strangers under the jury equivalent of a gag order, where I can't immediately say any of the things I've wanted to over the years.

He leans beside me against the wall, and we evaluate the other jurors, though our eyes continue to land on each other, both of us still in apparent shock over each other's presence here. My instinct is to create some distance, to grab my bag and head to the other end of the hallway or duck into the restroom.

But I can't.

Indifference.

Hawaiian Shirt Xavier continues making his rounds, and now everyone in the hallway is unified in our observance of him, including the two new additions from the next elevator load.

"Looks like someone's vying for foreperson," Damon says as Xavier offers a handshake and smile that is nothing short of dazzling to one of the other hallway dwellers.

I study Xavier. *I* want to be foreperson so I can ensure Margot gets a fair trial. And my job as a mediator would surely qualify me as an ideal candidate.

"He's so . . . chipper," Damon says, cocking his head in evaluation.

I nod in agreement, looking on as Xavier bursts into an over-the-top guffaw at something one of the other jurors has said. Judging him is a welcome distraction. Damon seems to agree. "I bet he claps after good movies and plane landings," I affirm.

Damon huffs through a barely there hint of a smirk, and the blue green of his eyes sucks me in a bit. We used to do this, before. As friends who saw those around us coupling up, we'd point out the things people did when in love that seemed unreasonable otherwise. Clapping at the end of movies. Same-side-of-the-booth sitters. Absurd pet names like Muffin or Butternut (Damon's old lacrosse teammate used this one often on his then-girlfriend). It's unnerving that, somehow, I've referenced an inside joke within minutes of seeing him after all this time, as if the reflex of it never grew rusty.

Damon holds my gaze, and I cannot seem to reconcile that, on the precipice of one of the most significant trials in pop culture history, Damon Bradburn is standing beside me. And I can't help but notice he's staring at me with a distinct focus that tells me he also has a lot of feelings about *me* being here, too.

3.

Voir Dire (n.)

1. an oath administered to a proposed witness or juror by which they are sworn to speak the truth in an examination to ascertain their competence to serve
2. my first untruth

A bailiff holding a basket steps out of the far hallway door, and everyone stands at attention. Everyone except Gray Man, because he's still staring at the wall, refusing to make eye contact with anyone and ensuring we are all aware of how dismayed he is to be here.

"Okay, phones, tablets, computers, smartwatches," the bailiff announces.

"Smartwatches, too?" the baby-faced juror whines from his corner.

"All of it," the bailiff responds, standing

impatiently beside him as he removes his watch.

Tamra, the older woman whose name I'd caught during Xavier's introduction, looks as though she may cry as she slowly gathers her items.

Gray Man grunts — a deep blast of stale air and anger.

Most of the other jurors frantically send last texts or scroll social media for their final bits of connection to the outside world before it all goes away indefinitely. I glance at Damon, whose thumbs fly around his screen. I look down at the phone in my hand. I could text my mom but decide against it, picturing her bouncing baby Genevieve around her dolphin-themed nursery, eyes to the ceiling, praying desperately for her colicky baby girl to calm. I could text my dad, though I don't even know which city he's in. And now that Damon is here, there's a pit of disappointment in my stomach thinking about them both.

I feel like I should tell someone in my life that Damon — *my* Damon — is also a juror, but there's no one to tell. My parents certainly remember him, but I couldn't possibly bring him up to them without dredging up a decade of forced-down grief. I'd love to tell Mel about him, but she came into my life after Damon, and ours is not a story I can relay in a rushed text. There's no time to contemplate why I've kept this big part of my history a secret from my closest friend. I shoot her a quick message:

Phone getting taken now. Shit's gettin' real!

She responds immediately.

WRITE DOWN EVERYTHING!

I press the screen to black and await the bailiff's approach.

"Who was your last text to?" Damon asks. He speaks slowly, carefully, as if there's a PROCEED WITH CAUTION sign glued to my forehead. He's not wrong.

"Best friend," I say, wondering if it causes him to consider the fact that *he* used to be my best friend.

"Mom," he says in response, flashing his phone at me, though I didn't ask. I attempt to swallow the mound in my throat, then bite at my lip anxiously. I think of his mom, Mrs. Bradburn. Mallory. Her daily yoga pants and bra tanks. I wonder what she's doing now. After.

We watch as the bailiff grows closer.

"So, no love of your life to send a final 'I love you' text to?" he asks.

"No," I say, attempting to determine if I should be offended that he's asking me about my love life so immediately after crashing into each other again. He looks at me, eyes narrowed in observance, and it's like a wave in the ocean, the blue green rolling wide, then shallow, then wide again.

"Hey there! I'm Xavier." Our potential foreperson has made his way over to us, hand extended to Damon.

"Damon."

Xavier repeats his name, and I wonder if this is some method he uses to remember, repeating names each time he hears one to ensure a mental stickiness. Xavier lingers for a beat, then turns his attention to me.

"Hi, Xavier," he says as we shake. His hand is clammy and his handshake so firm it hurts.

I smile. "Hi, I'm Sydney."

"Sydney," he echoes.

The bailiff, who's now collecting Tamra's electronics, clears his throat and offers a strict look in our direction.

"Why are we already not allowed to talk? The trial hasn't even officially started yet," Xavier whispers, having taken up on my free side. "And we're allowed to chitchat, right? Just not about the trial specifically."

"Practice, I guess?" I whisper back as the bailiff tags Tamra's Kindle. "And maybe they only want us conversing after officially reviewing all the rules."

Damon chimes in. "Maybe if we keep it up, we can get replaced by alternates."

"I can't get kicked off this jury," I counter reflexively.

Xavier shrugs and moves on, accosting a new juror stepping off the elevator with friendliness. When he's gone, Damon turns to face me and uncrosses his arms. "Why would you *want* to serve jury duty? Unless . . ." His face remains unmoved, except for the barely there flicker of something playful in his eyes. "Are you an *Authentic Moms* superfan?"

"Be quiet," I warn, suddenly hot at the notion this could be the thing that leads to my demise before the case even starts.

"You *are.*" He presses his eyebrows together, and his mouth falls open slightly as he awaits my response. *This,* his eyes say, *is a new development.*

"No," I hiss, though it's clear I doth protest too much. He presses his bottom lip into his top one, and I react without thought with an elbow into his side, perhaps a little harder than necessary. He doesn't flinch, and I hope he doesn't interpret the move as overtly playful.

The bailiff approaches. I hand over my laptop and phone. Damon lays a phone, iPad, and laptop into the basket. It's silly, really. We all knew we couldn't keep these things, but we brought them anyway, out of attachment or perhaps hoping they'd somehow be allowed.

Once there are fifteen of us in the hallway and all our electronics have been confiscated, the bailiff escorts us to the courtroom on the main floor. We are asked to assemble into a line, and Damon slides in right in front of me. Then we shuffle into the room, and I am stuck beside Damon.

It's a standard courtroom, the same setup I've repeatedly seen in movies and on TV (and through jury selection), though far less grand. Witness stand and jury box to the right of the judge's bench. Cherrywood pews and tables. Conference-room-style carpet, dark and patterned to disguise dinge. Air-conditioning on full blast despite the October chill.

We reacquaint with Judge Gillespy, an older woman with a sharp face and upturned cheekbones. She wears the same shade of deep red lipstick as she did during jury selection, and I find some comfort in her now familiar face. We sit for the first time in our respective juror seats, and I'm in the front row of the jury box, to the right of Damon, and we are hastily assigned as jurors three and four.

I press my eyes shut in dismay. Just like that, I'm going to be seated next to him for the rest of this trial.

Judge Gillespy welcomes us from her bench. She speaks in a projecting tone, one of authority that makes everyone take note. Everything up until this point has felt like a test run — the motions of jury selection, the call verifying me as a chosen juror, the bold jury ordinances. The past week was a frenzy of packing, letting my parents know while emphasizing the confidential nature of the situation, coordinating the leave with work, squealing with Mel — all the while, anticipation growing with each day that drew me closer to Margot and the role I could play in her fate.

But today, now, it's all become real.

And now that we are here and officially know the case we will be sitting for, Judge Gillespy explains that the attorneys have to verify there are no remaining potential pitfalls in the jury that has been assembled. I'm taken aback; I thought getting called in meant I had made it on to the case, but I could still be chucked from the trial.

Judge Gillespy asks two questions as part of voir dire that unnerve me.

"Do any of you have a personal relationship with the accused and/or the deceased that would prohibit you from serving on this jury in an unbiased manor?"

I don't speak up. I don't know Margot, technically. While I've watched the show, that is no different from the others on the jury who, unless they've been living under a rock the last seven years, know *about* Margot Kitsch.

The second question is the one that makes me suck in a breath.

"Do you know any of the other jurors?"

Damon's eyes shift sideways to me briefly, though he remains facing the bench.

If I admit to knowing Damon, I could be replaced by an alternate right here and now. Part of me would be relieved to have an opportunity to run away from Damon and all the feelings seeing him again has unleashed in me. But a much larger part of me is too invested in this trial and its outcome to not be a part of it.

I release my breath, a string of silent curse words accompanying it. "I do," I say. Damon presses his eyes shut, and I wonder why he hasn't spoken up himself.

All eyes lock on me, and I immediately regret the move, chastise my gnawing morals and penchant for rules. Judge Gillespy raises her eyebrows, and I answer her silent question. "I mean, I did, a long time ago. Juror number three." I point limply to Damon beside me. "He was my neighbor when we were kids." It's a slight, to call us neighbors when we were so much more. But I firmly believe those details are not relevant right now.

"Juror number three, is this true?" Judge Gillespy asks, her attention shifting to Damon.

"Yes," he says, though he doesn't offer more.

"I see." Judge Gillespy sighs, clearly unhappy with this news and the possibility of already having to shuffle the jury. "When is the last time you saw each other or otherwise interacted?"

"It's been ten years," I assert quickly.

Judge Gillespy confirms this with Damon. She pauses for a long while, and I hold my breath as I await her consideration, feeling my part in this case slipping out of reach.

She looks to the lead attorneys, both of whom are afforded the opportunity to weigh in. Beside me, Damon bounces his knee aggressively. Is he nervous? With his aloof exterior, I have difficulty believing he could be. I rip my attention away from him, unwilling to give him any more power. If he is once again the cause of me losing something I value, I don't know if I'll be able to hold back my disdain.

Eventually, they agree to let us stay given the amount of time that's passed since we've seen each other, citing it of no concern. I'm glad *they* can move on from it so effortlessly. But one thing is clear — by outing Damon and me as having had a previous relationship, whatever that relationship may have been, we now have an added layer of attention that I don't like.

With Damon's and my fate decided, Judge Gillespy reviews a number of rules with us, some of which were outlined in the preparatory email we received and some not — no talking about the case, no fraternization, and a demand for strict adherence to the no media and curfew rules. It's the no-fraternization rule that strikes me hardest. We are allowed to talk to one another, she clarifies, but we cannot discuss the case until deliberations. This point she makes clear, along with the need to follow curfew and other "location requirements," as she calls them — that is, no sneaking off and no after-hours visits, conjugal or otherwise. The emphasis she places on this last point makes me believe she's had to deal with a horny juror or two in her day.

"This is one of the highest profile cases this court has ever tried," she says. "There will be a lot of eyes on what happens in this room over the next several days. While these rules may seem . . ." She searches for the appropriate word. ". . . excessive, they are in the best interest of the case."

"As you may have noticed, it's a circus out there," she says after walking us through the intended flow of the proceedings, flipping a long, lean finger toward the front of the courthouse. "You have my assurance, I'll keep that nonsense out of this room." She doesn't smile, but her face softens a bit, and I feel a touch more comfort with her at the helm. "But," she says, her voice sterner than a second before, "know that not following the rules I have set forth could have severe consequences. Not only could failure to comply cause your dismissal from the jury, but it could result in a mistrial. It could even result in jail time."

Chairs squeak around me as jurors shift in their seats.

Well, shit. Despite my excitement for being a part of this, it suddenly feels as though

I am at my own sentencing.

I would have been perfectly fine with these rules had Damon not shown up and thrown a wrench into things. With so much unspoken and unfinished between us — like the confrontation I've fantasized about having with him over the years — there's a layer of concern about this no-fraternization rule I can't shake. As much as I want to be here, I also know I need to eventually talk to him about our past, no matter how intently I may want to ignore it. And him.

Judge Gillespy ends with our solemn oath, and the formality of our pledge to the court and trial tightens the fast-growing knot in my chest.

After our time with Judge Gillespy, the fifteen of us are packed into two passenger vans and shuttled to a hotel, which will serve as our accommodations for the length of the trial. Damon and I exchange a glance as he is shuffled into the opposite van, and I quickly look away, unwilling to give him too much of my attention.

It's a longer drive than I anticipate, given we will be making this trek to and from the courthouse each day. The downtown cram gives way to the fall foliage, and soon we're motoring along a lonely road off the I-5 that would be easy to miss. I catch the others looking out the windows, some intrigued, some disappointed, some seemingly confused. Tamra keeps looking behind us as if to ensure we aren't being followed. Perhaps the obscure location is for our anonymity, though, ensuring we are far enough off the beaten path that no one would think to find us here.

We pull closer, our destination becoming clear.

Off the beaten path we most certainly are.

4.

Sequestration (n.)

1. the isolation of a jury to avoid accidental or deliberate tainting of the jury by exposing them to outside influence or information that is not admissible in court
2. juror jail

Though I had no expectations of a high-end resort for our stay, what stands before us is . . . surprising. At first glance, the Singer Suites appears potentially deserted, with its dusty landscape and almond-colored stucco crumbling at the corners. Along its southern edge sits a row of overflowing dumpsters where a scraggly dog noses through a trash bag left on the ground beside them. There's a haggard strip mall to the right, though who its shops service out here is unclear.

As I stare out the tinted shuttle window at my new home, I think for a moment of Margot Kitsch's sprawling Malibu mansion, and the contrast between the two venues is hard to unsee. The one comfort is that the room doors of the Singer Suites are not external. At least it's not a motel.

There were two vacations we took as a family — my father, my mother, and me — both to Las Vegas. I was eight and nine. We stayed at the Highland Inn off the 160 Highway, the noise of semis whizzing by, our nighttime sound machine. When we first arrived, I stood at the unopened door of the ground-floor room as my mom and dad argued about staying at a motel, bags at our feet.

"An external door isn't safe," my mom had said.

He told her she was overreacting. I stared at my knockoff Converse, feeling the heat rise to the tips of my ears as another family passed and my parents did nothing to quiet their argument in light of onlookers. I did what I always did. I stood quietly to the side, working hard to avoid adding to their frustration.

Quiet and helpful, not a bother. It was my childhood mantra.

The family of four passed cautiously, and

I made eye contact with the younger child, perhaps a year older than me. We exchanged a look of solidarity. The other parents looked confused, if anything. My mother was young, too young by most standards, to have a child my age. And my dad, ten years her senior but already gray in his mid-thirties, made the three of us appear an odd group. My mom loved telling anyone who would listen that she was barely eighteen when she had me, basking in the salaciousness when people did the quick math. Sometimes she'd even go so far as to parade around pictures of infant me at their wedding, just to further play into our nontraditional familial origin.

Our days on those trips consisted of my mom and me wandering the strip and taking in the sights while my father played the penny slots at the MGM, downing as many free drinks as possible. The year I turned ten, just as I was hoping this would become an annual trip — that we could do *something* normal families did like take family vacations — my mom canceled the trip. She never told me why, but I was convinced I had done something wrong. Had I just been more fun, more agreeable, more what they wanted, there might have been another vacation, but that was it.

As I await my turn to climb out of the van, I wonder about Margot Kitsch's accommodations and if they are at all comparable. She is, of course, out on bail. I bet she's holed up at the Beverly Hills Hotel, where paparazzi often catch her lunching, or at the chic downtown penthouse of one of her wealthy connections. It's ironic, I think, as I stare at the automatic sliding glass door entrance of the Singer Suites, that Margot is largely free and the jury is on lockdown.

I see Damon again in the lobby as we await our room keys. He somehow ends up beside me again. His stance — legs apart, hands clasped behind his back — reminds me of high school him on the sidelines of the lacrosse field waiting to be called into the game. It's quickly becoming evident he isn't trying to avoid me the way I am him.

"So, what do I need to know from the last ten years?" he asks.

I try and fail to hold in an affronted sigh at his attempt to make small talk as if our implausible history doesn't exist.

When I don't immediately respond, he continues. "We're gonna be sitting next to each other all day, every day." He eyes me, and heat rises to the tips of my ears, some bothersome combination of unease and embarrassment.

His eye contact has always had a way of disarming me. He stares, but not in a creepy or awkward way. It's more of an *I see through to your soul* way, which is, currently, annoying as hell.

"I suppose we are," I say, looking back to the front desk. There are a million questions I want to ask him. What has *he* been doing for the last ten years? When did he get the tattoos? Who has his little sister, Kara, become? Why did he leave me?

"So I gather you're ecstatic to be here," he fills in when I fall silent.

I shake my head. "I'm not ecstatic. Just . . . intrigued."

"Intrigued," he says, as if it's a word he's never spoken before and is testing the weight of. He makes a noise, some cross between a *huh* and a *hmm.* It's effectively neutral. "So?" he presses. "The last ten years?"

The truth is I hate the question. And more important, I don't trust him. When shit went down, he just . . . left. Why should I give him the rundown of a life he made it a point to miss?

"It's okay, I get it," he says, his voice low once more.

This time when I look up at him, his eyes catch mine, and he flexes his jaw, that thin muscle slicing the right side of his jawline lengthwise into two halves.

What does he get, exactly? Why I don't want to open up to him, even with the slightest overview of my life? Does he get that after he left, I went into a shell? Or does he get why I'm interested in the case?

When I still don't respond, his eyes quickly sweep me, up and down, before he is called to the counter.

Right.

In line getting our key cards at the Singer Suites isn't exactly the appropriate time to revisit our tangled history.

I see him again as I scan my key card at the door to my room — he's entering a room two doors down from my own. He acknowledges me with a squint of those blue-green eyes.

I enter my room, close the door, and release a hard breath in relish of the solitude before evaluating the small space. There's a TV mounted above the dresser, but I know it won't work. A room phone sits atop the nightstand, but it will only call the hotel lobby for emergencies. Judge Gillespy made it clear she would take extreme measures to shut out any media access since the Margot Kitsch story is *everywhere.* Faded cream-and-gold-striped wallpaper clings to the walls, falling away at the corners, and a ceiling fan clicks at equal intervals as it spins aimlessly. At the window, I splay the sheer white curtains to find a view of the parking garage's empty ground floor.

Collapsing onto the bed, I find it gives so flimsily that I'm more enfolded in a hammock than flat on a mattress. I stare up at the too-low popcorn ceiling, trying to ignore the nervous hum at my core. Home sweet home for my foreseeable future with Damon just two doors down.

5.

Defendant (n.)

1. an individual, company, or institution sued or accused in a court of law
2. the reason I'm here

My alarm pings at six a.m., but I'm already awake and staring at the ceiling as the first flecks of early-morning light creep in through the gauzy curtains. I've focused on the crooked fibers of the popcorn ceiling for so long they've begun to take on intricate shapes, reminiscent of watching the clouds in my childhood backyard. Damon's little sister, Kara, used to love lying in the spring grass, staring up at the clouds. She'd see everything from puppies and kittens to a clown riding a motorcycle or a half-eaten taco. She'd point out each shape with a definitiveness that made me see exactly what she did every time.

I shake the thought and refocus on today. I can recall very few times in all my twenty-six years that I've been filled with more anticipation. Since becoming an adult, the days and weeks and years of my life have somehow bled together into a routine of chasing success. My childhood wasn't necessarily brighter; when I look back at it now, all I see is my parents' ugly divorce. Before that, their ugly marriage. Then my move a few hours south from Bakersfield to Los Angeles with my father at sixteen, when my mom finally left my dad and within six weeks was engaged to a truck driver in Sacramento. And finally, my graduation from Los Angeles Valley College, for which my dad was stuck in Orlando on an unintended layover because of a tropical storm. My mom did attend, with her newly minted third husband, Caleb. Genevieve's birth, which fell a week before my twenty-sixth birthday earlier this year, causing my mother to forget my birthday entirely.

Under these circumstances, and back in Damon's presence, I can't help but wonder what it's all meant. I've refused to spend significant time dwelling on these things. I've refused to feel sorry for myself. So many people have it *way* worse. But with

Damon here, my once-drowned memories are resurfacing, bubbling distractingly at the surface.

I dress quickly, opting for a cream crew-neck sweater paired with black slacks and shiny black mules. I blow-dry my dark hair straight, parted slightly off-center to work with my cowlick. I swipe on a bright magenta lipstick that I threw into my toiletries bag at the last minute. Knowing I'll be in the same room as Margot Kitsch today, it seems the appropriate accessory.

I make my way to the hotel lobby a few minutes later, where the other jurors have already begun to assemble. In the far right corner is a breakfast "buffet," which consists of individually portioned cereal boxes and a row of plain bagels, though I don't spot any accompanying cream cheese.

One of the other jurors — number twelve, I believe — accidentally bumps my shoulder as she returns from the breakfast spread and offers me a bubbly apology. She's a stay-at-home mom from Torrance, I recall. I overheard her describing each of her four kids in the van last night to juror number five, the quiet, polite older man whom I sit next to in the jury box. I have a habit of remembering details about people, as it often helps to do so in my job. Moreover, I am genuinely curious about them.

"Hi, I don't think we've officially met. Sydney Parks," I say to her, offering my hand. She returns the introduction, and I work to charm her quickly with my cheek-paining smile and agreeable nods. We'll all need to function cohesively to reach a verdict.

When I part with juror number twelve (Kate), I notice the baby-faced guy from the courtroom hallway at the tiered cereal shelf. He grabs one of each cereal (six in all) and throws them into his backpack. When he leaves, I take his place and grab a box of Frosted Flakes, realizing it's been more years than I can count since I've eaten Frosted Flakes — or cereal at all, for that matter. My standard breakfast ritual primarily consists of just fluids — coffee, OJ, milk. I own a lot of cups.

"Morning," I hear over my shoulder. I spin on my heel and look up, that saddle-leather scent storming my space. The way this new scent mixes with his natural musk again reminds me of Sagawa Horse Camp — a layered nostalgia I'm not prepared for, especially so early in the day.

"Damon," I say in neither a greeting nor an outright snarl.

"Not a lot here," he says, evaluating the

cereal boxes, then bagels.

"Yeah." I shake my Frosted Flakes box between us.

"Interesting choice." He flicks his pointer finger up lazily. I take note of his rolled sleeves, eyeing again the pair of angel wings inked across the inside of his right forearm. He picks up a cereal box and points the bottom corner of it in my direction. "I've always taken you for more of a Corn Pops kinda girl," he says.

I'm instantly offended. "I've never had Corn Pops," I assert, fairly certain it's a true statement.

He grins, barely, and it's odd and distracting how it doesn't hit his eyes. Like, at all.

"Cheerios are just as boring as Corn Pops," I say, referencing his choice.

He flexes his jaw, though the way his chin dimple bends into a swirl and his eyebrows raise at their arches makes him seem unbothered. "They're honey nut," he says, equally playful and defensive. "And I never said Corn Pops were boring."

If this were anyone else, I'd say we were just exchanging mundane breakfast banter. But this . . . this is *Damon.* Damon in adult male form like I *Weird Science*'d him from his sixteen-year-old self to be the most annoyingly attractive version of him I could imagine.

The two bailiffs accompanying us at the hotel announce it's time to go. I set the box of Frosted Flakes back on the shelf, too jittery to eat, knowing what awaits us at the courthouse.

We line up single file and climb into the two passenger vans. Damon takes the seat beside me. It's as if he's *trying* to be around me, which would certainly be a shift. I watch as he shakes a small handful of Corn Pops into his hand, presses them into his mouth, then positions the box in front of me.

"What happened to the Cheerios?" I ask.

He shakes his head once. "Too in your face, honey nut."

I begrudgingly accept, already regretting my choice to leave the Frosted Flakes behind, and the small box of Corn Pops is gone in three turns. Damon reaches into his worn leather satchel and pulls out another box for us to share, and I note we could have just eaten from separate boxes.

When we arrive at the courthouse, the jury is ushered to the side door of the courtroom. I'd assumed we'd have a few moments to regroup as the gallery settled. Instead, the fifteen of us are lined up according to juror numbers, me behind Damon. Xavier leads the line as juror number one. Behind me, juror number five — the elderly man whom I haven't heard speak. We exchange polite smiles and nods. I turn to face forward again, and my eyeline hits precisely at Damon's wide-set shoulder blades as we enter the courtroom. I shake my head, attempting to dislodge my attention from him. His broad back, specifically.

My senses are taxed as we enter, single file. Now that the gallery is full, the room feels far smaller than it did yesterday with an electric energy I feel like I may get zapped by. It doesn't smell bad necessarily, but there are too many bodies crammed in for it to smell particularly good. The air is stiff with anticipation and intrigue, and, finally, I find my people among the courtroom benches: those who are equally engrossed with this trial and Margot Kitsch's fate. I try to sneak a peek at her, but Damon is practically herculean and there's no way to look around him inconspicuously.

The case will not be televised, per Judge Gillespy's mandate, so there are only reporters scattered among the crowd, no cameras. Per courtroom rules, they don't snap photos of us as we enter, but they do gawk. Evaluating. Judging. Anticipating who might believe what about Margot and this case based on how we look. I can't help but glance down at my attire, wondering which side of the decision they might prematurely place me on. I wonder if they'll assume correctly that I'm here to ensure Margot isn't made a sacrificial lamb being led to slaughter.

I don't readily recognize any members of either Joe's or Margot's family, and I wonder if it's because they are possible witnesses or because they intend to avoid the hoopla. Anyone could be called to the stand at any time, and the thought is a bit intoxicating.

The eyes of the room continue to evaluate us as we evaluate them, and I feel again the pressure of expectation along my shoulders, atop my chest. All these people staring at us, each with their own desired outcome for this case. And they likely don't all agree. No matter what happens, people will be disappointed. Angry, even. And we the jury have the responsibility of those stakes.

I'm clammy.

Damon ahead of me shifts sideways in front of his seat, opening up my view of the courtroom, and I get my first look at Margot Kitsch.

6.

Opening Statement (n.)

1. an initial speech made by each side in a trial, summarizing the main points of the case they will make for the jury
2. where I learn what I'm up against

Her brown bob is stick straight, unreasonably shiny. I've noticed that shine on TV, but it's borderline distracting in person. She's tall, standing for *my* entrance (okay, standing because of a judge-ordered call to rise for the jury entrance generally), and her perfectly linear posture emphasizes her long, straight torso. There is no bend in her neck, no curve in her shoulder line, no jut of a hip. She is a razor-sharp vertical line, severe as her customary demeanor. She wears a subdued but stunning skirt suit, black with white frayed edges at the hem and wrists and gold buttons — a beauty filter personified.

The first time I came to know of Joe and Margot Kitsch was seven years ago, during the premiere of *Authentic Moms of Malibu* and the start of the franchise as a whole — Margot, the first cast member introduced. The scene began with a drone shot above the Kitsches' sprawling estate, owned by Joe for many years before Margot's arrival, afforded via his Hollywood production company, Kitschy Pictures. He produced no runaway box office hits but enough straight-to-streaming action films with solid B-list actors and actresses to keep him agreeably wealthy.

One night after two bottles of wine and the season six *Authentic Moms* finale, Mel and I looked up Joe's IMDb page and were surprised to see just how many low-budget movies he had produced that we had never heard of, and over decades. Movies with horrible plotlines and highly attractive lead actors. We chose one at random to watch that night, a film from the nineties titled *Hustle and Grace,* where a broke twenty-something lives on Fruit Roll-Ups and canned pinto beans while trying to earn a ticket to New York City via a big break in the competitive modern dance world. The film had a measly six percent rating on Rotten Tomatoes, the same as *Gigli.*

The acreage they had is rare in Malibu, as the other Moms were sure to point out when visiting her home for the first time for afternoon tea in episode two. Instead of oceanfront property, the estate is a green expanse, with topiaries shaped like cones and a spread of flat grass that looks too pristine to be real. But it *is* real, I know, thanks to the mouthy landscaper who landed a few cameos in later seasons. He once even called Margot's castmate Tenley Storms "trash" when he overheard her suggesting Margot's cork trees were purchased from the wholesale nursery down the street rather than imported from an independent tree farm in Portugal, as Margot claimed.

Margot paid for all three of that landscaper's children to attend private school.

In that first episode, the camera panned to the pool where Margot sat, clad in a black one-piece bathing suit with so many cutouts I wondered how one might successfully climb into such a thing, her face covered by a cartoonishly wide-brimmed straw hat. As the camera approached, she tilted her head upward, making eye contact with it, the slightest hint of a wiley smirk across her rosy lips. She was both familiar and mysterious, and she oozed main character energy.

I was nineteen, still living with my father, whom I stayed with after my parents' divorce. My mom set off to "find herself" and belatedly experience some version of the youth she'd missed because of me. The cliché of it didn't seem to give her any pause. My father, a pilot, flew ten days on, three off, and when home, he slept at indiscernible intervals. So I essentially lived alone. I desperately wanted to be *actually* on my own, but there wasn't enough money with my self-paid tuition funded by work at the sandwich shop down the street.

In college, I'd rush to finish my communications-based projects and papers before the show's seven p.m. airtime. For seven seasons, Margot and the cast have accompanied me from living with my dad and waitressing at the sandwich shop, to my job as a front office assistant at the law firm within walking distance from his house, to my arbitration job and eventual first apartment. And then, to Mel.

The woman I've watched all these years — the one who gave me some escape from the isolation of living with my dad, the fiercely measured and shielding mom I sometimes wish I had, the one with the jealousy-inducing gravitas she wears like a ball gown — perhaps some might call it pathetic or sad, but Margot has been indispensable to me in a multitude of ways. As silly as it may seem, she and the show have provided me with the long-standing stability and comfort that has otherwise eluded me my entire life. And now, I have a chance to do something for her.

Margot and I make eye contact briefly, and I have a hard time looking away. It's not just me, I soon realize. Members of the public gallery lean this way and that to steal a view of her. The bailiffs remain in their professional stances, but their eyes deceive them, beelining to her every chance they get. She's a magnet for observation.

One of the only times I can recall having all eyes on me (outside of arbitrations) was during my sixth grade choir concert, when my skirt was tucked into my underwear through the entirety of "Eleanor Rigby." Damon was in the audience that night, front row.

Judge Gillespy claims the room's attention to indicate it's time to commence, and opening statements begin before I've even had a chance to take in that the trial is officially underway. I take feverish notes, wanting to collect and remember every detail of the case.

D.A. Jackson Stern stands and buttons his suit jacket. He makes his way from the prosecutors' table and positions himself before us, pillowy hands clasped behind his back, a black ballpoint pen bouncing between his fingers.

I was first exposed to the prosecutor (and Judge Gillespy and the defense team) during jury selection, when I showed up to jury duty with no knowledge of case details or of who would be involved. D.A. Stern stood out to me then because of his imposing stature.

Today, D.A. Stern reminds me of a freshly shaven, modern Abe Lincoln — strikingly tall with a basset hound face, prominent ears and nose. He clears his throat, opens his mouth to speak, and I'm prepared for something akin to the Gettysburg Address.

"Joe Kitsch was a family man," he begins.

Damon, I notice, is jotting something down on his notepad for the first time. He's left-handed, and I'm distracted by the familiar way his hand uniquely curves as he puts pen to page.

His handwriting pulls me backward in time.

The letters.

The box of them still in the back corner of my closet.

He didn't text or call or even speak much back then. But he wrote. He wrote jokes. He transcribed song lyrics. He drafted meaningful things he was going to do and places he wanted to see.

He told me I knew him in a way nobody did.

"Better on paper," he used to say.

Stop. Focus. I press firmly into my seat to ground myself.

Damon stops writing and moves his pad toward me behind the jury box panel. I shift my weight and glance quickly around the room before looking down at the pad. It reads:

HIS NAME WAS JOCK ITCH?

I look up at Damon, and we make eye contact. He's got the barely there hint of a smirk, and I can't tell if he's serious.

No, he can't be serious.

I look around the room briskly again before scrawling my response.

What? No. JOE KITSCH.

I write back knowing my brain will now forever translate his name to Jock Itch every time I hear it, may he rest in peace. I know enough about Damon to know he's not intending to be insensitive; rather he's attempting to defuse the tension he feels emanating off me. At least, that's what the old Damon would have done. I tell myself not to fall for it.

I'm grateful for D.A. Stern's continuation. "He loved his kids, Dover and Emblem. He loved his parents, Glenn and Jackie. He loved his sisters, Jayne and Erika. And above all, he loved his wife, Margot." At this, he extends an arm, the tip of his pen pointed toward the defense table where Margot sits tall and still, watching, hands clasped in her lap. Under the table, her right foot taps vigorously at the indistinct carpet. I know from the show that she's not particularly skilled at being still or quiet, and I imagine this must be difficult for her in more ways than one.

D.A. Stern returns to the prosecution table and picks up a clicker. All heads turn to the pull-out screen adjacent to the witness stand as a slideshow begins. Photos of Joe and Margot on their wedding day. Joe on a golf course, the shaft of his putter in the air, pressed against his shoulder. Joe with his kids on Halloween, the three of them dressed in elaborate octopus costumes. I remember this photo in particular.

Margot had posted it alongside a video to her social media, showing off the motorized tentacles and professional makeup.

Joe was an attractive older man. He had that opulent aging quality where his features grew more defined and his face took on more character as he aged. Even in his late sixties, his blue eyes were wide and bright, he still held a thick mane of gray hair, and he maintained the physique of someone much younger. He always dressed in that casual way truly wealthy people do, still with an air about him even in jeans and a T-shirt.

The prosecutor continues. "His wife of nearly twenty-five years, Margot, to whom he gave the world, came from humble Minnesotan roots, and *Joe* introduced her to her lavish lifestyle. What Joe couldn't have known was that Margot Kitsch, Margot Frankel at the time, would end his life in a premeditated plot, fueled by vengefulness and embarrassment. And because of his deep love for this woman and the family they built, Joe Kitsch never saw it coming."

I miss what comes next in the D.A.'s statement, distracted by Margot's foot still pounding the floor and stuck on the characterization of her as vengeful and embarrassed. The description strikes me as misleading. What did she have to be vengeful or embarrassed about?

I snap back to attention as D.A. Stern finishes his belabored diatribe with, "Through the course of this trial, we will present to you the details of Joe's death, which will clearly show Margot Kitsch spearheaded a plan to poison her unknowing husband, making it appear as though he died of natural causes, then rushed to cremate his body to conceal what she had done — her own mother-in-law being the first to identify evidence that incriminates her." He turns to stare at Margot, who does not look away but whose eyes are wary and perhaps a bit scared. It's not a look I am accustomed to seeing on her face.

I shift in the wooden seat with no give and eye Margot's defense team, wondering if they will do her justice in their rebuttal.

Virtually all the allegations I heard prior to this case were grandiose and circumstantial at best. But I suppose with so much notoriety and a slow news cycle, the public needed a prominent witch to burn at the stake. And it looks like the prosecution is, in fact, going with the most popular theory circulating on social media — that Margot somehow poisoned Joe despite not being physically present when he died at their kitchen table that Wednesday morning last

September. With Joe's influential family at the helm of said witch hunt, I shouldn't have been surprised they could successfully get this case to trial.

Sure, Margot has exhibited some bad behavior on the show. She yells, has thrown a glass or two in the direction of her costars — even a pineapple once when the women were vacationing in Maui — but it's all for entertainment. Margot drums up drama for the cameras because she knows it's what viewers want. But the glimpses we get into her real life on the show expose her as an unwaveringly doting wife and mother. People just can't seem to separate the two. Or, perhaps more likely, they don't want to.

Margot's lead attorney, in complete contrast to D.A. Stern, is a winningly handsome man who appears quite a bit younger than his counterpart — late thirties or early forties, perhaps. While D.A. Stern sports an ill-fitting dark brown suit with sleeves hanging to the middle of his hands, Margot's attorney's suit is a perfectly tailored navy blue with off-color pinstripes so fine it's possible I've imagined them completely. He rises from the defense table slowly, buttons his jacket slowly, clasps his hands behind his back slowly, and finally approaches the jury box with great concentration. Between his finger-wave flapper-style hair, square jaw, and dramatic movements, he reads more like an actor playing an attorney than an attorney himself. His name certainly doesn't help: Lead Defense Attorney Durrant Hammerstead.

"Margot Kitsch is a reality star," he begins. "A fashion, beauty, and pop culture icon. A successful businesswoman. A doting mother." He presses his bottom lip into his top one in contemplation. Then he turns to face D.A. Stern, who sits at attention at the prosecutors' table, fidgeting with his pen between his first two fingers. The men eye each other, and I can't help but see the contrast. If Jackson Stern is a basset hound, Durrant Hammerstead is a Great Dane.

"There are things we unquestionably agree on, the prosecution and I, one of which is that what happened to Joe Kitsch is a tragedy. What we will show you, though, through the course of this trial, is that Margot Kitsch had an alibi at the time of Joe's death. That she had no motive to kill the father of her children. That she had no involvement in her husband's death.

"The prosecution will tell you that Margot somehow caused Joe Kitsch to experience a fatal cardiac episode alone in their family kitchen while she was miles away with several reliable witnesses. We will show you that Margot is, along with their two children, a victim as well. That her husband's death, while tragic, was of natural causes, with no evidence of foul play.

"Much has been made of Joe's cause of death in the pretrial media. The idea that a seemingly healthy man in his late sixties could have died of natural causes alone in his kitchen was deemed a far too lackluster set of circumstances."

I look over to Margot, whose face gives nothing away.

"Remember," Durrant Hammerstead continues, "your job here as jurors is not to weigh in on what you *think* might have happened, or to buy into whatever stories you may have heard online or otherwise before this trial." He shakes his head. "Your job is to decide whether my counterpart here" — he points to D.A. Stern at the prosecution table — "proves *beyond a reasonable doubt* that Margot Kitsch is guilty of murdering her husband of twenty-four years."

He makes some closing remarks and heads back to his table. Margot looks to him briefly as he takes his seat, a slight upturn of approval playing at her features.

And with that, with no pageantry or grandeur, we are dropped into the middle of a war zone as untrained, unarmed civilians with nothing more than notebooks and hope.

D.A. Stern calls his first witness.

7.

Bombshell Testimony (phrase)

1. testimony that is surprising, dramatic, or pivotal in its implications for a trial
2. Tenley Storms

The first witness, to my surprise and delight, is *Authentic Moms* cast member Tenley Storms.

Tenley made her *Authentic Moms* debut in season three and is perhaps best known for hiring a multitude of "interns" to serve as personal assistants, though there are ongoing questions among the cast as to whether she actually pays them. There was also her now defunct line of avocado preservers in a variety of colors with the ill-advised marketing slogan of "Always Ripe and Ready."

Tenley is notoriously *not* a fan of Margot Kitsch.

I sit up straight when her name is called, my heart punching against my rib cage. I hoped some famous friends might be mentioned, but I wasn't necessarily expecting another cast member on the stand, let alone so soon.

Tenley enters from the double doors in the back of the courtroom and struts the aisle like it's a runway, one pointed toe landing in front of the other as if she's marching along a taped line down the center. Her emerald-and-gold statement necklace clicks and clacks as the individual pieces bang into one another as she walks. Every head turns to watch her make her way. Well, every head except one. Margot stares staunchly ahead. For her part, Tenley doesn't look at Margot, either. Instead, her face is soft but focused as she approaches the stand.

I take in every detail of Tenley, knowing Mel will demand a replay. While Margot elected for a subdued but elegant black-and-white woven tweed suit that I assume is Chanel, Tenley has opted for a hot-pink skirt suit, the blazer unbuttoned to show off a tight white bodysuit underneath.

Tenley is undeniably beautiful. Younger than Margot, I know — early thirties to Margot's late forties — but her face is plumped with filler, making her appear older than she is. She's wearing very little makeup, her cheeks are clearly blushed and lashes coated with black mascara, but otherwise, her face is surprisingly and charmingly bare.

She and Margot did hit it off in the first few episodes of season three, I recall. When Tenley lost her mom to breast cancer just two episodes in, it was Margot who brought a bottle of Grey Goose and joined her on the floor of her closet. She did this for a woman she barely knew. The scene stuck with me because I had many of my own closet floor moments — the first when I initially learned of one of my father's affairs, not realizing at the time it wasn't the first or the last.

And then, finally, a last one at the liberation of their divorce. I cried quietly in my closet that night — out of relief, out of frustration, out of some sense of personal ownership of the failure — despite feeling like sixteen was far too old to be in my familiar spot in the far back corner. Damon had been gone almost six months by then, and in that moment, I thought of him as I cried.

I'm immediately intrigued as to why Tenley Storms would be taking the stand, especially as the prosecution's first witness.

Of course she doesn't like Margot, that's no surprise, but what evidence could she possibly bring to this case?

"How long have you known Margot Kitsch?" D.A. Stern asks after Tenley is sworn in. He asks all the basics of their relationship. "How did you two meet?" "What was your relationship like?"

Despite knowing the answers to D.A. Stern's introductory questions, I record her responses anyway. Tenley's known Margot for four years, introduced to her in season three of *Authentic Moms of Malibu* by one of the other cast members with whom she shares an ex-husband. She lives in the same gated neighborhood as Margot, three streets over. She was most recently married to Harry Tucker, a former professional baseball player for the Oakland A's, though that marriage ended with her dropping him quite unceremoniously two years ago when he was caught up in a career-ending doping scandal. As a result, her *AMOM* tagline is "My ex may have stolen bases, but I steal all the attention when *I* walk into a room."

Her new husband, whom she started dating shortly thereafter, is a plastic surgeon with a reality show of his own where he specializes in re-creating celebrity features. There are a lot of Angelina Jolie noses in and around L.A. thanks to him.

Damon gently knocks my thigh with his. It's happened so many times already I've lost count. It doesn't seem intentional, and it's not that he's manspreading necessarily. It's just that he's so . . . big. I look down, momentarily distracted by the size of his thigh. It makes mine look minuscule beside it, and I wonder what items I might place next to his thigh to gauge its size. A robust watermelon, perhaps.

I press my eyes shut. Nothing should be distracting me from Tenley Storms on the stand.

Just after a seemingly innocent question about Tenley's relationship to the Kitsch family as a whole, D.A. Stern drops a day-one bomb. "How long were you having a sexual relationship with Joe Kitsch?" There's a collective drawing in of breath across the courtroom, including from my own mouth.

My first reaction to the idea of a Tenley-Joe affair is that there's no way. In this age of invasive information glut, Tenley Storms having had a secret affair with Joe Kitsch seems, well, impossible — technologically and prying eyes impossible.

I watch Margot, who continues staring at Tenley, a look on her face that I can only describe as controlled revulsion. Her skin looks pulled taut, eyes slightly narrowed, jaw squared, cheeks hollowed as if she's biting at their insides.

My face burns as Damon clears his throat beside me. We both work to avoid acknowledging each other at this news.

Tenley glances down as she smooths her skirt, then looks back up at D.A. Stern. "A little over a year," she says, and there is another rumble through the courtroom.

A few members of the gallery shimmy to the ends of their respective benches and out the courtroom door. I imagine they each want to be the first to report this day-one revelation. The remaining journalists scrawl notes so forcefully I can practically hear graphite and ink slicing against legal pads. This news is about to break and immediately trend across most, if not all, social platforms and media channels. It's odd I won't be able to see it, read comments, analyze how the other Moms choose to weigh in. It's the first time I've truly felt the loss of access.

Shifting my attention back to Tenley on the stand, I think of the first time I saw Joe in episode one of *Authentic Moms of Malibu.* Halfway through the episode, he and Margot ate dinner together at their home, which Margot still technically resides in. They sat at their massive circular glass table, leaning over plates of chef-prepared miso salmon and roasted broccolini. They shared a bottle of cabernet from his family's vineyard in Temecula, baby Dover in a Stokke Tripp Trapp high chair beside them (a baby shower gift from Margot's friend and eventual costar Alizay DuPont), while they discussed an upcoming trip to the Seychelles. Joe joked that Margot would have too much luggage to fit on the private island they were renting for the next two weeks, and they shared a laugh. Between the way he kissed the top of her hand and how he looked at her so adoringly, I decided he was the type of doting husband a woman like Margot Kitsch indeed ends up with.

But now I know that Tenley Storms was sleeping with Joe Kitsch for over a year. All while the two women were filming the show. Together. Sitting at dinners in Tenley's beachside backyard, drinking champagne on chartered yachts, galivanting across the world on private jets, all with this unnerving secret. A *well-kept* secret, based on the response from the room.

I had no idea.

There have been rumors of Joe's infidelity, sure. It comes with the reality TV territory, having your life and loyalty questioned.

But never has there been specific and formidable evidence of it. I, like most fans, chalked it up to the insatiable rumor mill.

The anger inside me boils up to the tips of my ears. Yes, Tenley's relationship with Margot took a turn after those first few episodes, when Tenley was going through her divorce from Harry Tucker and she accused Margot of playing up her care for the cameras, but . . . how could she do this to the woman she once, albeit briefly, called a friend? How could she do it at all? More importantly, how could *he?*

Damon glances down at me and shifts his focus from my face to my legs and back again. I realize I'm kicking my crossed leg forward viciously. I interlock my fingers over my knee to halt the movement.

"From your understanding, how did Margot learn of your affair with Joe?" D.A. Stern asks.

"She saw some . . ." Tenley looks to the ceiling, searching for a word. ". . . sexy messages. Photos, specifically. I *never* send pictures with my face. I know better than that, but Margot, she must've recognized the live, laugh, love tattoo I have . . ." She pauses to press her first two fingers to the side of her right breast. ". . . here."

"Excellent," the baby-faced juror behind

me remarks amusedly.

I learned of my father's last affair via the salacious text messages my mother had printed out and left in a messy pile on the kitchen table after confronting him. It had been with Ms. Dwyer, a remedial English teacher at my high school. She wasn't even *my* English teacher, which somehow stung. My mother later brought up the texts again in the divorce proceedings, along with other evidence of far more affairs than I'd realized. I'm not sure why Ms. Dwyer was the final straw. Why of so many, some even more scandalous, it was the final straw that caused my mother to leave the marriage. I suddenly want to ask her.

Tenley lowers her hand to her lap before continuing. "Margot asked me to meet her for lunch. She told me I 'wasn't the first and wouldn't be the last.' Then she threw a full wineglass at me. There was crystal and wine everywhere. I apologized to the waitstaff on her behalf after she stormed out," she adds, as if there's some high ground to stand on here.

"Ms. Storms," D.A. Stern continues, "was there another odd situation you found yourself in around that time?"

"Yes!" Tenley proclaims as though reminded of something long forgotten. "I walked into my backyard, and it was overrun by *tarantulas.* Dozens of them! In all the years I've lived in Malibu, I had never seen *one.* And then this particular day, they are crawling *everywhere.* I was afraid to leave the house!"

Durrant Hammerstead objects, citing relevance as I ponder the sharp turn in questioning.

"A point is coming, Your Honor," D.A. Stern assures.

"Continue," the judge says, her voice as firm as I've come to expect. I, too, would like to understand the relevance of this soon.

"What day was this . . . this sudden tarantula outbreak?" D.A. Stern asks.

Tenley straightens. "It was the day after Margot confronted me about Joe."

Murmurs abound from the gallery.

D.A. Stern works hard over the next few minutes to make some absurd inference that Margot could somehow be responsible for a *tarantula outbreak* in Tenley's backyard — as though that could somehow mean she was capable of murder — and I'm amazed he's able to keep a straight face as he says it. It would be an outlandish storyline even by *Authentic Moms* standards. It's almost enough to distract me from the initial shock of Tenley's revelations on the stand, but not quite. I wonder why D.A. Stern would highlight an affair that defames Joe and undermines the "family man" claims he made in his opening statement.

But then I realize.

Motive.

8.

Adjournment (n.)

1. the temporary suspension of proceedings until the next scheduled session
2. when jurors come to life

We eat dinner at the hotel, in the same narrow dining area off the lobby where we grabbed breakfast. The evening of the first day of the trial, dinner includes clearly once-canned green beans, liquid-y mashed potatoes, powdery dinner rolls, and two mystery meat options. I opt for three dinner rolls.

I sit down next to Tamra at one of the five round tables. Today, she wears a brown-and-white-spotted muumuu that reminds me of a cow, though, somehow, it's incredibly flattering on her.

"Hi," I say, setting my plate beside her,

feeling a bit like it's the first day of school.

She nods politely, and we exchange form introductions before she returns to circling her spoon in her puddle of mashed potatoes. "My cousin was on a jury once. They got Outback Steakhouse," she muses, staring at her plate.

"Lucky them," I say, placing the roll I'd been holding back on my plate, opting to stare at it rather than eat.

I know I should be making small talk, building relationships with the other jurors, but I can't stop mulling over today's revelations in court.

Tenley met Joe on camera at a dinner during her first week of filming in season three, a birthday celebration for Meredith, another cast member. A few weeks later, he attended her book signing at the Ripped Bodice in Culver City while Margot took their kids to see *Wicked* in New York.

Tenley told us of how she and Joe began sharing phone calls. How he told her his marriage was "ornamental," which I found a curious description. How Margot learned of the affair two months in because of that naked selfie with her face cut out. How, on cross-examination, Durrant Hammerstead got Tenley to admit she continued the affair for ten more months after Margot found out. How, after confronting her, Margot never brought it up again, despite four more seasons and countless events and hours filming together. That Joe's reaction to Tenley when Margot learned of the affair was simply telling her, "Margot and I have an understanding."

The thrown wineglass doesn't seem to indicate an understanding.

Tenley then told us of how she eventually met the man who would become her now husband and immediately cut Joe out. That was nearly a year before he died.

Occasional bad behavior does *not* make Margot a murderer. But I know how these things go. Margot is likely to be judged more harshly for her lack of decorum at finding out about Joe's affair than Joe will be for the actual affair. I just hope the other jurors will give her the allowance to be human while considering her fate.

As her time on the stand wound down, Tenley was sure to take the opportunity to plug her book. "It's called *My Real House Life.* It tells of my life with my ex Harry, *all* the sordid details," she crowed, eyes circling the gallery. I picture the cover of her book as I did when she made the statement, which I've seen splattered across social media — hot pink with a close-up of her smiling face taking up most of the area, her blond curls wrapping around its edges.

I stare at the dinner roll on my plate as my thoughts shift to Joe, of the husband I had thought he was, of the love story I had thought he and Margot shared — all of it shattered with the first witness on the first day.

"Hold me closer, Tony Danza," I mutter to myself on an exhale.

"What was that?" Tamra asks, leaning closer.

"Oh," I say, only now realizing I spoke the words aloud. "It's just this silly thing I've done since I was a kid. If I'm nervous or in a bad mood, I say incorrect song lyrics. It's just this thing that somehow makes me feel better."

Tamra takes a long blink and then smiles kindly. "Hold me closer, *tiny dancer.* Elton John. I get it," she says with an accepting nod, and I appreciate that she doesn't seem to be judging my quirk.

Damon and the baby-faced one make their way to our table, Damon taking the seat beside me. Despite his niceties today and attempts to break the tension, my first instinct is still to flee, but I know I can't do that in front of the other jurors. I have yet to figure out how I'm meant to act when it comes to him or why he keeps materializing beside me.

"This food is shit," the young adult muses, though his plate is heaping. Tamra winces, seemingly at his choice of language. "I'm Cam," he says, eyes flicking between Tamra and me in a bare-bones introduction.

"Nice to meet you, Cam," Tamra says in what I deem an innate need for politeness.

"Sydney, hi," I offer.

"How 'bout that Tenley Storms today?" Cam leans in and grins at Damon like they're old buddies evaluating the "talent" at a bar over beers and a bowl of dirty nuts. Damon gives him a slight lift of the chin in a gesture I find indecipherable.

"We are not allowed to talk about the trial," Tamra gently scolds. "Not until deliberations."

"I'm not asking if you think Margot Kitsch offed her husband. I'm simply referencing something that happened today. How are we supposed to sit in the same room all day, listen to the same information, and then be expected not to talk about it?" Cam says, a forkful of green beans positioned in front of his mouth.

We all exchange glances. He's got a point. But I also need to stay in Judge Gillespy's good graces.

"Tamra's right," I say. "No trial talk."

She smiles at me with gentle appreciation, then grimaces at her plate again.

"Okay, okay. How 'bout a game then? To get to know one another? We've got so much time to kill."

"Poor choice of words," Tamra mutters to her green beans.

I look around the room at the other tables. Our fellow jurors are conversing lightly, seem to be exchanging general pleasantries, but mainly keeping to themselves.

We have Cam.

"Like an icebreaker? What is this, summer camp?" Damon says, crossing his arms, and his biceps grow. I take in the words etched along his left wrist: I'LL TELL YOU ALL ABOUT IT WHEN I SEE YOU AGAIN. He's mapped a world on his body since I last saw him.

"It's pretty much summer camp, isn't it? Except at this summer camp, instead of playing dodgeball or color wars, we have to sit and listen all day." Cam rips a roll in half and shoves one side into his mouth. "How 'bout two truths and a lie? Could be fun," he says, his words muffled through the bite.

"Is the fun here in the room with us?" Damon asks dryly.

I close my eyes while Tamra exhales forcibly beside me.

"But wait, you two already know each other, right?" Cam says, pointing at me, then Damon, undeterred. My hope that the other jurors (and the judge and attorneys) would forget this detail once the trial began is squashed.

Damon shakes his head dismissively. "Ten years ago. We don't know each other anymore."

Despite his words being true, and almost exactly what I conveyed to Judge Gillespy myself, they somehow sting. I consider if he is downplaying our history to support the judge's decision to keep us on the jury or if he's still as callous as he once was. Regardless, we're now committed on all fronts to minimizing our past. It should be fine. We are, after all, residuals of the don't-talk-about-it generation.

"I'll go first," Cam says, clearly not reading the lack of enthusiasm from the table. "I have forty-six tattoos, I'm thirty-two, and I once shattered my pelvis falling off a cliff at the Grand Canyon while trying to get the perfect selfie."

We all stare silently, unblinking, across the table at Cam. It's as though he's rehearsed for this moment.

"I find all three of these things to be lies,"

Tamra says finally.

I nod in agreement.

"Nope, two are true."

"There's no way you have forty-six tattoos," Damon says, looking around at the exposed bare skin of his ankles, wrists, neck, and face.

Cam shakes his head. "There are indeed forty-six. Strategically placed." I can tell Cam wants us to give him more — ask to see some of his ink, balk at the impressiveness of forty-six tattoos and his inevitable explanations for the meanings of each. We don't.

"You're not thirty-two," I say.

Cam points at me and smiles. "Correct. Almost twenty-one," he says.

"More tattoos than years on the planet," Tamra muses.

I wonder what Damon thinks, as I glance at his forearms covered in their own ink, about him and Cam sharing this common interest.

Damon leans into me and whispers, "Do you get the sense Cam is the online sugar-free gummy bear reviewer?"

I look up at him, brows pressed together.

"Do you not know the sugar-free gummy bear reviews on Amazon?" he declares.

I shake my head.

"I insist this be the first thing you look up when we get our electronics back." He looks down at me with a ruminant stare. His face is strict, jaw firm, but his words are playful. When I don't speak, he adds, "They're comedic gold."

I continue to stare at him, wondering what his angle is here. Does he think I will just ease into joking with him like old friends?

"Okay, you go," Cam says, pointing to Tamra.

"Alright," she says, leaning forward, her face contemplative. "I have six grandchildren." She pauses, looking up at the fluorescent light above us. "I've been married four times, and I once had a one-night stand with Bob Dylan after his concert in Nashville in '88."

I raise an eyebrow as I observe Tamra. That last one is highly specific.

"Who's Bob Dylan?" Cam asks, and Tamra and I give him a collective eye roll as Damon hangs his head and shakes it.

"You haven't been married four times," Damon says.

She nods. "Been married thirty-four years to my Charles."

I'm rather impressed with Tamra, both for the marriage and Bob Dylan.

Damon points at me before I can ask

Tamra any follow-up questions. "You're up," he says, a mild grin lining his mouth — one that seems to feed off my discomfort. I've seen that exact stingy smirk so many times before it's as though we're preteens again.

"Okay, fine," I say, sure to showcase a lack of enthusiasm for this game that rivals Gray Man's enthusiasm for being here generally.

I suddenly feel a bit hot. I don't care for the attention to be on me, especially regarding personal details. At work, I can command a room with confidence. But when you're the daughter of the town philanderer, you work mightily to draw no personal attention. And now, all three sets of eyes descend on me expectantly.

9.

Icebreaker (n.)

1. a game or activity used to introduce people so they feel more relaxed together
2. my formidable adversary

"I. . ." I look to Damon to find him watching me intently. If I didn't know any better, I'd say he's doing that soul-staring bullshit. I rush out the first three things that come to mind. "I work as a corporate mediator, my father is a pilot, and I . . . I love hairless cats."

I glance reflexively at Damon, wishing I hadn't brought up my father.

"That's it?" Cam says.

"Easy," Tamra scolds.

"I'm sure there's more," Damon says gently.

"You don't like hairless cats," Cam says,

not waiting for me to confirm. "Damon, you're up."

Damon clears his throat, his eyes lingering on me as if still dissecting my answers, before turning his attention back to the group. "Okay, fine. I ride motocross, as part of my job I write the sayings on the digital freeway signs, and I . . . also like hairless cats." He looks at me when he says the last one.

"You ride motocross? That's awesome. What kind of bike?" Cam and Damon launch into a discussion I quickly lose the details of, grateful to be done with Cam's game but lost in Damon's admissions.

My breath is caught somewhere in my chest. He writes the roadway signs I chuckle at and even look forward to during my daily commutes with Mel. I believed we hadn't had any contact over the last ten years, but in this unwitting way, we have.

And, perhaps equally compelling, he rides motocross. Back then, it was just an idea. One he'd tucked away in the safety of one of his letters. *I DON'T KNOW HOW I'LL AFFORD A BIKE OF MY OWN. I'LL HAVE TO SETTLE FOR RIDING SAWYER'S COATTAILS FOR NOW. BUT FROM THE TIME I'VE HAD ON HIS BIKE, I REALLY LOVE IT, SYD.*

How easy it would have been for me to

find these things out, I think. I've found myself ready to google "Damon Nathan Bradburn" more times than I'd care to admit over the years. But each time, something stopped me. I never felt prepared enough for what I might find. And after everything that happened back then, I shut down all my personal social media accounts and never returned.

I eat my three rolls, unsure of which of the many items rattling around in my brain to stew on — the disheartening details from the trial today, my poor showing in Cam's silly game, or these particulars of who Damon is now, ten years removed from when there was an us. So, I vacillate between the three as I chew, wanting desperately to confront Damon about our past but equally content in ignoring it.

Eventually, Tamra heads to her room, and Cam veers back to the buffet, shoving brownies into the many pockets of his cargo pants.

Damon has finished eating, as have I, but we linger.

"Road signs, huh?" I ask finally.

He nods, leaning in. These are the first words I've initiated with him, and he seems slightly uplifted by the gesture.

I should get up and leave, but I feel

compelled to ask, "The one a few months back on the 10 just outside Santa Monica, I think, that said GET YOUR HEAD OUT OF YOUR APPS AND DRIVE SAFELY?"

"That was me."

"And the one when Taylor Swift was in town? THE OLD TAYLOR CAN'T COME TO THE PHONE RIGHT NOW. SHE'S DRIVING."

His chin dimple twitches. "Also me."

This brute-sized man beside me, who can only seem to shape his face into a barely there smile with great effort, writes the punny roadway signs that warm me near daily.

Better on paper.

We look at each other for a beat too long over the acknowledgment that I know his work, and that perhaps he's even lifted my mood while stuck in traffic.

"Why do you hate hairless cats?" he asks.

"Why do you?"

He shakes his head. "Cats are too intelligent. I imagine them plotting against us all day long." He wipes his mouth with his napkin and then places it on his plate. "Like they're spies in people's houses to learn the ways of us humans."

"It seems like you've put quite a bit of thought into this, cats and their intended takeover of the world."

"It's worth the thought, isn't it? If I'm right?"

"I feel justified in being more of a dog person," I say, thinking of the reddish-brown indistinguishable mutt his family took in when his dad found it, scrawny and shivering, sheltering behind their recycling bin. Kara named her Phoebe after the *Friends* character, having taken to the show at a really young age. Phoebe was a quick fan of me — not something I was used to, since I grew up pet-less and was unsure of how to interact with them. Phoebe would find my lap first regardless of who else was in the room. "Dogs go to whoever needs their love most," Mr. Bradburn once told me.

Phoebe died of undiagnosed heart disease seven months later. A twelve-year-old Damon showed up barefoot at my front door, then cried silently with his head in my lap. It was the first time I'd seen him cry. It happened only once more — tears running along his cheeks — four years later when we said our abrupt goodbyes.

"Do you have a dog? Now?" I ask.

The corner of Damon's mouth quirks up, and I struggle, as I always have, with where to look first: his peacock-feather-colored eyes or his twitching chin dimple. He shakes his head.

We fall silent, and I again contemplate getting up. This is the first moment we've been semi-alone, and there is so much to say. But I'm afraid if I start talking, I'll begin to cry, and it will be a devastatingly embarrassing display of how much he still affects me. Besides, how would I explain a tear-inducing confrontation with another jury member on day one of the trial without conceding that we know each other as more than just childhood neighbors?

His voice clips my thoughts. "So was she everything you thought? Now that you've gotten to see Margot in person."

I breathe deeply at the shift in conversation. I clearly can't put off the superfan scent he's caught onto. And at this point, I'd much rather talk about Margot than us.

"She's beautiful. Even more of a force in person than on TV. What do you think?" I ask, trying to tread lightly and not talk about case details, just Margot.

"She seems . . . cold."

I *mmm* in noncommittal agreement. I think *cold* is a word one might use to describe this new version of Damon upon first meeting. Or even the one who went from best friend to never speaking to me again in a matter of a few days.

"And you're not?" I ask before I can filter the words. I can't help the dig. I want to hold him accountable for abandoning me. Abandoning *us*. "It's not that you have RBF, exactly," I say, "because you don't scowl. It's more . . . frozen indifference, your face." I say it teasingly, though I hope he picks up on the caustic undertone.

"Are we talking about me or Margot?" he says, the right side of his mouth twitching a millimeter upward.

"She's famous," I say, irritated he's managed to steer the conversation away from himself.

"Famous is a justification for being cold?"

"No, but . . . she's like the spring fling crown at the end of *Mean Girls* that Cady Heron breaks into pieces and tosses around until there's nothing left."

He looks at me for a beat, face unmoving, then says, "That's an obscure reference."

I wonder if he remembers me sitting him down in his living room after he made a big show of not wanting to watch, but then never pulled his eyes away from the screen, even chuckling when Regina asked if butter was a carb.

I shake my head. "*Unexpected* reference, perhaps, but not obscure. My point is, she has to be guarded."

He stares at me, and there's a glimmer of . . . something. It's like knowingness and un-pin-down-able sadness mixed into one. I watch as he grabs a napkin from an unused stack on the table and begins folding it, both purposeful and absentminded in his movements.

I look on, finding myself too interested in this interaction between us. In the silence, we are testing each other. Who will break and dive into our history first?

He looks down at our plates. "I would kill for some sushi right now," he says, backing down.

My stomach instantly rumbles. "Why did you say that? Now all I can think about is the yellowtail at Sushi Gen."

Damon shifts to face me more fully. "I love that place."

I've seen his road signs. We frequent the same sushi restaurant. Perhaps these are meaningless details, but they confirm that Damon and I could have crossed paths so many times before this trial in the last ten years. And in some ways, we already have.

"How's Kara?" It's an abrupt shift, but I've wanted to ask about his sister since the moment I saw him. She's a big part of what I'm still angry with him about. When he left me, he cut me off from her, too.

I knew her from the time she could barely speak, when a then-ten-year-old Damon and his family moved into the house two doors down. The blue one with the neglected yard and paint chipping at its base. Kara used to push up and down the street on a pint-sized red race car. I gave her a strawberry once when she wandered over, pointing to the bowl next to my seat on the front porch. My mom later scolded me for giving a toddler food she could have potentially been allergic to, which hadn't even occurred to me. But from then on, I was her designated strawberry stand, coming over to ask for "sawbayees." It didn't take much before she no longer had to ask, and I'd open the door with a bowl.

She's the reason I met Damon. He came jogging up the drive. His eyes caught me, even then. They were interesting. *He* was interesting. "Sorry," he huffed, scooping Kara up like a football, making her giggle — this high-pitched, kicky laugh, like the stutter of a struggling ignition. Never having had a sibling myself, she always felt like a little sister to me, too.

Now, I watch the jut of his neck as he swallows with what seems to be great effort. He concentrates on a fold of the napkin in his hands and then, satisfied, pushes it toward me before standing.

"Good night, Syd," he says, and I'm struck by his abruptness. He eyes me for a second before heading in the direction of our rooms. I watch him go and, when he disappears around the corner, pick up the napkin. It's folded with tight, crisp lines, now holding the clear shape of a well-practiced origami crane.

I press my fingertips to the tangle of emotion in my chest, trying and failing to unknot it.

10.

Adverse Testimony (n., phrase)

1. when a witness, expected to be supportive or aligned with the party they are related to, provides testimony that is unfavorable or damaging to that party's case
2. fathers who betray their daughters

Damon and I learned of my father's affair with his mom midway through our sophomore year. We snuck off campus for lunch when Damon asked me to run home with him to grab his bag for lacrosse practice. We were six years in as best friends, on the delicate cusp of something more.

We walked in the front door of his house, two doors down from my own, to find Mallory Bradburn fully naked, bent over the worn leather armchair that Damon's father always sat in, my father behind her. Unfortunately, my brain registered every detail, like one of those 360-degree cameras with hundreds of flashes going off at once.

My father was supposed to be fixing our leaking kitchen faucet before he left for a four-day trip. She was supposed to be on a conference call or otherwise working from the small desk in the corner of the main bedroom she shared with Mr. Bradburn. Damon and I fully intended to sneak in and out that day without her noticing.

It's odd, the thing I thought of as they scrambled for their clothes, Mrs. Bradburn's hair messy and swinging wildly as she searched the floor for each of her garments. I wondered how this man — my father — managed to get so many women to have sex with him. He was, by all accounts, ordinary. No better looking than any other dad on the street. Less so than, say, Mr. Bradburn. My father was polite and even charming, but not in a swoon-worthy way one might expect for a man who had managed to win over so many willing sexual partners.

"What the fuck." Damon's voice ping-ponged from every inch of ceiling and floor and wall as if we were pinned inside an echo chamber. I looked at him because I didn't want to see any more of my father as he fought to step into his boxers. Damon, however, focused in on him, eyebrows pressed so tightly together they merged into one, hands fisted at his sides, eyes searing with a hatred that scared me. He looked like an antagonized bull about to charge, locked in on one specific victim.

I had never seen Damon like that, so full of shock and rage, all of it directed at my father. I've never seen anyone as angry as Damon in that moment.

I don't particularly remember what they said. His mom cried. My father didn't look me in the eye, instead focusing on whether he'd need to restrain Damon.

For me, the scene was mortifying, but it didn't change my view of who my father was. I knew he was a cheat. I knew he wasn't someone who acted by a strong moral code. I was always waiting for him to ruin anything good, terrified his narcissistic behavior might have been genetically passed on to me, all the while still seeking his approval.

But for Damon, the situation sliced him in half. His parents had a loving marriage. They were happy. His family was one that had always been ardently intact. He loved his mom. He saw her as good, and we were still holding on to the days of defining people as good or bad with little conceptual acceptance of gray.

I felt us break right then, Damon and me. Not a fracture or a fissure. No. It was a visceral separation, like a chicken thigh cleaved from its body by a butcher. The door between Damon and me slammed unceremoniously shut, leaving me with the ominous ache of what could have been. Not even our friendship would survive, because I knew, despite how desperately I needed him to, Damon would not be able to look at me without seeing what my father had done.

I thought up so many desperate options. Convincing Damon to run away with me. Investigating an emancipation from my parents — I didn't need them anyway. Asking his parents if I could move in with them. Ultimately, though, I was too muted to take any real action to save my relationship with Damon. Besides, he should have known. He should have seen without me having to say it: *I am not my father.*

And, *I need you.*

For that — for him not being able to look at me and see past the actions of my father, for leaving me to suffocate in the wake of his disgrace — I've never forgiven him.

Mallory Bradburn confessed to her husband. I'm unsure who told my mom, but I knew it hadn't been my dad to share the news. But she knew within twenty-four hours. I heard my parents fight about it. About how he had been fucking the neighbor for months. About how it was sad *that* was the best he could do. About what a worthless loser he was.

Four days later, there was a FOR SALE sign in the Bradburns' yard. Two weeks later, a moving truck, and Damon erased from my life, with only a short goodbye in his parents' driveway.

"I don't know what to say. I wish I could do something to fix this," he said, his voice too firm.

I just stood there, staring back, silently begging him to tell me this was all a lie, a well-executed joke.

He stared at me with those eyes, the ones that could always see right into my heart. But it was different. *He* was different. There was never complication in the way he looked at me before. A mounting interest that was different and unexplored, sure. But his eyes on me had always meant love. Acceptance. Watching him stand with great effort in the driveway of the house that was no longer his home, he looked at me with so much conflict swimming in his eyes that I couldn't manage a response.

Silently, he wrapped his arms around me, seemingly in defeat, squeezing so hard I lost my breath. He pressed my face to his collarbone, and I fought the urge to press my lips to that spot of skin. I fought the urge to do a lot of things.

"I'm sorry," I whispered into him.

"Yeah" was all he said back before letting me go. That word echoed within me long after he spoke it, haunting me like an unshakable winter chill.

Our kitchen faucet leaked well past the Bradburns' permanent departure from the house two doors down.

On the second day of the trial, I head down to breakfast at 8:10, just five minutes before we are meant to leave for the courthouse. I can't help but notice Damon's absence.

It's not until we're climbing into the vans that Damon emerges, trotting out the front doors and into the line for the second shuttle just as I'm climbing into the first. His usually contained hair is slightly more askew than usual, eyes still carrying the slight swollenness of sleep.

We make eye contact and his gaze lingers, face firm, more alert than the second before. I hold up a box of Corn Pops and toss it in his direction. He catches it with ease, the dimple in his chin pushing deeper. He gives me a nod of appreciation and I nod back, then turn away so I don't appear overly invested.

My anger toward Damon is something I've quickly found myself having to stoke regularly to keep burning, admonishing myself for the lapse each time. It's tenuous, the unexpected complexity and range of emotions I am carrying as a result of his return to my life.

At the courthouse, as we line up to enter the courtroom, I anticipate Damon's smell before I actually inhale it. His scent again sends me straight back to Sagawa, to preteen me mucking horseshoes and brush-polishing saddles, to solo rides through the woods and the simultaneous calm and exhilaration I felt out there, alone. No parental anguish in sight, just freedom.

Those were the longest stretches I was ever away from Damon during the six years in which we spent virtually every day together. They were also the longest I spent away from my parents and their crumbling marriage. I think of Echo, my favorite horse — a light brown American quarter with a perfectly symmetrical white stripe up her muzzle. The day I got bucked and earned the scar on my forehead ended up being my last at Sagawa, my parents using the accident as a reason to no longer fund my attendance. The three summers I spent there were the best days of my life, outside of the ones with Damon.

Today, Damon sports a hunter-green wool V-neck sweater, and I'm struck by how flattering it is on him, wondering if he made such a spot-on purchase or if it was some stylish ex.

As if he can feel me observing him, Damon looks down at me over his shoulder. "Thanks for breakfast," he whispers. "I overslept."

"I figured," I whisper back.

His eyes linger another moment, and then he says, "You look nice," before the courtroom doors open and he faces forward again. I look down at the twist-front heather-gray knit sweater and black wrap skirt I was unsure of as I dressed this morning.

We begin filing in, and I am once again staring at the expanse of Damon's back. I imagine I'll know every curve and muscle of his back in great detail by the time the trial is over from how often I will find myself lined up behind him.

Today, I find when we are seated, Margot

is dressed in a light pink tweed blazer and matching skirt with black buttons and pocket accents that remind me of the outfit Jackie Kennedy wore the day JFK was shot. I wonder if this was intentional.

At the onset of our second day, we are introduced to Margot's life story — some details of which I knew, others I am hearing for the first time. I knew Margot came from little means with a humble Minnesotan upbringing. That she is an only child, and her mother passed after a sudden stroke shortly after Margot moved to L.A. when she was twenty-one, right before she met Joe. That she didn't gain her lifestyle via nepotism or connections, but rather, according to D.A. Stern, all because of Joe Kitsch.

Before the trial, I didn't know she'd had some challenging teenage years. And I certainly didn't expect that one of the prosecution's first witnesses would be Margot's own father, whom she has been estranged from for nearly twenty years.

Margot's father, Ken Frankel, steals glances at Margot as he makes his way to the stand. Margot stares at the ground, and I can't help but see a bashful child. I also can't help but see ten-year-old me, crying on my closet floor.

As Ken Frankel passes the jury box, I take

him in, observing the pockmarks along his cheeks and the wide-set frame of his bulbous nose, porous and red like a strawberry. The loose skin of his eyelids hangs dangerously close to blocking his eyesight. Despite their difference in age, it's evident he and Margot share the same oval face shape and full lips.

How could he take the stand for the prosecution? He hasn't even spoken yet, but I feel the betrayal of it burn through me as I look between him and his daughter.

In D.A. Stern's initial questioning, we learn Ken Frankel is still a laborer in the quarry where he has worked for more than half his life. He's likely in his early to mid-seventies, given Margot is nearing fifty herself. For a moment, I feel for him, taking in the details of four decades of physical labor — the curve of his spine and round of his shoulders, the wornness of his skin, the fatigue in his eyes that appears as constant as any other feature.

After establishing basic details about Ken Frankel and his relationship with Margot, D.A. Stern asks, "Mr. Frankel, why are you here today?"

I edge an inch forward in my seat.

He seems to hold his breath as he stares at his daughter. "I'm here to answer any questions about Margot," he says.

I try to read his face, his tone, to see if he offers anything like malice or arrogance. I've learned from my profession that people can only just barely hide strong feelings behind facades of harmony. And only for so long. But Ken Frankel remains outwardly calm.

D.A. Stern asks what Margot was like as a kid, and Ken Frankel's response is what I would expect. ". . . Audacious, center of attention, outgoing . . ."

"What was Margot's home life like?" D.A. Stern asks. "Would you consider it normal?"

What is "normal" exactly? Durrant Hammerstead agrees, objecting and citing the question as ambiguous. Judge Gillespy ponders a moment and ultimately allows it, though tentatively.

Ken Frankel smirks. "It was fairly normal, though not without some mess. Like any family."

"Could you describe what you mean by 'mess'?" D.A. Stern urges.

Ken Frankel leans into the microphone. "Margot was never great at following rules. She was a handful. And there were a few situations when Margot was young between her mother and me. Margot's mother had a penchant for throwing things when we would argue."

I lean farther forward, the toe of my black ballet flat pressed flush against the jury box. I glance over at Durrant Hammerstead at the defense table, who looks on the verge of bursting from his chair with another objection.

Beside me Damon shifts, crossing his right ankle over his left thigh, his bent knee hovering millimeters from my lap. Part of me wants to shove it back toward him. Another troublesome part urges me to rest my hand across it. I clear my throat, and he releases his leg, realizing he unintentionally crowded my space. He's like a giant in a dollhouse bumping into everything.

Ken Frankel continues, unprompted. "She threw vases that would shatter. Futile items such as laundry or throw pillows. Books. Anything in reach, really. The hardcover of *War and Peace* was particularly perilous."

I look on as D.A. Stern makes his point from this line of questioning. "So, you're saying Margot grew up with a violent mother?"

Ken Frankel hedges his answer, which seems more like a yes than a no, and fingers of discomfort grab at my neck. Ken Frankel has just pointed to a history of Margot being connected, even secondarily, to violent behavior. Like it's somehow in her DNA or embedded itself into her through exposure. If such a correlation were accurate, I'd be a philandering narcissist. Stomach acid churns in my gut.

11.

Prior Bad Acts (n., phrase)

1. when a witness provides information about the defendant's past behavior or actions, which may be used to establish the defendant's character
2. who we are at sixteen

D.A. Stern moves on, having adequately cemented his point that Margot's mother was violent at worst, aggressive when heated at best. "When did you last speak to your daughter, Mr. Frankel?"

"It's been years. She cut us out of her life completely. It devastated her mother. But our relationship with her was never the same after her disappearance when she was sixteen."

Disappearance?

I have whiplash from all the casual bombshells Ken Frankel is dropping.

I vaguely remember Margot discussing on the show — with Joe, in fact — how she had a "lively" run the last few years of her time in Minnesota before moving to L.A. But nothing related to a disappearance.

I instinctively look to Margot, as many in the courtroom do. She whispers busily into Durrant Hammerstead's ear.

Hold it in, I think, aiming the thought in her direction.

Her own father is incriminating her on the stand when her life is on the line. My father has disappointed me in significant ways, yes, but this . . . this is a whole different level.

"Can you tell us about Margot's 'disappearance,' as you phrased it?" D.A. Stern asks.

Durrant Hammerstead again attempts to object to the line of questioning, but once again Judge Gillespy allows it, though she warns D.A. Stern to tread lightly.

Ken Frankel runs a pillowy hand through his salt-and-pepper hair. "Her mother and I reported her missing to the St. Cloud Police Department after she didn't show up to school one day or come home after. It was in October of her sophomore year of high school." He pauses, seemingly to collect his thoughts on what to share next. "Her mother was in a panic. We had no idea where she'd gone. The officer we spoke with told us most teenagers who go missing show up on their own, having gone off with a boyfriend or friend on some adventure, either too aloof to tell their parents or to get back at them in some way." He drags his fingers against his cheeks, palm cupping his chin. "Given Margot's . . . rebellious streak, we thought that might be reasonable. But it was odd that nothing of Margot's appeared to be missing or out of place. She didn't take an overnight bag with her. We didn't have cell phones back then. That's why we returned to the police the next day when she still hadn't turned up."

D.A. Stern takes a beat to look to the jury box, his gesture implying, *Remember this.* "And what did the effort to find Margot look like?"

Mr. Frankel's eyes go wide and then retract. "She was a popular girl, so the community really dove in. Within hours there were flyers on every pillar, pole, and shopfront in St. Cloud. Some as far as Minneapolis. It was on the local news as well. Nobody seemed to know anything. Or if they did, they weren't talkin'. Lots of kids came forward trying to help, but none of it was particularly useful, I don't think."

I look on, wondering how this could have never come out after she became a celebrity? I wonder if once she reached the point where there could be particular interest in her life, Margot used her — and Joe's — power to suppress the "before" details of her life. If there's one thing I've learned after spending so much time in rooms with angry executives, it's that powerful people know how to remove obstacles from their paths and, specifically, how to scrub certain portions of their digital footprints from the internet.

"And how and when was Margot eventually found?" D.A. Stern implores.

Ken Frankel shakes his head, glancing over at Margot with a look both incredulous and questioning. "She just showed back up. After a week. A full seven days of vigils and strangers volunteering to look for her. And then, around dinnertime, she just showed back up at the house like it was nothing."

D.A. Stern takes a long pause, peering at the jury box, then clicks his ballpoint pen twice. "Did you ask her what happened?"

Ken Frankel runs a hand down his face again and stares at the floor thoughtfully. "We asked, but we didn't get much in the way of answers. Nothing, really."

"What do you mean?" D.A. Stern asks with bravado, eyes wide with feigned confusion.

"I mean, she said she couldn't remember anything. Not a thing. Said the only thing she remembered was being on Wisteria, our street, walking home. She didn't seem to have any idea what happened in those seven days."

"Had she been . . . harmed in any way?"

Ken Frankel shakes his head. "No, it didn't appear so. She was wearing the same clothes her mother had seen her leave the house in. She was unshowered but otherwise unharmed. They did a, uh, rape kit, which showed sexual activity, but they told us it was unclear whether that activity had taken place during that week or before. According to her mother, she was sexually active before."

I glance over at Margot and many do the same. She is clenching her jaw, but not in outward anger. It's more as though if she were to let go, the bottom half of her face might fall right off.

"Did you try anything to return her memory of that time? To get to the bottom of what happened in those seven days?"

He nods. "Yes. There was hypnotherapy, several intensive interviews by the police, even talk of a lie detector test. Nothing came of any of it."

D.A. Stern turns his back on the witness to face the jury when he asks, "Were there any drugs found in her system?"

Ken Frankel holds his daughter's gaze as he says, "We did not test."

D.A. Stern whips around to face Ken Frankel. "Your sixteen-year-old daughter goes missing for seven days, comes back with no apparent memory of what happened, and there was no testing for drugs? Why not?"

"Her mother and I declined. We were afraid . . ." He trails off as if fighting an internal battle of what to say next. Finally, on an exhale, he says, "We were afraid of what we might find out."

Durrant Hammerstead objects yet again, and I tune out the back and forth with Judge Gillespy. The break in testimony leaves the last statements hanging in the air, so we — the jury and gallery alike — are left to run through our own storylines of Margot and potential drug use.

Damon begins to jot something down on his notepad for one of the first times today, and I have to force my eyes away, too interested in what he might be writing.

"Mr. Frankel, where do you believe Margot was during those seven days?" D.A. Stern asks when the squabble is resolved.

Durrant Hammerstead is quick to object again, stating, "The witness's personal opinion is irrelevant to the facts of the situation back then and to the case here today."

"Judge Gillespy," D.A. Stern says in his down-the-nose way, "Mr. Frankel's discernment on the circumstances of a costly missing person case that was at the very least a waste of police time, but may well have involved various illegal and criminal activities, can point to characterization of the defendant."

Thankfully, Judge Gillespy agrees with the defense, her annoyance with the number of steps outside the lines D.A. Stern has taken obvious in the strain of her neck and narrowed eyes.

D.A. Stern nods and turns to walk back to his table. When he's barely taken a step, Ken Frankel leans into the microphone. "I think she made it up," he says. His words are rushed, flat. Nonetheless, I hear them clearly. We all do.

Judge Gillespy is quick on the gavel. "That is enough, Mr. Frankel!" she scolds.

Margot slumps, the first break in posture she's had in this courtroom. It's as though the weight of her father's betrayal has shoved her deeper into her seat, shrinking her into her childhood self.

Durrant Hammerstead is quick in response with a nearly indiscernible elbow into Margot's hip. She recoils, only slightly, her eyes catlike and predatory as she glares at her estranged father.

Judge Gillespy lectures Mr. Frankel about contempt. There's a swell of a low murmur within the room, and I feel like a bystander trapped in the middle of an argument between an angry parent and willful child.

I'm convinced the only reason Ken Frankel is allowed to remain on the stand is so the defense can get a chance at him. I squirm in my seat awaiting Durrant Hammerstead's cross-examination.

When the room has settled, Durrant Hammerstead rises slowly from the defense table, as I've come to know him to do. No rush in his movement, no panic in his face. Cool. Always cool.

"Mr. Frankel," he begins, "you mentioned that the community came together in search of Margot during those seven days?"

He clears his throat and looks up at Judge Gillespy, who is staring down at him with the sternest of looks, her jawline pulsing. "Yes, that's correct."

"Meaning, she was a beloved member of

the community?"

"In the way one becomes when missing."

"And when she returned home, the community once again rallied in support, isn't that right?"

"Some did. Others were skeptical, wondering what had happened."

"Well, there will always be naysayers, just go on the internet." Hammerstead smiles at the jury box as if he's just delivered the most fulfilling punch line. It does nothing to defuse the heightened anxiety of the courtroom. I glance at Margot, who looks small and frail, like a child whose parent is publicly chastising them. The situation isn't that far off.

"Am I supposed to respond to that?" Ken Frankel asks.

Hammerstead ignores him and instead says, "Must be someone of incredible likability, popularity, and character for a community to come together in that way."

The conversation meanders to an unfulfilling end, and I find myself not just tired after this testimony but to-the-bone weary.

So much has come to light in the last few minutes. I have trouble accepting any of it. Margot has been estranged from her father for almost thirty years, since she disappeared for a week at sixteen. While she's been living the high life in L.A., her father has continued working his labor-intensive job. Margot grew up in an often anger-filled household.

And while I've always held an affinity for Margot, I had no idea our kinship extended this far.

Damon shifts his notepad toward me, his large thigh tapping mine. It reads.

WHERE DO YOU THINK SHE WAS DURING THAT WEEK SHE DISAPPEARED?

I stare at Margot, who appears even more broken than moments ago despite her resolute face.

I need to know what happened to her during those seven days at sixteen, unwilling to believe any of it could point to her being capable of murdering Joe.

12.

Juror Misconduct (n., phrase)

1. when the law of the court is violated by a member of the jury
2. what happens in the presidential suite . . .

Three days into the trial, and I'm drained. Sitting in an unyielding wooden chair all day, doing nothing but listening and taking notes — it's somehow more exhausting than a day on the go.

Besides the damning testimony from Tenley Storms and Margot's father, we've heard from a handful of witnesses whom the prosecution has paraded to the stand, one after another, all to call Margot's character into question. A makeup artist who claimed Margot degraded her by getting her exiled from her *Authentic Moms* clientele after Margot was turned into a meme of a witch because of her heavy black eyeliner at a Sea Save Foundation charity event.

There was a former teacher at her son's elementary school, to whom Margot had left a lengthy, strongly worded voicemail about her dissatisfaction with Dover not being selected as the lead kindergarten role of Poppy Number One in the school's *Wizard of Oz* production. That same teacher also recounted a one-sided argument in the school parking lot about a girl in Dover's class to whom Dover had gifted one of Margot's diamond Cartier bracelets only to have the parents deny they had it. She said Margot threatened to have her fired.

And perhaps most damning, D.A. Stern called to the stand a former house manager named Sylvie, who claimed she witnessed Margot and Joe in a physical altercation where Margot slapped Joe's cheek with an open palm. Turns out, as we learned during Durrant Hammerstead's redirect, that slap was in response to Margot's learning of one of the growing list of Joe's sexual indiscretions. This time, it was the barely of age woman who worked the front desk of his chiropractor's office.

So far, Margot has been painted as an inept woman who needed a man like Joe to hand her a cushy life, only to grow dissatisfied and scornful, all while constantly displaying impulsive and outsized behavior. We are three days in and still with no direct path to or details of Joe's death.

After we've retreated to our rooms for the evening, I sit at the edge of the bed, staring at the inoperative TV. I've barely slept between thoughts of Margot and Damon. I'm definitely not thriving in my goal to get to know the other jurors, either. Damon has managed to sit next to me for every meal. I've stopped trying to evade him, though I have managed to keep him at arm's length.

Last night, I fell asleep thinking of the hours Damon and I spent on the couch (mostly his), watching movies — volume high so he could hear the dialogue over my incessant commentary. I made him watch *Beastly* and *The Perks of Being a Wallflower.* He countered with *Con Air* and *Speed,* calling out all the inconsistencies of '90s action movies.

I see him so vividly, lying on the chaise end of the couch, left leg straight out in front of him, right ankle crossed over his shin. I see Kara wandering in, perching on the arm of his end for a few moments before inevitably losing interest and heading off to string beads into friendship bracelets or play *Angry Birds* on Mrs. Bradburn's iPad. If life is measured in time spent, Damon and I were one during those six years.

I've changed into my mauve sweatsuit, washed my face, and thrown my hair into a messy bun, but it's only seven p.m. Despite a quickly approaching late October, it's still largely light outside. Without work or *AMOM* to distract me, I'm restless. I sigh, rustle a dollar bill out of my wallet, and head for the vending machine at the end of the hall.

"Hi, George," I say as our evening bailiff pokes his head around the corner from the elevators. I hold up the dollar bill. "Just grabbing a late-night snack."

George smiles and nods, glancing at the window behind him where the last strings of sunlight stream in. He returns to his position around the corner, out of sight, and I head in the opposite direction toward the small galley.

The vending machine choices are abysmal. Half the rows hold identical plastic-wrapped cinnamon-roll-like pastries and the other half are empty. As I'm about to give up, I spot the sole two-pack of peanut butter cups in the far bottom right row. I hastily insert my bill and press F5.

When I turn the corner back to my room, he's there. Damon, two rooms down from my own, pulling his door closed with silent care. He's dressed down in a white V-neck tee, gray joggers, and slides. I can see now that his sleeves of tattoos do in fact run up his biceps. The newness but equal familiarity of his body strikes through me. Something about the joggers and the observation of new skin results in a reflexive Kegel. He looks down to the opposite end of the hallway where Bailiff George sits just around the corner, then begins in my direction, halting when he sees me.

Me, in my mauve sweatsuit and aloe-infused fuzzy socks, with messy-bunned hair, holding a two-pack of peanut butter cups.

After a beat, he strides toward me — broad, confident steps but cautiously quiet to avoid detection from George. When he reaches my side, he lowers his mouth to a few inches above my ear and whispers through hot breath, "You coming?"

I want to ask where, to remind him we are under fifteen pages of strict rules, one of which is not to leave our rooms post-curfew. I want to tell him that whatever he is up to could get him kicked off the jury or, worse, cause a mistrial. But I can't ask those questions or remind him of the rules because he hasn't stopped moving. He brushes past me and continues making his way down the hall.

The Damon I knew was always seeking adventure. At twelve, I watched him break his arm cliff jumping at Kern River, though he barely let on anything was wrong until he ended up in a cast the next day. When we were fifteen, I got mad at him for exploring the abandoned commercial building on Union Avenue in some middle-of-the-night stunt with his lacrosse teammates. And, of course, there was motocross. In an unnerving way, this seems like the most natural thing in the world — Damon sneaking off in the name of exploration.

I have two choices: retreat to my room, eat my peanut butter cups in isolation, and read one of the three remaining books I've brought (all non-courtroom, per page five of the rules), or follow Damon. I know I should choose my room. That I must follow the rules to remain part of this case. I tell my feet to start in that direction, but they defy me. They spin instead — toward Damon, who is now several yards ahead. I take a quick glance over my shoulder to ensure the hallway is empty (it is), then trot to catch up to him.

"Does this little escapade of yours have the possibility of ending in injury of any kind?" I whisper when I've joined him, looking over my shoulder again.

"Virtually anything could result in injury if not done responsibly."

"It's ironic that you would mention responsibility when you're sneaking around just a few days into the trial."

"So if it had been a few weeks it would be okay?"

"What? No, you're missing the point."

He stops at the end of the hall and pushes open the door to the stairwell. "And besides, who's sneaking?" he says, holding the door for me.

I hesitate. This trial is, pitifully, the most exciting experience in my recent life. It's important and interesting and will be remembered. I'd be an idiot to do something to mess that up, to be forced to leave before helping to confirm Margot's innocence. I picture my life years from now, regaling acquaintances with accounts of this trial. If pressed to play two truths and a lie again, I will say I was part of the Margot Kitsch jury and people will lean in, wanting to know more.

I look into Damon's blue-green eyes, and for a brief, fleeting moment I think, *He's exciting, too.* I silently scold myself for the thought and instead tell myself that, once finally alone, we can address what happened all those years ago. I can give him the earful I've held in for ten years. I step into the stairwell, wondering how this will end. Because I can't imagine a scenario where this doesn't end badly.

He lets the door close slowly behind him, ensuring there is no thud just as he had with his room door, and we are alone in the dim stairwell scented with cigarettes and mildew, the only light — the quickly dwindling sun from the ceiling skylight two floors above us.

"Now what?" I ask, my voice echoing against the concrete stairs and walls.

He looks up, and I follow his gaze to the circle of stairs leading upward. He starts to climb. I do the same, because, well, I'm in it now. Climbing the stairs behind him, I can't help when my eyes flick to his backside, as it's in my direct eyeline. I wonder about his undoubtedly robust squat routine as we climb.

He reaches for the second-floor door handle and I expect it to be locked. There should be some obstacle to his plan — whatever that plan is — to indicate that we shouldn't be out of our rooms. But the door opens easily, the building seemingly welcoming our felonious antics.

We enter the second-floor hallway and it is quiet, vacant. The hotel, we know, is empty except for the jurors, who are all being kept on the first floor. It's hard to say whether our exclusive stay is because Judge Gillespy mandated it or because this hotel's undesirable location and lack of general appeal led to it being empty. I imagine it's a combination.

Damon briefly reads the sign on the wall, then starts toward the end of the hall, a destination in mind.

"Are you going to tell me what we're doing?" I ask.

He doesn't answer or even acknowledge my question. I'm nearly convinced I should have gone back to my room when I saw him. I probably should now.

We stop at a pair of double doors at the far end of the hall. The presidential suite, as the wall plaque indicates. Damon raises a daring eyebrow at me, then pulls a key card from his back pocket. He places the card against the reader, and the little red light turns green.

"Where'd you get that?" I ask, nodding toward the key card.

"I have my ways."

I narrow my eyes at him. "You know, this mysterious stranger bit? It's overkill."

"We're not strangers," he says so matter-of-factly I almost forget the last ten years don't include some version of us.

His eyebrows press into playful frowns that match his mouth. He doesn't say anything, rather he juts his chin at the room, urging me inside. I cross my arms as I enter the suite, and Damon follows, flipping on the light and slow-closing the door with expertise.

There's decidedly nothing presidential about the suite. Though it's larger than the box of a room I have, I can't imagine any presidents, past or present, opting for the Singer Suites. Straight ahead, there's a sliding door out to a balcony. Despite the dimming sky, I clearly see it has two burgundy Adirondack chairs that overlook the adjacent strip mall alley, which is mildly exciting considering the windows on the first floor don't open and we have been largely deprived of fresh air since the start of the trial. To the left is an open door to a bedroom, a king-sized bed inside. But the main space we've entered includes a dining table and small kitchenette, a three-seater sofa, a coffee table, and two chairs. The entire space is upholstered in a hunter-green fabric with gold scales of justice symbols — the curtains, the couch and chairs, even the wallpaper. It's like a White House forest threw up in here, its designer taking the term *presidential suite* quite literally.

"Wait," I say breathlessly, grabbing for the remote on the coffee table beside the couch. "There's a TV."

I position the remote to face the TV on the wall, assuming this one will have cable. I can't manage to press the on button, though my thumb hovers over it. Page four of the jury handbook clearly states we are not to access media of any kind, TV mentioned specifically.

"That's some admirable self-discipline," Damon says.

I hold out the remote. "But if *you* clicked it on, technically *I* won't have done anything wrong . . ."

I take note of the vein appearing along the run of his forearm crossed in front of his chest. I used to run my index finger across the same rise when he'd playfully press that arm across me from behind in an over-the-shoulder embrace.

"D'you really think if a bailiff came in here right now and caught us watching TV, they'd be concerned with who actually pressed the on button?" he says.

"Oh, you're suddenly a rule follower?"

He shrugs. "I know how much it means

to you not to get in trouble." He pushes himself to a complete stand. "Sneaking around the hotel is one thing, but accessing media, possibly seeing something about the case, that's another. I wouldn't want to compromise your role here." He says this last part with sincerity, though there's a playful mocking quality in his voice, too.

Does he think of me only as a tightly bound rule follower?

My mind wanders to just a few weeks ago when I was arbitrating a case between a pharmaceutical company and its former COO. The CEO and board cited many infractions as the cause of her abrupt termination. She raised her voice in a meeting. She demanded documentation of absences from her team members. She was "callous" in her interactions with peers, only caring about business and not people. She never apologized. I acknowledged silently that these were not necessarily markings of a progressive leader but were absolutely traits of many of the male leaders I had come in contact with in that same conference room over the years.

"I can't get away with what you can. Neither can Margot Kitsch." My throat clenches when I say her name. Sneaking out for a bit to avoid going crazy is one thing, but we should *not* discuss anything related to the case. Not until deliberations begin.

"You think because she's a woman, she couldn't possibly do something so unbound as kill her husband?"

I shake my head. "No. I think because she's a woman, she doesn't get the benefit of the doubt." A flash of his mom flares in my mind, and I wonder who she is now, what became of her, and, particularly, what happened to Damon's relationship with her *after.*

He seems to ponder my words for a moment, and the slight twitch of his brow indicates to me that he at least partially agrees. When neither of us seems to want to continue this line of discussion, he asks, "Are you gonna share those?" nodding in my direction. It takes a moment to realize he means the peanut butter cups I'm still holding.

"That depends. Are you going to tell me how you got the key for this grand palace of a room?"

He presses his lips together briefly before he speaks. "I swiped it from the maid's cart."

I shake my head in dismay.

"They shouldn't have left it hanging on a hook on the outside of the cart with a label above it that read presidential suite."

I throw the package in his direction, and he catches it easily.

"There's a minibar!" I practically squeal, reaching my knees ahead of the glass-front mini-fridge.

"Didn't take you long to come to the dark side." He turns to face me, still leaning against the thin wood-slat tabletop, an unpeeled peanut butter cup in his right hand.

I pull the handle of the fridge. "There's nothing to do here. The case itself is fascinating, but I'm also wired from it all and it's only seven fifteen." I pull two Natural Ices out of the fridge. We both grimace slightly at the only alcoholic selection — certainly not the presidential beer of choice. He watches as I untab my beer, set the can down, then take the second of the two peanut butter cups and peel the wrapper. "Cheers," I say, holding up the peanut butter cup.

He bumps his chocolate against mine, and we eye each other as we take our respective first bites. Then I sip the beer, feel it softening my edges almost immediately.

"The last time we drank together, your parents were in Ojai and I threw up in Kara's closet. In her laundry basket, specifically," I say, thinking of the summer before our sophomore year, how he stroked my hair until I fell asleep in his bed.

I expect him to smirk, to relive the light-hearted memory with me. Instead, he seems to wince.

"Did I . . . say something —"

"No, no." He shakes his head. "No."

I wonder if he can't manage to separate the good from the bad of our history. Or maybe he's thinking what I've been wrestling with for the last several minutes — that we should abandon this excursion to avoid getting in trouble.

He lifts his hand to his mouth, sucks gently at the pad of his thumb to collect the bit of melted chocolate into his mouth. I look on, transfixed, wondering how I'm meant to start a conversation about all the things between us that were never said.

13.

Discovery (n.)

1. formal process of exchanging information between parties about witnesses and evidence to be presented at trial
2. all the things I never knew

"What are you doing here?" I ask as the chocolate and peanut butter disintegrate in my mouth. I collect the waxy wrapper and shove it in my pocket to ensure no evidence of us having been here. We'll have to solve for the beer cans later, too.

"I told you, I took the key from the maid's cart."

"No, what are you doing *here*? On this jury."

He lifts up from the table and shoves his hands in his front pants pockets again, my attention drawn to his joggers once more.

There's something about the fit of them. They're not tight, not loose, either. Comfortably snug, perhaps. I swallow.

"I got called for jury duty, didn't think much of it. But shit, who knew it would be so intense." He takes another sip of his beer.

"You feel it, too," I say, though it's more of a statement than a question. I turn and look out the sliding doors, half-heartedly watching a Jamba employee heave three trash bags into the alley dumpster.

The reality is I was wholly naive thinking being a juror on this case would be thrilling. Margot Kitsch is fascinating, yes, but it's unnerving more than anything being fed the closed-door particulars of her marriage, not to mention the impending details of the abrupt end of Joe's life. It was far less real on my couch with Mel — an extension of the show's storylines, social media creating a layer of anonymity and entertainment to it all. It *was* all so much better when I knew just enough, when my views didn't have any real bearing on someone's life.

I take another sip, but it does nothing to lessen the stress of the stakes. I find Damon's eyes on me. "What?" I ask.

He shakes his head once. "Nothing."

"You're a man of few words."

"I've been called a closed book."

"More like the secret padlocked diary of a twelve-year-old girl."

His eyes and jaw constrict. "You didn't have a diary when you were twelve."

I take a step toward him. "And you didn't used to be this way," I say.

"What way?"

"So quiet." I think about how else to describe him. "Internal."

He squints. "How did I used to be?"

I cross my arms as I evaluate him. "More . . . happy," I say, eventually settling on a word that still doesn't feel quite right.

His jaw ticks. "Yeah, well, ten years is a long time."

I continue to watch him, wondering if I prefer this version of him or the old one. "So, this new you is quiet and adventuresome and writes punny roadway signs."

His blue-green eyes narrow. "You're making a list?"

"Purely for the sake of the trial. I should know what I'll be dealing with when deliberations begin."

We both take a sip, eyeing each other as we do. His gaze burns my skin.

Finally he relents, tilts his head back, and finishes the can. "I have a list, too," he says, setting down the empty can and taking a step toward me. "About you."

"Really?" I raise my eyebrows, imploring him to go on.

"An *Authentic Moms* superfan," he begins. I open my mouth to object, but he continues before I can. "Rule follower, or so I thought."

This makes me smile, the idea of his perception changing in such a short time. He goes quiet, staring at me, his eyes focused on me with an intensity that makes my stomach twist. I look away first, out the window at the remnants of the colorless sunset. "What else is on the list?" I ask, playing with the tab of my beer can with my thumb and index finger.

"Beer drinker," he says. I watch as he returns to the mini-fridge and pulls out the two remaining Natural Ice cans. He walks over and hands me another. I accept, though the one in my hand is still half full.

"This list makes me sound . . ." I trail off, wondering how much of this register was built from before versus now. If he has also found differences in me that he's attempting to reconcile.

"Fascinating?" he offers, though I can't tell if he is serious or teasing. His face never gives him away, always tidy with barely any expression. I find myself laser-focused on him when he speaks or when I'm looking for some kind of reaction, watching for a twitch of his chin or flex of that jaw muscle that curves around the bone for insight into his thoughts. They rarely offer much.

"Is that the whole list? About me?" I ask.

"No," he says, though he doesn't continue. He opens the new beer, takes a long sip, knowing I'm watching and waiting. I eye his throat as he drinks, regard his Adam's apple as it bobs.

"Are you really not going to tell me what else is on it?"

His mouth does that playful, barely there frown thing, and I bite at the inside of my cheek. This is the first time we've been alone — really alone — since the trial began. I want to bombard him with feelings and questions about the past. Say all the things I've kept bottled up for ten years. Ask him *why*. I'm annoyed that I haven't already. But I'm equally afraid to broach the subject, fearful I'll show him (and myself) just how much I am still consumed — and hurt — by it all.

As if reading my mind, he speaks into the silence the words I've waited ten years to hear. "I am sorry, Syd."

I attempt to laugh, act as though I don't know what he's apologizing for. But I know exactly what he means both because of the seriousness of his demeanor and some intuitive understanding that this is the time. "For what?" I say through an awkward chuckle.

"For back then."

I swallow a cough, causing my chest to ache.

"That I didn't handle it all better," he goes on. "That I didn't stay in touch." His eyes are sulky and narrowed, aged from a moment ago. It looks as though he has more to say, but I don't allow it.

"Please," I say dismissively. "We were kids. It was ten years ago." I swipe my hand in the air for good measure. I've been waiting for this moment — this conversation. But now that it's begun, I know I'm not ready. My self-preservation kicks in, willing me to shield myself from really going there with him.

"Yeah, but —"

Not ready to face it, not ready to alienate him with my upset, I make a sharp turn. "She's not a villain, you know." I press the tab of my can back and forth until it snaps off. I set it on the table. "Margot."

He leans against the table again, elbows back with his hands bracing the corners. He lifts his right hand and rubs at the back of his neck. He seems to be contemplating whether to allow my subject change or to press. Finally, he says, "No one is the villain of their own story."

His words singe my esophagus. My heart burns.

Needing to look away, I walk over to the sliding door and focus on the alleyway. "There's this one episode of *Authentic Moms,* season four I think, when Margot and Joe were eating with their kids at Neptune's Net," I say, then continue, largely in avoidance of the alternative conversation about *us.* "It was funny because picture Margot — *this* Margot" — I turn to face him and reference with my hand in the general direction of the courthouse — "sitting on an outdoor bench just a few feet away from the PCH, with paper baskets of fried shrimp and fish and chips next to a table of bikers."

He huffs, and the corners of his mouth bend upward, ever so slightly, in acknowledgment. I appreciate his willingness to allow me to turn the discussion.

Until that point in the show, I had only ever seen Margot consume arugula salads and lemon ginger kombucha, with the occasional emotionally induced double cheeseburger. "Anyway, they're sitting there, and Dover runs off to watch the water from the patio rail. Emblem was just a baby. And

Margot tells Joe she's had a miscarriage." I stop, wanting to gauge his reaction. Damon nods, losing the tension along his eyebrow ridge in a flash of empathy. Just a flash, gone as quickly as it came.

It's not hard to imagine what he thinks — or, at least, what he thought before this case. That *Authentic Moms* is a trivial show about rich, apathetic housewives living lives of privilege who drum up drama with one another because they're bored with their lack of responsibility and purpose. And perhaps there is some truth to that. But if there's one thing I've learned watching, it's that these women, though wealthy and glamorous, they deal with it — life and all its tithings.

"They'd been trying for a while, since just after Emblem was born. Thankfully she wasn't too far along, ten weeks I think, though I doubt that made it any easier. She fought back tears, stealing glances at the kids. And do you know what Joe's reaction was?"

Damon shakes his head. Once.

I swallow. I know I shouldn't be telling him this. It's a clear violation of jury rules. It could color his — our — interpretations of the case. But I want him to know. I want him to understand Margot as more than a character built for entertainment, more than the "cold" woman he sees in the courtroom.

I need him to be on the same side of something as me this time.

"He reached across the table, placed his hand on top of hers, and said, 'It's not your fault.' "

Damon presses his eyebrows together again, listening.

I shake my head lightly. "It wasn't pointed or derogatory. He meant it. And he said it because he knows her. *Knew* her," I correct. "And he knew she would blame herself. His first thought was not only of the baby they just lost. It was also for his wife."

I stand quietly, pressing my thumbnail into my palm and then releasing, watching the color rush back to the spot of impact. I think he knows what I've lost in the courtroom a few days into the trial. The picture-perfect family I invested so much of my time into over the last seven years, shattered with one sharp pull of the curtain. It may not seem so bad to someone else, but he knows why. That after living the breakdown of my own family, I needed the love story I've invested so much time into to be real.

He breaks our connection first, stares out the sliding glass doors with the vacancy in his eyes that seems to come in tense moments. I watch him closely, and it's clear he's gone somewhere else entirely. My pulse accelerates, though I'm unsure why.

"Kara died," he says. His words are delivered so flatly that it takes me a few seconds to register them. When I do, my chest is struck windless and nausea invades from my gut to my throat.

"What?" is all I can seem to manage in return. I'm certain I haven't heard him right.

He's silent for a long while, and I don't know what to do. Kara was barely seven years old when I last saw her.

I picture Kara sitting outside Damon's bedroom door, listening to our conversations, as she did so often. It was hard to get mad when we'd see her little feet pressed up against the space at the bottom of the door. She was our constant third wheel, always angling to be a part of whatever we had going on.

"It was a year after we moved," he says, and at once I shut my eyes, fighting back incensed tears.

She was *eight.*

I think of Gen, barely five months old, and my animosity toward that faultless micro-human, my *sister,* brings me a flash of fierce shame. "I can't believe it," I say, my voice cracking, and at first, I really can't. How could I have not found out about this? How did no one tell me? But, after they moved, I suppose nothing and no one really connected us anymore. I shut down all social media, and my whole world became intentionally only what was right in front of me. To this day, I have burner accounts, and only for the sheer purpose of following *AMOM* cast members and various pop culture accounts.

If only I *had* googled him or his family one of those many times I ached to.

He runs his hand down his face. "Turns out she had a heart condition nobody knew about."

I wince.

"People always seem so interested in *how*. More than anything, more than wanting to know about her, about who she was, they want to know how it happened. Morbid curiosity, I suppose." He rubs at his right earlobe absentmindedly, and I note its blazing red tip. "But you . . . you knew her."

I try to swallow down the new wave of nausea flooding my throat.

I've wondered about her over the years, of course. Every January thirtieth, on her birthday, I'd acknowledge her new age and wonder how she might be celebrating. I'd imagined her looking more and more like Damon.

Damon was sixteen when his family left, but Kara was just seven. I'm ashamed to admit she was an afterthought during it all. Had I only known what was going to happen . . . maybe I would have done something differently. Tried harder to stay in touch, with her at least. The nausea in my belly and throat swells, as I think of the last ten years. I cursed Damon, angry at him for leaving, for never tracking me down or making any attempts at reconciliation. I assumed it was because he never cared about me like I did him. I believed he couldn't get over what had happened between our parents. I never imagined he was dealing with another, far more significant tragedy.

His palm moves to the back of his neck. "When she died, I wanted to call you." His voice is deeper than just a moment ago, granular. "I needed to hear your voice to help me deal with it. I missed my friend, the person I knew would understand. I wanted *you.*"

Without hesitation or thought, I make my way over to him and throw my arms around his neck, press my body into his. I squeeze. I did know her. I *know* him. He wraps his arms around me and squeezes back, pressing my face into his neck, and my entire body is enveloped by his. He is warm. So warm. He exhales so forcefully as we embrace that it sounds like he's been holding his breath for ten years. His hand cups the back of my head. In our hold, it is sadness and comfort that surges between us. Since the start of the trial, he has fractured my shell one memory at a time. This feels like the irrevocable shatter.

I have missed him. So, so much. This notion is something that, just three days ago, I never would have been willing to admit to anyone, let alone myself. But it is a fact I can no longer refute.

I'm not exactly sure how long we stay this way, wrapped together. It is a moment of respite. The trial, Kara, the last ten years — all of it goes on pause as we hold each other. When we finally release, he pulls out a chair from the dining table and sits. I follow suit.

I watch Damon, the ache in my chest so expansive I feel as though I may pass out from the pressure.

"I'm sorry you had to find out like this."

"I'm sorry I didn't know. I would have . . ." I don't know how to finish the sentence or the thought. What would I have done? Would I have gone to him? Would I have shown up at his door, hoping all the embarrassment, disappointment, and disgust would dissipate, overtaken by the loss? In truth, I probably would have stayed away, out of fear I'd make things worse.

And because I still don't have the right words, I move my hand across the table and press it atop his. He looks at my hand, then into my eyes, his own eyes expansive and filled with so much I can't decipher. But now I get it. It is a sadness I've noticed in him since we've come back together. One he can mask everywhere except his eyes.

I've held his hand before. I held it on the bus back to school from a field trip to the Bakersfield College planetarium in the sixth grade when our bus nearly rear-ended a semi and skidded into a ditch on the 178. I held it when he led me blindfolded into his backyard on my fifteenth birthday to a surprise sushi picnic he'd set up for me and my few close friends, who, if we're being honest, were mostly his. But this is the hand of a man — thicker, rougher — with ten years of life I know nothing about. It's déjà vu and a brand-new experience rolled into one massive weight in my gut.

Then he says the thing that causes a tremble across the length of my body. "We all just do the best we can with the circumstances we're given."

Tears sting at my eyes, and I try desperately to push them back. I don't want my grief to upset him.

I think of my parents. How my mom was quick to move on and my dad seemed to always be counting the hours until his next flight to somewhere that wasn't with me. How hard I've worked to be a daughter they could be proud of, to seemingly no avail. But Damon's tragedy runs so much deeper and wider than my repetitive fractures. I realize trauma is not a competition, but his — his is as agonizing as they come.

"Seeing you again, this trial, it brings it all up again. Maybe it's the constant talk of the end of someone's life. I think about Kara a lot, about all the ways she could have been saved had we all been paying more attention . . ." I expect him to hang his head, but instead he looks at me square on. "How we're all just one decision away from a completely different life. How quickly it can all just . . . end."

We stare at each other, and I can't help the heat on my skin, the thump of my heart. I've gotten the slightest bits of him in these past few days, most of which have come in this suite, and I have the overwhelming desire to crack what's left of his eggshell against the pan, letting his remaining gooey parts ooze out. I'm anxious, knowing that his shell will likely regenerate again, quickly.

One decision.

It's impossible to hold the line with him.

I look down at my hand, still wrapped around his, and I squeeze. Our eyes lock, and his are both a mirror and a window, where I see so much — *too* much — all flashing through him like the still frames of his heart. Anger. Sadness. Regret. Something else, too. Something like . . . hope.

Heat surges between us, a scalding current through our sorrowed but powerful touch.

One decision.

The light ting of the elevator comes from the other end of the hallway, and we both sharpen, the intrusion of sound breaking the connection between us. We listen as a barreling noise begins and grows louder.

It sounds like the maid's cart. And it sounds like it's heading straight for us.

14.

Juror Attendant (n., phrase)

1. a person who assists in supporting the sequestration of a jury but doesn't work directly for the court; may include transportation, accommodations, meals, and other necessary support services during the trial period
2. our potential downfall

Damon grabs the two beer cans from the table, shuts off the light, and ushers me into the bedroom. I push in our chairs and follow, a can of my own in each hand.

As we hear the door to the suite — this suite — open, he pulls the closet handle and presses me in with his side, then shuts the door with his foot. My thighs push into the safe on the back wall, and Damon slides two robes to the far end of the hanging bar so we are smushed side by side in the dark, with only scant slats of barely remaining daylight finding their way in through the louvered doors. Pressure gathers in my chest, and I find it hard to breathe. He sips his beer, standing casually as though he's taking in a baseball game on a Saturday afternoon.

"How are you so chill?" I whisper as he swallows.

He shrugs. I expect him to be on edge, but the heightened stakes seem to have calmed him. "I can literally hear your heart pounding," he whispers back. We both look down at the visible heave of my chest.

There is shuffling around the suite, footsteps and the occasional bump or swoosh. I shrink back as far as I can when, through the slats, I see a fair-haired maid step into the bedroom, flip on the light switch, and stand directly in front of the closet doors.

If she grips one of the handles, I may pass out.

She stands there a moment, inches from us, evaluating the bedroom. I glance at Damon, though I don't move my head for fear of her sensing the movement. He is perfectly still, his posture rivaling that of Margot. The cans virtually disappear beneath his grip, and his fists' size makes me think of *Wreck-It Ralph.* He looks over at me, and that intense blue-green stare in the dark closet makes me feel something akin to attraction. Staring at someone in the dark, arm pressed against arm at the height of an adrenaline rush, will do that to you.

Heat threatening to overtake me, I focus forward to watch through the slats as the maid tidies the bed. She bends down, tugs sharply at one corner of the bedspread, then smooths the top with open palms. She places her hands on her hips, evaluating. Satisfied, she reaches into her light brown uniform pocket and pulls out a pack of cigarettes and a gold lighter. She taps one from the carton, lights the cigarette, steps to the balcony door across the room and opens it. She shrinks into one of the Adirondack chairs and disappears completely behind the wall, except for the toe of her stark white sneaker pressed against the rail. Shortly after, the smoke from her cigarette billows across the sliding glass.

Damon and I turn our heads to face each other.

"Looks like we found her break spot," Damon muses, his whisper heavy against my ear. He takes another sip of his beer.

"What if she stays for hours?"

Damon looks down at me. "Then I guess

we'll be here for hours, too." Even in the dark, his gaze pierces right through me.

Ironically, it's not the first time Damon and I have been in a closet together. Damon learned quickly when we were young about my father's continual cheating, his lazy effort to hide it. He'd know I had a particularly bad day when I'd go quiet, not asking him to watch movies or ride bikes down to the gas station for gum or twenty-five-cent Atomic Fireballs. He came to know where to find me.

He'd join me on my closet floor, wrap his arm around my shoulders, and press the side of his face into the top of my head. He used to be so tender, so . . . worried about me. Always worried about me. Like a toddler given an egg with a firm instinct to protect it.

He silently taps the tip of his can to the one in my hand closest to him. I watch as he takes a sip and then looks at me expectantly. I exhale. Might as well lean in at this point. I take a long swig that finishes my first can and raise an eyebrow at him. He nods at me in approval. I nudge him with an elbow to the side, and he exhales a breathy but otherwise silent huff that carries some semblance of amusement. After what he just shared about Kara, it's incredibly satisfying to see something besides sadness from him, however brief.

We stand pressed into each other for what feels like an eternity. His arm pushes against mine, gliding gently up and down with his breath. My heartbeats come in rapid-fire as his weight and warmth dominate the small space. Dominate me. It's claustrophobic in a rousing way, as though this closed, dark space holds no rules or boundaries. The air grows thick and warm, wet against my skin, as we watch through the slats as the maid eventually stands from the chair, flicks her cigarette butt over the railing, and slides the door open again. Once inside, she observes her reflection in the mirror opposite the bed, smoothing her hair at the part and then squirting two pumps of breath spray onto her outstretched tongue.

My pulse accelerates to a screaming pace as she steps closer to us. She looks over the room once more, seemingly to ensure she hasn't disrupted anything, and then, eventually, flips the light switch and steps out of the bedroom.

I lean forward, angle myself to watch through the slats as she runs her fingertips along the dining table as she walks. Midway she stops and sweeps up a small item her fingers have run into. She holds up the piece of tin to evaluate it. Damon and I both look down at the can in my left hand, tab missing. *Shit.* The maid turns on her heel, returns to her previous spot in front of the closet doors.

I think I'm ready for that passing-out situation now. The lightheadedness hits, and I would grip Damon's arm for steadiness if I weren't holding two beer cans. Noticing my state, he presses his arm deeper against mine to steady me, pinning me tightly between him and the wall.

The maid listens a moment longer, her face sharp. She walks back to the balcony's sliding door and looks out, left then right. She steps back in and reassesses the room. She looks to the closet, and I instinctively close my eyes — if I can't see her, perhaps she can't see me. She takes the few steps toward the closet door, and it's just the thin wood between us.

It's rather impressive how many thoughts make their way through my brain in a split second. I think of the mistrial this will inevitably end in, our names and photos leaked to the press. I think of Judge Gillespy scolding us, then placing us in contempt and throwing us both in jail. I even have a brief but visceral hallucination of Damon and me in the same cell in some prison fantasy gone awry. My heart leaps with each pump, and I feel its force across every inch of my wobbly body.

I open my eyes to find the maid staring right at me. Technically, she's staring at the door, but it feels like we're making eye contact. She cocks her head, perhaps listening more intently for another sound. She won't get it, though. I'm holding my breath.

Finally, after what feels like far longer than I should be capable of not breathing without dying, the maid, satisfied or perhaps no longer interested, turns and exits the bedroom again. The door to the suite slams shut in the distance, and I slowly release my breath.

We stay just as we are, waiting, listening, determining when it is safe to exit the closet. Damon's side is pressed firmly against mine, his arm now wrapped around the back of my neck. The cold of his beer can against the sleeve of my sweatshirt further jolts me alive. I feel his heart, too, as my shoulder fuses to his chest. Despite his calm demeanor, his heart is also thumping. It somehow soothes me, knowing he's not as unaffected as he seems. The compact space has taken on the scent of saddles and beer, and I find the combination decidedly intoxicating.

I close my eyes and inhale his scent, more erotic than nostalgic in this moment. I suddenly want to ravage him. It's a stark reminder of how little physical touch I receive in my daily life. One press of skin and I'm decidedly horny.

This is . . . Damon, I remind myself. My once best friend. My last real, meaningful kiss. The only person who knows so many both innocuous and monumental things about me.

The top slit of the closet door slashes him with a slice of dim light directly across his eye line, the full blue green of those eyes coursing into me. "You okay?" he whispers — a gentle, almost inviting declaration.

"Yes," I tell him, drawn into the halo of light across his eyes. As if on command, his heartbeat quickens against me.

He gently pulls his arm from around my shoulders, still looking down at me as he does. He lingers a moment, our eyes connected, and again I'm holding my breath. The electricity between us is nothing short of high voltage, zapping through me like a live wire. I wonder what's causing him pause. Before I can ask, he gingerly pushes the closet door open with his elbow. He silently inspects the room before I take a step out. At the rush of air, I find myself more grounded.

Damon is back in an instant, beer cans placed elsewhere. At his urging, I step out of the closet. The room is almost completely dark, the only light from the alley below.

"You sure you're okay?" he asks again, this time not in a whisper. Instead, it's a low, groaning sort of growl.

"Yes," I muster. "Just got a little lightheaded there for a minute."

Even so, he grips my elbow as if to steady me. Our eyes meet, his face sharp and raw. I want to wrap my arms around him again, tell him I'm sorry about Kara. So incredibly sorry. That I loved her, too. I want to tell him I wish we had been more mature back then, that we could have — *should* have — been better than our parents' worst decisions. That we shouldn't have let them ruin *us*.

Staring into his dimmed eyes now, I don't know that I can say any of these things without breaking. He continues to look into me, like he is the only one who could ever make sense of everything inside me. He was.

What I think of then, in a gush of memory that floods my brain and body in a massive, all-encompassing swell, is our first kiss. The only kiss we ever shared in all our time together. It was midway through our sophomore year, just a few weeks before the end. Those days were built of the fun and freedom I've often pointed back to as the best of my life. Moments of such uncomplicated happiness they made my skin tingle with satisfaction.

I'd gotten my hair cut that morning, opting for bangs and a bob as a reengineering, a rebellion against the "kid" version of myself that held consistently long, stringy locks halfway down my back. I regretted it the instant the stylist swiveled the chair to face the full mirror. I wanted *1989*-era brunette Taylor Swift. What I got instead was horrifyingly similar to the cuts I'd once given my Barbie dolls. I avoided Damon all day, though when I didn't return his texts, he showed up at my door.

"You're beautiful," he affirmed when I opened the door, before I could voice a complaint. "You're always beautiful."

I couldn't stop the slight shake of my head or the tears that threatened to fall, embarrassed by how much I was allowing it to affect me. He pulled me into his chest, wrapped his burlier-than-ever-before arms around me, and rocked slowly back and forth as we embraced. Even then, I couldn't fathom how he, at sixteen, knew the exact right words to say.

"Your bangs are tickling my chin," he teased before I could feel too sorry for myself. I shoved him. He chuckled, then pulled me back in. "You're beautiful," he said again, his features severe, and instantly, there was something different between us. As if everything — all our years and days and time — had taught us into this moment. His jaw muscle twitched. His eyes grew heavy. There was a flutter, though whether emanating from my chest or stomach, I wasn't quite sure. This person before me, *Damon Bradburn,* looked both brand-spanking-new and solidly familiar at the same time. Almost zombielike, overtaken by a lack of thought and need to act, I lifted my hand and cupped his jaw. He reflexively squeezed the muscle beneath my touch, and I felt the unmistakable ripple of excitement between my legs.

He moved like liquid, spilling toward me until his lips met mine. As soon as our mouths touched, I felt, more than anything, the rightness of it. Kissing him felt right. To this day, I couldn't tell you how long that kiss was. It could have been only seconds. It could have stretched on for several minutes. But in that kiss, I felt everything and nothing but it. I do know it ended abruptly, at the thrumming of my garage door opening, the rev of my father's Buick before it backed out.

Ten years later, here in the dark of the presidential suite, I know with certainty . . . I need another.

I lean in and kiss him.

Kara. Margot. Him.

Sequestration. The stakes of the trial.

Him.

I'm certain the kiss is a result of all these things rolled into a doughy mess. Regardless, I can't seem to help it. In this moment he is calling to me like a fucking foghorn.

He tastes hoppy and sweet, bitterness from the beer largely gone. He's a brand-new flavor, one I've never experienced but instantly like. It's only our second kiss, but it is very much a first kiss.

Damon pulls back first. The look on his face is a little shocked. *I agree,* I want to say. *I am also shocked.* The realization hits me then. Who knows how much longer we will be stuck together, sitting for eight hours a day in court, side by side in the jury box, and at this shitty hotel, and I have just kissed him unexpectedly, giving it all a weird complication.

He is still gripping my arms firmly as we are positioned just inches apart.

"I'm sorry, I don't know why I —" Before

I can finish what would have been a truly awkward apology, he leans in and kisses me.

He kisses *me.*

15.

No-Fraternization Rule

1. a prohibition against jurors socializing or forming personal relationships with each other outside of the official jury deliberation process
2. Judge Gillespy mentioned possible jail time

This time, the shock burns away quickly.

Damon kisses with intention — long, weighty stretches of deliberate movement against my mouth. His right hand cups my jaw, his thumb rubbing unconscious strokes against my earlobe. He speaks so little with his voice, as if he has a daily word count he must stay under. But with his mouth, he says so much. He says he knows what he's doing. He says command. He says pleasure. Kissing him is what kissing a man should feel like, I think as his tongue laps against mine. The bristle of his stubble, shaved though constant. The rough but gentle skin of his hands. Even the girth of his thumb against my face. That polished saddle smell. They all combine into one utterly masculine encounter. And it instantly makes me want to succumb.

His body sways into mine, and we touch from our lips down to our thighs. He tilts his head, and I instinctively do the same, our mouths fitting more deeply together. His tongue brushes mine in a sturdy wave, and the flutter in my stomach quickly evolves into an aching pulse that spreads down my body.

Mustering every bit of strength I have, I pull away again.

I expect him to look a little dazed after that kiss, but he's as fierce as when I first leaned in. And, yet again, he is a man of no words. He just stares at me, and the vulnerability I feel as a result pinches my gut.

I stumble backward, lightheaded. I can't read him. Not one bit. He just stands there without words, without movement, looking at me as if . . . as if I have no idea because he is giving me nothing.

Staring back at him, I know —

That was a mistake.

"That was a mistake," I say, aloud this

time. There are many things that drove me to kiss him, the rational side of my brain says. The need to uncap and release the emotion biting inside me about Kara. The overwhelming emotion I have toward him generally. It's as though kissing him was an exploration of the meaning of all those feelings. It's nostalgia, I tell myself.

I can't think of all the things that connect us or I'll lean back in. So instead, I think of all the hurt of losing him once, how I can't go through it again.

He flinches slightly, and I almost believe my words have stung him, though it's hard to tell because he's so damn silent. I can't imagine what is happening in his head, despite my attempts to figure it out. To figure him out.

He steps around me and grabs his beer to take a long swig, and it feels like he's washing away the remnants of our kiss. Of me. I can't believe this happened. What did I expect when I followed him on a mystery escapade as sequestered jury members under strict rules.

"I'm sorry," I say, but if I'm listening to myself, my body specifically, it's less of an actual apology and more of a formality.

"Don't be," he says, so immediately I'm unsure if it's genuine or perhaps meant to placate me. Desperate to dissipate the ick inside me, I'll accept either. We stare at each other again, his face — eyes specifically — looking conflicted as they narrow in an intense glower.

"And thank you," I say.

His eyebrows pinch. "For what?"

"For apologizing."

He huffs out a breath, which I interpret as some kind of unspoken understanding.

One quick apology doesn't solve all that exists between us, of course, but it does do some good. I recognize that something significant has changed in this suite. If I had to pin my feelings now, I'd say it's mostly just sadness. In one fell swoop, my empathy for Kara, for him, has replaced the anger. Empathy and anger can't seem to successfully coexist in me. For the moment, I am grateful for that.

Part of me — a part closely aligned with my center point — wants to pull him back into the closet. Because I know once we leave this room, this whole thing between us has to stay here — one small moment replaced by professionalism and jury member decorum.

He looks at me, conflicted, as if debating if my acknowledgement of his apology is an opening for more.

I clear my throat and look away. I can't handle more right now. "I really am so sorry about Kara." I cringe a little inside that I've just said the words he always avoided offering me in times of sympathy. "I wish I could have been there."

"I don't . . . I don't talk about her."

"I know," I say, because his words feel prophetic of a him I didn't see over the last ten years but know the movements of.

He clears his throat and straightens, as if someone has pulled taut a string from the ceiling attached through his body. Whatever stolen time we had in this suite, it's clearly over, his shield positioned in front of him again.

I open my mouth to speak, but before I can, he adds, "We should head back to our rooms."

I try not to deflate, knowing it's the right thing to do. "Yeah, we probably should."

After some deliberation, we place the beer cans into the bag from the trash bin, then throw it in the larger bin in the hallway.

He silently leads me back to the stairwell and holds the door open as I brush past him. My arm grazes his chest, and my body's Pavlovian response kicks in with a flash of his eyes cut by the light in the closet moments ago, sending a wave of both heat and sadness through me. Apparently, sadness and attraction *can* coexist. As we descend the stairs, it feels like the end of something. He opens the door to the first floor, and I step through. His eyes linger on mine as I do, making me believe he feels it, too.

We cross the hallway unspotted.

Facing each other again in front of Cam's door, the one tucked between ours, I'm about to turn and leave with no more between us when he whispers, "I'm sorry if . . ." He clears his throat, runs his hand down his face. ". . . if I made you uncomfortable."

"What? No, I'm sorry for starting it."

He nods. I'm intoxicated by the need to know what's going on in his head. He's a mystery greater than Margot Kitsch at this moment, and I want to solve it. Solve him. I want to know what else has happened in these last ten years — big, small, and everything in between. I want to know what beer he likes, because I'm confident it's not Natural Ice. I want to know what love has looked like for him, who has broken his heart. If the way he approaches relationships was shaped by what we walked in on that day. I want to know what life was like right after his sister died. I want to know how my feelings could betray me so quickly, choosing him over my ten-year stronghold of resentment. I want to know if he still thinks I'm beautiful, even tonight in my sweatsuit and no makeup. I want to know if he felt those kisses in his toes.

As we stand in the hallway, a swirl of things unsaid hovering around us, the door between us swings open. In an instant Cam is standing in his doorway, looking back and forth between us. He smiles, mouth wide, a grin full of accusatory glee.

"What're you guys doing?" Cam asks.

"Nothing," I say quickly.

"C'mon. Whatever it is, I want in," he pleads in a hefty whisper.

I look past them both to the corner where George is stationed. He's not visible, though I hear the quiet rush of what sounds like a football game, likely being watched on his phone. "Right, good night," I whisper in the general direction of them both. Reaching across Cam, I grab Damon's hand and shake it vigorously to emphasize the platonic nature of our interaction. But even the handshake sends a pulse between my legs.

Damon looks down at our hands and then back at me, his face unreadable.

I release his hand and abruptly take the few steps to my door, fish the key from my sweatpants pocket, and bulldoze my way in.

Safely inside my room, back pressed against the door, I cringe. I cringe at the handshake, the closet, the entire evening. My stomach hollows at the thought of Kara.

But then, I feel the phantom touch of his lips against mine and can't fight the twinge of heat that follows.

16.

Hearsay (n.)

1. an out-of-court statement that is being offered in court for the truth of what was asserted
2. lies, all of it

I don't run into Damon the next morning, as I arrive as late as possible for breakfast, grabbing a stale blueberry muffin and scarfing it down on the way to the shuttle. Most mornings, I've headed down early to talk with the other jurors, ensuring I know each of their names and a detail or two about them. Despite all the curveballs Damon's presence has brought, I still want to be foreperson. It stings when I finally emerge to find Xavier chatting up a group of four other jurors, right as they all erupt into roaring laughter at something he's just said. I make a vow to up my game.

It's not that I'm avoiding Damon — that's impossible when we'll be seated next to each other all day. I just don't know how to be around him after last night.

I tossed all night thinking about him, yes, but mostly about Kara. About her life. Her death. About what it must have been like in his house when they got the news. I pictured his mom crumpled in a heap on the floor, wrapped in the sunflower-covered sundress that was always Kara's favorite. I pictured his father staring at a doctor in shock, his gentle blue-green eyes (Damon's eyes) pleading. And I pictured Damon, tears falling silently down his cheeks as he bent to the cold hospital linoleum to console his mother. I can't imagine what their family has been through, and I don't know if it brought them closer together or tore them apart. There's still so much unknown space.

When we're lining up to enter the courtroom, he turns and addresses me over his shoulder. "Hey," he says, that jaw muscle flexing as soon as he closes his mouth.

"Hi," I return, losing the battle with the corners of my lips to keep them in place as they upturn.

He's about to say more, but the door opens and a bailiff ushers us into the courtroom.

Once seated, I'm dumbfounded at how much Damon has distracted me from the case. It's only day four of testimonies and my mind, once consumed by Margot and this trial, has quickly made too much room for Damon. I still can't reconcile which Damon it is I am finding myself drawn to — this new, hardened one or the best friend I used to wish would see me as more.

It takes a full few minutes to move my attention to Margot and the courtroom.

Today, Margot has donned a fitted pantsuit the color of an acorn, pant legs flaring slightly at the ankle, ending just before her subdued black heels. I take her in, surprised to find she seems almost upbeat. Though she doesn't smile, she's noticeably less tense than yesterday. I wonder if she's intent on staying positive. A fake-it-till-you-make-it approach to the day.

I'm getting to know the faces in the room a bit, too. Most of the gallery comprises the same people in the same seats each day. There's the woman with the bright blond locks who appears to be perpetually dressed in the same black suit. Next to her, the gangly man who constantly shifts his position on the bench, causing it to creak every few minutes. And on the other side of him, the older woman who, when not scrawling copious notes on her legal pad, swipes at her nose at regular intervals with the ever-present tissue in her hand.

There's no time to think about the repercussions of last night's revelations. The prosecution calls *AMOM* cast member Meredith Dixon as their next witness, and I shift my attention to the court proceedings. I expect to be excited about another one of the Moms in this room, but instead I'm anxious. I really hope we're not about to find out that Joe was sleeping with *Meredith,* too.

The double doors at the back of the courtroom open, and Meredith approaches the stand. She is raven-haired and in her late forties. Her hair is pulled back in a low, tight bun at the base of her neck, accentuating her long, thin face.

Meredith is widely considered the most "normal" of all the cast members. She wears stylish outfits, though they're far more subdued than the others'. She is rarely the instigator of arguments and often plays peacemaker between the women. The most controversial things about her are that she puts her twin toddlers on leashes at Disneyland and constantly says "irregardless." As a result, she is regularly called boring by the fan base. Her tagline is "You may judge me for being the voice of reason, but having class is *never* out of season."

I watch Margot evaluate her, eyes raking over Meredith, and her face twists in dissatisfaction. Any positivity Margot held is wiped completely from her face and overall demeanor, her efforts short-lived.

As Meredith is sworn in, Damon scrawls on his notepad. When finished, he passes the pad from his left leg to his right and angles it toward me. He's written in all caps but small print, his handwriting bold and slightly intimidating, like him.

YOU OK?

☐ ☐

YES NO

☐

STILL PASSED OUT IN A CLOSET

The first note Damon ever wrote me was the same format as this one. It was in Mr. Clayborn's first-period algebra class in sixth grade, when we felt like the only two people on Earth who didn't have phones yet. He reached across the aisle, holding a folded sheet while Mr. Clayborn scrawled equations on the board.

HOW MANY MORE TIMES WILL MR. C ADJUST HIS CROTCH BEFORE THE BELL RINGS?

☐ ☐

6 8

☐

THE LIMIT DOES NOT EXIST

Now I smile and place a checkmark in the third box, grateful for the easy out. *Fair enough,* he writes back, then moves his pad back to his other leg, but not before his eyes catch mine and we exchange a charged look, the shared secret of our escapade in the presidential suite last night between us. I appreciate that he doesn't press further, though a small, bothersome part of me wants him to.

D.A. Stern's co-prosecutor, Albert D'Agostino, dives into his questions to Meredith, and I am grateful for the distraction.

"Ms. Dixon, you've spent countless hours with Mrs. Kitsch over the years, filming for the show *Authentic Moms of Malibu* and otherwise, is that correct?"

"Yes, we've been on the show together since season one. We are both original cast members."

"Are you two friends?"

Meredith takes a moment before answering. "We have been, in the past." She is calm, factual, as she speaks in her distinct, croakier-than-one-might-expect voice. She sounds like someone on the cusp of losing their voice or a lifelong smoker, though I know she is neither.

D'Agostino asks more questions about their on-and-off friendship and then gets to a very specific point.

"Despite this history, we are here to discuss one event in particular. You took a trip with Margot and other cast members two years ago, correct?"

Meredith nods. "Yes."

There is one trip that immediately comes to mind that I assume as the one the prosecutor is referencing. Margot went on a girls' trip with three cast members during the past off-season — Alizay, Meredith, and Britain Buchanan, a onetime assistant to Dua Lipa. Between the four of them, they posted dozens of bikini boat shots. Even more bikini beach shots. There were also some bikini making-drinks-in-the-expansive-stone-kitchen-of-their-exclusive-rental shots. The trip wasn't filmed for the show, so I don't know the details of it other than what the women chose to post. What could have happened on that trip that's relevant to this trial?

At D'Agostino's urging, Meredith describes the trip. "We ate, drank, lounged. It was delightfully unexciting."

Indeed, this sounds like quite a departure from the televised trips the women usually take (at least one per season to some tropical destination), where they fight over who gets the best room and dance with unassuming waiters after too many glasses of pinot grigio. Meredith is perhaps best known for drinking too much and then falling into bushes. Margot, on the other hand, is usually diving naked into the pool or ocean or hot tub.

"What did you ladies talk about? On this trip?" Albert D'Agostino asks. The co-prosecutor is a stout man, portly and short-limbed with glasses he pushes up his nose with a pointed index finger. When beside each other, D'Agostino looks a bit like a child compared to D.A. Stern's long, towering frame.

Durrant Hammerstead's foot taps under

the defense table. I assume he is awaiting an opportunity to interject with an objection if D'Agostino doesn't make a connection soon.

"We discussed normal things mostly. Our families, what activities our kids were obsessed with at the moment. What we were reading. But Margot was reading this book, *The Poison Keeper.*"

She glances at Margot who looks sad, a defeated, sunken quality having taken over her eyes and cheeks. This isn't like the catty exchanges expected between the women on the show. It is, instead, one-sided.

I exhale as a murmur of confusion streaks across the room.

Albert D'Agostino returns to the prosecutors' table and picks up a clicker. He lifts it toward the screen beside the witness stand. When he does, a photo of Margot fills it, one pulled from her social media, including the caption and like count. She's wearing a shiny gold bikini and straw hat, lounging poolside, her bronzed legs crossed at the ankle on a lounge chair. She's on a terrace, sea glistening behind her below the balcony's edge. It's somewhat reminiscent of the opening shot of season one of the show. The caption reads "Misbehaving in Mallorca" and has more than one hundred thousand likes.

"This is a picture Margot posted on her social media. Can you confirm this is from the trip in question?"

"Yes, it is. I took that photo for her," Meredith says.

Albert D'Agostino clicks again, and a new photo appears, this one a pixilated close-up of the book splayed open on the end table next to the lounger, too blurry to notice in the original. The title fills most of the screen.

The Poison Keeper.

The title alone is damning enough, but it's about to get a lot worse for Margot, I realize, knowing most of the courtroom and jury likely haven't heard the details of the story Margot was casually reading poolside in Mallorca. I know them only because of a documentary I happened to watch a few months ago when deep into my true crime phase.

Albert D'Agostino clicks again. This time, he has pulled up the back of the book jacket. Words pop out at me like jabs to the eyes. Poison. Cruel death. Based on the legendary life of Giulia Tofana.

"The Poison Keeper," Albert D'Agostino reads as he steps toward the jury box. "A

novel all about the life of Giulia Tofana. On this trip, did Mrs. Kitsch talk about this book she was reading, just seven months before her husband died?"

Meredith leans forward and gazes at Margot, the two looking at each other as if strangers. As if they haven't shared so much of their lives with each other. I wonder what led Meredith to do this to someone she considered a friend. Tenley, I get. They had a falling out. Tenley was sleeping with Joe. But Meredith has always been the level-headed one.

"Yes. At dinner on the last night of our trip, Margot told us all about it. About how fascinated she was by the story. How this woman, Giulia Tofana, lived in Italy in the 1600s and was the daughter of an apothecary. Apparently, her mother was executed for murdering her husband. Margot told us how this woman went on to sell this product called Aqua Tofana, I think it was. This face cream or oil, or something, given to women looking to escape abusive husbands. As Margot described it, this Giulia was selling these women a mix of toxic chemicals so they could kill their husbands. The women would add drops to their husbands' drinks or meals. Margot told us about how it would happen slowly, over time, so most of the deaths were never attributed to poison but rather some unknown illness." She pauses. "She even told us how Mozart claimed he was poisoned by Aqua Tofana on his deathbed. Giulia Tofana was a bit of an icon, the way Margot described it."

I hear the word *objection* in my head before Durrant Hammerstead even says it. There's a slight squabble between Judge Gillespy, Albert D'Agostino, and Durrant Hammerstead, and I draw a tally mark in the corner of the sheet in my notebook, where I've taken to tracking the number of objections. I'll need a new sheet corner soon.

Once the objection is resolved, Judge Gillespy allows the line of questioning to continue, and D'Agostino asks, "Why is it that you remember this particular conversation so distinctly?"

"Because" — Meredith leans in again — "Margot was . . . excited. Like, enthralled by this book, this woman. She was talking fast and loud and went on and on about it, to the point where Britain — she's another cast member who was on the trip — and I talked about how weirdly obsessed she was with it."

Virtually everyone in the courtroom looks at Margot. Damon's eyes, though, shift to me. But not before I watch him underline a statement he's written on his notepad.

<u>WAS READING A BOOK ABOUT POISONING HUSBANDS</u>

Durrant Hammerstead's counterpart, Irena Medley, cross-examines Meredith. Irena Medley holds her own physically against the rest of the occupants of the defense table. She towers over both Margot and Durrant Hammerstead, long and lanky lean like a supermodel. She wears her hair pulled back tightly and has the sharp cheekbones and jawline to match, giving her an exquisite androgynous quality.

Irena Medley asks a rapid-fire series of questions, attempting to poke holes in Meredith's account of the evening in question. How many drinks did Meredith have that night? "Two tequila sodas." Were there side conversations going on? "No. When Margot speaks, she commands the whole room." What was Margot wearing? "I don't remember, probably something long and floral," Meredith says.

"Was her hair up or down?"

Meredith shakes her head delicately. "I couldn't say."

"So, you listened to Margot go 'on and

on,' as you describe it, about this book she was reading, and you were paying close enough attention to remember exactly what Mrs. Kitsch said but don't remember what she was wearing or any details of her appearance that night?"

"I didn't say I remember *every* detail of what she said. But I remember the gist of it."

Satisfied, Irena Medley emphasizes how thousands of people have read this particular book, one that is a *fictionalized* retelling of Giulia Tofana's life, none of whom have then gone on to kill their husbands, that we know of.

"Reading a book that thousands of others have read . . ." Irena Medley wrings her hands thoughtfully. "It's an incredible stretch to assume a correlation to this case."

"Is that a question?" Meredith asks, looking up at Judge Gillespy.

"No," Irena Medley concedes, accomplishing, as I see it, very little of substance in her cross-examination.

It's Albert D'Agostino's redirect that truly hammers home the prosecution's goal with this witness. "Ms. Dixon, were there any other relevant details of that conversation or others with Margot along similar topics, since my counterpart has suggested that the topic of a book Mrs. Kitsch may have been reading doesn't apply here?"

"Yes," Meredith affirms. "A week after that trip, Margot and I grabbed coffee after school dropoff. She was designing this flyer for an upcoming Sea Save event. I told her there were people who could do that, but she wanted to do it herself. She had a vision." Meredith flips her hand in the air as she says *vision.* "Anyway, she left her laptop open when she went to the restroom, and I noticed the article she had pulled up in another window."

"What was the article?"

"It was about this woman. Nancy something Brophy."

"Nancy Crampton-Brophy?" D'Agostino fills in.

"Yes, that's it. It was this news article about this woman who wrote romantic thrillers and became known for one blog essay in particular."

I'm not familiar with this new reference.

Durrant Hammerstead and Irena Medley whisper to each other, likely discussing whether to object yet again.

D'Agostino continues quickly, as if sensing he's on borrowed time. "Ms. Dixon, were you able to read the full article before Margot returned to the table?"

Meredith shakes her head. "No. But it was . . . interesting enough that I researched when I got home." She raises her eyebrows at Margot, who stares as though she's looking right through Meredith.

"What did you find in your later research of this woman Mrs. Kitsch was reading about?"

"So, this woman, Nancy Crampton-Brophy, became 'famous' for writing an essay." Meredith leans forward again, painfully close to the microphone, and I can't help but follow suit. She pauses for what I can only assume is dramatic effect, trained well by the show. "The essay title was 'How to Murder Your Husband.' "

I glance at Margot, who shakes her head ever so slightly as if to say, *You are wrong, you're all wrong about me,* in a desperate plea.

Meredith continues. "Apparently, after she wrote this 'How to Murder Your Husband' essay, she was *convicted of murdering her husband.*"

The expected whispers make their way across the room.

Knowing how things usually play out, I have a hard time believing these conversations would have occurred without Meredith or Tenley bringing them into the show as an attempted storyline. An Authentic Mom potentially plotting the demise of her husband? The other Moms and producers would have jumped on the chance to exploit it — just the kind of hyperbolic storyline that would have been ratings gold for the show.

Judge Gillespy wraps her hand around her gavel, though she doesn't lift it, the movement alone threatening enough to silence the gallery. D'Agostino is sure to note a summary of Nancy Crampton-Brophy's case will be included as an exhibit, before focusing again on the jury. "No further questions," he affirms, before setting in the direction of the prosecution table to join a clearly content D.A. Stern.

Damon looks over at me, eyebrows raised.

I attempt to hide my dismay.

17.

Restitution (n.)

1. the act of restoring or making amends for something that was lost, damaged, or borrowed
2. can be applied to snacks

We eat lunch in one of the courthouse rooms, a spread of sandwiches, chips, cookies, and room-temperature sodas piled in the middle of the large, round table.

"Is there anything ever on the lunch menu besides sandwiches?" gripes Gray Man, directing his words to the turkey on rye in his hand. True to the first day, he has worn very little besides differing shades of gray suits. It's the first time I've heard him speak except to ask our van driver to blast the air-conditioning harder on virtually every ride, freezing the rest of us out. He is the only juror I haven't gathered any fun facts about.

"There's never anything organic, either," says juror number twelve, the usually perky mom of four, Kate. To no one's surprise, Gray Man ignores her. Juror number eleven (the blond man I've come to know as the perpetual courtroom sneezer) grabs the last package from the turkey tray, and juror number two (a short, bald man who waves to Judge Gillespy each time we enter the courtroom) scoffs in dismay.

I sit down next to Tamra at the round table, then Damon takes the seat next to me. Cam quickly takes the seat beside Damon. We've become an unexpected little foursome.

"Four days in and we haven't even heard from the defense yet," Tamra says. We all look at one another, then the others, dejected. I'm not quite at the level of despondence they seem to be, but I do feel the fatigue of it all.

"It's wild that woman wrote a book about killing her husband and then killed her husband," Cam's voice projects, garnering a few looks from around the table. He speaks as if he's mid-conversation about the morning's developments, though he's just sat down. I notice juror numbers five and six nodding in agreement.

"An article," I correct, just as one of the

bailiffs — Carolyn, I know her name to be — clears her throat toward Cam and me.

I wonder whether the revelation about the book Margot was reading will damage her case. Whether it *should* be damaging. I've read books about murder. It most certainly didn't make me a murderer or more likely to murder.

"No case talk," Xavier, our self-appointed jury leader, scolds jovially from a few seats down, then bites into the club in his hands. He seems to love sandwiches.

"Sorry," Cam says to no one in particular, pulling his chip package open before leaning across the table to the center and grabbing two more bags. Tamra stares sadly at her bag of Lay's. They didn't even offer a variety of flavors today, it's just a pile of yellow bags of Classics.

Damon leans in and speaks so softly only I can hear. "How are you holding up? Still a superfan after all you've learned?" His chin dimple twitches.

I smile politely at Damon, though do not otherwise reply, shoving my pastrami on wheat to my lips and sinking into a bite too large to speak through.

We eat primarily in silence for the remainder of the meal, and as our lunch break wears down, I duck into the restroom for a moment to myself. I stare at my reflection, see the barely there markings of a flush. There's more color in my cheeks, and not the artificial kind. My eyes seem dewier, my eyebrows more arched. Despite the stress of the case and several nights of poor sleep, I look like I've just returned from a relaxing Caribbean vacation. A twinge of guilt singes the back of my neck as I think about Kara. About Joe Kitsch. I've had some semblance of enjoyment here, Joe's death the catalyst for the new life in my cheeks.

Exiting the bathroom to head back to the makeshift lunchroom, I face-plant directly into Damon. Specifically, the right side of my face lands squarely between his pecs. I instinctively know it's him, his smell and build immediately recognizable, even as my body collides with his. He is a wall, no softness or give.

He clasps my arms, just above the elbows, to straighten me as I step back.

"You fall a lot," he says when we've separated.

"No, I don't," I respond automatically, though I instantly recall the almost-passing-out situation from last night, realizing how much the damsel in distress I've managed to be with him and how much I hate it. Like an unlikable rom-com heroine.

As I pull away, I realize I've left a foundation stain smack dab between his pecs on his sky-blue button-down. His eyes flick to the front of his shirt and then do this sort of flutter thing that tells me he doesn't care.

We stand staring at each other in the hallway in front of the women's restroom entrance and it feels dangerous, being alone with him, despite the many people just yards away behind various courtroom doors.

Still passed out in a closet, I think. I feel as though I am. A big part of me wishes we *were* back in that closet, everything else shut out.

He pulls a package from his back pocket, hands it to me. "A replacement."

"Thanks," I say, taking the peanut butter cups. I open it and hand him one, keeping the other for myself.

"Cheers," I say, holding it up.

He bumps his cup to mine. The chocolate has softened, likely from the placement in his back pocket. Peanut butter cups have quickly become my favorite treat.

Despite telling myself to walk away, I linger. "You really still ride motocross?" I ask through the bite. No matter how much I want to stay mad at him, I just can't seem to make it stick today. It's unnerving, more than anything, how little time it has taken for me to see *him* again.

"What made you think of that?"

I shrug. "It's one of the only things I know about you now." Other than the taste of your mouth.

He leans against the wall just beyond the ladies' room door, crosses his arms as his right foot moves in front of his left. "It's where I do my best thinking."

The answer surprises me. "While flying through the air and avoiding collisions over earsplitting motors?"

He huffs and his mouth parts. "Yeah."

"What do you think about? On your bike?"

"I don't know." He straightens. "Life. Roadway signs. Hairless cats."

"How does a man of so few words write such punny roadway signs? This feels like one of life's great mysteries."

"Better on paper," he says, as if it's an obvious answer.

"Like the pages of a twelve-year-old girl's padlocked diary," I confirm.

He releases his jaw, and perhaps I imagine it, but the corners of his mouth curl up farther than I thought possible.

"Wait, is that a smile?" I muse.

His mouth falls. "I can smile," he says, though his face makes no movement in the direction of said smile.

"Right," I say, crumpling the peanut butter cup package in my hand and walking past him toward the courtroom. I feel him watching as I do, and I can't help the extra sway in my hips this notion causes.

After lunch, D.A. Stern and the prosecution continue their parade of Margot slander, this time in the form of her self-built business. Bess Waterford is called to the stand.

Margot's former business partner plods to the front of the courtroom, her black patent leather Gucci loafers squeaking as she walks. The irony of those shoes is not lost on me. They were a gift from Margot two years ago for her birthday, the handover of the expensive pair aired during the finale of season six.

Bess looks like the "after" picture of a former plain Jane who's undergone an expensive makeover, with her heavy but well-blended makeup, highlighted cheekbones, and svelte frame. There's an ongoing debate online over whether she is actually pretty or simply meticulously crafted. People on the internet have very strong opinions about her face.

Once Bess has taken the stand, at D.A. Stern's urging, she explains, "I was Margot's business partner for GotMar when it launched and for the first year."

"And for those who are not familiar, what is GotMar?" D.A. Stern asks.

"It's a line of push-up bras, which Margot launched in season three of the show."

And sells exceptionally well, I know. I've seen the GotMar display at Nordstrom, right beside a table of Skims. I shift uncomfortably in my seat, realizing I'm wearing one of her products under my A-line dress right now. I instinctively tug at the neckline of said dress to ensure no evidence of this coincidence is visible. I will note mine is from the everyday line and, though adequately supportive, not push-up.

Having Bess Waterford on the stand talking about bras makes me think of the shopping trip to Walmart at age eleven with my mom for my first bra. I needed one several months before, having taken to layering and sweatshirts to hide the growth below, but this was the first time my mom attended to the need. She kept calling it a "training bra," which I deemed archaic. What was I training, exactly? My breasts how to stay put? They were hardly ample enough to go anywhere.

I don't particularly remember what that first bra looked like or if we argued about which one to get. What I do recall is that my mom was nice. Doting, even. I don't know what made her especially attentive that day, but I took in every bit of it. I went home with two "training bras," a sugar high from a Rocky Road cone, and a hardcover copy of *Cinder.* I hadn't thought of that day in a long time. I still savor the rare glimpses I remember of an attentive mother. It's all I ever wanted from my parents when I was young.

My baby sister Gen's cherubic face flashes across my mind, and I wonder what her first bra-shopping experience will be, if I'll be there for it.

Next to me, Damon clears his throat, and I look at him. We make eye contact, and just that link causes a jolt along my spine. His eyes are always filled with so much, but I never quite know what. I shift in my seat uncomfortably, fighting the urge to take Damon's hand in mine, right here in this courtroom, and squeeze it.

18.

Character Witness (n., phrase)

1. testifies to a person's positive or negative character traits and reputation in the community
2. possibly of the backstabbing kind

"Tell us what your relationship with Margot was like when you worked for her," D.A. Stern asks Bess Waterford, returning my attention to the stand. A pen bounces wildly between Stern's fingers as I interpret his question: *Tell us all the reasons you hate Margot.*

Bess Waterford looks to Margot briefly, then flutters her eyes to the gallery. "She was . . . intense. Demanding."

"How so?"

"Nothing was ever good enough. She was always appalled by our 'lack of professionalism.' " She uses air quotes. "Meanwhile, she did a bunch of weird shit herself."

"What do you mean, exactly, by 'weird shit'?" D.A. Stern asks. I can sense Cam fighting a chuckle behind me.

Bess Waterford leans in conspiratorially. "Once, I walked into her office, and she was binge eating vanilla wafers. Like, she had a family-sized package open, half missing, mouth full with, like, seven of them. Crumbs everywhere. And she's supposedly gluten-free. They were *not* gluten-free wafers. Another time, I opened the hall closet in our office to grab a trash bag, and she was standing there, in the dark, just staring at the wall. Weird. Shit."

Juror number five, to my right — the lovely older gentleman named Luis who has no immediate family except his two bright white Westies, Lance and Chucky, I've recently learned — writes slowly on his pad, his hand holding a slight tremor. When I look closer, I see it's not trial notes he's taking down, rather, he is playing tic-tac-toe. With himself. I make a mental note to spend some time determining how this particular juror might behave during deliberations.

Right on cue, Durrant Hammerstead objects, citing relevance. I never realized how many objections there could be in one case. In one day of one case, even. The antics are never-ending. I take in the eleven lines between Judge Gillespy's eyebrows and imagine they've grown deeper in this very courtroom from her constant need to reprimand skilled attorneys like arduous toddlers.

I feel for Margot in this moment, too. Who *hasn't* stress-eaten a box of wafers or stood in a dark closet so they can lose their shit in private? If anything, these examples of "questionable behavior" humanize her.

I get it. I just hope the rest of the jury does, too.

Before the testimony continues, Damon leans over, his arm covertly stretching across my lap to strike a tally mark with his pen alongside the others. Apparently, he's noticed my little game of tracking objections. His arm, warm and bristled, grazes mine as he retracts it, and a zap shoots through my core. When I look up at him, his attention is focused on the D.A., who has resumed his questioning.

"Tell us, Ms. Waterford. When and how did your business relationship with Mrs. Kitsch end?"

"About a week after we landed the Nordstrom deal, which *I* did all the legwork on. Margot called me into her office. She directed me to sit. And then she told me I was 'not a good representation of the brand.' " She uses air quotes again.

"What did that mean exactly? 'Not a good representation of the brand'?"

Bess looks down at her chest, and her chin rubs against the white of her turtleneck, leaving a small peach-colored makeup stain the size of a penny. *Of course,* I think, forcing myself not to glance over at Damon's own makeup-stained shirt. Bess Waterford unknowingly mocks me from the stand.

"I had gotten implants the month prior. Apparently fake tits don't fit the GotMar brand."

Cam, behind me, snickers. Damon shoots him a look.

"So, she fired you for making a personal decision about altering your body?"

"Yes." Bess crosses her arms. "Margot's a Scorpio. Once she thinks you've done something wrong, she doesn't forgive or forget. She just gets even."

There's another objection, the sixth of the day so far. I draw a tally.

D.A. Stern transitions despite the overruling. "Ms. Waterford, from your vantage point, what did you make of Joe and Margot's relationship?"

"It was like any other relationship in our

circle. Transactional."

"Can you explain?"

"He was with her for her looks. She was with him for his money and power. Tale as old as time. Cliché and passé, if you ask me, but whatever floats your boat." She flips her chestnut hair with an aggressive toss. "But Margot, she didn't play by the rules."

"The rules?"

"Yeah, she decided she wasn't willing to play her role anymore. She got on the show, got some modicum of fame. Started Got-Mar, got rich. Money *she* earned. She threw off the balance of power, the unwritten agreement of their relationship. She rocked that boat till it capsized."

The defense objects yet again, and I vaguely hear Judge Gillespy agree that Bess's response is indeed speculation.

Beside me, Damon rubs absentmindedly at the back of his neck. I wish he'd stop.

Finally, it's the defense's turn at Bess Waterford.

Durrant Hammerstead remains lax in his seat and lets his counterpart redirect. Irena Medley doesn't smile often, but when she does, I am struck by her bright white teeth that remind me a bit of Damon's. It's a shame he doesn't show his off more.

"You don't know what it's like, working

for someone like that," Bess goes on, unbidden, before Irena Medley can even get a question out. "She's got this larger-than-life presence. She's . . . perfect. On the outside, at least. Having to exist next to someone like that, it's awful." She says *awful* as if describing a puss-laden sore.

"Ms. Waterford," Irena Medley says with authority, attempting to rein Bess in. "Isn't it true that just before Margot purchased your shares of the business two years ago, there was a concern raised to you, by Margot, about shipments of product coming in from the Mexico plant?"

Bess shifts in her seat. "A concern, yes, but nothing was ever proven."

"What was the concern Margot raised to you?"

Bess huffs into the microphone, smooths her hair, her skirt. Finally, she says in the most dismissive of tones, "She heard a rumor from the warehouse manager that black market Botox was coming in with the product shipments."

Irena Medley enacts a severe lift of her brows as if it's the first she's hearing of this revelation.

"It was never proven!" Bess declares.

Judge Gillespy strikes her gavel — one firm, hard blow. "Watch your volume, Ms.

Waterford."

Bess is clearly heated, her chest rising and falling, hitting her chin at each heave, deepening the makeup stain on the front of her shirt, mocking me further.

Judge Gillespy, clearly over this witness, asks the defense to wrap it up.

"Ms. Waterford, you had quite the falling out with Margot, it seems," Irena Medley says. "First, there were allegations of illegal goods being moved in the product shipments, then this claim that you no longer fit the brand. Did you ever . . . do anything geared toward Mrs. Kitsch that was . . . out of anger? As a result of this falling out?"

Bess swallows hard. "I was upset," she says, her voice flimsy.

"You were upset when you did what?"

Bess glares at Margot, then forces herself to look away, while Margot's eyes grow dark, their sadness remaining.

"I keyed her car when I saw it in the parking lot of Erewhon on Santa Monica."

"You keyed the word *twat* into the side of Margot's Range Rover, is that correct?"

Cam snickers again.

Bess closes her eyes. "Yes."

Irena Medley makes a *hmph* sound in judgment of Bess's admission. "It would seem *you* are the one who seeks revenge at all costs, not Mrs. Kitsch," she declares.

Judge Gillespy pounds her gavel.

Margot turns her head sharply to the gallery, as if to say, *Are you getting this?*

"No further questions," co-defense counsel Medley states, and then takes her seat, leaving Bess Waterford glaring at Margot from the witness stand.

19.

Legal Loophole (n., phrase)

1. a gap or ambiguity in the wording or application of a law or rule that allows individuals to exploit it to their advantage
2. not a crime, technically

Thirty minutes after I've retired to my room for the evening, after I've changed into sweats, washed my face, and gone through my skincare routine, I sit at the edge of the bed riddled with worry. So far, Margot has been made out to be a scorned wife in a marriage for show, a difficult teen who disappeared for a week, a cutthroat business partner, a gold digger who married her way into luxury, and a mildly unhinged closet-hiding wafer binger. The woman described in that courtroom is so very different from the one I've watched over seven seasons of

AMOM, and I can't help but wonder which is the true version. It's certainly made me realize that I might not know as much about Margot as I thought I did. I'm itching to get into that deliberation room and lead discussions.

A shuffling sound at my door catches my attention, and I look over in time to see a sheet of folded paper sliding under it. For some reason, I instantly think of the handwritten note I received in the eighth grade from Jared Moore, handed to me in our junior high hallway between English and lab. Damon was the only person to have ever written me a physical note up to that point. I opened it anxiously, some small bit of me daring to think it could be a declaration of romantic interest, only to find it read, *Is it true your dad is sleeping with Ms. Paige?* It would turn out my father had a thing for teachers. I was no longer invisible; tagged instead. After I told Damon what happened, he got his revenge on Jared Moore that afternoon at a particularly aggressive lacrosse practice.

I know who this note is from: the same person whose notes fill that Tiffany-blue shoebox in my closet. My heart thuds with anticipation as I unfold the note and begin reading.

SYDNEY,

IF YOU COULD BINGE-WATCH ANY SHOW RIGHT NOW, WHICH WOULD IT BE? MINE WOULD BE TED LASSO BECAUSE I'LL NEED A LONG-TERM BREAK FROM DRAMA AFTER THIS TRIAL. AND IF YOU SAY THE NEW SEASON OF AUTHENTIC MOMS OF MALIBU AFTER ALL THIS, I MAY HAVE TO RETHINK OUR FRIEND-SHIP.

SINCERELY,
DESPERATELY BORED DAMON

I reread the note still standing in the doorway, the smile invading my lips unavoidable. He's so solidly reserved most of the time, but there have been a handful of moments where he has popped open to me, and I find myself honored each time he does.

Better on paper. More comfortable with written words, certainly.

I'm immediately taken back to my teenage years, lying in bed, smiling because of his words. The paper was always worn, like he had folded it and carried it around in his pocket all day, unfolded and refolded several times before delivery.

I plop down on my bed, grab a book to place under the note, and scrawl my response, thinking this is a much better option than sneaking around the hotel. We are *technically* abiding by the rules, remaining in our rooms and not discussing the case.

Desperately Bored Damon,
I think I need to go back to our old favorite, *The Princess Bride,* on repeat. Nothing could get me out of this trial funk like Westley's mask coming off on his roll down that hill, revealing his true identity to Princess Buttercup. And no, I think I'll have to take a hiatus from *AMOM.* Maybe from reality TV altogether.

Sincerely,
Sadly Seeking Shows Sydney

Without thinking, I bend the paper along its existing fold lines, open my door, and peek around. When I see the hallway empty, I stride past Cam's room and slide the sheet under Damon's door.

When safely back in my room, I lie on the bed and open my current read to the bookmarked page. I read the page. I reread the same page. I sit up. The adrenaline rush I feel at something as childlike as passing notes with Damon makes me almost embarrassed.

When I've read the same page four times over, I hear the swipe of paper against the bottom of the doorframe.

SAD SYDNEY,
I'M SORRY TO HEAR THAT YOU'LL HAVE TO FIND SOMETHING TO FILL YOUR AMOM VOID AFTER THIS. I CAN THINK OF A FEW OPTIONS. I PLAN TO START WITH FOOD NOT WRAPPED IN PAPER OR OFF A BUFFET.

DESPERATELY HUNGRY DAMON

P.S. I CAN STILL RECITE PRINCESS BUTTERCUP'S ENTIRE SPEECH TO PRINCE HUMPERDINCK (THE SLIMIEST WEAKLING EVER TO CRAWL THE EARTH).

I draft my response.

Desperately Hungry Damon,
I was so annoying reciting that speech so loudly you could never hear the TV! And please share said food options? I, for one, plan to never eat a sandwich again. The first thing I want is Thai food. Or Sushi Gen, of course. Or maybe Indian. Anything with flavor. Great, now I'm hungry again.

Starving Sydney

His next note takes a bit longer. I stare up at the ceiling particle foam until I hear the swoosh again. *SYD,* it begins. My eyes catch and can't seem to move past the first three letters on the page. Damon calling me Syd is one thing, but writing it in the same way he addressed every letter and note he ever gave me softens my defenses against him further still.

I'M HEADED STRAIGHT TO DIN TAI FUNG, GORGING MYSELF ON SPICY NOODLES AND CUCUMBER SALAD UNTIL THEY HAVE TO CARRY ME OUT.

I stop reading and stare at the back of my door as if he's standing just on the other side, reading his note to me from the hallway. I love Din Tai Fung. I picture sitting across from Damon in a booth, bamboo steamers between us, his sexy gaze on me as he positions his chopsticks.

I've been only once, a birthday surprise from Mel. It's the type of place meant for sharing. I wonder briefly who Damon may have shared a booth with.

BESIDES FOOD WITH FLAVOR, I'VE ALSO BEEN THINKING A LOT ABOUT KARA.

And then the note just ends. It's as if he sat and stared at the page, contemplating what else to write, and eventually gave up.

I stare at my own page, unsure what to say back. I consider several chest-splitting opening lines:

My heart aches for you.
I've always worried my parents don't love me.
I have a sister who is just a baby, yet I've somehow managed to resent her.
I've felt sorry for myself until this moment.

But I chicken out before drafting any of them. Instead, I write:

Because you care about her. And that doesn't just go away. I'm sorry seeing me has brought it all up again.

My pen hovers over the paper, ready to chicken out again. This time, I force the thought into ink. I add:

But I'm so grateful to be near you again.

I step into the hallway again, and just as I am propping my door open with the door-stop, Cam's door opens beside me.

"Hey," he whispers, backpack slung over his shoulder.

"Hey," I whisper back, hoping my face doesn't give away how incredibly caught I feel.

“What’s that?” he asks. He glances over his shoulder toward the elevator where George sits around the corner and then points at the sheet of folded paper in my hand.

Instinctively, I scrunch the paper into a ball in my palm. “Oh, it’s nothing.”

He eyes me with a playful grin.

“Where are you going?” I ask, desperate to shift his focus.

He repositions the strap of his backpack on his shoulder and shakes his head. “Don’t worry about it,” he says, then eyes my closed fist, paper inside.

I nod. Right. I’ll ignore whatever bad decision he’s making, and he’ll ignore mine. I’m okay with that. More than okay. And while I certainly don’t want Cam to cause a mistrial with his antics, his sneaking off does give me a bit of comfort that it’s not just Damon and me rocking the judicial boat. It seems more than one of us is willing to push court-appointed boundaries for our own reasons.

Cam takes off down the hallway, and I slide the note under Damon’s door before scurrying back to my room.

20.

Jury Excursion (n., phrase)

1. a controlled and supervised event where jurors are temporarily allowed to engage in an activity outside the usual sequestration setting
2. *not* a date

It's Saturday, which means no court. And in a surprising gesture, the bailiffs notify the jurors that we get a day out in the world. You would think we'd been awarded a basket full of puppies for our court-appointed service with how overjoyed we are at learning we get to go cosmic bowling, then to Outback Steakhouse for dinner.

I dress in one of the only casual outfits I packed that is not sweats: a burgundy cable-knit sweater that hits at the high waistline of my wide-legged jeans and white platform sneakers. I chalk my own enthusiasm up to the fact that for five days we have seen nothing but the inside of the courtroom, the shuttles, and the hotel. But I know more than a little of the excitement tugging at me is that I get to be out in the world with Damon.

We passed notes back and forth last night for nearly three hours until, finally, I drifted off with his sheets of paper splayed about the bedspread around me. He told me about a few of his tattoos and their meanings, one of which is a lightning bolt up the right side of his rib cage that he inked after losing a motocross race and corresponding bet. That the angel wings on his forearm are for Kara. He told me that reading the sugar-free gummy bear reviews online is an admittedly odd but favorite pastime of his.

THERE AREN'T MANY THINGS THAT MAKE ME LAUGH, he had written. *THOSE DO.*

He told me he plays video games, though was sure to add *only occasionally,* as if it were a first date and he didn't want to scare me into imagining him glued 24/7 to a controller. He told me his favorite game is *Arsonist Betty,* where the player is a vigilante hero chasing an elderly arsonist around L.A. I must admit, based on his description, it sounds like something I'd enjoy playing.

He told me he likes to cook. That it's a

bonding activity between him and his mom, to chop and dice, roast and sear, in comfortable silence together in his parents' kitchen. That a lot of what his family does now are activities in comfortable silence. He told me one of his favorite meals to make is curried lamb chops with sweet potato hash, and my mouth practically watered as I read.

I learned a lot through what he shared in those additional notes. I now know he and his mom are close again. There was a twinge of jealousy in learning he managed to find his way back. I thought of my relationship with my father and how it never recovered. Then again, recovery implies returning to a place of health, and I don't know that we — my father and me — ever had that.

I shared more than I typically do, too. I told him about my parents' ugly divorce. That, despite what happened with our families, it still took six more months and at least two more affairs. About how they don't speak and haven't been in the same room together in nearly nine years. How I doubt they will be again. EVEN FOR YOUR WEDDING ONE DAY? Damon asked back in one of his notes, and I affirmed, *Probably not.* Though in reality, even as I wrote the words, I had a hard time picturing a wedding at all, knowing I've never come remotely close.

I told him about Mel and our friendship, how important she is to me. About our near-daily nighttime ritual of white cheddar Popchips on our Los Feliz couch and the reality show of choice. He told me he has friends, but none like what I describe with her. His world is small, like mine. It gave me a pang of appreciation for Mel.

He ended the conversation around midnight with *I'LL LET YOU GET SOME SLEEP* and the last sentences that made my stomach free-fall — *IT'S NICE THAT WE CAN TALK ABOUT OUR FAMILIES AND NOT HAVE IT BE SO RAW. THANK YOU FOR BEING HERE.*

In those notes, we tested the waters, stretching a little further each time into the delicate pool of our history and the people held within it. And, to my immense relief, neither of us drowned.

The bowling alley is cleared out for us, and as we exit the shuttles, escorted by guards to our private venue, it's like we're celebrities rather than prisoners, as it sometimes feels.

I find Damon at the shoe rental counter. "Thirteens, please," he says to the attendant as I step beside him. He's also dressed down today in dark jeans and a worn red High West Distillery tee. I see the Park City, Utah, location advertised on the shirt and wonder if he's visited. I wonder a lot about him.

I take in the tattoos above his elbows, all an endless stream of Damon trivia. I regard the intricate compass pointed due north along his right upper arm, which he told me last night in one of his notes is a matching tattoo with his dad, who is a fisherman and believes it to be a sign of good fortune. I've always held a soft spot for Mr. Bradburn.

Damon's body is a map of his life and the people in it, a legend notating the important people and things and moments. Passion in this particular form, and on him, is undeniably sexy. It's a new feeling to explore — outright sexual attraction to Damon Bradburn. I was attracted to him back then, sure. But it was more of an appreciation for him and exploration of what he meant to me, versus the escalating itch of craving I now find myself having to push down.

He takes his shoes and turns around, leaning against the counter. It's a bit odd to see him now in person after a night of note passing. The list of material secrets between us keeps growing.

"You confident enough to take me on?" he asks.

"Definitely."

He raises a chestnut eyebrow. "Great."

Damon waits while I get my shoes and follows me to the bay of my choosing.

We end up sharing a lane with Cam and Tamra. The scoreboard reads: TAM, CAM, DAM, AND SYD.

"When's the last time you went bowling?" Damon asks as we wait for Tam and Cam to take their respective first turns. He sits beside me on the hard bench with the color and shine of cherry nail polish.

"I don't know that I ever have," I say, the realization hitting me. Another one of those things most people did for the first time in childhood that I somehow missed.

"Seriously?"

"You know how my parents were. We never did stuff like this." I tuck my knee under my chin, watching his throat as he swallows.

He stretches his arm along the back of the bench, grazing my hair as it rests. I get a flash of the day he got his driver's license, honking outside my house in his dad's silver Tacoma truck. I was his first passenger. He stretched his right arm behind my seat as he backed out of my driveway, forearm pressing against my loose hair. My stomach fell through a trapdoor at the excitement of it all that day, at the notion that Damon and I could go places freely. Anywhere. Everywhere.

He doesn't immediately speak, but his eyes offer an *I'm sorry* in their squint and quick release. Eventually, he says, "I guess part of me hoped they'd change after everything."

I shake my head. "It meant I could go get into serious trouble without anyone caring, though. Sex. Drugs. Robbing banks. I did it all after your family left."

He huffs. "You didn't do any of those things."

"No. I read. Watched TV. Got good grades. Tried to be invisible but worthy of their attention at the same time."

His eyes flash with something like guilt. A week ago, I would have gladly welcomed guilt from him. Now, I don't want him to carry any of it.

"Thus your love of reality TV and Margot Kitsch was born," he says.

I'm dying to know what he thinks of Margot, of the case. I've been wondering since that first day. But I can't ask him outright.

"What about you? When's the last time you went bowling?"

"With my parents and Kara. After everything happened, they leaned into being the quality time types."

"Oh?" My chest burns. I think about how his family dynamic changed. How mine didn't. "What was that like?"

He considers for a moment. "It was okay. I think it was mostly for Kara, I guess, to have us all spending time together. I found it incredibly performative. Though we could definitely get a bit competitive. Don't ever play Monopoly with us."

"Deal." I evaluate Damon, reality surging through me. I cannot imagine being particularly welcome at any Bradburn family game night.

I used to wonder if his parents stayed together all these years. My assumption was always that they would, that they would make it. Something inside me is pleased with the notion that they did. And this casual conversation about our families, well, a big part of me is astonished by it. Does this mean we've both gotten over it all? Or does it simply mean we're ignoring it? Either way, I'm at least momentarily content.

"Damon, you're up, man." Cam points to the scoreboard, where Cam and Tamra are tied with eight points each.

I slide forward on the bench as Damon approaches the line with his ball. He bends, swoops the ball forward, and earns a strike. He strides back to me and takes the seat by my side, his arm returning to the back of the bench. I think of him in middle and high school, how I'd watch him play lacrosse. How he moved with such ease, innately athletic and staunchly capable.

"It's really annoying how naturally good you are at everything."

He turns to face me, though he doesn't affirm or deny.

"Name one thing you're bad at?" I press.

"Why?"

"Because I have to know something you suck at. It will make me feel better about you."

He wrinkles his brow, seemingly at my choice of words. After a long pause, he says, "I suck at relationships."

I work hard to avoid my expression giving anything away, neither intrigue nor disappointment. I can't help but think it's a warning. Or at minimum, a thing guys say to keep expectations low.

"Same," I offer back.

"Sydney, c'mon! You're holding us up," Cam says from the bench across from us.

I grab my ten-pound ball with the purple swirl and line myself up, throwing it halfway down the lane, hitting three pins. I don't particularly care about the game or my score. I do wonder what Margot is doing today. I try to picture her bowling in the lane beside us, and the vision is comical.

I throw the second ball of my turn, this time hitting four of the remaining pins. When I return, Damon grabs a napkin from the stack on the built-in side table and fiddles with it.

The cosmic lights swirl around us, and it suddenly feels like we're at a nightclub. He's silently tinkering with the napkin, and I take the opportunity to ask, "What did you mean when you said you're bad at relationships?"

He raises an eyebrow.

"General curiosity about my courtroom seatmate," I say, answering the question that eyebrow is asking.

He leans back and folds his arms across his chest. His jaw muscle flexes. "Why are you?"

I shake my head. "No. You can't answer a question with a question."

"So many rules," he teases.

I knock his knee with mine.

"I'm not good at it," he says finally, eyes still concentrating on the napkin.

"Not good at what?"

He straightens. "Dating. Relationships. Any of it."

"Why?" I'm not egocentric enough to assume it's because of *me* or what happened to us, but I do wonder if it's made him gun-shy, as it has me. It has to have influenced him, changed him. Made him a little less trusting, or at least far less optimistic.

His head swivels to face me, and I force myself to hold his gaze. Love is a topic we've managed to elude up until this point.

"I had a girlfriend in college. Things didn't work out. I haven't really put myself out there since."

"You haven't dated anyone since college?" I try and fail to contain my surprise. He's easily definable as desirable — a *Billy on the Street* poll would undoubtedly result in a staggering number of affirmations of this. I've watched eyes linger on him in the gallery of the courtroom. He certainly *could* date.

He shakes his head. "A date here and there, but nothing substantial. I guess . . . it's just easier this way."

"Easier than what?"

"You don't let anything go, do you?" His right eyebrow twitches.

"It's called a conversation."

He huffs. "Yeah, okay."

"So?" I press, leading him back to my question.

"Easier than being disappointed. Easier than *disappointing.*"

I don't think he means to, but his words make me unsure of what to say next. He's right, I think. I don't particularly excel at being present with other people, either. He, like me, keeps people at arm's length, his interactions prescribed and controlled.

"What about you?" he asks.

My cheeks flush. I don't particularly want to tell him I've never had a serious relationship. That instead, I avoid dating situations altogether until I grow so lonely I open my Dater Baiter app and accept the first date I find and hook up just to feel the weight of a man on top of me.

"I don't really date. Haven't dated."

"At all?"

I shake my head. "Not really, no."

"Why? I can't imagine it's from a lack of interest from potential suitors."

I raise an eyebrow. " 'Potential suitors'?"

"I was going to say 'opposite sex,' but I didn't want to presume."

"There is no abundance of potential male suitors," I say. "Thus my qualification as bad with relationships, too."

"We sound like the perfect pair." He rises to take his next turn. But before he makes his way over to the lane, he turns and hands me the napkin he's been fidgeting with. It's neatly folded into the shape of an origami owl.

He rolls an easy strike and returns to the bench.

"First a crane and now an owl?" I ask.

He takes it gently from my hand, twirls it between his fingers in front of us. There's something rousing about his sizable hand delicately pirouetting the fine paper. "Before Kara died, she took this origami class at the library and got really into it. For her eighth birthday, my parents got her this book of hundreds of different animals and flowers and things." His eyes flicker a shade lighter when he talks about Kara. He looks down at the ground and smirks. "She got pretty good at it. The owl was her favorite. I think mostly because it was one of the first she mastered, but also, I think she appreciated the meaning of it. Wisdom. Good luck."

He slowly lifts my arm at the wrist, curls his fingers around mine, guiding them backward, and opens my loose fist, dropping the owl softly into my palm.

21.

Premature Deliberation (n., phrase)

1. jurors engaging in discussions about a case without following the proper procedural guidelines set forth by the court
2. an innocent discussion over nachos

We bowl two rounds, and Damon wins both, with Tamra coming in a close second. Cam is such a horrible bowler that I land in third despite it being my first time. Xavier checked in twice, his top half popping over the bench from the lane beside us to ask, "Everyone playing nice?"

Damon and I sit at the alley bar post-game, sharing a paper plate of nachos slathered in pumped cheese and pickled jalapeños. We each sip bottles of Michelob Ultra, the agreed-upon best option from the bar.

"Tell me about your job," I say, sliding a jalapeño over to a chip before picking it up. "Is writing punny digital signs a full-time gig, or are there other components?"

He chews, the dimple in his chin growing prominent, further shadowed by the overhead light. "That's a small part. But it's a cooler description than transportation engineer, which basically means I design and prepare plans for bridges, highways, et cetera."

"Do you like it?"

"I do, actually. It's kind of rewarding, planning the infrastructure that helps support the community."

I huff in appreciation. Even as kids, he needed to understand how stuff worked — how things were built, the mechanics of those things. I went to his house one day after school — our freshman year, I think it was — to find him tinkering in the garage with an old remote-controlled car. He had parts strewn about, stripped to undecipherable pieces.

"What about you? Do you like being an arbitrator?"

"I do. There's this big sense of accomplishment in helping two parties avoid litigation. Most of the time, people just want to be heard and have some semblance of validation. Whenever there's an agreement, I feel like I've saved something. And . . ." I pause, allowing the thought to fully form. ". . . it makes me feel in control of something."

He *mm-hmms* in understanding as I speak, and there's an attractive layer of engagement in it.

"I bet you're good at it," Damon says, wiping his fingertips with a napkin.

"Oh yeah? Why?"

"Because you're easy to talk to. And you care about people. Look at the way you've taken up for Margot, someone you don't even know."

I open my mouth to argue but think better of it. I've shown my cards so clearly to him on how I feel about the case, and so early on at that. There are "real" people in my life I've spent far less time with and know far less about than Margot, though some of the evidence this past week has planted small seeds of doubt about her in my mind.

"You think Margot's guilty, don't you?" I blurt out. Until now, I've done well not talking about the case. Sure, I've broken a few other rules, but I have not directly conversed about case details. But as I get to know Damon, in so many different ways in such a short period — through his handwritten notes, his presence beside me in court, our time in the presidential suite, the bits he shares with me through our talks — I can no longer ignore the thing that's been nagging at me since seeing him again.

"Did you really just ask me that?" he says, eyes narrowing playfully.

I clasp my hands in my lap. "I'm serious. I want to know." Actually, I *need* to know.

He looks at me thoughtfully, the dimple in his chin deepening as he pushes his bottom lip into the top one, seemingly careful to choose his words before he speaks. "It's still early in the case," he says, cocking his head to one side.

I raise my eyebrows at his nonanswer.

"I really don't know what to think yet. Isn't that the point? To hear all the evidence presented and then make your determination? Anything before that would be . . ." He sucks at the corner of his lip.

"It would be what? Wrong?"

"I was going to say unfair."

Right. So he thinks I'm being irresponsible by possibly siding with Margot. But he doesn't have the seven seasons of backstory I do.

"For the record, I'm not saying you —"

"I get it," I say, trying to ward off the annoyance gnawing at my belly. "I get it," I repeat, this time more softly.

I know there will be people who don't view this case the way I do, who don't know the things I do about Margot. But Damon . . . the more I get to spend time with him again, the more I can't bear the thought we might disagree on something as important as someone's life. That once again, some outside factor causes us to end up in opposite corners of a maze where we can't manage to find the midpoint.

I won't share details of Margot's life with Damon again like I did in the presidential suite. I know it was wrong to do, that it messed with the integrity of not only the case itself but of how Damon wants to approach his role here. But there are things about Margot I wish he knew. That I wish all the jurors knew. I wish I could tell Damon the things about Margot that make her so much more than what the prosecution is presenting her to be.

Like when her favorite charity, Sea Save, was struggling financially and almost had to close down four years ago; she and Joe anonymously donated $500,000 to keep it afloat. The only way the money was tracked back to her was via a Reddit thread that I guarantee no jurors would possibly know about. Those types of acts don't make headlines. Joe didn't care about Sea Save. He did it because it was important to Margot.

Or how they used to read books together. How they'd each get a copy of the same book and read separately together, silently side by side in bed or poolside on a quiet afternoon. The show caught several small moments over the years of the two of them razzing each other about being further along than the other, jokingly threatening to divulge spoilers.

They read *The Alchemist* and *Beloved,* memoirs like *When Breath Becomes Air* and *Men We Reaped.* They read books that always landed on the Books That Matter lists, that included commentary on societal shortcomings and race relations — books I aspired to read but only occasionally saw through to purchase. They both cared about the state of the world, despite being part of the select few who netted most from it. Sure, they had moments of being out of touch or acting selfishly; Joe, as we now know, most of all. But shouldn't the good matter, too?

I don't want to go too far down that road, so I change the subject. "How do you come up with the signs?" I ask.

He pauses a moment at my abrupt change

in direction, then answers, "I don't know, I just try to get people to look up."

"My favorites have been when big-ticket artists are in town for concerts."

He nods and semi-grins, and I appreciate his willingness to follow me down this windy road of conversation.

"There was so much Taylor Swift content," I say.

"CUT OFF? DON'T GET BAD BLOOD, SHAKE IT OFF. Yeah, that was me."

"That one on Valentine's Day?"

"NO VALENTINE? YOUR SEAT BELT WILL HUG YOU. Also me."

"I almost spit out my coffee when I saw that one!"

His eyes grin and it's boyishly prideful. I take delight in prying it out of him.

"And the one at Christmas . . ."

"ONLY RUDOLPH SHOULD DRIVE LIT."

I shake my head, smiling. It's as if Damon never left, his words finding me on my morning and evening commutes for years now.

Just as we're relaxing into our old, playful selves, Cam finds us and unintentionally swipes a knife straight through the energy between us.

"Hey," he says, sidling up beside Damon. He grabs a nacho — the most cheese-slathered one left — and speaks before he's done chewing. "Come to my room. Say, tomorrow night? I wanna show you guys somethin'."

Before we can ask any questions, Cam is off to return his rental shoes.

22.

Outback Steakhouse (restaurant name)

1. a popular casual dining restaurant chain known for its Australian-themed atmosphere and Bloomin' Onion appetizer
2. restaurant of choice for the California State court system

We cross the parking lot to our next destination at twilight. As we step in, I'm pleased to note that Outback Steakhouse sounds like sizzle and smells like butter. It's almost embarrassingly exciting to continue our outing with a meal that may include more flavor than too much salt and stale pepper. As a kid we ate out a lot, but mostly fast food or take-out pizza — an emphasis on quick, easy, and cheap. In response, I taught myself to cook a rotation of basic meals early on.

Cam bumps my elbow and points to the TVs hitched to the bar ceiling. There are four in total facing our direction, all set to various ESPN channels. The thrill is short-lived, though, as the hostess leads us to a private back room where four tables of four are set up, no TVs. There's a spark of disappointment that we don't get to sit out with the masses where I can take in new faces. I rebound quickly, though, the high of this day out still rippling through me.

Almost robotically, Tamra, Cam, Damon, and I take over the table in the room's far corner. Damon sits beside me as he always does. Cam is to my right, and Tamra takes the seat across the table.

"I'm ordering a big-ass steak," Cam declares, tossing his menu to the center of the table.

"What are you getting?" Damon asks, perusing his menu.

"Not sure," I say, attempting to stave off the feeling inside me that is declaring to my gut that this is a date. It's not, of course. It couldn't be further from a date. But my gut isn't listening, as it fires flares of excitement.

"What's the most opposite thing from a turkey sandwich?" he asks, then flexes his jaw.

I evaluate the options. "A big-ass steak?"

Damon sets down his menu. "Yep. That's what I want."

"Actually, same," I say, placing my menu neatly atop his.

After our orders are taken and drinks arrive (there was an eruptive cheer when George announced we could order more alcoholic beverages), Cam and Tamra dive into a discussion of their respective zodiac signs. I take a sip of my cabernet and shimmy my shoulders up and down in delight.

"Did you just do a happy dance?" Damon asks. He leans in, cupping the top of his pint glass. I imagine the inevitably bitter taste of his mouth after he sips that beer.

Heat spreads in all directions from my gut. "I did."

"I like it," he says, chin dimple twitching.

He's known me to do food happy dances since I was a kid. He used to join in occasionally, usually on pizza nights and with a hysterically bad robot.

"Do you remember that ugly hamster statue thing we used to hide back and forth?" I ask. It's nice to reminisce about the joyful points of our history, rather than what ended our friendship. I feel foolish now for having blocked all the good out for so long. Our years of good should not be erased because of a disappointing end, I decide.

He bites at the inside of his cheek. "Yeah."

"I can't remember who hid it last."

He leans back in his chair. "It was you. You put it in my underwear drawer."

I snort, nearly choking on my sip of wine.

"I almost broke my ankle after seeing that thing staring at me when I pulled out the drawer."

I press my hand to my chest as I shake with laughter. "I wish I could have seen that," I say, wiping a tear from the outer corner of my eye. He watches me closely as my laughter calms. I observe Damon's attentiveness, his fingers still curled around his glass. He's always done this, watched me laugh rather than participate himself.

At fourteen, Damon and I found a hamster statue on a table of ceramic knickknacks marked for fifty cents each at a neighbor's estate sale. Though I still don't particularly know the difference between an estate sale and a standard garage sale, this event was most certainly the latter, with tables full of folded holiday sweaters and washed-thin tees, scraped-up toys and tattered paperbacks. Damon picked up the statue and tapped me on the shoulder with it, and when I turned to find it staring at me, I screamed — an embarrassingly loud reaction that caused Damon to bend forward, hands on his knees, laughing. He bought the hamster (gave the woman manning the till a dollar and told her to keep the change), then proceeded to torture me with it for the next two years. We often debated whether it was a hamster, gerbil, or guinea pig and the minimal differences between the three. Ultimately, we settled on hamster, though we couldn't be sure. It became a thing between us, hiding the hamster/gerbil/guinea pig where the other would unsuspectingly find it.

He leans forward. "D'you remember —"

"The bucket," we say in unison.

"I think I actually peed my pants on that one," I confess. It's vividly still in my mind, Damon texting me to come outside. When I opened the front door, I was met with the orange ceramic hamster statue — one leg broken off from when it fell from Damon's back fence (my placement) — swinging from a turned bucket above the doorframe, string tied to it so it fell to dangle in front of me, face-to-face.

Damon rolled in the grass, cackling until his stomach ached.

In this moment, this memory, we are our younger selves again. Hopeful and staunchly resilient. Mercifully unaware.

My laughter calms, and we both go quiet.

"I still have it," he says.

I lean in. "You still have Prince Hamsterdinck?"

"I had forgotten his name," he admits.

"How could you forget? Kara named him," I say. We got her hooked on *The Princess Bride* early, always fast-forwarding through the gory fight scene at the end.

He crosses his arms and runs a hand down the side of his face. "That's right," he says thoughtfully.

Cam and Tamra across the table burst into laughter and it draws our attention. It reminds me where we are. That, should someone overhear our exchange, they'd learn that our history runs far deeper than we've let on.

"Did you ever want to do something besides being a mediator?" he asks, as if he can sense the anxiety brewing within me and needs to defuse it.

I try to think of my childhood dreams, what I might have shared with him when we were younger. I lean forward. "Well, no young adult says, *I want to be a mediator when I grow up,*" I say.

"Same for transportation engineer," he muses.

"Right?"

He flexes his jaw, seemingly deciding whether to voice a thought his tongue is wrestling with.

"Did you? Have something you wanted to be?" I recall him having an ever-changing list when we were young, everything from firefighter to veterinarian to professional motocross racer.

He rubs at his jaw. "For a while I thought I might teach. History."

I think of a teenage Damon sprawled on my living room floor, reading nonfiction — comparative studies on the pyramids in Egypt or logistics and supply chain strategies from World War I — wondering how he could find these types of books enjoyable. Then I picture him in front of a classroom, dress shirt rolled to his elbows, wide stance, slapping a yardstick against his open palm. I shift in my seat.

"Why didn't you go that route?" I ask.

"After Kara, it just didn't seem to fit anymore."

I'm immediately hit with a pang of embarrassment for turning his onetime dream into the start of a sexual fantasy.

"I thought I'd travel, maybe end up living in another country."

"Why didn't you?" I ask, but intuitively, I

know. He couldn't leave his parents. I don't make him say it. Instead, I ask, "Do you ever think about blowing it all up and starting over? About starting a teaching career?"

He shakes his head, once. "No. I'm where I'm supposed to be."

"I am, too," I say, reflecting on my life, my career in particular, in these terms for perhaps the first time. "It's disheartening at times, seeing people reach a point of so much hurt they can't imagine arriving at any common ground. But helping them find it, proving that you can come back from a seemingly unsalvageable situation, there's a high I feel each time."

"You make it sound like a divorce proceeding."

"It's similar, I suppose. People who feel slighted. Real, fractured human emotions. People blinded by hurt." There was no saving my parents' marriage. I thought there was no saving Damon and me. But seeing relationships mended, in part with my help, gives me hope.

Both of us have shifted our chairs to face each other, and just like in the courtroom, when our knees bump, I don't particularly mind. "Why haven't you had a serious relationship?" he asks.

I sip my wine for some time. "I just

haven't met anyone that . . . fits." I think back to Dominic, the guy I met two years ago in line at the CVS pharmacy as we both awaited antibiotics for similar bouts of strep throat. We expressed our disdain for the woman in front of us who was demanding the pharmacist fill her prescription immediately despite the line. Grumpy and throats inflamed, we bonded over our deep disapproval of people in public, generally.

Dominic and I messaged over the course of the next three days, comparing symptoms and TV binging choices. On the fourth day, we met at a mom-and-pop coffee shop equidistant from our respective apartments and ordered an array of all the carb-heavy items on the menu.

"Food is amazing," he said, eyes as glazed as the doughnut before him after four days of limited intake.

"Carbs good," I grunted through a bite of chocolate croissant.

We saw each other two to three times a week for nearly six months after that, though neither of us sought to define the relationship. For me, it was because I wanted to match his aloofness. For him, I found out later, it was because he had several casual relationships he'd been juggling at once, a few of which had even been double-booked with me on the same days, I came to learn.

Dominic was the closest thing I've had to a relationship. I don't even know that I particularly liked him.

"Why do you think that is? That you haven't found anyone?" He leans back and crosses his left ankle over his right knee, and I'm distracted by the sheer spread of him. I resist the urge to volley the question immediately back to him.

"Like I just said, I guess it's because I haven't met the right person."

He squints his peacock-feather-colored eyes at me. "That feels like a cop-out."

I raise an eyebrow at him. "Does it?"

"Yeah." He rubs his thumb along his bottom lip absentmindedly, and it's the epitome of distracting.

"Okay, real talk?"

He places both feet on the ground and leans forward, hands clasped ahead of him. "Always."

"My parents' marriage, it was borderline abusive. D'you remember how many times I showed up at your place around dinnertime just to escape it?"

He nods.

"I can't imagine hating someone that much. I don't ever want to hate someone that much."

"It *was* abusive, Syd. Things don't have to be physically violent to be abusive." He swallows.

I know this, of course. But putting that label on things somehow makes it all less sweep-able under my ten-year-old rug.

"You're not them," he says, then takes a sip of his beer. Intellectually, I of course know I'm not them. But they are my DNA.

"What about you?" I ask, keen to turn the spotlight.

"I had that girlfriend in college," he says. "But things didn't work out. She was great. Really great, actually. But I just never got to the point of wanting to take the next step. She wanted to move in. I wasn't ready. She left, found someone who was ready, got engaged and married all within the next year." He spins his pint glass in little circles atop the table, spreading new arms of the glass's watery ring. "I told myself I didn't care about her enough to give her what she wanted. But sometimes, I think maybe I cared too much. So much that I was terrified."

"Of what?"

"Of losing her. Once you lose someone, loss is this thing that is sort of . . . waiting. It felt like a ticking time bomb. Like if she stayed with me, she'd eventually die." The tips of his ears are red. "I know how that sounds."

"How does it sound?" I ask, my throat tight with recognition.

"Paranoid. Morbid."

I shake my head, cross my arms against the table. "I think it sounds honest."

We stare at each other, and I can practically feel the heat of his face spreading to mine.

Tamra taps her knife gently against her glass, forcing our attention. "I have a toast," she says, cheeks bright pink and eyes glassy. It appears Tamra is a bit tipsy after half a glass of pinot noir. She stands, raises her wineglass, and looks down at the three of us. "I'd just like to say," she begins, then presses her eyes shut in deep concentration, or perhaps contemplation. "That of course this situation is less than ideal. I know we all miss our loved ones, would rather be with them than on this jury." Her eyes grow full. "But I just want to thank you" — she makes eye contact with each of us at the table — "for giving me some semblance of a little family while we are here. Friendship is the wine of life, as they say! To new friends!" She raises her glass emphatically and sloshes a raindrop-sized dollop of wine onto the center of the table.

"One drink and she's Maya Angelou," Cam muses, then pats her on the back, seemingly more entertained by half-glass-of-wine Tamra than touched by her toast. "To new friends," he says merrily, lifting his beer and clanging it against Tamra's glass. Somehow, Xavier has made his way to our table, wanting in on our little lovefest. He taps his soda glass against Tamra's.

We all join in, Damon and me toasting last.

"To new friends," Damon says, tilting the top of his pint to meet the lip of my wine-glass.

"To new friends," I echo, surprised by my sudden breathlessness.

Damon's stare lingers. I don't move away when his knee once again gently bumps mine.

23.

Trial Enthusiast (n., phrase)

1. a person who takes great interest in trial processes and outcomes
2. a complete buzzkill

As we near two hours in the back room of Outback Steakhouse, the bailiffs don't seem in any rush to shuttle us back to the Singer Suites. We show our gratitude with the room's collective happy energy, with thank-yous and offers of glasses of wine and pints of beer, though they decline. Still, they are far more upbeat and chatty than ever before.

We learn George, our usual first-shift overnight guard, lives in East L.A. with his wife of nearly thirty years, alongside two of their four adult children and two grand-children. These details endear him to Tamra, and soon they are exchanging particulars of grandbabies, swiftly agreeing how much better it is to be a grandparent than a parent.

When I order my third glass of wine, I expect George or one of the two other guards to stop me. But they allow it. And suddenly, the room feels like a reunion of old friends catching up, a corporate party after the bosses have headed home and the DJ starts playing '90s hip-hop.

Perhaps most entertaining is watching the other jurors ostensibly, happily unravel. After a glass and a half of red wine, Tamra's blinks extend, and she laughs at most everything anyone says. Cam finds her particularly amusing, working to say anything remotely funny to get her to break into a table-slapping cackle. It warms me to look over and see my courtroom seatmate Luis (juror number five) smiling through a discussion with Kate (juror number twelve), the mom of four. Even Xavier at the table beside us seems to have temporarily yielded his mission toward wide likability to lean back in his chair and enjoy some drink with smoke steaming off the top. The atmosphere is so carefree that I've almost forgotten we are the jury on the Margot Kitsch case.

And then there's Damon. His jaw loosens. He even chuckles at points, mostly in reaction to Tamra's laughter. These things come out of him with little effort, and I'm both intrigued and pleased by how much more leisure there is in him tonight.

When I stand from the table, Damon looks up at me. "Where you goin'?"

"Just to the bathroom," I tell him.

He nods, and then hangs his head and shakes it, as if feeling silly for asking.

Alone in front of the sink mirror in the generically tiled bathroom, I expect to think about Margot, about the case. But I find myself thinking of Damon instead. Of the swirling dimple at the center of his chin. Of his immense size. Of his sealed inner parts, lid slightly ajar. I shake my head, attempting to pack away my attraction. It's just familiarity, I try to tell myself. It can't be more. Not now, because of the trial and certainly not after given the complication between our families.

After washing my hands, I throw the paper towel into the bin and push the heavy swinging door open with my shoulder and elbow, eager to return to the table. I halt in the narrow hallway when I nearly run into someone standing just outside the ladies' room entrance.

"Oh, sorry," I mumble, rocking back on my heels to avoid contact with the man's midsection. Damon was right, I do seem to fall a lot. I expect the man to step back and make room for me to go by, but he doesn't. He just stands there, staring at me.

We make eye contact, and he doesn't break it, his hollow brown eyes both drowsy and, somehow, also boring into me with an intensity that makes me uncomfortable. His chin is rather pointy, oddly shaped, and his skin has a sallow quality that reminds me of oatmeal. When he continues staring, I attempt to maneuver around him, but he steps across what little of the hallway he isn't taking up to block me.

"Where you going?" he asks. His breath is an abhorrently pungent mix of beer and Bloomin' Onion.

I have no idea who this man is. He's not a member of the jury or a guard. He seems to just be an ill-behaved, overserved restaurant-goer. "Excuse me," I say, throwing on my most authoritative tone.

"Why you guys with those officers?" he asks, an amused grin on his crimson lips, ignoring my request. When I don't respond, he says, "I bet I know why." His speech is slow, slurred, and more than slightly adversarial. "You guys are a jury, huh? *The* jury . . . for that bitch. That Malibu Maneater. Why else would cops be taking a big group out to eat?"

He doesn't even get Margot's media-dubbed nickname right, which somehow, even in this situation, manages to annoy me. "I'm going back to my table," I say, attempting to step around him again. But once again, he takes a sidelong stride, blocking my path. He isn't particularly tall or bulky, but still, he's sizable in comparison to me. Enough to use our size difference as a tool for intimidation.

He steps forward where there wasn't space to be had, and I am immediately pressed against the wall. I wonder nervously if he might attempt to shove me into the empty women's room and lock the door. He is drunk and obstinate and has that feral gleam in his eyes that women have good reason to be afraid of. I mentally prepare for a fight, just in case.

The bustle of the restaurant continues on just around the corner. The murmurs of conversation. The occasional booming voice or burst of laughter. The clang of plates and pans, muffled, from the nearby kitchen. There are many people close by, yet I am trapped and far away.

I contemplate a list of possible next moves. Make a scene. Retreat to the ladies' room and attempt to lock the door before he can follow me in. Give him a sharp elbow to the throat or finger jabs to the eyeballs.

"Excuse me," I say, as forcefully as I can muster. There's not even a flicker of movement from him.

"I saw y'all walk in, and I knew right away who you were," he says, so close his words practically singe my ear. "My uncle golfed with Joe Kitsch once. That bitch definitely did it."

I continue to vacillate between annoyance and fear. Of course his uncle sharing a golf outing once makes him an expert on all things Joe Kitsch. And I wonder how many women he's referred to as "that bitch" in his lifetime. My best guess is *many.*

"Get out of my way," I say, ramming my forearm into his side in an effort to create enough space to escape.

At this, he raises his hand, and it looks as though he might grab me.

Fuck this guy. I will absolutely knee him in the groin.

"Syd?"

The man and I both turn to find Damon behind us, his large build creating even less space in the narrow bathroom hallway. I have never been so relieved to see a familiar face.

The man is noticeably smaller than Damon — most everyone is. Despite this, he doesn't flinch, and he remains stationed between me and the exit where Damon stands.

Damon and I make eye contact, and he must see my concern because he doesn't hesitate. He presses his shoulder into the man and steps between us, and I'm immediately staring at the broadness of his back. "Is there a problem?" he asks, taking on his Secret Service–esque stance — legs spread wide, arms wrapping behind him. I look down at his hands, clenched into fists.

"No problem," the man says, as flat and even as before, seemingly unfazed.

Damon reaches his right arm behind him, placing his open palm against my elbow, ensuring he knows my exact location.

"Great," Damon responds to the man in the hallway, encircling his fingers around my arm, squeezing slightly.

It's an uncomfortably familiar scene to us at fourteen, Damon stepping in when my father turned his frustration on me after an argument with my mom. I don't remember the particulars of that fight — about one of his affairs, I assume.

I do recall, however, Damon and me in my room, door closed, his eyes filled with compassion I didn't know what to do with as my parents' voices speared into the room. He knew this happened, had heard it play out from outside or through my recounts. But this was one of his first times serving as a close-quarters witness. When my father called for me, anger seething from his lips, Damon was to his feet in a heartbeat. When my father burst into my room, Damon said nothing, just stood between us.

My father never hurt me physically, though I cannot say I wasn't fearful of it happening. I stood in my bedroom, staring at Damon's back — thinner then — thankful for him but equally mortified. My father glowered at him, part daring, part viciously angry, part amused. But Damon didn't budge. My father eventually huffed and stormed out, though not before flicking his hand toward Damon in a show of dismissal. And not before Damon reached out for me, his hand stretching backward and cupping my forearm, as it does now.

I press my other hand against Damon's lower back, leaning to look around him. Finally, the man says, "Right. Good night then." He eyes me for a long while until Damon steps to block his view. When he finally exits the hallway, Damon immediately follows, stopping in the archway that leads into the main dining area. I watch his eyes move to the far right and stay there — the direction of the restaurant's entrance. I observe the tight muscle straining along the side of his neck, his fisted hands at his side. The angry red that extends from the tips of his ears down through the lobes.

After what feels like several minutes, satisfied, he turns and takes two long steps to me.

"You okay?" he asks.

"Yes, fine," I say, forcing a smile.

"What was that?" he presses. "What did he do?"

"He just . . . he was drunk. He put two and two together that we are the Margot Kitsch jury." I hadn't intended to tell him this last part, but I trust Damon. I didn't know I did, hadn't even thought about whether I needed to until now, but it's a decision already made.

His eyes narrow and then release once he processes the words. He looks over his shoulder at the archway and back at me. "We should tell the bailiffs."

I shake my head. "No, it was just some random guy."

His concerned eyes search my face, disbelieving.

"It was nothing," I say, shrugging a shoulder, attempting to sound far more flippant than I feel.

His eyes narrow in question, and if he hesitates to believe my levity he doesn't show it. "We should tell George. Just in case."

My hand is cuffing his forearm before I can stop it. "No," I say.

He looks down at my hand, then back to my eyes. I stare at him and see the boy who used to be my best friend, and sharp, glass-like flecks scrape through me. Up until this point, he has been, in many ways, a man I just met. Someone with hints of a boy I used to know — same bright eyes and dimpled chin, same affinity for written words over spoken ones. It's taken until now to see them as the same, to reconcile the two. But looking into his eyes, feeling his concern and protection, he's every bit my old best friend.

I release his arm. "It was nothing," I repeat. "Just some jerk who took his opportunity to voice his opinion about the case. Everyone has an opinion." I hope I'm putting on a convincing act. The thought of what might have happened had Damon not shown up — it leaves me far more than flustered, wanting to seek Damon and his safety more than ever. But if we let the guards know, who knows what could happen to the case. I'm not sure if this incident would be enough for Judge Gillespy to call a mistrial, but I don't want to risk it.

He's momentarily thoughtful, then says, "Yeah, but the guards should know. Let them decide whether it's important or not. That guy threatened you, Syd."

"Look," I say, then release my breath. "It was nothing. I promise you. Let's not get everyone riled up for no reason. This whole thing is stressful enough."

Again, he assesses me silently before responding. "You sure you're okay?" he asks.

"Yes," I murmur, feeling him come around. "Now let's get back to the group before Tamra steals my wine."

The tightness in his face relaxes, just slightly, and his left eye twitches dangerously close to a wink. "I'm sure she's dancing on tables by now," he says, stepping back so I can exit the hallway first, but not before I catch the unwaning glimmer of concern in his eyes. It's a look I know was once reserved only for Kara and me, the two people he felt the fierce need to look after.

24.

Security Directive (n., phrase)

1. specific instructions or directives to safeguard jurors and ensure their well-being during trial proceedings if a judge perceives a threat to the safety or security of the jurors
2. handcuffs tightening

First thing Monday morning, Judge Gillespy calls the jury into the courtroom. When we enter, we are met with an empty room, the only exception being the judge and two bailiffs.

"What's this about?" Cam whispers to no one in particular.

The courtroom is eerily vacant, the usual energetic rush I feel walking into a full gallery replaced with striking silence. I can't help but eye Margot's empty chair at the defense table. We take our seats and stare at

Judge Gillespy. She sighs and takes a long blink, and those actions alone cause me to sit at attention.

"I don't want to alarm anyone," she begins, resulting in immediate alarm. The frequency of the room changes, as if controlled by a knob someone has just clicked a few notches higher. A few jurors shift in their seats. Luis, to my right, abandons his current tic-tac-toe game to lean forward. "But an incident from over the weekend was brought to my attention."

Damon beside me acts completely unfazed, his ankle over his thigh, right knee pointed toward me.

"It seems a member of the public approached some of you while out on Saturday."

There's a murmur among the other jurors. I force myself to remain focused on Judge Gillespy, refusing to look at Damon. This explains why yesterday, despite it being Sunday and having no court, we were largely confined to our rooms.

Judge Gillespy continues, "While it appears there is no direct concern, out of excess caution, there will be no additional outings for the remainder of the case."

Cam behind me groans. I feel Damon's eyes on me, but I refuse to look at him. I asked him not to say anything, and he went behind my back. My ears burn with frustration. Why couldn't he just trust my judgment?

Judge Gillespy reminds us of her many rules, including the "no boning" rule, as Cam has come to call her no-fraternization decree, and she's sure to hammer home once more the potential punishments, which, of course, include *jail time.*

"Syd," Damon calls after me in the hallway when Judge Gillespy gives us a five-minute break before we return for the day's proceedings. I spin to face him, unable to stop my arms from aggressively crossing against my chest.

"I asked you not to say anything," I whisper-yell at him. He knows this case is important to me, but he's overlooked me and what I might need or want once again.

His eyes contract, and I'm immediately confident he knows my anger is about more than just this one thing. He stares at me, and I find him as obnoxiously unreadable as ever.

"Are you gonna speak?" I ask eventually, hoping he hears the irritation in my tone.

My ability to recall the anger I've held toward him for so many years is too easy, bubbling just below this new surface of calm. It screams to me that no matter how much I tell myself I've forgiven him, how much I might like him now, I can't just rid myself of ten years of resentment in a mere few days. It was foolish to ever think I could.

He rubs at the back of his neck before dropping his arm and calling my eyes to his. "I can't let anything happen to you," he says, his voice a cavernous chamber.

My heart's rhythm halts a moment before regulating. Like me, his feelings are about so much more than this situation. I see it all in the etch of his features, a brief vulnerability seeping through the pores of his otherwise rigid face. He lost Kara. I am, in some small way, a chance at a do-over.

Despite my internal protest, I feel some of my irritation melt away. It's so hard to stay mad at him when he's so protective. Even more so when I think of why.

He steps dangerously close. "I'm sorry," he says, and it's more grumble than words. He lifts his hand slightly and then retracts it as though he wants to touch me but then thought better of it. Our presidential suite kiss flashes through me, and I have to remind myself where we are.

At the most inopportune moment, Xavier exits the men's room and starts toward us. Damon takes a step back as Xavier passes.

He eyes us briefly, then lines up at the courtroom door several yards down, sending another curious look our way again once there.

I refocus on Damon. Perhaps I'm imagining it, but his face tells me a distinct story. He's not sorry for saying something. He'd do it again, no matter my feelings about it. He's only sorry I'm upset. It's enough, though, my frustration dissipating further. "Sweet dreams are made of cheese," I mutter under my breath, hoping for a serotonin boost.

"Watermelon sugar pie," he says back, practically an automatic reflex.

Once again, Wrong Lyrics Only does what it's meant to do. This is, of course, another thing we share. Another remnant of him. A silly but sticky fragment of us in another life.

"If I could sit you down and force you to watch *Mean Girls* on repeat as punishment right now, I would."

"That wouldn't be a punishment," he says in that same grumbly tone, ensuring his hand brushes mine as he moves past me toward the courtroom door.

The first witness D.A. Stern calls for the day is Jackie Kitsch, Joe's mother. As I watch her enter the courtroom and amble cautiously to the stand, I'm surprised by her appearance. In my pretrial deep dive, I didn't come across a single recent photo of her. I expected an old money glamorous woman with plastic surgery and pearls. Instead, Jackie Kitsch is unassuming, adorned in an unremarkable black sheath dress below a tight white cardigan and no jewelry other than her plain gold wedding band. She's charmingly frumpy, her gray hair a little frizzy. It's an endearing surprise, how ordinary she appears, despite being the mother of a Malibu near-billionaire.

As she grows closer, I see the blue-hued bags under her eyes and forehead lines etched deep even when her face is at rest, and despite her testifying against Margot, I feel a swelling ache of compassion for this mother who has outlived her child. What a thing to go through in the last years of her life.

I look to Margot, imagining her mash-up of emotions toward this woman. Margot looks on longingly, as if she wants to stand, rush to Jackie's side, and hug her.

As Jackie Kitsch is sworn in, I attempt to recall what I know about this woman. Joe was raised in the Pacific Palisades in a 1940s Spanish colonial passed down from Jackie's parents, whose family wealth dates as far back as the California gold rush. She stayed home with Joe and his sisters, Jayne and Erika. Joe spoke about her briefly but lovingly on the show, though never in detail, and she was never filmed. I can't recall Margot ever even mentioning her, now that I think about it.

D.A. Stern approaches the stand with his lips flattened together in a sympathetic frown. "Mrs. Kitsch, let me first just say, we are all very sorry for your loss."

Her eyes are immediately wet, and the ache in my chest grows. She raises the already frayed tissue in her hand to the outer corner of her right eye and taps it there briefly, before returning it to her lap. "Thank you," she offers.

At D.A. Stern's prompting question about "who Joe was," Jackie Kitsch tells us of how Joe wasn't particularly good in school but always seemed fated for "something more." How he was funny and outgoing and always managed to find himself in "mild trouble." She speaks with pride, and it's not hard to be endeared to her or her description of Joe.

"When did you first meet Margot?" D.A. Stern asks.

Jackie Kitsch straightens expeditiously, as if having taken a shock to her spine. "A few weeks after they got engaged."

D.A. Stern feigns surprise. "From my understanding, that was over a year into their relationship. Joe waited that long to introduce his fiancée to his family? Why?"

"We didn't meet many of his women."

D.A. Stern looks on as if she might say more. When she doesn't, he asks, "What was your initial impression of Margot?"

Jackie Kitsch exhales mightily enough for the microphone to amplify it, looking in Margot's direction for the first time. Margot's eyes plead with her, and the women exchange a full conversation in those few silent seconds, one I wish I could decipher but am sure I don't grasp the complexities of. "She was polite, well-mannered."

Again, D.A. Stern awaits more words that don't come. "Did you two get along?"

"We did. We didn't have mother-daughter date nights or spend much time one-on-one, but we were mutually pleasant. She ensured we were invited over for holidays and that we see the kids regularly." Her eyes pool at the mention of the children.

"How did you learn of Joe's passing?" D.A. Stern asks, his voice insinuating he must be as fragile as possible with this particular line of questioning.

My breath catches in my chest as I think

of Mallory Bradburn, of her commonalities with Jackie Kitsch. I look over at Damon, whose eyes are wary as he stares on at the witness stand, and I know he's thinking about his mother, too. I wish I could take his hand, offer him some connection in this room full of strangers.

After learning of her son's death from her daughter Jayne, who learned via a call from Ms. Pembrooke, the house manager (*not* Margot, she points out), D.A. Stern fast-forwards to the day of Joe's funeral. Jackie Kitsch hesitates, concentrating on her lap where she picks at the small bits of tissue clinging to her dress, before addressing the circumstances around that day. "Margot had him cremated within three days of his death." She stops and looks to the jury. "She was just so . . . cold after he died. Void of emotion."

She shifts in her seat with a pained expression. I find myself struck by the way everyone keeps describing Margot as "cold." How many women have been maligned simply because they aren't endlessly warm and bubbly?

"After the funeral," she continues, "we went back to their home for an intimate gathering, just family and close friends."

"How did you spend your time at your

son's funeral reception?"

"I greeted guests, thanked them for their condolences." She hesitates, and I can feel her growing closer to some pivotal element of this case. I infer from the sharpening silence that the gallery can sense it, too. Jackie Kitsch continues, "Later, I was visiting with Emblem in her room. She didn't want to go downstairs and be required to talk with everyone. And she was frustrated with the itchy dress Margot had her wear that day."

"What happened in Emblem's room?"

"We got to talking. She was showing me her collections. She loves collecting things. She had seashells from every beach she ever visited. Rocks, too. Some interesting and unique, some plain old rocks." She smiles, her pruned lips growing thin. "She even showed me a collection of tampons once. She'd steal them from under Margot's sink or from restaurant bathrooms, then she'd pull the cotton out and use them as pillows for her doll beds."

"Charming," D.A. Stern muses. "Did Emblem show you anything that day that caused you . . . alarm?"

My heartbeat quickens at D.A. Stern's choice of words. Between pretrial social media theories and opening statements, I know something happened the day of the funeral. Something that made Jackie Kitsch question Margot's involvement in her son's death, enough so that it just may have been the catalyst for this trial.

25.

Unreliable Witness (n., phrase)

1. someone whose account of events, observations, or experiences may be inaccurate, inconsistent, biased, or influenced by external factors
2. a five-year-old

Jackie Kitsch clears her throat. "Yes. Emblem did show me something concerning," she says, in reference to D.A. Stern's last question. She lifts the tattered tissue to her eyes again. "She pulled a teddy bear off the shelf. She laid it on the floor, face down, then ripped the Velcro back apart. It was one of those nanny-cam bears. A video camera in the eye. There, she pulled out a new collection. One I hadn't seen before." She pauses, looks at Margot again.

Margot listens intently, her expression pained, the corners of her mouth pulling downward. Her eyes are round, as though they were pinned open, forcing her to watch.

"What was the collection?"

Jackie Kitsch hesitates. It's like all of us in the room are in a collective nosedive, and I'm unsure where and how we crash land. I, like the others, hang on her every word. On the silence between. Finally, Jackie Kitsch says, "It was a collection of eye-drop bottles. Three of them, all empty."

A wave of low-decibel noise makes its way around the room. *Hmm*s and *humph*s and under-the-breath mumbles. Not enough for Judge Gillespy to strike her gavel, but enough for D.A. Stern to look over the gallery and jury in acknowledgment.

"Where would Emblem have found three eye-drop bottles?"

"I asked her," Mrs. Kitsch says. "She said in the bathroom garbage in her parents' room. I asked her when, but she couldn't seem to give a straight answer. 'A while ago' was all she'd say. That's how it goes with a five-year-old. She was only four then." Mrs. Kitsch looks to her lap mournfully.

"What did you find concerning about the bottles?"

"Well, I found it odd there were three empty eye-drop bottles. Those things last forever in my house, years even. So, I wondered how else they might have been emptied so quickly. Emblem *insisted* they were empty when she found them. This question kept nagging at me for days. Curious, I started googling. Uses for eye drops and such. I'm a bit of an internet sleuth. That's what Joe used to call me." She chuckles sadly and looks to her lap again, focused on the shredded tissue bits she holds there. "I came across an article about a husband in North Carolina who poisoned his wife by putting eye drops in her drinks. It was in the first page of results. It caused her to die from a cardiac episode." She lets her words linger so we can make the intended inference.

A cardiac episode. Just like Joe.

She continues, "He killed her that way to collect her life insurance. That article . . . it made me pause." A tear escapes, trailing down her cheek. "It made me question if Margot would do something like that. It was suspicious, to say the least. Her rush to cremate him, her inheritance, her . . . motives in their marriage. It all felt quite suspicious."

I look around the room, rubbing at my chest. Jackie Kitsch is a sympathetic witness. She doesn't come across as bitter or accusatory. Just factual and heartbroken. And as I sit here thinking about Mallory Bradburn, I feel for this witness in a visceral way I wasn't prepared for.

Durrant Hammerstead cross-examines Jackie Kitsch, and it's relatively straightforward. He emphasizes that Emblem did not specify in that conversation the day of the funeral *when* she found the bottles and that we cannot be sure if it was even all together or individually over time. He gets Mrs. Kitsch to confirm she has no evidence of Margot's wrongdoing, just a hunch, a gut feeling. Durrant Hammerstead's points are sound, but Jackie Kitsch's testimony nags at me nonetheless. Likability is a huge factor in court cases. Jackie Kitsch is as likable and nonthreatening as they come. And I have to admit, the whole thing *is* suspicious.

Coming into this case, I had zero question of Margot's innocence. But so much keeps coming to light . . .

The affairs.

Her disappearance at sixteen.

The book on poison she was reading in Mallorca.

The string of adverse character witnesses.

Now, the eye-drop bottles.

What does it all mean?

After Mrs. Kitsch steps down from the

witness stand, there is little time to contemplate or recover. And soon, I understand why — D.A. Stern wants us to feel the connection and continuity between Jackie Kitsch and the next witness.

We all look on as the same screen where D.A. Stern displayed pictures of the Kitsch family during opening statements is pulled out again. Once everything in the courtroom is to his liking, D.A. Stern introduces five-year-old Emblem Kitsch as his next witness, before directing our attention to the screen and pressing play.

The prosecution and defense mercifully agreed to interview her on camera in a one-on-one setting versus parading her in this courtroom with its gallery and jury box full of gawking strangers. Even so, the thought of five-year-old Emblem Kitsch influencing the outcome of this trial, or being involved at all, causes a queasy wake in my gut.

In the prerecorded interview, Emblem sits in a conference room that appears to be somewhere in this courthouse. She wears a fluffy purple one-piece zip-up with the unicorn hood pulled up over her head, and I'm unsure if it's pajamas, a costume, or something else. The length of her deep brown hair spools out on either side of her neck, and she props up a stuffed penguin to look as though it's seated atop the table beside her. She is nothing short of adorable.

She resembles Joe far more than Margot. She inherited and thus preserved his blue eyes and prominent nose, heart-shaped mouth and nearly nonexistent eyebrows. I somehow equate this fact as likely to work in the prosecution's favor.

The courtroom is pin-drop silent. This feels like the most important testimony to date. Perhaps it's the anticipation of what unfiltered words might barrel out of a five-year-old's mouth. Perhaps it's because Margot Kitsch is sitting at the defense table, watching a video of her daughter's testimony being presented as evidence for the *prosecution.* Perhaps it's the stark reminder that there are children whose lives will be forever affected by the outcome of this case. Whatever it is, the courtroom is holding a collective breath.

It's not D.A. Stern or Durrant Hammerstead who interview Emblem, but a court-approved child witness expert. I imagine there are several minutes of making Emblem feel comfortable, asking innocuous questions like how school is going and what her favorite foods are, cut for time. Our version goes straight into questions about her part in this case.

"Emblem, tell me about your collections," the woman off-screen inquires.

"I like to collect things. I have lots of treasures I find, but I only keep the ones I can add more things to."

"I used to collect key chains when I was your age," the interviewer comments.

Emblem gives a congenial giggle.

"Do you usually show people your collections?"

"Mmmmmm . . ." Emblem scrunches her face and cocks her head in consideration. "Sometimes."

"When your Grandma Kitsch was over the day of your dad's funeral, did you show her some of your collections?"

Emblem's face falls, seemingly at the mention of her father, and my heart cracks for her. "I showed her the nanny-cam bear. His name is Taylor Swift."

"What a lovely name."

"She's a real person. A singer."

"I know. I love her songs."

"Yeah, me too."

"What was the collection you kept in the back of Taylor Swift?"

"They were little bottles." She holds her fingers up about an inch apart to indicate their size. "I thought they'd make good water bottles for my doll to carry in her purse. Her name is Judge Judy. She has high heels." Emblem begins bouncing her penguin up and down against the table, seemingly losing interest in the interviewer and her line of questioning.

"That's a very smart idea. Tell me, where did you find those little bottles?"

Emblem continues to bounce her penguin, adding a side-to-side motion, and her face grows serious as if she knows this is a point of contention. "In the garbage. In Mommy's room."

I note that she says "Mommy's room" instead of "Mommy and Daddy's," and that crack in my heart widens to a split.

Damon's knee presses gently into the side of mine. I look up at him, but he's not looking at me. He's looking at the defense table. I follow his gaze to find Margot staring straight ahead at her daughter on the screen, tears streaming down her cheeks so easily she doesn't seem to notice them.

Seeing Margot crack is disturbing. On the show I've seen her yell, throw things, attack. But she never cries.

I have to look away so my own composure doesn't fracture.

"I'm not supposed to take things out of the trash. Daddy used to get mad at me for it. They were under the garbage bag."

"*Under* the bag. Under the trash bag, you mean?"

"Yeah, but in the bin."

Damon writes this last part down. So does Luis to my right, under his current tic-tac-toe game.

"How many bottles were in that collection of yours?"

"Three."

"And did you find them all at once or one at a time?"

"All at once, I think." She fiddles with the hem of the penguin's red-and-black scarf.

"You think?"

"Yeah, I mean, I don't know."

I wonder how she remembers the bottles were under the trash bag, between it and the bin, but not how many there were. I try to think back to Kara at that specific age, the last kid I've spent any real amount of time with, but I come up short on pinning down the consistency (or lack thereof) of a five-year-old's memory and, thus, ability to articulate details from it.

"Was it before your daddy died or after that you found them?"

She shrugs, moves her penguin to her lap, and leans back in her chair.

"If you really think hard, can you try to

remember?"

Emblem closes her eyes, pressing them firmly shut, as if to demonstrate that she is thinking hard like the interviewer asked. "I think it was right after."

"Right after what?"

"Right after Daddy died. I found them right after."

"What makes you think it was *after* your daddy died?"

Emblem pulls the penguin to her chest, presses her eyes shut again. "Because I knew he couldn't be mad at me for taking them." She opens her eyes and looks to the interviewer, eyes wide and lips parted as if to ask, *Did I do good?*

26.

Admission (n.)

1. a voluntary concession of the existence of certain facts
2. a confession ten years coming

We ride back to the Singer Suites after a full day in court, my head spinning from the day's testimony and the questions it's left me with. Having empathy for those who lost Joe does not make Margot guilty, I remind myself as our shuttle exits the freeway, greeted by the fast-coming early dark of late October. I work to ignore the gnawing doubt that continues to creep into my once resolute stance on this case. On Margot.

I'm lost in thought until we are just a few blocks from the hotel, when Cam leans forward from the back row of the shuttle, positioning his face between Damon and me. "Let's meet up tonight instead," he says, then falls back into his seat. It takes a moment to grasp what he's saying.

I had forgotten entirely about Cam's invitation from the bowling alley on Saturday: *Come to my room. Say, tomorrow night? I wanna show you guys somethin'.* After my Outback Steakhouse bathroom hallway run-in and then our subsequent confinement to our rooms yesterday, I was content to follow the rules and stay in my room. But Cam doesn't seem to want to let the idea go.

"What do you think Cam wants to show us?" I whisper to Damon beside me. "Are you gonna go over?"

"Not sure," Damon whispers back. He shifts his eyes to me. "Do you want to?" It's as though he's willing, but only if we go together.

"I don't know," I say, staring up at his darkened face.

He leans in. "It's just Cam."

Well. Perhaps Damon can't think of any sinister options with "Just Cam," but my mind forms an immediate list of possibilities. Maybe the trial has sent Cam mad and he plans to butcher us in his room with a dull butter knife from the breakfast buffet. Maybe he silently followed Damon and me up to the presidential suite that third night of the trial and plans to blackmail us in exchange for silence. I could go on and on. It's perhaps my most accomplished trait, catastrophizing. And with Judge Gillespy's newest security directive just this morning, the idea seems incredibly foolish.

We climb out of the vans and head to the dining area for dinner. The crowd, generally, has returned to the somber humdrum of the previous week, all remnants of Saturday's uplift squashed by Judge Gillespy's announcement this morning and subsequent heavy day of testimony.

Despite my mental exhaustion, I make a concerted effort to chat with a few of the other jurors (outside of Cam, Tamra, and Damon). However, most beeline for their rooms the second they've finished eating tonight's dinner selection of chicken fingers and fries. Xavier pats each person's shoulder as they pass on their way out of the dining area as if he's a coach consoling his locker-room-bound players after a tough loss. Gray Man steps around him to avoid his touch.

Later, as we stand in a line in front of our respective doors, Cam and Damon look over at me questioningly. I promptly shove myself inside my room, letting it close with a thud behind me.

I've told myself to keep things platonic with Damon. I can't exactly keep my distance, but I can avoid situations *like this.* Like the presidential suite. I'm here for one reason: to ensure Margot gets a fair trial. But Damon's presence screams at me in a way I can't seem to ignore. He's adventure. He's all the good from my childhood — every bit of it still resides in him. I can't seem to say no to it, to the opportunity for more time with him. Even if it means Cam, too. And after today's testimony, that of both Jackie Kitsch *and* Emblem, time beside Damon feels more like a need than a want.

I stare at my reflection in the bathroom mirror and present my argument. "We're not going to talk about the case," I tell her. "We're probably just . . . blowing off steam. From being so cooped up all the time." We stare at each other, and I blink first. As soon as I've spoken the words, I know I've already decided.

I walk past Cam's door and knock quietly on Damon's. As I do, I hear the elevator beep from around the corner. Shit. There's a fifty-fifty chance whoever exits the elevator will come this way. I can't risk a guard catching me break curfew. Damon's door swings open, and I shove my way into his room. He eyes me in silent question.

Close it, I mouth, motioning toward the door. His hand still clasping the handle, he does as I say and quietly presses the door shut.

"What is it?" he asks, his voice still low though we are now alone in his room.

"The elevator dinged. I thought someone might see me," I say.

He looks out the peephole for a long moment and then turns to face me, shakes his head to indicate the hallway is clear. Now, though, I'm distracted by the details of his room. My eyes catch on the bed, comforter pushed to the foot, flat sheet messily stretching across it, a ripple along the fitted sheet where he sleeps. I clear my throat and force my eyes to focus elsewhere. Scanning the rest of the room, I survey the stack of books on the nightstand and the pair of jeans neatly folded over the armchair in the corner. The room is incredibly small, with no way to keep a physical distance from him.

He presses his back into the door and steals my attention. "So, does this mean you want to go see what Cam's up to?"

"I'm slightly curious," I say.

He runs his hand along the back of his neck, head bent down, then looks back up at me. That combination of movements from him, it's alarming the fire they create in my gut.

"We should give it a minute, though. Ensure the coast is clear?" I say, pointing toward his door. He nods, takes a step into the room so we are both inches from his disarrayed bed. I survey the room some more for something to do besides staring at him. "Is that what I think it is?" I say, swiping the item from his nightstand. "You may own the last remaining Walkman. May I?"

He nods, and I start flipping through his music selection, a black nylon case of CDs slid into plastic protectors, four on each page.

"Figured this was the only safe electronic device the bailiffs wouldn't take."

I think of the bottom drawer of his old bedroom dresser, which held a collection of cassette tapes and CDs found at garage sales and thrift shops around town. How, despite my protests that he could listen to any song via Spotify, he preferred the tapes, painstakingly rewinding to listen to something again. I can still hear the squeaky run of the tapes. I like that he's held on to this bit of himself from his past.

We share a knowing look before I go back to flipping CDs.

"What are you in the mood for?" he asks.

I bite at the inside of my cheek, wondering if he remembers how I used to play the *High School Musical* soundtrack on repeat for most of the years we knew each other. How he'd exhale with marked annoyance each time a song would repeat. How I'd sometimes catch him humming "We're All in This Together" on our walk to school.

I feel him observing me closely as I flip the pages of his CD case, his eyes never leaving the side of my face. I pretend not to notice.

Eventually, I find the CD I want and, after amusedly directing the CD player, blast "I'm Like a Bird" by Nelly Furtado loud enough so we can hear it through the headphones.

He smirks again.

I cross my arms, and his eyes follow the gesture briefly to my chest, then back up again in a flash. We stand in silence listening, both lost in the song. I wonder if the sheer act of listening to music together takes him back the way it does me. I picture him sprawled on my bedroom floor, hands clasped behind his head, mouthing lyrics. For the four whole minutes of the song, we stand silent, listening and watching each other.

As the song comes to an end, he takes the

CD player from my hands. "Hey," I say, feigning protest.

"My turn." He rotates his back to me as he leafs through the book of CDs, a destination seemingly in mind. He pulls out a disc. I try to look, but he blocks me with his body. I press into his side, but it takes barely a nudge for him to ward me off. Size-wise, I'm like a Chihuahua at his heels.

Once his CD of choice is in the player, he turns to face me. We watch each other for reaction as the familiar intro to "Empire State of Mind" barrels from the player.

I grin. "Are you trying to get me to sing? Because this is a great way to do it."

He leans against the dresser, crosses his arms against his broad chest. "The stage is yours," he says, throwing an arm out toward the strip of carpet between the bed and dresser where we stand. "Wrong Lyrics Only?" he suggests, knowing we're both thinking it.

"Empire State of Mind" was one of our most common wrong lyric references. When my dad left after that fight where Damon stepped between us at fourteen, Damon turned around to face me, and after a minute of silence, he said, "Concrete jungle wet dream tomato."

My tension broke with a shatter.

I shake my head. "I need alcohol for Wrong Lyrics Only."

His face changes, hardens in knowing. I think about the last drinks we had together, at Outback Steakhouse, our legs touching under the table.

Confirming his mind has also wandered back to Outback Steakhouse alongside mine, he says, "I'm sorry I told George about what happened at the restaurant."

I shake my head. "It was nothing, Damon. I appreciate your concern, but I promise it created more trouble than it's worth."

He rubs at the back of his neck, evaluating me. Finally, he says, "Even so, I guess I'll just have to keep an eye on you. Make sure you're safe."

I expect a hint of a smirk, but when I can't find one upon inspection of his lips, something inside me softens further still. Around him, I am a stick of butter melting slowly in the sun. I think I'll say, *I can take care of myself,* or *I don't need you watching over me,* but instead what comes out is "I guess so."

He takes a step toward me. "Should we talk about that kiss?" he asks, and my muscles reflexively tighten.

"What? Why?"

He shrugs. "I don't know. Because it happened, and we haven't really had the opportunity to talk about it."

"Except for every moment of every day that we spend together when we're not sleeping."

"Yeah, but we're never alone."

I become highly aware of our aloneness now. "Can't this be a padlocked diary topic?" I try.

He stares me down, eyebrow raised.

It seems odd timing to bring it up. I'm not certain it needs to be brought up at all. That presidential suite kiss seems like many moons ago, with all that's happened in the trial and otherwise since. "Okay, so talk," I say finally.

He licks his bottom lip, and I'm reminded of how he tasted. Warm. Wet. Hoppy.

"Well, you seemed like you regretted it. Like maybe it was a heat-of-the-moment kind of thing."

I don't confirm or deny.

"I just wanted to apologize again, if that's the case. If you really do regret it." He speaks with intention, like he's been thinking about it, choosing his words, looking for an opportunity to bring it up.

I think of his fiery tongue, how it spilled into my mouth like lava. "I kissed you first," I say. "I don't want you to think you did anything wrong. You didn't."

He runs his hand along his neck again. "Other than potentially cause the mistrial of the century." His eyes flicker in what I've come to know as his own form of a smile, and I do the same so I don't think about the possible consequences of my questionable activities.

"It was fine," I say, attempting to reassure him again.

"Just fine?" he asks, his face so inscrutable I almost believe he's offended.

I shake my head and avoid a smile, refusing to give him more.

A new song plays — familiar, but not a Wrong Lyric song. The one that pulsed out the window of my father's Buick as he backed out of our garage, ending our first kiss. "Thinking Out Loud" by Ed Sheeran. It had just come out and was constantly playing everywhere, a marking of that point in time. I wonder if he remembers.

His face hardens as he looks at me, and we're silent for most of the song. Finally, he speaks. "Did you have feelings for me? Back then?"

I swallow, continue to hold his gaze. "We were teenagers," I say.

"And?"

"And you were my best friend. I'd be lying if I said I never thought about it. Never thought about . . . more between us."

His pointer finger taps at his thigh.

I clear my throat and ask, "Did you?"

He continues to hold my gaze. "I think whatever we had got cut short."

"That's a fact, not an answer," I press. This moment, this bit of conversation, feels important in a way that's too complex to define.

He lets out a breath, something between a huff and a sigh. "I did. Of course I did," he says.

A spark of lightning strikes from my stomach down between my legs at the admission I've waited ten years to hear.

27.

Contraband (n.)

1. illegal or prohibited traffic in goods; smuggling
2. *I* didn't do it

"So," I say, still staring at him in the close quarters of his hotel room. "Maybe that kiss was . . ." I bite at my bottom lip, trying to ignore the throbbing heat pulsing through me. ". . . seizing the opportunity we never got back then." I try on the explanation, see how it fits. It doesn't seem wrong, but also, not wholly right.

He breaks our gaze, looks to the window. "Yeah, maybe," he says, then moves his attention back to me. "But honestly, there was opportunity back then. We were together almost every day. I was always afraid you wouldn't feel the same and it would end our friendship. If things didn't work out, we wouldn't be able to go back."

My lips part, and a dull ache invades my chest. He's offered far more than he's usually willing to say. And I'm sure he realizes the irony of his words. Our friendship *did* end, and we never *were* able to go back, just not because of our mounting interest in each other.

It suddenly feels incredibly intimate, being in his room, right next to his slept-in bed. I imagine his bare, inked skin pressed into those stark white sheets. Innocently sneaking around is one thing, but falling for this man — again — when it took me so long to get over him the first time is another charge entirely.

"Right, well, should we get on with our debauchery then?" I say. I have to get out of this room.

Damon nods, though makes no motion toward the door. I see his internal struggle — say more or relent. It's a constant battle between us and within ourselves, of how hard to push backward into the particulars of our past. One too forceful press and we may lose whatever small ground we've gained.

Eventually, he chooses the door. He listens for a moment and, when satisfied, opens it in that silent way he has perfected. I don't even hesitate in following. I can't seem to stop myself, no matter the potential consequences.

Damon pokes his head into the hallway. He motions for me to join him, and we step out of his room, quickly pressing against Cam's door. Damon knocks three times, so lightly I can't imagine Cam hearing it. But the door swings open almost immediately, as if Cam has been watching out the peephole.

We file in silently, and Cam shuts his own door with precision. "Glad you guys came," he says.

Damon and I evaluate his room. We know so little about one another despite spending eight straight days with the other jurors. A view into someone's room, where they sleep, is a wealth of information. Cam's bed is perfectly made — corners tucked and comforter smoothed. None of his personal items are strewn about, and at first glance one might assume this room has been turned down and is ready for a new occupant. I wasn't expecting him to be so orderly.

"What'd you want to show us?" Damon asks.

Cam grins — this wide, secretive smile that stretches his whole face. We watch as he heads to the closet, retrieves the same black backpack I saw him leave his room with the other night, and sets it on the bed. He grins at us again, then dumps its many contents onto the brushstroke-patterned bedspread.

My mouth drops open.

Before us, splayed across the bed in a messy pile, is a collection of practically every item banned from the jury: two cell phones, a printed magazine with Margot's face on it, a small AM/FM radio, a plastic baggie filled with brownies that look a lot like the ones from the buffet, a half-empty bottle of vodka, and a box of Trojan BareSkin condoms. It's like *Orange Is the New Black* in here with all this poorly hidden contraband.

Damon picks up what looks to be a prescription bottle and observes it.

"Gummies. You want one?" Cam asks, still grinning proudly.

Damon tilts the bottle toward me in question. I shake my head.

"Where did you get all this?" I ask, staring at the pile of goods but too afraid to touch any of it. I envision Bailiff George dusting the pile with fingerprint powder once it's inevitably seized.

I expect some harrowing tale of how he wrapped things in plastic and swallowed them or shoved them into unmentionable orifices, or a complex bribery system with the guards. He shrugs. "Nobody checked my backpack."

"Seriously?" I say, feeling a bit disappointed there isn't a more dramatic story behind the pile of items on the bed.

"Figured it was time to share the wealth." Cam plops down on the bed and opens the plastic baggie, removes a brownie, and takes a bite.

I sit on the corner of the bed. "So, what do you know? What's the word on the street about the case? About Margot?"

Damon sits beside me, hooking his knee atop the bed to face both me and Cam. "Really?" he says.

I know. It's completely hypocritical of me to ask when I've been preaching adherence to the rules. I know I'm putting the case itself — and perhaps Margot — at even greater risk. But I have to know what the media is putting out about her. If they are painting her in a favorable light.

"It's not good," Cam says, handing me the magazine. "This one I swiped from the lobby. Seems they didn't think to temporarily hold off on setting out their weekly magazines."

I hesitate for a brief moment but then,

intrigue winning over, grab the magazine. I look at the date. It released today.

Margot's face takes up most of the cover with five words scrawled across it: "Who Is the Malibu Menace?" To the side, the subhead that makes my stomach sink: "Scorned by Joe's multiple affairs, reading books on women who poison, and a secret disappearance at age sixteen."

I think back to Margot's father's testimony just a few days ago, as I have often. With all the case's revelations thus far, his is still the one that nags at me most. Where was Margot during that week when she was sixteen? What happened to her over those seven days? I don't know why exactly, but I can't help but believe whatever happened back then put her on the trajectory that led us all here. I was the same age, after all, when the defining moment of my life happened. Aren't we all just products of our formative years? Margot's no exception.

I flip to the article, which shows more pictures of Margot, Joe, and their kids — a sad scrapbook of what used to be. Skimming the article, I find an anonymous source from the courtroom quoted, referencing Margot as "unapologetic and spiteful" during the trial and that "the jury does not seem to connect with her."

Really?

It's a far stretch, all of it. How are we meant to "connect," exactly, when sitting silently in a courtroom?

"The defense hasn't made its case yet," I announce, tossing the magazine back into the pile. What shoddy journalism. I hastily grab the bottle of vodka. Cam smiles, tips his chin at me as an approval to drink straight from the bottle, so I do. We both look at Damon, seated beside me. I raise my eyebrows at him in a dare. He sighs and takes a swig. I wonder how he'd taste if I were to kiss him now.

"We can't do this here. Too loud," Cam says, grabbing the contraband and replacing it in his backpack, then sliding a strap over his right shoulder. He heads for the door. "Follow me."

Damon and I exchange a glance as Cam quietly pulls the handle. I shake my head in defeat.

The overwhelming desire for time with Damon, in any form. This newfound sense of adventure.

Of course I'm going to follow.

28.

Collective Juror Misconduct (n., phrase)

1. a group of jurors, rather than an individual, engaging in behavior that goes against the court's instructions or rules
2. jurors gone wild

Damon, Cam, and I make our way silently to the stairwell and begin to climb. Just as I'm thinking perhaps Cam has also swiped a key to the poorly secured presidential suite, he passes the second-floor door and keeps going, stopping at the only other option: the door to the roof.

This one's got to be locked. It's the roof. External access. But nope, Cam shifts the handle down, and sure enough, it's also unlocked. I doubt these security measures are up to Judge Gillespy's standards for this high-profile *murder* trial.

We step onto the roof, and I am immediately struck by the pungent odor of what I believe is a combination of desert rain and animal urine. The strip mall below is still lit up, providing ample light to the otherwise darkened evening sky. I immediately wrap my arms around myself as the moist breeze catches my hair.

"Oh, here," Cam says. He bends around the corner of the door and hands me a gingham flannel blanket.

I wrap the blanket around my shoulders, wondering just how many times Cam has snuck up here.

Cam slides down against the stairwell wall, and Damon and I follow suit. We sit in a line — Cam, Damon, then me — looking on as two Jimmy John's employees share a smoke break.

Cam positions the backpack in front of him and unzips it. "Either of you want to use the phone?" he asks, pulling one from the bag.

I contemplate, but making a call seems a step too far with all the rules we're already breaking. I do briefly contemplate calling my mom, checking in on her and baby Gen, but I quickly think better of it. Besides, a call to the outside world would place a pin directly into the bubble we are in, and I don't want that.

"I'm good," I tell him.

Damon shakes his head, and Cam replaces the phone.

"How 'bout one of these?" Cam pulls out the prescription-sized bottle of blue gummies.

Damon and I exchange glances, and he raises his eyebrows in question.

"Might as well," I say, leaning around Damon and swiping the bottle. We're already fraternizing on the roof, having snuck out of our rooms post-curfew with Cam's full bag of contraband. One bite of a gummy to ease the beehive in my gut can't make any of this particularly worse should we get caught.

"You sure?" Damon says, watching as I spin the cap off the bottle.

I grab a light blue gummy and bite into it, collecting half into my mouth. I hold out the other half in offer to Damon. He wraps his hand around my wrist, raises my hand to his mouth, and then takes the gummy with his teeth from my fingers. My stomach free-falls as his bottom lip grazes along the pad of my thumb.

"Excellent," Cam muses, taking a whole gummy for himself.

"I told you, Amazon gummy bear reviewer," Damon whispers, bending close. His breath steams against my ear, in direct contrast to the biting evening air, and the rousing combination sends a shock up my spine.

Thirty minutes and an additional half gummy later, the three of us lie atop one of Cam's blankets on the cement roof, me in the middle, staring up at the evening sky. It's clear and smogless — an L.A. rarity, though the air is both wet and crisp with the faint clay smell of distant rain. Though I can't seem to focus on much else besides the whole left side of my body pressed against Damon's right. He's like a warm, crackling fire, and I fight the urge to cuddle into his body heat.

As Cam's voice grows groggier, slow and more placid with each minute that passes, I wonder why I don't feel any different. "I'm not feeling much. Can I have another?" I ask without moving my eyes from the smattering of stars in the sky.

"Give it a few minutes," Cam says. He pushes himself up to sit, the entirety of his face upturned. His expression is noticeably slack, more than usual.

"Cam, how many gummies did you have?" I ask.

"Two," he says.

"When? We took one," Damon says, his voice seemingly echoey and inside me all at once.

"I took one in my room before you guys showed up. Don't worry, I have a high tolerance." He's still smiling.

Damon picks up the bottle and inspects it. "He's had . . . a lot. And, from what I can tell so far, these are the extra trippy kind."

Damon and I exchange a look, then observe Cam again.

"We should have invited Tamra," Cam says, grabbing another brownie from his bag. "I bet she'd be fun high."

It's hard to worry about him with that dopey look on his face.

I turn my attention back to the sky, unable to form anything resembling concern. Lying on a rooftop next to the guy I like, I feel like a teenager in the best possible way. Tonight encapsulates everything I know I missed after he left — friendships, thrills, bad decisions. I focused instead back then on being the perfect daughter to avoid adding to any tension between my parents while simultaneously building my plan toward independence.

"Do *you* have a high tolerance?" Damon

asks, clearly attempting to dissect my statement about not feeling much of anything. It's clear he and Cam do. The more time passes, though, the more his voice sounds like it's originating from behind my face.

Mel and I take gummies fairly regularly, though ours tend to be more "sleepy" than "trippy." "I don't like losing control," I say, a sidestep for no apparent reason.

"I remember," Damon says so quietly I almost miss it.

Distinct shapes begin to form in the sky. I find the Big Dipper directly overhead. A slight stretch down and to the left, the Little Dipper. Extending to over Cam, Ursa Major and Minor. Above Damon, Orion with his belt and sword. And after some searching, I find the North Star, shining just a bit brighter than the others. *It's so beautiful,* I think, believing I could visually dissect this sky forever — even if the experience is being facilitated by a cold cement roof likely covered in stray cat pee.

A lightweight sensation takes me over, as if I am floating toward Orion himself. I picture Kara up there, holding a giant sheet of black construction paper, small holes poked into it, shining a flashlight through to create the scene we are transfixed by. I rather like this notion. I don't look over at

Damon, but I feel him staring intensely at the sky just the same. I wonder if he is seeing what I'm seeing.

Cam's voice interjects. "Why do we have eyebrows?" he asks, seemingly transfixed by his own inquisition. Silence follows as we collectively ponder.

Apparently losing interest in finding an answer, Cam eventually wanders to the far side of the roof, leaving Damon and me staring up at the ebony sky.

"He's really high," I say. A distant part of me suggests perhaps we should keep an eye on Cam, but then another part of me — a much more insistent one — asserts that I should just let go.

I watch the sky, awestruck, as Orion swats his sword toward the Little Dipper, slicing it in two.

"Are you?" Damon asks, turning to face me, gathering the loose strings of my attention. It's a unique angle to take him in from. I've never seen adult him lying down. For a moment, I believe we are in a bed.

I look back to the sky to see stars falling like confetti. I feel like I'm in a snow globe. "I believe I now am." I turn my body to face him again, all parts of him more lucid than ever before. I resist the urge to sweep my finger along the crease under his eye.

Each time he blinks, it's as though I can feel the skin of his eyelids as they slide against the wetness of his eyeballs.

"Why are you looking at me like that?" he asks.

"Like what?"

"Like you want to eat me or something."

"It's your eyes . . . the way your eyelids move . . ." I can't find the words, so I just keep watching the slipperiness of his blink.

Damon's jaw muscle twitches and expands, and he opens his mouth, his perfect teeth wet like his eyeballs. "You're definitely high," he says, turning himself back toward the starry sky.

I look up just as Orion takes a seat inside the Big Dipper, his arms and legs dangling out in all directions. I laugh — at Damon's eyelids, at Orion's antics, at the fact that I am, in fact, very high. He huffs back, amused, and it's a simple, knowing exchange at the absurdity.

"You should date more," I say after a while, the unfiltered thought crashing out of my mouth like a crested wave. "It seems to me you belong out in the world, sparkling."

"Did you just call me 'sparkling'?"

I face him again. "Yes. You sparkle. It's an objective observation. You know you do."

His eyes crinkle as the tightness of his face

further recedes. "I've never thought of myself as sparkly, Syd. That's a new one."

"You are indeed sparkly. People notice you. You have a presence that makes people take note. Kind of like Margot." I look back to the sky but feel his eyes on me still.

He props his head up with his hand, elbow pressed to the blanketed cement. "You don't see *yourself.*"

I consciously swallow, attempting to coat my dry throat. "Sure I do."

He shakes his head. "No. You don't." He states his response so factually I have to question whether I'm indeed wrong.

"Then what am I?" I say, my voice a dare.

He doesn't hesitate. "You're smart. I like the way you think. Like how you resisted turning on the TV the other night in the presidential suite. If I were a fan, I don't know if I could have shown such restraint."

I roll my eyes when he brings up my fandom again. "Yes, clearly I am restrained," I say, gesturing at the air in reference to our current half-baked situation.

"You constantly surprise me," he says in response. He pushes the sleeves of his sweatshirt up to just under his elbows, and I take in the ink on his arms again. I think I now know them all on these two plots of land. I feel a bit of pride in that — that I've spent enough time in his vicinity to know every forearm tattoo and how each adjusts with his movements.

"You're thoughtful. Like how you grabbed me a box of cereal that morning I accidentally slept in."

"I'd do that for anyone," I say, which is solidly a lie.

He keeps going, more words escaping him than I'd thought possible in one sitting. Who knew all I had to do was get him high and the compliments would spill out of him. "You're beautiful. There's that. Even more beautiful than I remember. I didn't think that was possible."

I force myself to hold his gaze rather than look down at the cement. I've been called beautiful only by two other men in my life, both right before casual sex.

Damon, though, has called me beautiful before. The first was ahead of the homecoming dance freshman year, when he arrived to pick me up, though we were going as singles in a group rather than as couples. It was my *She's All That* moment, complete with a trip on the bottom step. When I regained my balance, his eyes flicked down and then back up over my lavender floor-length sweetheart dress. "You're beautiful," he said, with a wistfulness in his voice that made me want to question him.

The other time was right before our first kiss.

Damon dips his head to catch my eyeline. "I was gonna say you're *fucking hot,* but . . ." He seems to search for the appropriate end to his sentence, but when he doesn't find it, he instead lets the unfinished bit hover between us.

My stomach flips. Beautiful, sure. Fine. But never "fucking hot." His eyes sear me from the insides of my throat to the pit of my stomach.

We both watch my hand rise from the blanket, fingertips landing on his exposed forearm. We follow the trace of my index finger as it examines the tattoos of his forearm one at a time, each having grown in meaning and appeal the more I get to know him again. My fingers flutter over the angel wings to the intricate mandala just above. We watch as the tips of my nails brush the hairs of his arm as they move, like legs sweeping through a field of wildflowers.

"Is that on the list you've been keeping about me?" I ask, my voice unreasonably husky as our eyes stay trained on my hand and its movement.

I see him nod in my peripheral. "It's a hell

of a lot longer than just that, but yes."

I stop to look up at him, fingertips still against his skin. Damon's face takes on a familiar stoniness. His eyelids having ceased in their blinking. I look to the sky for comfort, only to find Orion has picked up the North Star and is spinning it atop his outstretched index finger like a basketball.

I turn back to Damon to share this news with him only to find him staring at me with what I'm certain is desire. His eyes are soft, filled with that cool that never seems to leave them. But also, I see now, rimmed with longing. It's been there all along tonight, I realize — a set-in, unwashable stain. A wave of emotion washes from my abdomen to my chest and back down.

I take a quick look to where Cam disappeared to. He's lying on the ground on the opposite end of the roof, still but peaceful, as if he's fallen asleep.

Damon cups my chin, drawing my attention back to him. He positions his thumb squarely below my bottom lip, brushing it slowly back and forth. I watch him as he stares at my mouth, the focus of his observation so intense that I reflexively rake my tongue over my bottom lip. He swallows roughly in response. His eyes flick up to mine, and I demand his gaze. Our faces hover so painfully close that, even in the near dark, I can see the finespun lines of his skin and the thick navy-gray rims of his irises.

I don't know what to do. I don't know what I want. My heart is crackling like cellophane, tearing at the preemptive thought of this man breaking my heart again but, equally, fracturing at the idea of not leaning in anyway.

Before I can ruminate further, he leans in and kisses me. It's tender, delicate even. So silky and gentle I wouldn't think the softness of it possible from someone built like him. I press into him, attempting to indicate with my movement that I don't want him to be gentle. He responds, driving his tongue against mine, moving my mouth open more fully.

I find myself uninhibited, particularly with Cam just feet away — even if he is seemingly fast asleep. Perhaps it's the rooftop setting under the stars. Perhaps it's this night and its echoes of the teenage and college recklessness I never had. Perhaps it's the gummies. But somewhere in the recesses of myself, I know it's because of him. Damon does something to me, something I've never quite experienced since being with him before.

Before I can think it through, I'm climbing into his lap. Damon responds, sitting up against the stairwell wall and straightening his legs in front of him to allow me in. My knees press into the solid wall behind him as I lean in. He bends his knees, dragging his legs closer, cradling me.

Our eyes race, both contemplating what happens next. The tug-of-war between "should" and "want" wrenches through us both.

Impulsively, I grab each of his cheeks with a thumb and forefinger and pull the skin upward, taut.

"What are you doing?" he asks, though it comes out muffled because of my control of his mouth.

"I just want to see if it's possible." I pull the skin of his cheeks higher, and he presses his eyebrows together in question. "If you can smile. If your face works," I say.

He holds still, allows me to treat him like a puppet. Finally, I drop his face, satisfied that it can, in fact, move the way of a smile. That the gesture is available to him, if and when he was to choose it.

When I release his face, he cups the back of my neck with his hand. I instantly flood with want, my senses pushed to an alertness I haven't felt all night. I examine his eyes, nose, mouth, and skin, and my vision goes blurry as it fuses my two versions of him — past and present — together. His hand holds firm to the back of my neck.

We stare at each other, and the sadness that never seems to leave him is momentarily replaced with desire. Still, I know it's there. A flicker of a sentiment has been swirling in me all night, and, staring into his eyes now, I am finally able to define it. I would do just about anything to work that imprint of pain from his eyes and body and heart. This idea is scary and impulsive. It feels like a free fall — uncontrolled and thrilling and terrifying at once, knowing I might die at the bottom when I finally land. Even so, what a ride.

I lean in and kiss him, not at all softly.

Everything feels . . . more. My skin more sensitive to his touch, my tongue more tactile, my whole body tingling with excitement. Somewhere in the depths of my mind, I thank the gummies. As our kiss grows deeper, I scoot into him where there's no room to be had, my hips rocking toward his stomach. He presses into me, our bodies connecting at several points. His hand snakes around to the front of my neck. When he squeezes, I feel the pulse of it between my legs. When I shift more firmly in his lap, I feel his erection rising against me, so closely aligned to its intended place it makes me moan into his mouth.

"I want you so bad," he murmurs into my ear. His voice is like fingertips grasping the edge of a crumbling cliff, and it makes me writhe against him. He exhales, leans his head against the wall, closes his eyes. I feel powerful, sitting on top of him, causing his arousal. I've never felt more capable. Damon is the thrill I've never fully had but now, exposed, need to continue to feel.

His hand releases from my neck, moves down to my waist, then back up underneath my sweater. His hands are ice cold from the evening chill. Their touch causes an immediate eruption of goose bumps across my entire body. He releases his breath, seemingly enjoying being the cause of my skin's reaction. His fingertips press into the small of my back, and I practically whimper. We stare at each other a moment, the strand of connective tissue between us thick, throbbing. He looks at me like I'm the most intriguing thing he's ever seen. Like I've stopped him in his tracks. Like I have a presence akin to Margot Kitsch. *I get it,* I think, as I stare back at him. I get how valuable this power is. How addictive. I lean back in and kiss him more deeply than before, my hand making its way down to his erection just below his jeans. I envision the solid mass below and believe I may come completely undone right here on this rooftop. Right here in his lap.

"I knew it!" Cam's voice infiltrates, and Damon and I freeze. He's still lying several feet away, though he's lifted his head in our direction, clearly observing our intimate moment. Damon reacts by covering me with the discarded blanket beside us as if I am naked, though we are both fully clothed.

As quickly as he burst in, Cam lays his head back down and closes his eyes again as if he were a corpse experiencing a phantom muscle spasm. Damon and I look from him back to each other, me still atop his lap, his hands still clasping the bare skin under my sweater at my sides. Our laughter is immediate.

29.

Communal Property (n. phrase)

1. assets and possessions owned jointly
2. after last night, Damon's lap

Tuesday morning, we are introduced to Shane Windham, Joe's longtime business manager and executor of his estate. Though the same age, Mr. Windham looks as though he could have had a good ten years on Joe. While Joe defined as he aged, Shane Windham has a worn, reddened face and hair receding severely at his temples. He reminds me of a melted candle, his skin folded and molded over, winding paths down his face, collecting at the center point of his neck.

As we await Shane Windham being sworn in, Damon scrawls a note on his pad and shifts it toward me on his right leg. *HI,* it reads. I look up at him, and the muscle in his jaw clenches. *Hi,* I write back, then promptly look away, pressing my eyes shut. Last night I dry-humped Damon Bradburn on the roof of the Singer Suites while high on smuggled gummies with Cam lying just a few feet away. There could be no greater indication that I am making questionable life choices.

Something about this environment makes me feel young and stupid. It's as though the more parameters are placed around me, the more I regress to being incapable of rational thought and decision-making.

The cedar and nutmeg scent of Shane Windham's cologne wafts toward us from the witness stand, and it makes me sneeze.

"Bless you," Damon whispers beside me, and his hungry tone reminds me of his whisper to me last night. *I want you so bad.* I shift in my seat, suddenly feeling so exposed I might as well be naked from the waist down.

Damon tilts his notepad toward me once more. Under our exchange of hellos, he has written: *I HAD A DREAM ABOUT YOU LAST NIGHT.* Before I can react, someone clears their throat, and I look over to find it's one of the courtroom bailiffs, Maurice, stationed just to the right of the jury box. He's looking directly at me. Jurors eleven (the quiet young man) and twelve (the mom of four) also seem to take note of the exchange. I smile awkwardly and shove Damon's notebook back to him.

Last night was a low point. Technically, it was a high point — a very high, best-make-out-of-my-life high point. But I'm acting impulsively, and my actions have real potential consequences that supersede my own wants. I sit up a little straighter. Today, I draw a line in the sand. I won't tell Damon that not only did I dream about him, too, but that, once back in my room last night, I pleasured myself thinking about our rooftop encounter.

D.A. Stern dives in, and I am grateful. He asks Mr. Windham about his relationship with Joe, which we learn dates back an impressive thirty-five years. Mr. Windham describes their friendship, which extended far beyond their business relationship, including dozens of sails to Catalina Island on his catamaran and private viewings of Joe's upcoming films in the Kitsches' theater room. After this background information, D.A. Stern gets to it. "Mr. Windham, will you tell us the details of Joe Kitsch's will?"

Shane Windham clears his throat and leans forward, bumping his top lip against the microphone. It's become a slight amusement of the trial, seeing how few people can speak into the microphone with appropriate clarity and spacing. He leans back slightly. "It was actually quite basic, despite his complex income streams and wealth."

"What do you mean by 'basic'?"

Shane Windham clears his throat again and looks to us in the jury box as he says, "He left everything to his wife. To Margot." He motions a hand toward the defense table where Margot sits, right ankle crossed behind left, legs at a forty-five-degree angle, just as she usually does. She looks on, rather stoic today. I think of the magazine article, the gallery member who described her as unapologetic and spiteful. *Is she?*

There's something different about her today. She's dressed sharply, as always, in a perfectly tailored black midi dress with a draped mock neckline and pointed nude heels. Her hair hangs straight and smooth, just as it has each day of the trial. Her makeup is neutral but present. Though perfectly groomed and styled, there's a sunkenness to her eyes. Maybe the trial is getting to her. I wonder if she's been sleeping. Is it trial fatigue or guilt?

Shane Windham clears his throat again and regains my attention.

D.A. Stern strolls to the jury box, rests a hand on the small wall ahead of me. "So

Margot stands to inherit how much, exactly, as a result of her husband's passing?"

Shane Windham's response is immediate, eyes clearly full of contempt and on Margot as he answers, "Just under eighty-five million."

A murmur breaks out across the courtroom.

"Eighty-five million dollars?" D.A. Stern asks.

"That's right. All of his bank accounts, his investments, his production company. They all list Margot as the sole beneficiary."

D.A. Stern quietly assesses the jury, ensuring the information Shane Windham has conveyed sinks in. "That seems . . . unheard of. That there wouldn't have been a trust of some kind, with a portion of that money set aside to take care of his aging parents or for the children."

Shane Windham leans forward, too close to the microphone again. "It was unconventional. And to be honest, I advised against it. But his parents don't need the money, and Joe didn't want a complicated financial structure. He trusted Margot. He wanted her to have it all."

I glance quickly at the rest of the jury as most everyone scrawls feverish notes. *Was it his way of buying her silence about his af-*

fairs? I think, looking at Durrant Hammerstead as I do, hoping he points to as much in his cross-examination.

"And what about GotMar, the undergarment line that Margot is the face of. Can you tell us more about the structure of that business?"

Shane Windham clears his throat yet again, a cacophony of loosening phlegm. "When it was founded, it was rolled under Joe's umbrella corp."

"What does that mean exactly, in terms of ownership?"

"It means Joe is . . . *was* the majority owner of GotMar. He funded it. And when Margot bought out her ex–business partner, Bess Waterford, it was legally Joe who did so. That move gave Joe one hundred percent ownership of GotMar Incorporated."

There's another grumble across the courtroom, a collective understanding of where this discussion leads.

"And did Joe and Margot have a prenup?" D.A. Stern asks, riding the wave of intrigue in the room.

I shift in my seat. With Damon by my side, Cam behind me knowing what happened last night, D.A. Stern leading perpetual-throat-clearer Shane Windham down an inevitably Margot-damning path right in front of me, I'm feeling increasingly claustrophobic. I tug at the neckline of my burgundy boatneck sweater and glance at Margot. If I feel the walls closing in around me from *my* vantage point, I can only imagine what it must feel like for her.

For her part, Margot looks on with no malice. She appears tired. Perhaps too tired to make the details of Shane Windham's testimony matter.

"They did have a prenup, yes," Shane Windham states.

"And what are the details of that prenup, regarding Joe's business dealings, should they have gotten divorced?" D.A. Stern wanders back to the prosecution table, completing his triangulation between the stand, jury box, and his seat. His favorite black pen bounces between his fingers as he does. He has yet to stand at the podium at any point of this trial.

Shane Windham clears his throat and leans forward. "Margot would not be entitled to any of his businesses."

"Margot would not be entitled to any of his businesses," D.A. Stern echoes as he makes his way toward Shane Windham on the witness stand. He references an exhibit, Joe's full will, a shockingly short document of only five pages. "Just so I'm perfectly clear, what you are telling us is that should Margot have decided she was . . . unhappy in her marriage, and opted to simply leave Joe —"

"She would have left with very little," Shane Windham finishes. "And Joe would have retained full ownership of GotMar."

I think of Margot in one of her last episodes of *Authentic Moms* before Joe died, which aired last fall. In an interview, she spoke directly to the camera, her words overlaying scenes of her rushing around the GotMar offices. She spoke with conviction, animatedly even. She said her hardworking grandfather always instilled in her that it doesn't matter what you do, just be the best at it. There is money and opportunity in everything — anything. "I used to call it his 'be the best garbageman' speech," she had said. "In response, he told me, 'Find me the best garbageman. I'll bet he's the billionaire head of a garbage empire.' Sure enough, he sat me down and we searched online and found a guy in Sydney who started with a shovel and sold his business for half a billion dollars." The scene cut to Margot staring fiercely at the camera, that brief joviality replaced with her classic sternness. "It's not the 'what' that matters, it's the 'how,' " she said.

D.A. Stern puts on a performative frown. "How is that possible, in the state of California where community property laws allocate fifty-fifty ownership of assets in divorces?"

"Because they had a prenup, and because she signed her business over, those things supersede property law."

"Interesting," D.A. Stern muses. "But if he dies —"

Shane Windham does not wait for D.A. Stern to complete the question. "She gets everything," he says, staring again at Margot as he does.

"She gets everything," D.A. Stern repeats. He wanders back to his seat. "No further questions, Your Honor," he says before unbuttoning his jacket and plopping down.

It's as though the air has been sucked out of the room. For all the murmuring over the last week, the gallery is now silent.

Durrant Hammerstead cross-examines, though I don't hear much of it.

She would have lost it all if she left him. It's a hard fact to argue.

Damon beside me presses his palm to the back of his neck.

I watch him, a swirl of emotion roiling in my gut. For the sake of the case — and the safety of my heart — I have to figure out how to avoid Damon when we break for lunch, knowing I want nothing more than to find out if this courthouse has an accessible roof.

30.

Autopsy (n.)

1. a postmortem examination to discover the cause of death or the extent of disease
2. a heart ripped out

I grab a paper-wrapped sandwich from the center of the large round table in the room adjacent the courtroom and sit between Tamra and Gray Man. Damon takes an open spot across the table. I've managed to largely avoid him since we snuck down from the roof and back to our rooms last night. I purposely made my way to the hotel lobby at the last minute this morning and chose the van he wasn't in line for. He did toss me a box of Corn Pops, for which I gave a short but appreciative smile.

I eat quickly and linger in the corner of the room, waiting for the guards to open the doors and let us out, feeling like a caged animal. More and more, it's clear we are all prisoners of this case. Of Margot's. And more and more, it's equally clear I am not doing nearly enough to prove my leadership to the other jurors. Hell, I wouldn't even vote for me for foreperson at this point, given my antics. I wonder if my goal is still salvageable and, if so, how.

Damon crumples the paper from his sandwich and, still chewing, makes his way over. He tosses the paper ball into the waste bin and leans against the wall beside me.

"Pastrami or turkey today?" he asks after he's swallowed, flipping his chin toward the dwindled pile of sandwiches.

"I went crazy and chose ham," I say, my disappointed stomach gurgling on cue.

"So you went ham?"

"You've never struck me as a dad joke kind of guy," I say.

He shakes his head. "Punny road signs, remember?" He rubs at the back of his neck, his mood shifting to something more indeterminate. "So, last night was fun," he says.

"Yeah," I say, looking up to the ceiling to avoid his gaze. The fluorescent lights make my eyes water.

"And you accuse me of being short on

words." He flashes me a look that's almost invasive in its warmth.

I take him in and am met with his flexing jaw muscle and twisting chin dimple. I cross my arms and mimic his side lean against the wall. "Shouldn't we just shove it under the rug and never talk about it again like normal humans?"

He crosses his arms, now mimicking me. "My therapist says that isn't healthy." He purses his lips in a gesture I've rarely seen from him.

"Do you? Go to therapy?"

He nods. "I do."

I uncross my arms and straighten. "Oh. That's great," I say, reminded there are still so many new things to uncover about him.

His eyes crinkle slightly. He takes a step closer so we are practically touching, a bold move in a room full of other jurors and guards. He leans in so his lips are inches from my ear. "I get that you don't want to do anything to mess up this case," he whispers into my hair, "and that we have a lot of complicated history. So, I'm probably a bad idea. So, I'll back off." He lets his hand bump mine. "But just know I don't want to. And that if you change your mind . . ."

When he doesn't finish the thought, I look

up and immediately lose my breath. His face is inches from mine, his peacock-feather-colored eyes narrowed, jaw rigid, lips pressed tightly shut. He doesn't have to finish his sentence. His face says it all — all the things I wish it wouldn't — his expression wayward and sexy as hell.

I need to keep my distance, I remind myself, for the sake of the case *and* my heart. I cannot put it past him to break me again. And it's not lost on me that we haven't actually resolved anything from our past, other than a brief apology from him that I barely acknowledged. With the revelation about Kara and the feelings I've fostered since the start of the trial, I've let the ten years of resentment slip away. I know, though, it's not entirely gone.

I break our gaze to dull the pulse in my core. Glancing at the table instead, I make eye contact with Xavier, who observes us closely, prompting me to step back.

We return to the courtroom after lunch, and I'm immediately on edge. It's the part of the trial I've been dreading — the details of Joe's death. The prosecution is winding down its case and we've yet to hear the particulars of the day he passed. Regardless of what has come out about Joe in this trial, he was a person, and whatever his shortcomings, he deserves a fair trial.

The idea that this man whose life I know so much about is now gone, and that his life is, in many ways, on trial as much as Margot's, has left a consistent knot in my stomach that seems to grow with each testimony. Even Margot, dressed in her subdued black fitted dress, came outfitted for some semblance of a funeral today. My stomach roils, and I wish this testimony came in the morning rather than right after the shitty lunch ham.

Just after we've taken our seats, D.A. Stern calls Medical Examiner Teresa Jessel to the stand. I evaluate her as she's sworn in. She's noticeably thin, lanky in a bone-heavy way that reminds me of D.A. Stern. She wears round spectacles that magnify her eyes and strike me as ironic. I take in her long, talon-like nails, painted with some intricate purple-and-black snakeskin pattern, and I'm intrigued with how those nails don't interfere with her line of work.

D.A. Stern wastes little time, prompting Dr. Jessel to explain the process of Joe's autopsy and subsequent toxicology testing. "In an autopsy, we look primarily for four things: cause, mode and manner of death, the state of health of the person before they died, and whether any medical diagnosis and treatment before death were appropriate." Teresa Jessel has a unique accent, a mix between Indian and a Southern drawl, an interesting combination that draws me in.

"Dr. Jessel," D.A. Stern says in a voice that seems deeper, more authoritative than usual, "as a result of the autopsy, why did you deem Mr. Kitsch's cause of death as undetermined?"

"Well, Mr. Kitsch was otherwise healthy but suffered a massive cardiac event. And I was unable to find an underlying issue or specific trauma to point to cause."

D.A. Stern appraises the jury as Dr. Jessel speaks. When he doesn't immediately ask a follow-up, Dr. Jessel continues. " 'Undetermined' simply means there could have been other factors at play that we couldn't glean from the standard state toxicology reporting and coroner findings."

D.A. Stern presses his lips together so they prune like the pit of a peach. "Were there any underlying health issues uncovered during the autopsy that could have accounted for his death? An illness or deterioration of some kind that could have gone unnoticed?" he finally asks.

"Nothing like that was found."

D.A. Stern moves to the jury box and rests his hands atop it. He taps his pen on the wood. "And are there additional tests that could have been run on Mr. Kitsch to look further into the cause of his sudden death?"

"Yes. Additional testing can be done at the request of family members."

"Did Mrs. Kitsch request additional testing? To find out the cause of death of her husband of twenty-four years?"

"No, she did not."

"No, she did not," D.A. Stern echoes. He circles the defense table, then ambles back to the witness stand. "And Mrs. Kitsch actually took claim of the body as soon as the autopsy was complete, is that correct?"

"That's right."

I think of the argument the D.A. made during opening statements, pointing to his theory that Margot rushed to cremate Joe's body to hide any evidence of foul play, and how Jackie Kitsch raised questions about the nature of Joe's death only *after* the cremation had taken place.

"Tell me, Dr. Jessel, have you ever testified in any cases where additional toxicology reporting *was* requested and it helped to determine a cause of death?"

"Yes."

"What were the details of that case?"

Durrant Hammerstead objects, citing relevance, and after a long pause, Judge Gillespy allows Dr. Jessel to continue.

"Well, standard tox reporting doesn't screen for everything. But in a case I had a few years back, the widow requested additional reporting. An extended drug panel, poison and toxic agent testing, advanced metabolic testing, she did it all. She wanted to be thorough because her husband had been otherwise healthy. Because of that additional reporting, we were able to identify subsequent traces of tetrahydrozoline in his system. This finding ultimately played a key role in determining the events that led to her husband's death."

"Tetrahydrozoline?" D.A. Stern asks.

"The active ingredient commonly found in eye drops," she explains.

The gallery expresses one collective murmur. I guess we know why Dr. Jessel is the medical examiner of choice to testify on behalf of the prosecution. My legs grow restless as I await the expected outcome here.

"And what were those events? In that case?" D.A. Stern asks.

"The teenage son had placed eye drops into his father's morning coffee after an argument about a scratch on the family car's front bumper. The boy thought it would give his father diarrhea, not kill him. A common misbelief."

Margot blots at her nose with a frayed tissue.

"Tragic," D.A. Stern says after evaluating Margot. "But that testing wasn't done in this case because Mrs. Kitsch didn't request it. And by the time we came to pretrial testing?"

Dr. Jessel answers the implied question. "Any remnants of said chemicals would no longer appear in the testing after so many months. And since the body was cremated, we could only rely on the samples retained from the initial autopsy."

D.A. Stern nods. "No further questions."

Damon shifts in his seat, casts his eyes toward me briefly. A bead of sweat trickles down the small of my back. It all feels like information I shouldn't know. My head is spinning. I used to want to know everything possible about Margot Kitsch and the people in her life. Now, I wish I could go back to only knowing what she wanted me to. I wish I could undo the growing doubt that scrapes at my thoughts with each new witness.

Durrant Hammerstead's turn with the witness comes quickly and so does the shift in questioning. "You said that when you examined Mr. Kitsch's toxicology results, there were no indications of foreign substances?"

"Mr. Kitsch died from sudden cardiac arrest. I ruled it undetermined because of his otherwise good health."

"Undetermined? So, to reiterate your earlier testimony, your belief is that Mr. Kitsch likely died of natural causes?"

Dr. Jessel swivels her head in a figure eight. "I found nothing in my evaluation of the body or the toxicology results that would indicate anything other than natural causes."

Durrant Hammerstead turns to the jury box and grins laxly, sure to impress upon us the importance of this statement.

Finally, something in Margot's favor. I can't help but think, though, that it's nowhere near enough after the prosecution's time with this witness.

31.

Trial Attorney (n., phrase)

1. a lawyer who engages chiefly in trying especially plaintiffs' cases before courts of original jurisdiction
2. unnecessary BDE

I am hopeful Judge Gillespy will end the day early and grant us a break from the heaviness of the case. Instead, we are met with a forensic toxicologist who D.A. Stern parades to the stand. This witness is sure to sear into us that three eye-drop bottles worth of tetrahydrozoline were more than enough to create the cardiac episode that resulted in Joe's death. Furthermore, he states that the window of time for such a poisoning to result in a similar cardiac episode would have required consumption sometime that fateful morning. Durrant Hammerstead is sure to inform us this witness's testimony is all speculative.

And then, finally, the D.A. calls his last witness — the police officer in charge at the scene takes the stand to describe the circumstances she walked into at the Kitsch home the day Joe died.

The initial responding officer, Officer Chavez, is a woman I estimate to be in her mid-forties, dressed in uniform with her black hair pulled back into a low, strict bun. D.A. Stern helps fill in the basics. She has seventeen years of service, all with the Los Angeles County Sheriff's Department. Before that, she graduated top of her class from the police academy. During her time with the force, she's secured "dozens, if not hundreds" of crime scenes in her time, including twenty-four potential homicides.

"Who called 911 on the day Joe Kitsch died?" D.A. Stern asks after these introductory particulars.

"The house manager, Ms. Pembrooke."

"And where were the children?"

"It was my understanding they were at school. It was mid-morning, ten forty-seven a.m., when the call was received."

"Walk us through what you found when you arrived at the Kitsch home as the first officer on scene."

"My partner, Ellison, and me, we arrived

seven minutes after the call was made. We were met at the front entrance by the house manager. She was what I would call hysterical. Crying, screaming, not speaking particularly coherently. She kept saying, 'He's not moving. His eyes are open. His eyes are open.' " Officer Chavez's eyes slide to Margot, then quickly back to D.A. Stern, as if she's slipped by sneaking a peek at the defense table. I wonder if she is an *Authentic Moms* fan, if she knew whose home she was walking into that day. "Ms. Pembrooke showed us to the kitchen, where we found the deceased."

"What was Mr. Kitsch's state when you entered?"

"He was seated at the kitchen table, slumped in his chair. Livor mortis was present, his lips were purple. We checked for a pulse. He was already gone."

All the money and favor in the world, and it couldn't buy him a long enough life.

A single tear meanders down Margot's left cheek at the defense table. She presses a tissue to it gently.

Kara. Joe. The death of Margot's marriage and what I thought I knew of it. These past several days have been consumed by death, and I've reached my tipping point of grief. My eyes pool. I feel a bit silly at my emotion, but it's so much bigger than this moment of the trial. Damon looks over at me, concern written across his brow. He presses his thigh into mine, sturdy but soft, and holds it there, solidly there. I look up at him, and his eyes are narrowed in concern. Concern for me.

D.A. Stern turns to face us. "And wouldn't a mother, looking to protect her children, ensure they were far away when something like this happened, sure they wouldn't be the ones to find him?"

"Objection!" Durrant Hammerstead screams just as Judge Gillespy pounds her gavel. His scream indicates the D.A.'s actions are so egregious he doesn't need to state the nature of the objection. Judge Gillespy seems equally angered — nostrils flared and chest high — clearly tired of the D.A. constantly testing the boundaries of her tolerance.

D.A. Stern is brash, arrogant in a way only a man of his stature and title seems to be. I worry other jurors will find his dominance worth following all the way through, like an authoritative platoon leader.

"Clear the room," Judge Gillespy demands, eyebrows pressed together, raised at the center like a steeple, and we are quickly escorted out of the courtroom.

■ ■ ■ ■

"That was intense," Cam says as we enter the hallway. We linger there for several minutes as Judge Gillespy scolds D.A. Stern for his antics, I assume.

"You okay?" Damon asks as we take up in a far corner of the hallway away from the others.

"Yes. No. I don't know, really."

He runs his palm up and down my bare arm, seemingly forgetting people can see us. I take a quick look down the hall, and everyone seems consumed by what happened in the courtroom. I am, too.

"That must have been hard to hear," he says, still running his palm along my arm.

"I feel like an idiot," I say, looking up at him as he inches closer.

"Why?"

"Because I was excited to be on this trial. I lost sight of the fact that someone's life is over. What that actually means." The tears flow forcibly, gliding down my neck and collecting at the collar of my mint-green linen dress. They are mostly for Kara. And him. I've been holding in all my emotions about his return to my life, and the revelations associated with it, in a tight internal coil, and it's now unfurling before him.

Damon doesn't hesitate to pull me in. I press into him, my face curved into his chest, feeling my tears dampening his light gray dress shirt, all the empathy flowing out of me. But I don't care about the optics of it right now. I don't care how the two of us embracing in the corner may look to the others or how tear-stained his shirt will be when we part. Right now, he is the comfort I need.

"It'll be okay," he says into my hair. His saddle scent surrounds me like a halo of safety. He says those simple words now because he knows I'm upset about him. For him. And this time, he *can* assure me.

The bailiff clears his throat as he eyes Damon and me from the doors. His presence indicates it's time to go back inside. I don't want to go back inside. I want to go to the roof, the presidential suite, Damon's room . . . anywhere that means I can be with him in private.

We reenter the courtroom after what I can only imagine was a significant reprimand of D.A. Stern by Judge Gillespy. The gallery already returned prior to our arrival, and they look on in anticipation, likely wondering if D.A. Stern will overstep again.

Once we are all seated, D.A. Stern eagerly continues with his witness as if there had been no frenzied pause. "Approximately how long had Mr. Kitsch been deceased when you arrived at the scene?" he asks.

"That's not my call," Officer Chavez affirms.

D.A. Stern nods. "And what was Ms. Pembrooke's statement of what she was doing that morning during the time Joe passed?"

"She was home. It was just her and Mr. Kitsch. Stated she was upstairs straightening the kids' rooms and folding laundry for at least an hour. She came downstairs to refill her water bottle, found Mr. Kitsch, then immediately called the police, according to her statement."

I make a note to review Ms. Pembrooke's police statement in detail during deliberations.

I think of the elaborate camera and security system of the Kitsch family home, highlighted on the show. According to Durrant Hammerstead's opening statement, nobody was seen coming or going between Margot leaving with the kids and Officers Chavez and Ellison arriving. This detail works solidly in Margot's favor.

But the same thought that's been nagging

at me creeps in once again. Just because she wasn't physically there doesn't mean she wasn't responsible. I silently chastise myself for the small betrayal of thought.

D.A. Stern's continuation forces my attention. "Your report indicated Ms. Pembrooke prepared a smoothie for Mr. Kitsch earlier that morning. Were there any remnants in the kitchen or house of that or anything else he had eaten or otherwise ingested that day, prior to his death?"

"No. Ms. Pembrooke had already cleaned up. The blender and cup he drank out of had been hand-washed, all ingredients put back into the refrigerator and pantry."

"So very on top of it, Ms. Pembrooke was," D.A. Stern says with hints of a cunning grin.

"D.A. Stern," Judge Gillespy warns, gavel in hand.

He nods subserviently. "No further questions," he says.

The defense, to my surprise, does not cross-examine.

D.A. Stern looks down thoughtfully at the prosecution table as the officer exits the courtroom. When Judge Gillespy nudges, D.A. Stern declares in an almost daring tone, "The prosecution rests, Your Honor."

At the onset of Officer Chavez's testimony,

I wondered why D.A. Stern called the coroner before the officer. That perhaps it was an out-of-sequence mistake or over-sight. But now I realize it was indeed intentional. D.A. Stern wanted the vision of poor Joe Kitsch, slumped over, eyes open but lifeless at his kitchen table where he sat every morning, to be the image we the jury are left with from his case.

I stare at Durrant Hammerstead behind the defense table as he shuffles the papers before him, wondering if, come tomorrow, he will be able to remove the meddlesome doubts I, and likely others on the jury, now carry about Margot.

32.

Jury Stress (n., phrase)

1. when the nature of the evidence or details of a case have a significant emotional impact on jurors, affecting their well-being and ability to make impartial decisions
2. we cannot be held responsible for our actions

At dinner, we all eat in heavy silence.

I sit at our usual table with Tamra, Cam, and Damon. I know I should avoid Damon, but I need him nearby in a way I don't want to think too hard about.

Tamra runs her fork absentmindedly over her Caesar salad, which is mostly croutons.

"How are you doing, Tamra?" I ask. Damon has offered me continual escape and support throughout this trial, whereas Tamra has been going through it largely alone.

"I'm okay," she says, giving me a thin smile, one I find more brave than friendly.

"I need a brownie," Cam says, sliding his chair back and heading toward the buffet.

I stare at my plate, raking my fork over my crouton salad and dry chicken breast. God, I miss flavor.

"How are *you* doing?" Damon asks.

I look up at him, unsure how to answer. It's as though I've just binge-watched horror movies for eight straight days, and I'm both exhausted and wired. I say nothing, and he seems to accept this as an answer. We've somehow pitched our chairs so close they are touching, and I don't slide away. Halfway through our meal, he slides his hand to mine under the table and positions it atop my thigh, holding it tightly there until most everyone else has retired to their rooms.

When we eventually part, I head to my room while Damon lingers to avoid it looking like we are leaving together, per my request. He doesn't argue. When I enter my room, there's a small item on the floor that I nearly step on. He must have slid it under my door before dinner. A small, misshapen origami elephant, complete with large ears and a delicate upturned trunk, constructed from one of the buffet napkins. I pick it up and gingerly place it next to his owl and crane atop the dresser.

I head to my nightstand and tear a new sheet of paper from my notebook. I start to fold, unsure exactly what I'm attempting to make. I've never done origami. I fold this way and that until the paper is too thick to continue. It's a lopsided rectangle. I draw a bear on it and write, *I tried,* on the back, then slide it under his door.

It comes as no surprise when I awake unrested. In reality, it's less that I woke up and more that I gave up and climbed, wired, out of bed when it was time.

Damon sits next to me on the shuttle. We share two boxes of Corn Pops on the way to the courthouse, though one box each would have worked just fine.

We passed notes until two a.m. when I fell asleep awaiting his next note. My dreams were like time travel, returning me to my early teen years in Bakersfield. Summer rain. The smell of jasmine, unbridled vines along the concrete bricked wall of his backyard. Damp blades of grass stuck to my bare feet. Kara's laugh. Him and me. The *best* of who we used to be.

He wrote about Kara. Some things I knew, others I didn't. About how she'd find something she liked and deep dive into it (like origami). How he took particular pleasure in introducing her to his favorite movies from when we were her age — *The Princess Bride* and *Spy Kids.* How he used to read the Percy Jackson books followed by the Heroes of Olympus series aloud to her until her devastation when Leo was presumed dead in *The Blood of Olympus.* Kara is a passageway into Damon's deepest parts, and, last night, pen to paper, he allowed me in.

So many of his memories of her include me. As it turns out, I was present for almost all her life. I was even able to share things *he* didn't know about her. How Kara came to me in the first grade, devastated that she had become the subject of a game at recess called Kara Killas where half the class chased her around the soccer field, the winner being the one who finally caught her and knocked her to the ground. I told her to throw a punch the second she felt hands on her. How I borrowed his baseball glove and had her practice those punches into my palm.

I told him how, that summer right before they left, she told me over a plate of shared apple slices in my kitchen how she was going to marry Austin Davies, the blond curly-haired boy from her second grade class —

that they would live on a farm and have six kids. That he would take care of the animals while she worked as a veterinarian. She had her whole life planned out. Sure, it would undoubtedly change, and this particular version would become some funny story that would get shared at the dinner table with her eventual family, should she choose to have one. But still, it was the future she saw for herself at the time.

I feel like I read Damon's autobiography last night, as if each beat of his heart were the punch of a key on a typewriter, filling in all the parts I missed. He told me about his girlfriend in college, Bryn. He told me about his parents and his relationship with them, before and after. He told me a little more about why he doesn't date, afraid he won't be able to give enough of himself to someone.

As I read his notes, I tried to picture Damon as the boy he was before he became a calloused man, but more and more, there's only one of him. One that holds both the endearing boy I knew and the incredibly solid man I've gotten to know, woven brilliantly together like the images on Mel's watercolor canvases.

I told him things, too. I told him more meals I can't wait to eat when we get out of here. I wrote that, completely opposite to him being up by 4:30 every morning to go to the gym and be at work by six, I set three alarms to be up by seven. I told him about my parents, our lack of relationship. The distance and insecurity I've always felt in my own family. How I longed for a family like his, the way they were in the before. How life has been a lonely walk, and I've always assumed that was the card I was dealt, that my fate was sealed.

Something happened in the early-morning hours. We shared deeply in what felt like a lack of sleep hangover mixed with a fever dream. Our private thoughts, our scars, our worst moments. It was unguarded. I've never been so vulnerable. With anyone. Ever. Maybe with him when we were young, but that was a soft, uncomplicated vulnerability that came with pure trust before it had the chance to be broken.

Summer rain.
The smell of jasmine.
Kara's laugh.
Him and me.

I'm anxious as we enter the courtroom. We haven't heard from the defense team since the opening statements over a week ago, except for what I consider light cross-examinations of the prosecution's witnesses.

Durrant Hammerstead came ready to shine today. He's dressed in a deep blue suit with a white silk tie and matching white shirt that reminds me of something Ryan Gosling might wear on a red carpet, and I'm certain he's applied some form of under-eye concealer, the whites of his eyes extra bright.

Margot also seems lighter, more hopeful today, dressed in a pale pink dress with a playful ruffled hem. It's a bit of a departure from her strict suits and understated dresses thus far.

Durrant Hammerstead's first witness is Gloria Pembrooke, the Kitsches' house manager. The woman who was home alone with Joe when he died.

She is younger than Margot, likely in her mid-thirties, with thick fake eyelashes and reddish-brown hair that flows halfway down her back. Today she's wearing a gorgeous brown pantsuit — a departure from the jeans and sneakers she usually dons. Margot gives the flash of a smile as Ms. Pembrooke takes the stand, and it's the most affectionate exchange in the trial thus far.

Oh, the secrets this woman must know.

"Ms. Pembrooke, how long have you worked for the Kitsch family as their house manager?" Durrant Hammerstead asks after she's sworn in.

"Almost six years. I was hired right before Emblem was born." She and Margot exchange a nostalgic smile, and I continue to be struck by the warmth between them.

"Tell us a little about your job responsibilities," Durrant Hammerstead says.

"I do a lot of things. I cook meals, run errands. Take the kids to school when Margot isn't available to do so. I manage the other helpers to ensure things get done, like the gardening team, the babysitters."

"What do you recall most about your time with the family before Joe's passing?"

"It was nice. They are a loving family." She smirks to herself, staring into a memory. "Margot always says to the kids when they don't care for some healthy meal, 'You are what you eat!' " Ms. Pembrooke smiles longingly at Margot. "Joe would nudge Dover's shoulder and whisper, 'I'd rather be a Big Mac,' and they'd laugh and laugh while Margot flipped a towel playfully at Joe. It just sort of stuck. Every time someone ate something they didn't particularly care for, they'd say, 'I'd rather be a Big Mac.' " She stares at the patterned brown carpet. "It's funny, the things you think of when someone dies. One of the first things I wondered about after Joe passed was whether or not the kids would keep saying 'I'd rather be a Big Mac' without Joe." She huffs. "Sorry, perhaps that's not what you were asking."

"No, that's lovely, Ms. Pembrooke. Thank you for sharing. Tell me, what has your relationship been like with Margot specifically over these past six years?"

"She's fair. Kind. Very kind. And I love the kids very much. I love working for her."

Margot gives an affirming nod.

"Can you give us an example of some of Margot's kindness?"

"Well, just a few months before Joe died, my father passed unexpectedly. I found out when I was at the Kitsches'. It was just Margot and me there at the time. She was in the middle of getting ready for a charity event. It was her own event that she was hosting for Sea Save, I think. She had her full glam team there at the house." Ms. Pembrooke pauses and makes eye contact with Margot again. I examine the exchange closely. Despite their lack of physical indications, it's evident there's a well of connection between these two women. Ms. Pembrooke continues. "Margot dropped everything. She sent everyone home. She missed her event. She made cardamom tea and held me while I cried."

Durrant Hammerstead pulls a tissue from his pants pocket and hands it to Ms. Pembrooke. She dabs at the corners of her eyes, then crumples the tissue into a ball and lowers it to her lap.

"What was your relationship like with Mr. Kitsch?"

Ms. Pembrooke dulls a bit, like a moody manager just walked into the room or someone bumped her in a cashier's line. "It was fine. Pleasant. He wasn't around often, so I didn't spend much time with him." She looks down at her lap, reflecting. "He always said thank you if I did something for him, if I ran down the hill when he was craving his favorite Mediterranean wrap or if he saw me walking in with his dry cleaning. But other than that, we didn't speak much."

"Tell us, Ms. Pembrooke, what were those last days of Joe's life like? Were there any changes to his routine?"

She shakes her head. "No, it was pretty normal. Though by normal, I mean every day was different. But Mr. Kitsch was in town that week. He was working locally, on the set of that Kit Harington film *The Never Days.*"

A few people around the courtroom nod in recognition, likely pleased they'll get to mention an actor's name in their reports from the day, possibly gaining more clicks for their respective articles. I know of it, too. *The Never Days* is a postapocalyptic thriller set to release next week. And thanks to the attention around Joe's death, it may now see more significant box office numbers than otherwise anticipated.

"And what about on the part of Mrs. Kitsch? Did you observe any changes in her behavior in the days leading up to Joe's death?"

"No. She was home that morning, got the kids off to school. Then she usually went out about her business and would return by late afternoon most days to spend time with the children."

Durrant Hammerstead makes eye contact with several jury members so we catch the not-so-subtle subtext. Margot was a doting wife and mother, even on that last day of Joe's life.

I hear the ticks of a clock's second hand reverberating in my ears as we inch into the specifics of Joe's final moments.

33.

Exculpatory Evidence (n., phrase)

1. evidence the defendant did not commit the crime
3. when jurors should take notes

"Tell us about that final day," Durrant Hammerstead says, and I shift in my seat. "What do you remember?"

Ms. Pembrooke swallows hard and leans forward. "Joe came down for breakfast around seven forty-five, just as the kids were wrapping up their toast and eggs. Margot was trying to gather the kids' backpacks and shoes to get them out the door."

I try to picture Margot in a bathrobe and slippers, hair pulled back in a banana clip, ushering her kids out the door to get to school on time. The vision doesn't come easily. I rarely saw my own mother in the mornings. She left for her job at the collection agency at six forty-five every weekday to try to beat the relatively minor Bakersfield traffic. If I was up early enough, I might catch her on her way out the door, carrying her travel mug full of too-strong black coffee and a strawberry Nutri-Grain bar.

"The kids had been gone three hours by the time . . ." She looks down. "They hugged him goodbye, pressed quick kisses on his cheek, then rushed out the door as they always did."

I picture Dover and Emblem, adorned in their navy school uniforms, kissing their father goodbye. I've seen this exact scene play out on an episode before. Margot has kept them shielded since Joe's death. The only pictures in the press have been quick exits from a car with sweatshirts covering their faces. Our view of Emblem's court interview is far more than the world has seen of her in the last year.

Gloria Pembrooke continues. "I offered to make him his morning smoothie."

"Did he have a morning smoothie often?"

"Oh yes. Pretty much every day."

"And did Margot typically partake in these morning smoothies?"

She nods. "Yes. I usually filled the blender and they both would have one."

"And what was in these smoothies?"

"I use a variety of things. Spinach, bananas, honey, chia seeds, protein powder, juices. Whatever they might be needing. That morning was most all those things."

"And the police questioned you, didn't they? About the ingredients of that smoothie, of those in the days leading up to Mr. Kitsch's death?" Durrant Hammerstead looks to the jury, indicating this as an important point.

"Yes, they did."

"What did they find?"

"They found no evidence of anything wrong with that smoothie. Or any of the others."

But she had fully cleaned up any remnants, I think, the devil's advocate in me piping up.

"Was this the last thing Joe consumed before he died?"

Ms. Pembrooke shifts in her seat. "I believe so, but I can't be certain. I wasn't with him every minute after. Or before, for that matter."

"So, Joe came downstairs at approximately seven forty-five, kissed Margot and the kids goodbye. They left shortly after, and then it was just you and Joe."

She nods. "Yes."

"Did Margot have a smoothie that morning?"

"No. She was rushed. She was dropping the kids off and heading straight to Alizay DuPont's home to prepare for her event."

There's an uptick of pens to paper at the mention of another *Authentic Moms* cast member.

"And you made his smoothie after Margot had left the home?"

"Yes, that's right."

"So, just to be clear, Margot was gone from the home about seven forty-five a.m. and did not return until alerted of Joe's death over three hours later."

"Yes, that is correct." Ms. Pembrooke looks to Margot again, and again they exchange a charged look.

Durrant Hammerstead verifies, per the garage cameras at the Kitsch home, that Margot did indeed leave the house with the kids at 7:48 a.m. He then walks to the defense table, reviews a sheet of paper, and gives Ms. Pembrooke his attention again. "There's a record of a call from you to Margot at eight thirty-two that morning of Joe's death. It lasted twelve minutes. What was that call about?"

The details of the smoothie. The call. I can't help but feel like Durrant Hammerstead is making the prosecution's case for them. I have to believe he knows what he's doing. Maybe it's a tactic — address straight on the questionable parts of Ms. Pembrooke's testimony to show there's nothing to hide. It's risky, I concede.

"I had an errand to run for Margot. Saks packed two different-sized shoes into her bag a few days before, and she wanted me to go back that week to collect the correct pair. I called to ask where the shoes were because I couldn't find them in her closet. I meant to go that day."

"Simple enough," Durrant Hammerstead says, addressing the jury. "Ms. Pembrooke, who in the Kitsch home uses eye drops?"

Ms. Pembrooke glances at the defense table so quickly it could be taken as an eye spasm rather than a peek in Margot's direction.

"Both Mr. and Mrs. Kitsch on occasion. Margot tends to use them before public events or photo shoots, which she attends fairly often. It was always an item on our 'in stock' list — things I ensured we had extras of on hand, that we never ran out of."

Durrant Hammerstead nods. "Joe's mother, Jackie Kitsch, testified to finding three eye-drop bottles hidden in the back of a teddy bear nanny-cam in Emblem's room.

What can you tell us about this?"

Ms. Pembrooke flips a flimsy wrist in the air in the most dismissive manner I've seen from her. "Emblem is always collecting and hiding random household items in her room. I once found one of Margot's Louboutin shoeboxes under Emblem's bed. When I opened it, thinking it might be holding a pair of Margot's shoes, I found it crammed full of restaurant condiments: salt and pepper packets, raw sugar, even individual jam pouches and mini ketchup and sriracha bottles. She's a bit of a hoarder, that one."

Juror number eleven behind me huffs, amused.

Satisfied, Durrant Hammerstead ends his time with the witness.

D.A. Stern cross-examines, having been tapping his pen wildly against his knee as he awaited his turn. He leads with asking Ms. Pembrooke why a call about the location of a pair of shoes might take twelve whole minutes. "Seems a long call to simply ask where a shoebox is?" D.A. Stern presses. They go back and forth on it to no clear outcome.

Twelve minutes *is* a long call. I strain to picture a call to ask about shoes taking twelve minutes. Instead, my mind redirects to a panicked Ms. Pembrooke calling Margot. Margot having to calm her down to see their murderous plan through. I attempt to swallow the growing mound that feels like compacted sawdust in my throat.

Eventually, the D.A. moves on. "Ms. Pembrooke, how long would you say one eyedrop bottle might last, before it be thrown out?"

She juts her shoulders into the air. "I don't know, a month or two."

D.A. Stern *hmms* in what I can only describe as accusatory condescension. "Those little bottles last me forever. I usually end up throwing out half-used bottles after they've expired." Ms. Pembrooke stares at D.A. Stern, awaiting a formal question. Finally, he adds, "Do you happen to know the expiration date of those bottles found in Emblem's teddy bear?"

"No," she answers flatly.

"Well, it's interesting." He walks over to the prosecution table and picks up a manila folder, opens it. "All three of those bottles held the same expiration date, almost two years out from the day Joe Kitsch died" — he closes the folder — "meaning they were all retailed and purchased within a short period."

"I don't know how that works," she says,

closing her eyes in seeming exasperation.

D.A. Stern belabors the point, referencing research his team has done on the manufacturing and distribution of the product in question, outlining the extreme likeliness that the three eye-drop bottles were purchased in close date proximity, if not all at once, though this doesn't dispel Ms. Pembrooke's statement that she buys them in bulk.

Finally, he moves on. "Ms. Pembrooke, would you consider your relationship with Margot a close one?"

"Yes, I suppose I would."

"As someone close to her, as you've just described, did Margot ever share with you the details of where she was during those seven days she went missing when she was sixteen?"

Durrant Hammerstead objects. I mark the tally and look to Damon, who winks in approval.

D.A. Stern nods before Judge Gillespy can make her determination and quickly pivots, his goal of getting the room to think again about Margot's teenage disappearance, her corresponding estrangement from her parents, achieved — though clumsily, in my opinion. "Did you actually witness Mr. Kitsch consuming his smoothie?"

She shakes her head. "No. I cleaned up the kitchen, then went upstairs for some chores. I couldn't say if he had started drinking it when I headed up. I came back down after about an hour, and the glass I had filled for him was empty in the sink. So I washed it out. Then I went back upstairs."

"Where was Mr. Kitsch?"

She closes her eyes, a seemingly unwilling owner of this last memory of him. "He was at his usual seat at the kitchen table, looking at something on his phone."

"And then what?" D.A. Stern demands.

"Then I headed back upstairs."

D.A. Stern riffles through the papers at the prosecution table, the silence long enough that a few jury members begin growing restless. "Ms. Pembrooke," he says finally, stepping toward the witness stand, then halting. "Do you know anything about the tarantulas that suddenly appeared in Tenley Storms's backyard roughly two years ago, the day after Margot confronted her about her affair with Joe?"

The callback to Tenley Storms's day one testimony is unexpected. Many brows in the room furrow in unison at the line of questioning.

"No," Ms. Pembrooke says, though she doesn't seem as surprised by the question as the rest of us.

"Tell us, what did you go to school for, before going into this current line of work."

Faces in the gallery twist in confusion, wondering D.A. Stern's angle. I expect the defense team to interject, but they don't. Durrant Hammerstead seems too curious about where the conversation might be headed to intervene.

"Arthropodology," she says, switching the cross of her legs.

I catch Durrant Hammerstead whispering into his co-counsel's ear. Wherever this is going, it appears the defense is not well-versed.

"Explain what that means?" D.A. Stern urges.

"It's the study of arthropods. So, insects, crustaceans —"

"Spiders?" D.A. Stern interjects.

Damon's hand is across my lap before Durrant Hammerstead officially objects, and I have to hold back a smile as he ticks a tally mark to the top right corner of my notebook page.

After some thought, Judge Gillespy asks Ms. Pembrooke to continue.

"Yes," she says. "Technically, spiders fall into this field of study."

"So, just to ensure this is all clear," he

says, "you have an incredibly close relationship with Mrs. Kitsch, and then the day after Margot confronted Ms. Storms about her affair with her husband, her backyard is overrun with tarantulas, and we've come to find out you studied arthropodology, the study of, among other things, *spiders*?"

Gray Man scoffs from behind Damon, and I can practically hear his thoughts. This is unreasonably ridiculous. I'm inclined to agree. Still, it's on par with the outrageous storylines on the show. I can practically guarantee that this specific detail from the trial will be a topic in the next season, one that garners ample screen time.

Durrant Hammerstead objects again, and Damon and I both rush to be the first to draw the tally mark. I beat him by a hair, grabbing his arm with my free hand to slow him down. I look up at him, and he glares so defiantly that I have to hold back a laugh. I can see him bite at the inside of his cheek to hold back his. I realize our actions are juvenile, but to be fair, the D.A. and witness are discussing backyard tarantulas that the prosecution seems to think are some kind of nefarious revenge plot.

Judge Gillespy once again cautiously allows D.A. Stern to proceed, and Ms. Pembrooke, for her part, holds her poise. "Tarantulas can be common in southern California, especially during mating season. Haven't you ever seen *The Kardashians*? Kourtney had an infestation in her yard once."

"I don't watch *The Kardashians,*" D.A. Stern says flatly. He presses his lips together tightly in contemplation. "That's quite the career shift," he muses, "from studying arthropods to becoming a house manager."

"Not a lot of money in entomology," she concedes.

"No? What about in house management? How much does Mrs. Kitsch pay you?"

D.A. Stern is all over the place. I wonder if this is some ploy of his, to disarm her with a bunch of curveballs.

"Objection," Durrant Hammerstead proclaims, just as I catch Margot pressing her fingertips to her right temple. "Relevance."

"Your Honor, I'm merely trying to understand the specifics of Ms. Pembrooke's working arrangement with the Kitsch family."

"I'll allow it," Judge Gillespy says, then squeezes her eyes shut in a long blink of frustration.

Durrant Hammerstead tugs at the sides of his suit jacket aggressively and sits.

D.A. Stern approaches the witness. "I'll

ask again. What is the compensation for your work as house manager for the Kitsch family?"

"Two hundred thousand dollars per year."

There's a rumble across the courtroom, and Cam mutters, "No shit," under his breath behind me.

"I can only imagine the lengths one might go to keep a job like that," D.A. Stern says, his back turned to the witness.

This time, neither Damon nor I dare to draw a tally mark.

The D.A. holds his hands up in concession. "No further questions." He returns to the prosecution table, sits, and crosses his left ankle over his right knee as if kicking back at a neighborhood barbecue.

34.

Alibi (n.)

1. a claim or piece of evidence that one was elsewhere when an act, especially a criminal one, is alleged to have taken place
2. a true best friend

Over the next two days, the defense calls a handful of character witnesses and a medical expert of their own. It's no surprise their medical expert states that Joe having died of natural causes is "highly likely" and that there are many reasons someone seemingly healthy might drop dead as the result of cardiac arrest. He is also sure to emphasize that to prove there was tetrahydrozoline or any other similar active ingredient or "poison" in someone's system, there would need to be additional bloodwork, which was not done. Through his testimony, the defense's case that Joe's death did not involve any sort of foul play is hammered home.

Today, Durrant Hammerstead calls Alizay DuPont to the stand. Another *Authentic Moms of Malibu* cast member and heir to the DuPont family microwave empire, Alizay's real name is Alice, though I suppose her stage name is better suited for her thriving OnlyFans. Ever the entrepreneur, she also has a line of canned rosé called Alizay All Day, sold exclusively at Whole Foods for a whopping twenty-two dollars a can, and spends summers on tour as the headliner of a one-woman cabaret show. I immediately perk, pen gripped tightly in hand, the tip already pressed to the notepad in my lap, ready to document all her details.

Alizay DuPont is Margot's best friend, at least on the show, and was with her the morning Joe died. Her solid, verified alibi. This is one of the details the media covered extensively pretrial.

Alizay enters the courtroom, and I'm immediately struck by how petite she is. On TV, her persona is sizable. But in real life, she's more of a Chihuahua (with the feisty personality to match).

Alizay is also the meme queen of the show, with several of her televised moments having circulated social media. The most viral is the moment she had glitter slime rubbed into her hair by Tenley Storms at a party for the launch of her fictional children's book about a little girl named Zay who, despite the many naysayers in her life, chases her dream of becoming a reality TV star. I gifted a copy to my mom for Gen when she was born. The incident caused a two-season-long legal battle between the two. Eventually, they settled out of court. Notably, Alizay's *Authentic Moms* tagline is now "I'm a glitter bomb of fun."

With her fresh face and RBG pearls, Alizay is dressed as though her Halloween costume is that of "courtroom witness." She wears a sturdy black pantsuit with a white button-down shirt beneath, collar folded over the blazer, and oversized black-rimmed cat-eye glasses, which I am fairly certain she doesn't have a prescription for. They don't do much to hide her aggressively laminated eyebrows. And this is the first time I've seen her don sensible black heels. Her shoe closet is like a view into a textile factory.

Alizay takes a seat on the witness stand, is sworn in, and smiles at Margot. Margot smiles back, though it's more of a cautious frown than anything.

"Ms. DuPont, tell us how you know Margot Kitsch," Durrant Hammerstead inquires.

"We are both cast members on *Authentic Moms of Malibu,*" she says, looking around the room. "We met in season one, almost eight years ago now."

"And how would you describe your relationship with Margot?"

"We are great friends. Margot is a very loyal person."

"And as friends, has Margot ever confided in you about troubles in her marriage?"

"Yes. We talked a lot about our husbands, as friends do. But all normal stuff."

I picture Alizay's husband, a burly, red-faced man who buys and flips houses on a Netflix reality show of his own, *Melrose Mansions.*

"Were you with Margot the morning of Joe's passing?"

"Yes. She came to my home at about eight fifteen a.m. We were having our hair and makeup done together ahead of a Sea Save luncheon. I suggested she come over for mimosas and glam after dropping the kids at school, that we'd make a morning of it."

"And how far away do you live from the Kitsch residence?"

"It's a few miles, roughly ten minutes between."

"So, twenty minutes just to drive back and

forth, if not more? And Margot was at your home the entire time with you and your glam team, as you call them, from approximately eight fifteen until the police called a little before eleven a.m.?"

Alizay nods. At his prompting, she verbalizes her affirmation. "Yes, that's correct."

The defense's time with Alizay is short — the shortest we've seen with any witness — as she's clearly here only to verify Margot's alibi.

Soon enough, it's the D.A.'s turn. His pen shakes vigorously between two fingers as he approaches the stand. D.A. Stern is efficient, acting as if he might even be bored. "So, you and Margot were getting your hair and makeup done at your home around the time of Joe's passing." D.A. Stern smirks to himself. "No wonder Mrs. Kitsch looked so incredibly camera-ready on the news that day."

Alizay huffs and the microphone picks it up, a static hum echoing into the room. Judge Gillespy, clearly fed up with D.A. Stern, looks ready to climb over the bench and lunge at him. She gives him a scolding, no longer caring to shield us from her fiery warnings to the D.A. I shift in my seat as if she's yelling at *me*.

Unfazed, the D.A. continues his questioning. "I understand, according to you, Margot never left that morning, but she did receive a phone call. According to phone records, Margot answered a call from Ms. Pembrooke at eight thirty-two a.m. Were you with her when that call came in?"

"I was."

"And what was the nature of that call?"

"Well, she did step into the hallway for the discussion, so I only heard bits and pieces, but when she came back in a few minutes later, she said it was something about Saks having put two different-sized shoes into her bag a few days before when she was shopping in L.A. and not having time to go in person to deal with it. She answered right next to me as we were getting ready, then stepped outside as her eyelash glue dried." I note that Margot's recount of the discussion is nearly identical to that of Ms. Pembrooke.

"How long was she gone?"

"Like, five minutes."

D.A. Stern walks back to his table, lifts a sheet of paper, and takes it to the judge. "Let the record show that both Mrs. Kitsch's and Ms. Pembrooke's phone records indicate that call was nearly thirteen minutes in length."

Alizay stares at D.A. Stern, letting her eyes

flick only briefly toward Margot at the defense table. "I can't say for certain. Only that it didn't seem like that long."

I take in Alizay's subdued demeanor on the stand, noting it's a far cry from her on-screen self. She was once served a restraining order by Tenley Storms for throwing a punch after a disagreement over who got the better room on a Cabo trip. Her defense was that she couldn't form her hand into a proper fist because of how long her nails were, making throwing the punch impossible. She was released from all charges.

D.A. Stern pauses, looks through a manila folder at his table before continuing. "Tell us, Ms. DuPont, do you have any pets?"

I hear one of the jury members huff, certainly wondering the relevance of such a question, likely hoping we are not going down another tarantula-laden path. While I know the uncommon answer, I, too, wonder the relevance.

"Yes, I have several."

"Could you list those pets for us, Ms. DuPont?"

Durrant Hammerstead objects, and D.A. Stern assures Judge Gillespy he will establish relevance soon.

I allow Damon to draw the tally mark so I can experience the small thrill of his shoulder pressed into mine, his forearm brushing against my upper stomach.

When Judge Gillespy allows it, D.A. Stern nods at Alizay to continue.

"We have four dogs, two cats, seven chickens, a donkey, and a squirrel monkey."

"Sounds like quite the time," D.A. Stern muses, smiling first at Alizay, then at the jury. "Tell us more about this monkey. That's quite an unusual pet."

"Her name is Deborah. She was a gift from my husband for my fortieth birthday. The kids love her. Dover and Emblem adore her, too. They come to play with her often."

"Did Mr. Kitsch like to spend time with these animals?"

"N-no. He didn't particularly like animals."

"And is it true Mr. Kitsch was allergic to Deborah, your pet monkey?"

"Yes, he'd break out in a horrible rash, have trouble breathing. It was the strangest thing. He didn't seem to have allergies to any of the other animals. Just Deb."

"Sounds horrific," D.A. Stern states. "Tell me, once you all learned of Joe's severe allergy to this monkey of yours, was he ever around it —"

"Deborah," Alizay corrects.

"Right, Deborah. Was Joe ever around

Deborah again?"

Alizay shifts in her seat. "Perhaps once."

"Oh? And when was that?"

Alizay's eyes dart to Margot at the defense table. "Margot was kind enough to offer to watch Deborah for us when we were headed to the Caymans and our usual handler wasn't available."

"How generous. And when was this that Margot offered to take in the monkey that her husband was severely allergic to?"

"I wouldn't say severely . . ."

Judge Gillespy chimes in. "Ms. DuPont, please answer the question."

"It was just after we had wrapped season five, I believe."

"Just after filming season five," D.A. Stern quips. "If I have my timeline correct, this would be right around the time Margot was learning of Joe's affair with Tenley Storms."

It's not a question. D.A. Stern looks to the jury again to ensure we know it's a statement.

"It's getting a little *Legally Blonde* in here," Cam whispers from behind me. Juror number eleven snickers.

Damon adjusts in his seat.

I exhale until my lungs are empty. We are reaching the end of the trial, and it's clear Durrant Hammerstead is out of his depths when matched against D.A. Stern. There's little time to right this ship.

Especially because come Monday morning, Margot is set to take the stand.

35.

Bailiff (n.)

1. responsible for security in the courtroom and for the safety of all participants
2. my fate, their hands

Long after retreating to my room for the evening, I sit at the foot of my bed, twirling Damon's napkin elephant delicately between my thumb and forefinger, thinking about the trial. Could Margot really have done it? Convinced Ms. Pembrooke to squeeze three bottles of eye drops into Joe's smoothie that morning? Could she have sat in Alizay's bathroom, laughing and sipping mimosas, casually glancing at her watch, wondering if it was yet done? Two weeks ago, I adamantly believed there was no way. But after all this testimony and witnessing firsthand Margot's courtroom behavior, I'm jarred by the doubt that has crept in.

Staring at the napkin elephant's folded edges, I feel the keen desire to press it in between the halves of a book, like I once did with the single red rose Damon handed me on my fifteenth birthday.

I think of being pressed beside him in the closet. Of sitting on his lap on the roof. Of his tatted forearms and general broadness. A restlessness has been brewing inside me since the first few days of the trial. I feel it taking over in the tap of my foot and jitter of my hand.

Before I can talk myself out of it, I dash to my door and look out the peephole. With no one in sight, I pull the handle carefully and step into the hallway. In a flash, I am at his door, knocking quietly.

"Need something?" I turn toward the elevators where George has risen from his seat around the corner and taken two steps toward me.

Shit.

"Oh, hi, George. No, no. He just left this at dinner." I hold up the origami elephant still in my hand, then motion it toward Damon's door before me. "I was just returning it to him."

George watches me bend down and slide the folded napkin under the door.

As I rise back to a stand, Damon's door swings open. "Hey," he says quietly with a primed look before I eyeball him, then George. He bends down and picks up the elephant.

"I was just returning that," I say, loudly enough for George to hear. "You left it at dinner."

"Thanks," he says, his eyes shifting from George to me. We three stand exchanging glances for what feels like an hour.

"My origami support elephant," Damon says to George, tilting his head and raising his shoulders.

"Okay, back to my room now." At my door, I see them both still watching. Right. I'll have to go all the way in and retreat completely. So, I do just that. I step into my room and fall onto the bed, defeated.

Ten minutes later, as I lie in bed staring at the ceiling, finding new shapes, I hear the now familiar swipe of paper. In some undetermined reflex, I jump out of bed and am at the door in one motion.

I find the origami napkin elephant atop a folded sheet of paper. I can't pull it open fast enough.

NOT-SO-STEALTHY SYDNEY,

WHAT WAS THAT? I THOUGHT GEORGE MIGHT HANDCUFF YOU RIGHT THEN AND THERE.

DISTRESSED DAMON

I immediately grab a pen from the dresser and jot a response.

Distressed Damon,

I pause. What *is* my response? Do I tell him I was headed to his room to . . . what? I'm not sure I know what I planned to do once I got there. The possibilities are disturbingly endless. The truth is I'd take any excuse to interact with him. After considering a few moments, I write:

I realized I never properly thanked you for the elephant. Or crane or owl. So, thank you.

Sentimental Sydney

Warier than ever about leaving my room post-curfew, I stand at my door in contemplation. Cautiously, I check the peephole and open the door again. I walk barefoot past Cam's room, where I hear music playing, then stop at Damon's door. Before I can shuffle the paper into the space below it, it opens, and I have to swallow a yelp of surprise. There stands Damon, index finger pressed to his lips as he steps aside so I can enter his room. There is no time to think. I quickly glance to the corner George is tucked behind, and there is no sign of him. Before that can change, I step into Damon's room, and he expertly closes the door behind me.

We stand facing each other in the narrow entryway of his room, and I am immediately hot. My heart was already thrumming against my rib cage as a result of the escapade itself, but now I realize the sneaking around is some kind of furtive foreplay. I am in over my head entirely.

Damon stares back at me, and his chest rises and falls with effort — though not as forcefully as mine.

I attempt to clear my throat and emit some sort of warbly screech.

"Far stealthier this time," he whispers before I can speak. He's still dressed in his navy dress shirt from court, top button open so the beginnings of his collarbones jut into view.

"How'd you know I was at your door?"

He cups the back of his neck and bends it

forward, then looks at me with his brows and eyes pressed together as if one. "I was waiting for you."

I stare at him, the tips of my ears burning. "Just in case I came back?"

"Yes. Consider the note bait." He hangs his head and folds his arms in front of him. I struggle with where to look, his eyes or that chin dimple. I shuffle my attention between both.

"Bait for what exactly?" I tease. "Should I yell so George can ram the door down and save me?"

"You don't need saving." He shakes his head lightly, and I take note of the more serious edge to him tonight. "I want to know why you came to my door in the first place. It wasn't to return the elephant."

"It was to say thank you for the elephant." I look down at my hand, though this time I'm holding the note and not the elephant.

"You could have written that down instead of coming over in person," he says.

"I did." I hold up the paper.

"No, I mean before. You could have just written a note and slid it under the door. Why'd you come in person before?" He leans against the wall and crosses his right foot in front of his left.

"I . . ." Again, I don't have much to say,

because I did want to come in. I wanted to be here. He raises his eyebrows in question, almost pleadingly. "I wanted to see you," I say finally.

We don't break eye contact. It's this high-octane, pulsing eye contact that makes me want to say fuck it. Fuck this case, fuck Margot, fuck everything. I just want to stare at him awhile longer, let that searing stare of his melt my sharp edges.

A noise in the hallway breaks our stare. We both lean toward the door as we hear George's billowy laugh and then muffled speech. I glance at the alarm clock beside Damon's bed. Nine p.m. George's transition with Raphael, the nine p.m. to six a.m. bailiff.

I swallow, feeling the force of it down my throat. Damon jerks his head toward the room, and I take his cue to move away from the door. I sit on the edge of the bed, and Damon sits in the chair in the corner, though the room is so small our legs are practically intertwined.

While George tends to stay in his seat around the corner at the elevators, Raphael is a walker. He prefers to pace the hallway, highlighted by the clang of his metal key chain against his belt buckle, that noise falling and rising as he paces farther away and back.

And with his shift now on, I'm bound to Damon's room indefinitely.

36.

Cabin Fever (n., phrase)

1. a state of mind that can develop when a person is confined and unable to have social interaction
2. a mounting need

Damon and I stare at each other, the walls of his already compact room seeming to shrink with every moment that passes. We spend so much time together every day, sitting beside each other in court, during meals. But rarely have we had the opportunity to really talk. And rarely have we been completely alone. Each time we *have* found ourselves alone, I've thrown myself at him.

Damon reaches over and grabs something off the dresser. "Vending machine mystery pastry?" he offers, the cellophane crackling beneath his grip.

I shake my head as I tuck some loose hair behind my ear. We continue to stare in some sort of weighted standoff. I'm not sure why it's so muggy in here. "Why do you make me the origami animals?" I ask. It seems a silly question once I've asked it.

He leans forward in the chair, rests his forearms on his thighs, and clasps his hands in front of him, his fingers slowly interlacing. I can't look at those hands without imagining the feel of them on me. "Elephants are symbols of strength, remembrance. Cranes are good fortune. Owls are my favorite. They're guardians. It's meant as a protector. To protect."

"Protect me from what?"

He leans back. "I don't know, this case? From getting too swept up in it all? From drunk guys at Outback Steakhouse?"

I hate that I think it, but I wonder if my heart also requires protection from *him*. "Thank you," I say, though it comes out weak.

"You already said thank you."

I reflect on all I've learned about him, mostly through our notes. I know a lot, thanks to those notes. But I want to know so much more. "Tell me more about what you're like outside of here."

He leans forward again, takes on his previous position. "What do you mean?"

"What's your life like? This isn't normal, living in a hotel room on lockdown, listening to a murder case day in and day out. What's your normal?"

"I told you, I go to work, ride motocross on the weekends. Meet up with friends. Pretty basic."

Basic is the last word I would use to describe Damon. He is so much more than basic. "No, I don't buy it. What's something most people don't know about you?" I say "most people," but I mean me. Because I relish the idea that I already know much more than most.

He smirks.

"There's totally something! What is it?"

He rubs at his chin with the tips of the fingers of his right hand. "No, I'm reacting to you. Why do you assume everyone except you has these crazy, extravagant lives?"

I contemplate his question. Do I? I suppose I have assumed most everyone is out there doing extraordinary things and I'm the only one who has opted for small, safe.

"There's one thing that comes to mind," he says eventually, looking at the door as if Raphael might burst in at this very moment to stop him from divulging.

I lean in, and our knees graze.

"You know all those wild animal documentaries on Netflix? I watch one almost every night. It's like my weird comfort before I go to sleep."

I smile, picturing Damon — big, wide, tatted Damon — curled up in bed watching Antarctic penguins singing for mates under Barack Obama's or Morgan Freeman's narration.

"I can't believe I just told you that."

"I'm glad you did," I say.

"You're not laughing. I thought it'd make you laugh."

"I don't think it's funny. I think it tells me a lot about you."

"Oh?" His eyebrows raise.

"Yeah. I think it's your way of coping with the world. It's so heavy out there." I flick my hand in the direction of the window. "Sometimes you need to shut it all out and focus on something not so heavy. That's what *Authentic Moms* is for me. Or was, at least. I don't know that I can watch it anymore after all this."

He tilts his head as if surveying me, and my cheeks grow hot. "I suppose you're right," he states. He exhales and presses his hands atop his knees, ready to change the subject. "What about you? What's your weird thing?"

"I don't have a weird —"

"Stop."

After some thought, I say, "Okay. But if you tell anyone —"

"Who would I tell? Cam? Judge Gillespy?"

He has a point.

"Okay," I say emphatically. "Every time I pass a fountain, or any body of water of any kind, really, I have to throw a coin in and make a wish. I purposely keep change on me at all times specifically for that reason. And I always make the same wish."

"What's the wish?" he asks.

Perhaps it'll lead me off a cliff, but I choose to stand with my toes against the edge anyway. "I wish for love." I don't elaborate because the admission already feels pathetic on some level, but that wish isn't necessarily for something romantic. It's about someone, somewhere, filling the void of a lifetime of feeling unwanted.

I watch him, too invested in his reaction. His left eye twitches, and then both narrow in concentration. His eyebrows inch closer together, though not all the way. Just a millimeter or two. His face hasn't significantly changed. But I see a world of surrender in it.

"I hope you never have to make that wish again," he says. He says it like he says everything — so matter-of-factly but with a deep entanglement of vulnerability — so much so that I have to believe him.

Now would be a good time to address our past, beyond surface-level apologies. But if I'm honest, I don't want to risk ruining what we've built back over these last few weeks.

In need of a distraction, I stand and take the step to his dresser. I lift a squat black bottle and evaluate it. "Trail." I read the name from the label, then tap a spray of the cologne into the air between us. He looks on, amused. The smell of him envelops us, and it sends an immediate, undeniable pang of want through my core.

"Why do you choose to smell like a horse saddle?" I ask, not wanting to let on how fond I am of the scent.

"It smells like horse camp."

I cock my head. "You never went to horse camp."

"I did. Once."

He stands and takes a half step toward me, unmistakably broody, his eyes fixed on mine. Looking into those infinite eyes, I'm smacked with understanding that nearly buckles my knees.

Sagawa. The summer before sixth grade. I rode Echo, a resplendent American quarter, the entire summer. She was moodier than the others, rearing at anyone who brushed her without a purposeful technique or chomping harder than necessary at a held carrot. At eleven, I thought I was special. That she held a sweet spot for me. That we had this indescribable bond that made me some sort of majestic animal whisperer. Looking back, she likely chose me because I was the least threatening — nervous and gentle, more attentive and less boisterous than the other kids.

Damon and I exchanged letters all summer. Better on paper, he absolutely was. It was crazy how much he had to say in those letters, more words exchanged via the post office than we likely would have in person all summer. He wrote about the training he was doing to "get fit" before school started, which was mostly running and push-ups. He told me all the cute new things Kara was learning, including all the new words she adorably mispronounced. He told me how boring it was without me there, which I secretly relished.

In the final week before my scheduled return home, I took Echo out on an afternoon ride on one of the back trails. It was my favorite ride, alone with her through the tree-covered path. The ancient evergreens and mossy earth made it feel like I could be somewhere far away, anywhere else with so many varied options of different life circumstances. I loved the idea of that. Each time I was out on the trails alone, I'd imagine up a new life. Me as the only daughter of a lonely widower who doted on me as the last living love of his life. As one of six kids in a chaotic brood where I always had someone to play with. Me as an Olympic equestrian, looking out at adoring parents from the podium as the national anthem played in the background. It was one of my favorite things about camp, that they trusted us to go out alone.

Thirty minutes into the ride, something spooked Echo — a speedy rodent or snake that rustled through the brush and across our path. She bucked. I fell backward as she spun, hitting the side of my face on the dirt, a tree root protruding just enough to split the skin of the right side of my forehead, just below the hairline.

Echo calmed fairly quickly, though I was too afraid to climb back on. I took hold of her reins and limped back to camp (over an hour on foot), all the while dizzy from the pain in my head and worried about the amount of blood still dripping from my forehead. I grew fully terrified only when I arrived back at camp and one of the counselors ran to me, eyes wide and panic-stricken.

"She's lucky she didn't pass out," I overheard that counselor say to another. "Or worse," the other said back. They called my parents, and two hours later, I sat with a stitched forehead from the called-in doctor and an ice pack pressed to it as I watched my mom's burgundy Corolla pull up from the office window. Something explosive happened inside me when I saw Damon bound out of the back seat toward the office before my mom had even turned off the engine.

He came.

Even at eleven, I knew how monumental it was that he showed up for me. That this was and would continue to be something rare.

"We were chatting at the mailbox when the call came," my mom said as she stepped in. "He insisted on coming." She said this before even asking if I was okay or evaluating my head. I couldn't tell if she was annoyed or impressed with Damon, but either way, I immediately knew I needed him there, perhaps more than her. That I needed him in a way I didn't yet know to be scared of.

I only cried for the first time with the good

side of my face burrowed into his neck.

I didn't quite understand it yet, but I loved him then. I loved who he was to me, what he gave me. I loved that he *knew* me. At eleven years old, having someone know me was like being chosen by the sun.

Standing in front of him now, watching his chest slowly rise and fall, his eyes invading mine, I know for certain that I loved him at eleven. Before I knew what it meant.

I don't know that I ever stopped.

I need to sit. I take my seat on the edge of the bed once more. He sits beside me. My body is on fire as I watch him raise his hand to my face, cup it. It takes great effort not to nuzzle into it like a cat arching into a back scratch. I stop breathing when he gently rubs his thumb along the scar at my hairline and I know he's back in that memory with me. "Do you still ride?" he whispers, and it sounds like *Do you still love me?* as if he's just seen my thoughts.

I look to the carpet. "No."

He releases his hand back to his lap. "Why?"

Why.

I could say it's because my parents wouldn't take me any longer or because I lost interest after I was thrown. But I know these aren't the real reasons. I now know it's because the last day I rode was the day I knew I loved him, and I can't untangle the two.

Since he's come back into my life, I've tried so hard to suppress not only the bad at the end but also the good. The parts that were too good to ever fully get over.

I watch as his free hand swipes forward and back three times along his jeans, over his thigh. Damon is grainy and textured, making me want to run my hand across him just to see what his coarseness feels like against my skin. I try desperately to shake the thought.

"Can I ask you something?" he asks, his voice huskier than usual.

I nod.

"I don't know how to act around you. I don't want to get you — us — in trouble. And I get it, it's serious trouble. We could be held in contempt. I want to respect your dedication to this case. I want to respect our complicated past. I don't want to promise things I can't give. Like right now, I want to kiss you. But is that okay?"

My heart thumps against my sweatshirt — the same one I was wearing when we kissed in the presidential suite. I think of the rooftop again, sitting in his lap and pressing my lips to his, my hand against his groin. Most kisses I've had in my life have felt like a means to an end. The way Damon kisses, though, is deliberate. His lips move with intention and purpose, as though the kiss itself is an exploration of sense. A kiss with him is like sitting side by side, placing the pieces of an elaborate puzzle, each slow movement another found piece. I just don't yet know what the finished picture is.

I inhale. He smells like sexual attraction feels.

Unable to resist, I lean in and kiss him.

I feel his breath catch and then release heavily into me. His hand goes immediately to the back of my head, under my hair, and presses firmly. I tug at the front of his T-shirt, collecting a small mound of fabric in my palm. He pulls away softly and leans his forehead against mine. "You deserve it all," he murmurs. I lean back in, seeing him — us — clearly for perhaps the first time.

His other hand curves around my face, under my chin. He presses his tongue against mine and it is firm and searching. I wish in this moment I could bottle the comfort of him to uncork when emptiness sometimes takes me over.

He leans into me, his chest firm and drumming against my palm. He moves his lips from my mouth to my neck, grazing the skin of my cheek, then chin, as he goes. I close my eyes and tilt my head back. I inhale, intoxicated by how comforting his smell is. How everything about him is so good. I grasp for him — my fingertips pressing against his back, his biceps, his neck. He lets out a low sort of growl, and the hunger of it sends an electric shock out from my base in all directions.

I find it hard to think as he plants his lips on my neck, his teeth grazing the curve to my shoulder. Despite the bliss of it, doubt creeps in. We've tiptoed around our past, never addressing what happened. Perhaps we don't need to, I think, as his tongue gently traces up the length of my neck to my ear, sending my body into an outbreak of goose bumps. It was ten years ago, after all. So much has happened since. Perhaps the past is gone and we don't have to revisit any of it. I'd accept just about anything I told myself right now, just to keep his tongue on my skin.

He takes my earlobe between his teeth and tugs, the action forcing my eyes to roll back. I lean into him, desperate for more of him, for all of him.

Just as I'm about to give in fully, I pull away sharply, startled by a noise from the hallway. We sit, listening — his hand still pressed against the back of my head, mine still pressed against his neck. I place the noise quickly — the distinct, muffled clang of Raphael's key chain jumping forward and back against its clasp. It reaches its height as he walks by Damon's door, the shadow of his feet carving into the dark brown carpeting of the room. Damon and I watch each other as the sound dissipates down the hall, eventually disappearing where he would have turned the corner to the second wing.

Damon's eyes don't leave mine. They ask if I'm okay. They ask what happens next. They beg for permission to keep going.

"I better go while I have the chance," I say, barely able to get the words out over my escalated breath. I tell myself it's not a test. I'm not saying it so he'll counter. I say it because I know I need to.

"Or . . . you could stay?" He cups the back of his neck with his palm and looks through his lashes at me, the peacock-feather blue of his eyes searing me like a laser.

I stare back at him, intensity corking my airway and desire drumming between my legs.

Or, I could stay.

37.

Testimony (n.)

1. a formal written or spoken statement, especially one given in a court of law
2. the opportunity to be heard

Margot rises from the defense table and glides regally to the stand. Today, she wears a cream-colored skirt suit with a burnt sienna laced edge and an understated olive-colored silk top underneath. Her stick-straight brown bob is parted down the middle and pulled back in a barely there ponytail at the nape of her neck. She appears calm, confident, and ready to finally speak.

Once seated, she turns to the jury and forces eye contact, one by one, offering us each unique smiles of acknowledgment. She is sworn in before she can get to us all. I wonder if whatever might be happening inside her compares to the electrical storm in my own stomach.

I left Damon's room last night, desperately wanting to stay, avoiding the disappointment in his eyes as I snuck out. I put myself to sleep with visions of him adorning me with various forms of affection. The feel of his hand squeezing my knee. His lips pressed to my forehead, lingering. I suppose it was my form of cute animal shows, if those animals were all in heat.

Today, Damon is striking. He's wearing a deep purple, almost maroon button-down shirt that makes his eyes more piercing than I previously thought possible. We exchanged quick pleasantries this morning, and I did take the seat beside him on the shuttle, though we were both quiet. Nonetheless, I felt the comfort of him as I always do.

He tilts his notepad toward me on his knee. I can't help but smile. He's drawn a small owl on the top right corner of the sheet.

It's an exceedingly unexpected development — that the day Margot takes the stand, it's Damon who dominates my thoughts. When I reiterated that I should leave his room last night while I could still get the words out, he hung his head, then kissed my forehead — one long, lingering kiss — before releasing his hold of me. That forehead kiss, like so much of him, was protective.

I took a lukewarm shower when I returned to my room, hoping the blast of water would soothe the nagging want at my base. Instead, I pictured Damon behind me, his broad chest pinning me against the wet tile. My fingers slid back and forth as I envisioned his tongue making the motion. It was the fastest climax I've ever reached.

The courtroom buzzes with excitement. Margot on the stand is the grand finale the collective gallery has been awaiting — less, I imagine, for the sake of proving her innocence, but rather because everything she says or does on the stand today will be scrutinized by the masses as soon as it's reported.

Durrant Hammerstead slowly rises and approaches the stand, buttoning his deep gray pin-striped suit with one hand. He rests his hands atop the rail, his face only a few inches from Margot.

"Let's start at the beginning of your time in California," he says after his standard pleasantries to ease his prime witness in. "What brought you here?"

Margot leans forward, and her deep,

punctuated voice instantly captures my attention. She's sat so silently in this courtroom for nearly two weeks, I'd almost forgotten her voice. "I had spent my entire life in Minnesota. I felt like I was . . . meant for something else. A different life. I was itching to get out. And I thought L.A. was the place to go for something more."

"Take us back, if you will, to the beginning of your relationship with Joe once you were in California."

Margot stares forward, taking a moment before she begins. "I was twenty-one. I met Joe during my second year in L.A. My roommate Kelly and I were eating at Don Antonio's, our favorite Mexican food spot. Joe was seated at the table beside us at some business dinner." She smirks to herself, flicks her eyes briefly to the ground. "Kelly and I were getting ready to leave, and the waiter told us our meal had been paid for. Joe and I closed the place down after that, drinking and talking. He made me laugh a lot. I told him he was funny. He told me he had to be, with his face." She hints at a smile. "That was important to me, someone who could make me laugh and who could laugh at himself."

"And how did your relationship progress after that first night?"

"He courted me pretty heavily. I'd told him that first night I missed the Polish sausage from Von Hanson's, this small place in St. Cloud. That I couldn't seem to find anything as good in L.A. There was a bouquet of sausages at my front door the same week. I didn't even know how he figured out where I lived. I was sharing a tiny apartment in Westwood. It was far more phallic than he likely intended that sausage bouquet to be. That became an ongoing joke between us as well, one we retold often, how ill-advised that bouquet was. Somehow, it only added to his charm. After that, there were extravagant parties and dates, even a private jet to a beach dinner in Tulum."

"How did you feel about all of it? About him?"

"It was overwhelming, honestly. I was young. I had barely been anywhere but St. Cloud. I had no frame of reference, so I didn't know if this was just how men and relationships in L.A. went."

"What about the age difference between you two? How did you feel about being courted by a man twenty years your senior?"

She makes a motion of tucking a hair behind her ear, though it's already pulled back. "He was definitely the oldest man I'd ever considered dating." There's a light chuckle from the back of the room.

Margot is coming across well. She's not antagonistic or cold, speaking calmly and openly in a way that allows us to connect with her. Then again, D.A. Stern hasn't had his turn with her yet.

Margot continues, "But he was funny, as I said. And I felt overwhelmed when I came to L.A. He became a bit of a safe space."

I think of Damon, avoid glancing at him.

"And when was the first time you learned of his infidelity."

I swallow hard. Damon beside me looks over, and we make eye contact. It's charged, a plug smashing into a wall socket.

"It was five months in."

He courted her extravagantly, then was cheating on her almost immediately, and then ongoing for the next twenty-four years?

"What were the circumstances that first time?"

"She was a model. I found that very, I don't know, insulting. The idea of being cheated on by my forty-two-year-old boyfriend of five months with an L.A. runway model. A text came up on his phone while he was in the shower. A . . . picture. It turned out he had a thing for collecting pictures." She speaks with certainty, a factual retelling of events she is equally sentimental about and detached from.

"What was Joe like when you confronted him?"

She exhales a hard breath. "Glib. He downplayed it, told me it was nothing."

"How did that make you feel?"

"Confused. But also, it sort of was what it was. I accepted it as part of my life with someone like him."

I venture a quick sweep over the jury. Is Margot doing enough to win them over? Is she doing enough to win *me* over? Coming into the trial, there was no need. I was already on her side. But I can't unlearn all the damning things that have come out since then. How could these things *not* make me question her?

"And how many more times did this happen throughout your time with Joe? Where you found out about other women in his life?"

"There were fourteen that I know of."

A light gasp echoes from the far corner of the courtroom.

"This is why I'd choose the bear," juror number twelve, Kate, mumbles behind me.

How many affairs did my father have? There were six I knew of, though I'm positive there were more. He never remarried after my mom, which I took as a selfless act on his part.

"What number was Tenley?" he asks, and I wonder why this matters.

"Number twelve, I believe."

Durrant Hammerstead hangs his head as if in mourning. Then, "On the topic of Tenley, I have to ask, since the prosecution seems quite fixated on it," he says almost apologetically. "Margot, do you know anything about the tarantulas in her backyard?"

Margot huffs. "Under normal circumstances, I wouldn't even dignify that with a response."

"Yes, well, here you must," he says with a broad smile in an attempt to minimize his scold. Margot assures us she does not know anything about tarantulas generally nor about the ones specifically from Tenley's backyard, and I'm growing frustrated with Durrant Hammerstead and his line of questioning. But then, finally, I see where he is going.

"In any of those instances of Joe's affairs, did anything ever grow . . . concerning? More concerning than just the idea of your husband's potential indiscretions?"

I hold my breath, anticipating something headline-inducing.

"Yes. There are three I can think of. The first was two years into our marriage. She was a fitness influencer," Margot says with a flippant eye roll. I wince, knowing how hard Margot has been working throughout this trial to come across as kind, poised, humane. Sure, she can be crass and even a bit bullish on the show, but it makes her unapologetically successful. And the unequivocal star of the franchise. How easily all her hard work could be undone with the slightest lapse of composure here, now. Margot continues, "I came home from a lunch to find her scrawling all kinds of foul words across the windows of our home with red paint." Margot gives an impassioned shudder.

"That must have been awful."

"It was. When she saw me, she just walked off casually down the driveway. She only stopped to tell me, 'I could have him.' "

"Did you or Joe ever press charges?"

"No."

"Why not?" Durrant Hammerstead questions.

"Because that would have made the incident public. We valued discretion."

"And what were the other two situations?"

"The next was when I was pregnant with Emblem. This particular woman he met in his cycling club. She emailed saying she had been sleeping with Joe for several months and that he deserved to die for what he did."

The ever-waiting murmur recurs from the gallery.

"What is it she claimed he did that he deserved to die for?"

Margot shakes her head. "She never said."

Durrant Hammerstead allows a quiet moment to lapse so we can sit with this news, and I shift uncomfortably in my seat. I wonder if that email will be an exhibit me and the other jurors will be able to examine during deliberations. I imagine it will be.

"Did you ever follow up?" he asks eventually.

"No. I hardly saw the point of grabbing lunch or drinks with a woman who wished my husband dead."

Margot goes on to explain the third woman was a Whole Foods sommelier who showed up at her kids' school during pickup, claiming Joe had been "with her" for several months.

I had come to terms with Joe as a cheater after Tenley Storms's testimony, but hearing the details of multiple affairs from Margot's point of view . . . I don't know how she was able to tolerate it. I attempt to swallow down the angry mound in my throat as memories of my father flood my mind.

"So, clearly, there's a slew of women over

the years who have had issues with Joe Kitsch, who have felt scorned by him."

Judge Gillespy agrees with an objection from D.A. Stern.

I sense Damon's movement before it begins, and the sheer notion of the innocuous thing he's about to do causes a sharp zap between my legs. He leans into me as he marks a tally in my notebook. He does it all so achingly slow and deliberate he might as well be running his fingers along my naked body.

Everything in me is heightened after last night, after these past twelve days. *Too* heightened. And Damon's slightest touch is absolutely the crack that can burst the whole dam.

I clear my throat, shift in my seat.

Durrant Hammerstead continues. He pulls at the bottom edges of his suit jacket, though it's already straight and wrinkle-free. "After any of these fourteen affairs, did you ever attempt to seriously injure your husband?"

Margot looks to the jury and sets her sights on either me or Damon, I'm not quite sure. "No," she says.

Then why would she after the last one? I allow myself to go where Durrant Hammerstead leads us.

The courtroom is silent as Margot rubs her lips together, forward and back. The gallery seems to hang on her next words while she concentrates intently on the jury, her eyes roaming purposely among us. Then, in the attentive silence, she catches a tear with her forefinger before it can fall.

The thought I have next is one I can't shake. Margot can cry on command. It's a party trick of sorts, which she has demonstrated on the show. The most recent example I can recall was when Alizay's seven-year-old daughter, Besos, gifted Margot a handmade Christmas ornament of glitter and clay, and Margot feigned touched tears.

I stare at Margot.

Fourteen affairs. A slew of scorned lovers. His ownership of her business.

I could even understand why she might want to burn it all down.

A foreign feeling overtakes me as I evaluate Margot on the stand. I wish I could hug my mom right now. Tell her that I, perhaps for the first time, understand why after all of it she might want a do-over family.

"Margot," Durrant Hammerstead says, his tone clipped, indicating a change in direction. "Much has been made by the prosecution about your disappearance at sixteen, about where you were and if it significantly impacted you. Your father alluded to the fact that your estrangement from your family came directly after. Can we talk about that?"

I press the tip of my pen to the pad, ready to transcribe every word. Of all the things that have come out in this trial about Margot and Joe and their lives, this is the thing that has nagged at me most.

I need to know that whatever happened in her teenage years didn't wholly determine who she would become.

38.

Spoliation (n.)

1. when someone intentionally alters, destroys, conceals, or otherwise tampers with evidence that may be relevant to a legal proceeding, investigation, or potential litigation
2. not applicable here

Durrant Hammerstead continues, "Your father said you returned home after those seven days and didn't remember what had happened. Is that true?"

"Not entirely, no."

The room buzzes. It seems this bit of unanswered history has captivated the gallery, too.

"Can you tell us what happened back then?"

Margot is thoughtful before she speaks, a rarity from the woman I've seen on the show. She is typically quick-witted, sharply intelligent, and can often devise a scathing retort so fast the other women on the show can't hold their own against her. She looks to the ground and then sort of rolls upright in a wave, as if working up the courage to say whatever comes next. "I was . . . bullied quite a bit in school. I never told my parents. It all became too much. Right before the week in question, this group of girls — the worst of the lot — cut a chunk of my hair off while I sat in class. A *big* chunk, right out of the back." She touches the back of her head for emphasis. "I never reported it. That next week, fed up, I decided to meet up with a friend in Minneapolis. We holed up in this cheap motel, watching TV, sleeping in, and living off of pinto beans and Fruit Roll-Ups just . . . taking a break from it all."

The whisper of the room swells, and I see the confusion in each individual face. They don't know whether to be sympathetic or distrustful. Is Margot lying? I used to view her as abrasively honest. It *would* explain a lot. Why she left home and moved so far away. How distrustful Margot is of the other women on the show. How hard she has worked to make a name for herself. Something gnaws at me, though, a thought inching to the tip of clarity but not quite there. It tells me there's some connection I should be making but am not. I work to ignore the prodding notion, knowing if I reach too forcefully for it, I'll push it further away.

"Margot," Durrant Hammerstead says, his voice cradling. "Why didn't you tell your parents, or anyone, that you were taking off for a week?"

Margot looks to the jury. "I didn't think. I just needed to get away. I regret that. In hindsight, I know it was foolish."

Durrant Hammerstead allows us to stew on this new information before he clears his throat and refocuses. "Let's talk about Got-Mar, your lingerie business. Why did you embark on this particular endeavor?"

"I wanted to build something, have a legacy."

"But you were married to a successful Hollywood executive, had two beautiful children, were doing good in the community through your charitable activities. Why more?"

I work to ignore the misogyny in his question.

Margot pauses. "I can't imagine a world where we don't try to be more than we currently are. I had a vision, and Joe helped me achieve my goal of launching this business.

I never dreamed it would see the success it has." Her smile is humble but proud.

I ponder on this as Durrant Hammerstead goes over many of the details of the day Joe died, Margot reiterating much of what we already know. That she was at Alizay's house, with witnesses, when it happened. She didn't have a smoothie that morning, nor had Ms. Pembrooke even begun preparing one by the time she left. She verifies the just-under-thirteen-minute call from Ms. Pembrooke was about returning mismatched shoes.

Soon, it's D.A. Stern's turn, and on cross-examination, he is authoritarian. Harsh, even. His intention is clear. He is irritated by Margot and her crocodile tears, and we should be, too. To ensure no room for empathy, his time with her is surprisingly short. But there is one point he insists we focus upon.

"Your husband of twenty-four years dies unexpectedly, and you somehow manage to have him cremated in three days." D.A. Stern pauses. Margot's eyebrows press together. "I just can't imagine having the wherewithal to do that, to make all those arrangements so quickly. When my father died, my mother lay in a heap in their bed for nearly a week and was barely capable of eating, let alone working out the particulars of what to do with his body."

Durrant Hammerstead objects, and there's no hesitation in Judge Gillespy's warning to D.A. Stern to stay on track. I'm like one of Pavlov's dogs, immediately drooling at the word *objection* because I know it will mean body contact from Damon. He delivers, marking the tally, eyes on mine as he does, his arm pressing into my left side. He's testing me, and I don't particularly mind.

Margot answers the question he has not asked. "I was fortunate enough to have Gloria on hand to sort it all. She had been with Joe and me long enough to know what our preferences would be when it comes to such matters." There's a murmur across the courtroom, and I huff in annoyance. *There's* a headline that will feed the "housekeeper helps murder husband" stories. She continues. "The kids were devastated. I wanted to let them have the opportunity to say goodbye as soon as possible."

"Why cremation?"

"Joe and I had talked about it." She looks down at her lap and smiles. "We were in the Maldives, seven years ago now, in one of those over-the-water bungalows. We were lying in bed, staring out at the water, and out of nowhere he said, 'Bring me here when I die.' I laughed, made a joke about how logistically that would be challenging, and he said, 'Cremate me.' So simply, so . . . assuredly. And then he said, 'I mean it.' " There's a waver in her voice as she recounts his words. "I'm just a girl who grew up in Minnesota in the nineties. I had never thought of the Maldives or Hollywood or cremation. So many of these things were foreign to me until I met Joe."

Something clicks into place. That buzzing fly I've been trying to swat away finally lands.

The nineties. Minnesota.

That movie of Joe's that Mel and I watched, one of his obscure first films that nobody saw except for us and maybe a few hundred others. *Hustle and Grace.* For most of that movie, the main character was in her hometown, a small port city on Lake Superior, in Minnesota near the northern Wisconsin border. I remember this because Mel and I kept commenting on how charming the town was, one of the few highlights of the film.

Pinto beans and Fruit Roll-Ups. Just like in Joe's movie. Details so random they are specific.

Doing the quick math in my head, that

movie would have been filmed around the same time Margot went missing, in the same year at least. Meaning Joe was likely in Minnesota when Margot disappeared for a week when she was sixteen.

Is this confirmation that she was with Joe when she disappeared at sixteen? Or perhaps they met innocently, only to reconnect again years later in L.A.? Or is she making a game of it, taking one of the plots from Joe's early films and trying it on for size?

Joe has filmed movies all over the country, all over the world. But the idea Joe and Margot could have met back then, that there could have been more to their story . . . that he was a grown man and she was *sixteen* . . .

It tilts the axis of their lives — and this case — completely.

I have no way to fact-check any of this, of course. I have no phone, no access to the internet. I can't bring it to Judge Gillespy or the attorneys because it's something I know outside of the trial. And even if it is true, that they were both in the same state at the same time, it doesn't prove that they ever met, let alone that she was with him when she disappeared. Perhaps it's far-fetched. Still, my mind fuses both situations into one. And this information, this secret, burns a hole in my pocket and lights a flame of tension in my gut at once.

Having nothing to do with this information, this theory, this . . . whatever it is . . . I sit on it. Frustrated, I press my hands under my thighs and tuck it away, knowing I likely won't ever know if there's any truth to be had here.

I've missed some of Margot's testimony, though I catch that they are still discussing Joe's cremation. I force myself to refocus.

"If Mr. Kitsch made this request to be cremated, why was it never noted to Mr. Windham, his business manager? Or anyone, for that matter?"

"He told *me.* I was his wife. There was no reason to have to do more than that." Margot tries but fails to hide her consternation, her tone clipped, and it's a glimpse of who she is on the show.

D.A. Stern turns his back to Margot and looks instead to the jury box as he asks his next question. "Have you fulfilled this alleged wish of Joe's? To take his ashes back to the Maldives?"

"No, I haven't," Margot says, eyeing his back. I half expect her to pull a knife from some secret compartment under her clothes and fling it between his shoulder blades based on her scowl alone.

D.A. Stern turns back to her. "Why not?" he says with forced incredulity.

"I've been a bit busy," she states, and there's a caustic chuckle from the gallery.

D.A. Stern and Margot stare at each other in a loaded exchange, and I can't quite determine either's aim in the silence. Margot, still fixated on D.A. Stern, softens, as if remembering something or someone's whispered a directive in her ear. She releases her shoulders, her lips, her eyebrows. Her eyes round. She speaks before D.A. Stern can stop her. "I miss him." Her voice cracks. "I miss his touch. I miss feeling his hand against mine. I miss the charge of it. I miss his kiss. I wish for his touch more than anything." Her voice is trembling, an unsteady wobble. A plaintive cry.

D.A. Stern calls out, "No further questions," over Margot's words, but she's the one with the mic.

I watch Margot before me as she seemingly breaks. Her perfect posture slumps and her eyes look more wilted than anything.

Durrant Hammerstead redirects, as I imagined he would. He wants the last impression with this his most important witness.

"Margot," he says, his tone noticeably

smoother, carrying an added layer of something delicate. "After everything Joe put you through, did you still love him?"

I lean forward, eyes fixed on Margot's, though I catch the line of a deep swallow in her throat. She presses her eyes shut before realigning her attention to her attorney. "Joe and I were married for twenty-four years. It's a long time. I loved him, I hated him, and felt everything in between during our time together. That's marriage." She looks at the jury, and my pulse quickens when we make eye contact. Her words strike me as ruefully honest. It would have been easy for her to take the stand as the weeping widow who made her husband perfect in death. Instead, she is . . . subtle.

She speaks to me as if we were seated beside each other. "After you've been with someone awhile, you tend not to see them anymore. They can become this bodily mass that exists around you. But every once in a while, I'd look up and catch sight of him just as he was entering a room or telling a joke at a party, and for the briefest instant I'd forget who he was and think . . . *Wow, look at that charming, mysterious guy.* Those were the moments when I remembered why I loved this man, why I married him." She turns her attention back to Durrant Hammerstead. "He was with me in every best moment of my life. The ones I will always look back on with tenderness. So yes, I still very much loved him. Despite it all." She swipes at the outer corner of her left eye with the length of her pointer finger. "And I have missed him every single day since he left."

I turn to Damon, and he looks down at me, his eyes pulsing like a kaleidoscope. The intensity of his gaze causes a chill across every inch of my body.

Damon's leg touches mine and it doesn't feel accidental. There is a spurt of electricity — the attraction of a positive and negative charge. The surge of our undeniable connection.

I have missed him every single day since he left.

Before us sits a woman who can never experience her lover's touch again, despite a desperate desire for it. All the while, I've been fighting against the feel of the man beside me. I *do* have a second chance.

The defense rests its case.

39.

Oral Arguments (n., phrase)

1. presentation of a case before a court by spoken word
2. activities of the tongue

There's so much ready to burst out of me, but I don't know what, and I don't know where to place any of it if it does. Having Margot on the stand today, in some grand finale to the two weeks we've spent on this case, it's as though my heart is strapped to a gurney, having met its limit.

In the van back to the Singer Suites, we emerge from the courtroom's underground garage, and I'm surprised to see the sky ashen, fat raindrops splattering against the windows like thick tears. We're quiet during the ride, all of us seemingly spent or lost in thought about what happened in the courtroom today and over the last two weeks. I glance back and see Xavier, usually the most upbeat of us all, with his head bent back against the headrest, eyes shut. Luis, my older jury seatmate, is fast asleep, mouth ajar with his arms crossed in front of him.

I stare out at the street, the van's silence amplified by the hard rain outside. When we reach the approximate halfway point to the hotel, Damon beside me removes his jacket and places it on his lap, where it flows across the small space between us and over my right leg. Underneath it, his hand finds mine, cups it. There's a surge across me as our fingers twine, his curling to my palm.

I turn and look at him, but he stares ahead, out the front windshield.

He seems to always know exactly what I need.

He runs his thumb gently across the thin, sensitive stretch of skin between my thumb and forefinger, back and slowly forth.

I close my eyes and lean against the window, savoring the cold against my cheek. Damon is calm and warm and comforting in a way he can't possibly know the depths of. I don't know how I survived the last ten years without him.

Somewhere along the way, Damon's touch turns from comforting to something more. The press of his thumb against the tender skin of my hand shifts slightly firmer. He adjusts in his seat. I begin to feel the bump of the road between my legs, my entire sense of touch heightened to a state of blood-rushing sensitivity. I squeeze his hand tighter.

Twenty minutes later, I pace the small space between my room door and window, roiling with nervous energy. Thoughts of Damon tickle across my belly and thighs, rippling me with an itchy sensation. Things hum restlessly open between us, and I feel the overwhelming need to satisfy all that is unsettled in me. When I saw Damon that first day in the courtroom hallway, I thought it was a punishment of some kind, being trapped here with my past. Now, I might just believe it's a gift. A settlement, at least. We get to exist, together, in this sphere of separation from the outside world, where we don't have to consider the real-life ramifications of us. The end is looming. What if this case is all we'll ever get? I can't let it end without more of him.

Before I know it, I am tapping softly at his door.

I glance nervously at the corner where George is stationed, silently begging him not to turn. As I wait, there's a zing through me from the back of my throat to the pit of my stomach, as I think I should have taken the time to fix myself up. Smooth my hair, change my clothes, brush on some lip gloss. But I didn't — the force of Damon pulled me straight to his door.

When the door opens, my heart practically leaps from my chest to him. He's wearing those joggers, the gray ones that hug his backside (and frontside). He's shirtless, which only adds to the utterly unfair scene at his hotel room door. He leans, forearm above his head against the doorframe, the skin of his side pulled taut over the ridges of his midsection from the stretch. He is the hottest fucking thing I have ever seen.

I inhale him.

Horse camp. *My* horse camp. Me.

I've been thinking about it since I found his cologne bottle the other night. If love is gradual or all at once. I know that when I saw him climb out of the back seat of my mom's car at Sagawa, face twisted in soft concern — it's the moment I began loving him. I didn't know it then. I didn't know it until now. But the answer is — falling in love with him was both gradual, sneaking up on me in our everyday moments, and also a lightning bolt of realization. One instant, like that very first kiss on my doorstep, to make me see clearly.

I loved him.

I never stopped.

He stares at me, and, as I have come to expect, he says so much in the weight of his gaze. His jaw muscle flexes. I'd say he's looking in my eyes, but it's more than that. He's mirroring my wants, desires, and fears all back to me through his silent, intrepid eyes.

He steps forward, so close that our chests touch with each rise, leans farther into me to close the door silently behind me so we are alone. I bathe in his heat.

He is not surprised to find me here. No. It's like he knows. Like he could feel my need through the walls and came rushing to the door.

He still doesn't say anything. Why would he? There's so much to say, but none of it matters right now, and none of it would suffice. He doesn't speak from his mouth. He speaks from the blue green of his eyes, the curve of his lips, the intensity of his jaw. He speaks from the surge of his chest. From his hands that are clenched then released, then fists again. I watch as each time he clenches a vein running up his forearm presses against his skin, causing the angel wings to pulse.

I scan him, some unconscious thought gnawing at me to pay attention. His chest. It's largely bare of tattoos, in stark contrast to his arms, a blond happy trail spanning from the bottom curve of his belly button and dipping below his waistband. But there is one tattoo etched across his inner left pec. I'd laugh if I didn't know better, because it would otherwise seem obscure. So out of place.

But I can't laugh. Instead, there's a searing heat between my thighs.

Round eyes. Three perfectly spaced whiskers sprouting from each side of its muzzle.

A gerbil or hamster or guinea pig. It could be any.

Prince Hamsterdinck, stationed directly over his heart.

His hands remain tension-filled fists at his sides while I stare at him, at that tattoo. His body is a living history of all the people and things that have ever mattered to him. His passion for motocross. Fishing with his dad. Kara is everywhere, from the wings to the owl. But me — I am etched over his heart, on the otherwise blank canvas of his chest. *Me.* Us. There is no other reasoning. That ridiculous yard sale ceramic hamster didn't mean anything to anyone else. Only us. It was — is — the representation of what he meant to me back then. My solace, my safe place to be silly and free. An escape from all that was broken.

He clenches his jaw again, and the muscle along it flexes tightly against the skin. His lust could be mistaken for anger, the intensity just the same. But I know when I look at him, he is brimming with want.

I raise my fingertips to his chest, then my eyes to his in question.

"You've always been with me, Syd." His pec twitches under my touch. I don't move my hand. "I've tried to give you space. I'm clearly failing." His eyes go down to my fingertips pressed against his skin. His heartbeat accelerates beneath my touch.

"I don't want you to stay away."

His eyes search mine, and I recognize the struggle in his. "I meant it when I said I'm bad at relationships, Syd. I don't . . . I don't know if I can give you —"

"I haven't asked you for anything," I tell him.

"No, you haven't," he concedes. "But I can't go there with you without being clear about that."

"Go where?" I ask, my voice breathy and vulnerable in a way I can't fight. We are still as close as we can be without being pressed together.

"To take you the way I want to. The way I haven't stopped thinking about since I saw you that first day at the courthouse."

My throat goes dry, and my center pulses. I make myself hear his warning. And I do hear it. But I don't care. I want him while I can have him, even if it means only for the remainder of this fast-closing case, even if it's just for this one night. I hadn't realized how so much of my life went on hold when he left, how stunted and dispassionate I have been, and that being back with him now has allowed me to press play once more.

I am sixteen again, but in a body that holds ten years of pent-up want.

He lifts his hand and cups the right side of my head, his thumb rubbing gently along the small scar on the right side of my forehead. I lean into his touch. Though changed, it's still a bodily reminder of his previous version of me.

I cannot fight it any longer. The cabin fever has left me utterly inflamed. I step urgently forward and jump onto him, arms around his neck, legs wrapping around his waist. He responds effortlessly — his arms immediately around my lower back, one hand wrapped under my backside. He rarely has words, but right now, he doesn't need any. He knows what I want. And I know with complete certainty his body demands mine, too.

He holds me up, pressing his lips onto my waiting mouth. Our lips pinned together, just as his tongue forces its way to mine, he takes three steps forward and releases me onto the bed, then follows, landing atop me. He stops his fall with his elbows, hovering just above me, only our legs intertwined. His kisses up until now have been stable, a layer of control always within his reach. Now, they are fiery and uncontrolled and desperate, like there are ten years of desire and longing pouring out of him, too, our lips and tongues the conduits for the explosive exchange.

Our mouths separate briefly as the bed bounces, though it's only a split second before we connect again. He shifts his weight to one side, his outstretched palm making its way to the bare skin of my stomach under my blouse, his firm touch made more intense next to the silky fabric of my top.

His hand skims my back, inching closer to the clasp of my bra. I close my eyes and nod, lifting slightly so he can reach around and unclasp it. He does, and immediately his hand is separating me from it, my right breast in his palm as he squeezes gently. Then a second time, harder, which sends a wave of need across my midsection. Part of me thinks I should stop him, slow things down to leave more to savor. But I couldn't stop the rolling force even if I tried. I lift into him, needing to be as close as possible but frustrated by the layers between us. I create some space so I can remove my blouse and loose bra. He watches.

"Get to work," I say, and he obediently removes his pants as I shimmy out of my A-line skirt. And that smell, horse saddle leather — I must mount him immediately.

He's down to his black boxer briefs, and me, to a nude thong. I reach down and grab the thin straps of my underwear to remove it when his hand grasps my wrist to stop me.

"I'll do it," he says, his blue-green eyes locked on mine.

I release my grip, as does he, and I lift to my elbows to watch as he slowly lowers until his face hovers just above the delicate fabric. He's so close I can feel his hot breath penetrating the thin cotton. That sensation alone causes me to throw my head back in pleasure. He remains there a moment too long with no movement. Impatient, I raise my hips ever so slightly so the scruff of his five o'clock shadow brushes against the triangle of fabric. He exhales mightily, and the warmth of it finds the skin above my pubic bone, sending a ripple of goose bumps across my stomach, down my thighs. He brushes his fingertips along my inner thigh, forcing the goose bumps to further mound. As I'm about to voice my torment, my need to feel the weight of him, he lays a tongue-led kiss to that same spot of fabric, and my eyes and head roll back in reply.

Unexpectedly, he rises, his mouth greeting mine again. He kisses me slowly, then breaks apart and grumbles out, "Are you sure you want this?"

The answer, of course, is more complicated than just yes or no. There are dozens of reasons I do want this, but also possibly hundreds for why we shouldn't. But this is not a moment for the scales of reason. I have held out — pushed aside my desire for Damon — for as long as I possibly could. For perhaps my whole life. I cannot imagine sitting next to him in that trial box a day or even a moment longer without knowing the feel of his full skin.

My body needs him desperately, but my heart needs him more.

I look deep into his eyes and say, "Put your hands on me."

There is no further hesitation. He swoops down to my feet and with him goes my thong. He also stands, removes his boxer briefs, and is back on top of me so quickly I can't catch a view of his fully naked body. But I feel it, pressed against me as he covers me again. He's like a furnace, warm and giving.

He takes both my hands in his, fingers interlaced, and raises them above my head, pinning them roughly to the bed. He kisses me deeply this way, our tongues vying for placement. His erection throbs against me, practically scalding with heat.

To the world, he is quiet. Gruff, even. Sad. But here, now, with me, he is — at least momentarily — tender. I want to wash away the last ten years that didn't include him. I writhe against him, desperate for more.

"I don't have a condom," I say, the devastation of the realization hitting me. I cannot comprehend not seeing this through . . .

"I do."

"You brought condoms to jury duty?"

He shakes his head, once, hovering over me. "No. Cam did."

"You asked Cam for a condom?" I say, breathing hard, recalling condoms as one of his many smuggled items.

"Absolutely not. But after the roof, he

found me the next day at breakfast and slipped it to me under the table."

"That was presumptuous of him."

He huffs, and at this angle, the bulging veins in his face and forehead remind me of a superhero in battle. "It *was* presumptuous. And I was going to tell him later it wasn't like that . . ."

"But?"

"But I hoped it was."

My hand slides down him, and I let my fingers stroke him, my thumb brushing the tip, then down the length. He closes his eyes and hangs his head in response.

"How many did he give you?" I ask.

"One," he says, also breathing hard.

I cup his length in my palm, wrap my fingers firmly around him. "Then I guess we better make it count," I say.

He responds with a groan and leans into me again, his kiss ferocious and demanding. I respond with equal force, releasing my grip on him so I can close the space between us and feel his kiss more deeply.

I have never looked at or touched or longed for a man the way I do Damon. The yearning I have for him is like a tummy ache after too much sugar, a bee trapped in my sternum. It hurts, the ache of desire for this man.

As if he knows this is exactly the right moment, he takes his hand and smooths the hair from my face, presses his lips to mine once more, then buries his head into the side of my neck as he enters me. I rock forward to allow him in, and we both release a breath in unison as he finds his way. His mouth suctions to the top of my shoulder when he's pressed deeply inside me, and I shudder. He bites firmly at the same spot on my neck as he pulls out, then slides back in again, and I'm mentally pleading for time to stop so this feeling can last indefinitely. I press my fingertips into his ass, urging him along. He obliges, moving with faster, more distinct effort. And for an indiscernible moment in time, we are one, connected in every way, moving together and apart at the exact right frequency, a surge of pleasure between us both. I beg for it not to end, for him not to stop, and it's more vocal than I expect myself to be. He seems to enjoy it — my pleading — bulling into me with more abandon each time.

As my tension builds to near release, he pulls himself out of me and smirks at the resulting frown that overtakes my face.

"I can't let this end yet," he huffs. He rolls off me and sits up, pulling me into his lap. I eagerly oblige, lowering down onto him. His eyelids twitch as I take him in fully, and I feel nothing short of powerful as I ride him. I rest my forearms on his broad shoulders, tug at his hair as I move. He buries his face into me, biting again at the curve of my neck as my pace becomes frenzied. He thrusts his hips with me, and together we slam into each other with reckless surrender.

In this suspended time, it's as though he was built for me. He fits me perfectly, filling all the places that have felt so empty for so long. Somewhere along the way, he has taken over, pounding into me, and I can do nothing but bounce and moan in pleasure.

When his final thrust comes, I clench, holding him inside me for a last moment of bliss.

"Holy shit," he exhales into my neck.

I agree. "Holy shit." I feel a release so deep I only realize the presence after it's gone, like a chiropractor has worked out a longstanding kink.

I climb off him and lie flat, and he stretches out onto his back beside me. We laze quietly for a moment, and as we do, he runs his fingertips gently along the top of my right thigh, and it causes a new eruption of goose bumps across my damp skin.

Here, beside Damon, I am more alive than

I have ever been.

I run my fingers along his arm and chest, admiring his ink, recognizing again it's the first time I've seen him without a shirt and, thus, the first time I'm seeing some of his tattoos. His skin holds a backward map of his life, and I want to drive every road, see the moments of each, all the way back to their origins.

He props himself up on his elbow to face me when we've both caught our breath. "That was . . ."

"Nice?" I offer.

"More than nice. Epic."

I laugh. "I like that. Epic."

He presses his lips lightly to my forehead, then cups the side of my jaw and runs his thumb gently across my bottom lip. I wonder if he knows how intensely I feel his forehead kisses.

"I've thought about this since the first time I saw you," he says, his voice gravelly.

"We were ten."

He huffs. "Okay, maybe not the first time, but definitely shortly after."

"Why didn't you ever tell me?"

"You were my best friend," he says, as if it's answer enough. And it is. We were kids when we met. When and how were we meant to transition to more? His hand grazes my thigh. "I did plenty of things, thinking about you."

I let my tongue rub at the tip of his thumb, and he flicks his eyes down to the movement.

"Oh?" I say, unsure if he means during our time on this trial or back then.

"Yeah."

"Tell me," I murmur, arousal humming between my legs again, as though it never waned.

He moves his hand to my stomach, his fingertips fluttering across my bare belly. "I fantasized about you, about what it would be like to kiss you." He leans down and kisses me, as if to prove to himself that he now can, in fact, do it outside of his fantasy.

"Is that it?" I ask.

"No. No, it's not. I imagined you naked. I imagined the feel of your skin." He runs his palm up my thigh. "You're even softer in real life."

"What else?" I whisper, needing to hear it all. It's a unique form of power I'm not used to, knowing Damon has lusted over me, thought of me as he pleasured himself.

"I've imagined several times what it would feel like to fuck you."

My lips part and I huff. He takes it as a sign to continue.

"I thought about bending you over the side of my bed and fucking you from behind." He lets his fingers meander down, lightly fluttering against my inner thigh. "I thought about you moaning my name."

"Damon?" I barely get his name out.

"Yes?" he says, the movement of his hand stopping as he grips my thigh.

"Go ask Cam for another condom."

40.

Judge's Chambers (n.)

1. the office of a judge where the judge conducts various activities apart from the public courtroom proceedings
2. the reckoning room

Judge Gillespy's chambers look a lot like my grandpa's old home office, with rich floor-to-ceiling mahogany shelves lined with books and paperweights, plaques and frames. Judge Gillespy's robe hangs on a hook on the back of the door. She wears a simple fitted black dress, hair collected at the nape of her neck and lips swiped with her signature burgundy lipstick. She looks up from the file in her hand at the table in the corner as we enter.

"Have a seat," she says, dropping the legal file onto the table and circling to her side of the desk. We take the two chairs opposite her.

Damon and I don't make eye contact. My heart wallops against my navy-and-white-striped blouse as Judge Gillespy evaluates us. It's like my first outing into the world after losing my virginity. The feeling that everyone I encounter instinctively knows I had sex last night. Twice. Like the sex is oozing out of my pores in a scent they don't know they can smell.

As soon as we arrived at the courthouse this morning, Bailiff Maurice pulled Damon and me aside and escorted us here. My heartbeat chimes in my ears at the thought that perhaps this is Damon's doing. Did he feel guilty about what happened last night and tell Judge Gillespy? He did, after all, tell George about the Outback Steakhouse guy.

I steal a glance at him and immediately shame myself for questioning him. He wouldn't. This has to be about something else entirely.

Judge Gillespy clasps her hands atop the desk tightly and continues to stare at us. Her eyes move slowly from Damon, to me, back to Damon, before she clears her throat and leans in. "I don't have to tell you what goes into a trial like this. Hundreds of thousands of taxpayer dollars" — she pauses to audibly exhale — "not to mention the three-ring circus of media and 'fans' outside the courtroom daily." She makes air quotes when she says *fans,* then pushes her rolling chair backward and walks to the window, which overlooks said group of fans, who I know without looking are already parked outside with their signs and chants. "A mistrial would be incredibly damaging for everyone involved, *especially* when the case has already been fully presented and we are just about to start deliberations. And it would be an embarrassment to me, personally." She turns to look squarely at me. Not Damon, just me. I swallow with great focus, the saliva in my mouth having grown thick. "Have I not made the ramifications of derailing this case abundantly clear?"

I speak first. "You have. You very much have."

She returns to her seat, leans forward. "People have noticed how . . . *close* the two of you are. Perhaps closer than you let on in voir dire. So," she says, crossing her arms, finally turning her attention to Damon, "I will ask you both directly. Is there anything I should be aware of that would cause me to be compelled to call a mistrial in this case?"

I look to Damon, whose eyes remain forward. Neither of us immediately speaks.

Judge Gillespy huffs at our silence. "Let me be more direct. Is there anything involving the two of you that would violate court rules regarding juror relationships?" She peers between us again.

I swallow hard and feel with certainty that Judge Gillespy knows everything about the presidential suite, about the rooftop, about my two very vocal orgasms last night. I have a choice to make: tell the truth that Damon and I had the most insanely hot sex of my life just hours ago in my tax-payer-paid hotel room, or lie.

We're all just one decision away from a completely different life. His words from our conversation in the presidential suite echo in my ears between the beats of my thumping pulse. If I admit to a relationship of some kind with Damon, Judge Gillespy will call a mistrial, resulting in a slew of dominoes falling. Wasted time for everyone involved, including Margot and the other jurors. It would humiliate Judge Gillespy. It would cause emotional turmoil for Joe's family, his kids. His poor kids. And, of course, there's the prospect of jail time.

If I lie, I am no better than the worst parts of this trial, prioritizing my self-preservation above anyone else's needs or best interests. It would make me like my father.

My views and priorities coming into this trial have completely shifted. My attention has fallen more on Damon than the case. My steadfast belief that Margot couldn't have killed Joe is waning. I've made minimal effort in my goal to secure the role of foreperson. I don't even know my purpose here anymore.

I think of Damon in bed last night. How his hands felt against my skin. How he felt inside me. Of his tongue and fingers invading me together. Of his soft forehead kisses after. How he could be so forceful at all the right times, so gentle in all the others. Of how he's taken me back to being sixteen again, but also shown me how far we've both come.

Despite it all, I cannot deem myself more important than the overall judicial process. Everyone involved deserves a clean trial. I glance at Damon, who is pleading with his eyes. *I'm sorry,* I tell him silently as I feel him slipping away as a result of what I'm about to do.

I've been a substandard juror up until this point. It's time to right this ship and stop being selfish.

"We had sex last night," I announce. I look

back at Damon, who presses his eyes shut. "And this morning," I add, because I assume it's relevant.

Judge Gillespy releases a breath, and the weight of it strikes me like the blast of a gale-force wind as it pushes me back in my seat.

My worst-case scenario has come true.

"I don't have to tell you how negligent you have been," Judge Gillespy says, standing again, this time with what I assume as intended intimidation. "Or how incredibly disappointed I am in you both. Your neglect of the rules, the severity of the situation. Someone's life is on the line" — she presses her fists to the top of her desk — "another's justice in death. There are no greater matters."

She stares at us for a long while. Damon and I remain silent. I cannot think of a single word to make this better. There simply aren't any.

"You do realize there is more than a mistrial at stake here? Although the weight of that should be enough. I can cite you both with juror misconduct, hold you in contempt, and give you jail time. Was that not made clear?"

My mind spirals from what I should be doing to get myself out of this situation to all I haven't yet done if Judge Gillespy holds to her threat. There's a significant amount of living I've missed. Being here with Damon, experiencing the highs we have, makes me want to start *doing.* I need to see the pyramids in Egypt and eat at Din Tai Fung at least one more time. I need to fly somewhere with a seat in one of those fancy sleeping pods and attend BravoCon with Mel. I need to watch the last season of *You,* which I had to stop watching because I found myself lusting over a fictional serial killer. I need to love.

"It's my fault," Damon says. "I was the one who —"

Judge Gillespy throws a palm in the air and closes her eyes. "I do not need the details of your trysts. Nor will you be rewarded for some measly attempt at chivalry now. Please stop there."

My ears burn with embarrassment, and I swallow with great difficulty as my throat swells. I've ruined everything. I think of Tamra, of her time away from her husband and grandkids, now for nothing. I think of Luis, elderly and exhausted. I haven't considered myself truly selfish until this instant, but I am. And not just because of Damon. Because of my omittances during jury selection to be chosen for this trial.

And well before that, my view of my parents' divorce as only my pain. In many ways, I've always been selfish. I am my father's daughter.

Judge Gillespy begins to pace the room. I turn to watch her. Damon remains stationary, facing toward her empty desk. I wonder if he is upset by my admission. I want to ask, reach out and grab hold of his hand, but I can't do any of it.

After a few moments of tense silence, the only noise the muffled weight of Judge Gillespy's heels against the thin black carpet, she says, "I'll be back in a moment," before exiting the room.

"Shit," Damon whispers as soon as she's gone, and I close my eyes and wince against the sound of his voice. "I'm sorry I got us into this," he says.

"It's not your fault," I say. It's mine. I'm the one who cares about this case. I'm the one who sought a spot on this jury to help Margot, only to find *I* could be the reason this all ends badly.

He turns to face me, and his acute sincerity makes me lean away. "I don't regret it," he says, the dimple in his chin constricting as he clenches his jaw.

I don't either, sitting here, looking at him, with his earnest face and strong pull. How could I possibly? But the stakes are too great. I don't even know what I believe about the case anymore after everything we've heard, but still, I absolutely didn't want to be the cause of a *mistrial.*

"Every time you go away, you take a piece of meat with you," he says, and I have no choice but to smile. There really has never been a time when our wrong lyrics haven't made me feel better, in some small increment.

I wonder if there's a way we could pass notes in jail. I bet Cam could help with a plan.

The door opens, and Judge Gillespy strides in aggressively, crumpling a paper towel from the restroom between her hands. She tosses it into the bin under her desk and takes her seat. Her stare bores into Damon, then me. The stern clench of her jaw makes me think for a moment the two of them could be related.

Finally, she releases her jaw and opens her mouth, though it takes her several seconds to speak. "A mistrial would be devastating," she says. "Even replacing you with alternates at this point would draw unnecessary scrutiny to already highly scrutinized proceedings. Any hiccup at all results in a negative headline or viral post." She flicks her hand in the air in annoyance. After some time, she sighs in reluctant defeat. "Have you discussed the case?" she asks. "During any of your . . ." She gives up on finding an appropriate word and instead thrusts her hand in quick circles in the air.

"No," Damon and I both say in unison. Margot has come up in our conversations, sure, but we haven't specifically discussed the details of the case. At least, not in the way I believe she means.

"Are you two capable of a course correction, if given the opportunity?" she asks pointedly. We both look up immediately. "The last thing I want to do here is have all this time and all these resources wasted only to have to start over completely. So tell me, if we move forward from this, can you two be trusted to . . . remain professional?" She says "remain professional," but it's clear her words are code for *not fuck*.

"Absolutely," I offer. "I am so very sorry, Judge Gillespy. I can assure you, it was a lapse in judgment. A by-product of being isolated for so long. I take this case, the judicial system and process, very, *very* seriously. If given another chance, I promise we would have no future involvement." I motion my thumb at Damon, who remains unmoved.

"Juror?" Judge Gillespy urges Damon.

He clears his throat and leans forward. "It won't happen again."

Despite having just expressed the same sentiment, somehow his words still cut me. The idea that last night can't happen again is excruciating. It makes my desire for him grow, an immediate burst of craving at my core.

"Assuming that is true, that I can trust you both to keep your focus for the last leg of this process, then" — she pauses, sighs — "I am willing to keep this between us. For now. I suppose this . . ." She looks back and forth between us, searching for the right words. "This situation of yours isn't directly impactful to the case . . ." Her voice trails off as if questioning whether she believes it.

I audibly exhale.

"We are so close to the end," she says, making her way to the door to open it for us. "Get through deliberations, then after that, well, that is up to you."

I am floored as we exit the judge's chambers. I thought for sure Judge Gillespy would call a mistrial and our names would be leaked, our likenesses splashed across TMZ. Thankfully, she has shown us some mercy, even if it is for the benefit of the trial and not us.

There is one lingering thought — I have no idea how we were found out. Did Cam give us up after Damon's condom request? Did one of the bailiffs see us sneaking around? Or was it someone I would have least expected to be paying attention? Gray Man perhaps? We may never find out, though it hardly matters now.

Damon and I head to the courtroom to join the others, stepping into the same elevator I saw him step out of at the start of all of this.

He presses the button to the fourth floor, and as we descend, the air in the elevator car grows immediately viscid. The idea that I cannot touch him, the stakes even higher than before, makes me want to tackle him to the floor of this elevator. He feels it, too. I know he does. He stands unnecessarily close to me, his forearm grazing mine, and I have to fight to ignore the growing flutter between my legs. He leans against the elevator wall, quiet and unreadable. When he doesn't speak, I take the opportunity. "Maybe after," I say in almost a whisper, and I lose myself entirely, joining him against the back wall.

"Maybe," he says.

After this trial, after this deliberation, which will likely last only a few days at most, there is the potential of us. One where we can get to know the new versions of each other further, in the real world, without having to hide or sneak around. I know he warned me that he's not capable, but perhaps he just doesn't see it yet. Sure, there are complications outside, too, but my heart pinches at the prospect. As long as there is a small window of possibility, there is hope. My lust is replaced with the excitement of a potential future. That he might want it as much as I do.

Closing statements remind me of debate class in high school. D.A. Stern goes first, speaking for nearly an hour, the only reprieve about two-thirds of the way through, when Durrant Hammerstead "accidentally" knocks his water glass to the ground just as D.A. Stern begins talking of Margot's assumed vitriol toward her late husband.

He lays out again the details of the prosecution's case. That Margot had several reasons to want her husband gone, dead specifically. The multiple affairs. His full ownership of her successful business. His will, leaving everything to her. D.A. Stern outlines how the autopsy and toxicology reports did not point to a clear-cut natural cause of death. How the timing of Joe's smoothie consumption that morning and subsequent time of death align to the window of affect given by the forensic toxicologist. How Margot "rushed" to cremate her dead husband's body to destroy any potential evidence. He reiterates how Jackie Kitsch found three eye-drop bottles, hidden by Emblem. How even *she* suspected Margot, her own daughter-in-law and the mother of her grandchildren. He references that she could have easily had someone else do it for her — someone indebted to her — a clear nod to Ms. Pembrooke. He paints Margot as a manipulative mastermind, and having watched her for seven seasons of *AMOM,* I can't argue the mastermind part.

Margot stares on, tracking D.A. Stern as he strides, bouncing his pen between his fingers as he talks.

When it's his turn, Durrant Hammerstead rises slowly, goes through his now expected laborious motions of adjusting himself to a stand. "Margot had ample time — years of affairs — to seek out 'revenge' if that were her mission," he begins, gesturing his hands toward us. "She is not the first woman to be tied financially to her husband. You heard from our medical expert and even from the state's medical examiner that Joe Kitsch's death was caused by cardiac arrest. A tragic though natural occurrence. The likely result of genetics or lifestyle or age — not foul play. And let's not forget, Margot has an alibi." He says this last part as if ignoring it would be incredulous and irresponsible. He talks us through how Emblem very well could have collected those eye-drop bottles over several months and how being "disliked" (he glances at D.A. Stern as he says this — a clear reference to the onslaught of witnesses he brought forth to display their distaste for Margot) is not grounds for determining someone a murderer.

He tells us, just as he had in opening statements, that D.A. Stern must have proven *beyond a reasonable doubt* that Margot was responsible for Joe's death in order for us to find her guilty. "And what we have here, at the end of this trial, is an abundance of reasonable doubt," he tells us sharply.

I study the other jurors when he says this, though I don't garner much from their neutral faces.

He does take one shot at D.A. Stern, saying, "I know it would be a career-maker for the D.A. to pin the Malibu Menace in the trial of the century." He speaks with such taunt in his voice that it surprises me. I didn't think Hammerstead had it in him.

"But this case is not about D.A. Stern building his résumé. It's about this woman's life. Don't lose sight of that as you deliberate."

Sliding back into the Durrant Hammerstead we have seen throughout the trial, he ends his statement with "Remember: If she wasn't there, a guilty verdict's not fair," in what I glean as an attempt at his own notorious "if it doesn't fit, you must acquit" aphorism. It's not his finest moment. He's made the case in his closing arguments, though, that the prosecution has not clearly shown Margot killed Joe, directly or indirectly. Hell, they didn't even prove that he was, in fact, murdered. But still, something nags at me. A cumbersome little voice that says this case is not as cut and dry as I'd like it to be.

Margot smiles gratefully at Durrant Hammerstead as he returns to the defense table, seemingly in agreement that he has laid his defense out well.

The end of the trial, and thus Margot's fate, is looming. And we twelve jurors are about to determine the outcome.

41.

Jury Deliberations (n., phrase)

1. process during which members of a jury discuss and consider the evidence presented in a trial in order to reach a verdict
2. where karma's gonna track you down

We step into the deliberation room, and it's as though my pounding heart has been cut into two, each half shoved into one of my ears. I'm beyond anxious for what this conversation will hold. And after what transpired in Judge Gillespy's chambers earlier, I'm more determined than ever to ensure fairness in deliberations. But the more I stew over the testimony and what I know of Margot, the more I worry that perhaps I was wrong for my steadfast belief in her innocence.

I look around the space where we will spend the next undetermined number of hours. Days, potentially. Now that the three alternates have been removed for deliberations, it feels a bit smaller in here. Just the core twelve remain. I've shared the past two weeks with these people. We've sat together through all the testimony, listened to the same words, seen the same faces, heard the same accusations. We've learned intimate details about Joe Kitsch's life that strangers shouldn't know about someone else. Hell, Damon aside, I've learned more about Tamra and Cam than I know about most people in my life. And now here we are, about to discuss whether we heard it all the same.

When we've all sat around the table, I realize we've shuffled in according to juror numbers like the well-trained civil servants we are, Damon to my left and to my right, Luis, whom I'm ashamed to admit I've exchanged barely more than nods and hellos, which I feel particularly terrible about now that the trial is sunsetting.

There's a buzz in the room, a heightened energy as the power in this case has officially shifted to us. In this room, our thoughts, our opinions, and our voices matter.

When everyone is seated, Xavier is the

first to speak. "According to the judge's instructions, we should begin with introductions, then decide on a foreperson." He clears his throat. "Right, so anyone care to go first on a formal introduction?"

Everyone looks around the room, avoiding eye contact like it's the first day of school. We've been together for two weeks. We've all conversed at this point, some more than others, and so it seems rather pointless to introduce ourselves after sitting in the same jury box for eight hours a day — over eighty hours in total, which I calculated while contemplating my poor life choices in Judge Gillespy's chambers just a few hours ago. But Xavier seems determined, his eyes still circling the room.

"I'll start," he offers when the room remains silent. He stands, which seems highly unnecessary, and I wish he hadn't been the one to start because now standing is some precedent we will all have to follow.

Still rattled by Judge Gillespy's scolding, I realize I've missed my opportunity to take the lead. I wanted to be foreperson, but I fear I've unconsciously stepped back from pushing for the role as the doubt about Margot began creeping in. And Margot's account of what happened when she disappeared at sixteen — her uncannily similar description to one of Joe's film plotlines — I can't reconcile what it means. What it should mean, if anything, for this trial. I can't bring it up here, though, because the connection between Margot's testimony and Joe's film was not made on the stand and is therefore not permissible in our deliberations. Part of me is relieved this can remain my own personal case complication that I'm not required to share with the others.

Can two weeks of questionable testimony undo seven years of knowledge? Taking on the role of foreperson is still my best chance to redeem myself, refocus on my goals here, I decide.

"I'm Xavier. Thirty-six. I live in Van Nuys, though from Saginaw, Michigan, originally." He holds up his hand as a map of Michigan and points just below the indent between thumb and forefinger in what I know to be the standard Michigander greeting. "I'm a technology consultant. Married for eleven years to my husband, Lockwood, and we have two kids, Sienna and Corbin, twelve and six. And fun fact, I played Minor League Baseball for the Cubs until I tore my rotator cuff during a spring training game in Arizona in '07."

Yes, definitely wish Xavier hadn't gone

first. Why did he have to throw in a fun fact? The only one I can think of is that I spend most of my time watching reality TV, but that's highly inappropriate to share here.

The other jurors nod, smile, and share quiet hellos to acknowledge Xavier's introduction. Most of the eyes in the room land on juror number two, as he is the person to the right of Xavier. The short, bald man — who I know to be named Amir from our brief breakfast discussion last week — clears his throat and stands, and I press my eyes shut in defeat. Had I gone second, I could have gotten away with staying seated, but now juror number two has set the tone that this is a thing. I miss his introduction entirely, and now it's Damon's turn.

"Hi, everyone, Damon. I'm twenty-six. I live in Glendale. I'm a transportation engineer, worked as a construction foreman before that, though please don't vote for me for that here because I don't think it translates." He gets a few chuckles from the room. "I love motocross and hairless cats," he adds before returning to his seat.

Right, it's my turn. I stand and clear my throat. "Hi." I wave and immediately regret the wave. How am I so bad at this (the talking about me part) when I am so confident and solid in a mediation room? "I'm Sydney. I'm also twenty-six. I live in Los Feliz. I work as a corporate mediator, so I'm basically a lawyer without the pay." Tamra grins, but there are no chuckles like there were for Damon. And because this is feeling too much like some subverted speed dating event, I do go ahead and throw in a fun fact. "And a fun fact about me, I have a newborn sister. Genevieve. Gen, we call her Gen." Normally I wouldn't share baby Gen as a point of pride. In fact, though she's technically my sister, before the trial I thought of her more as my mother's baby than in terms of her relationship to me. But the longer I'm here, the more I long to hold her again.

Tamra *aah*s from across the table, and I sit back down. Damon looks at me with a twist of confusion across every feature of his face. "You didn't tell me you have a little sister," he whispers, and if I didn't know better, I'd say his tone sounds accusatory.

I try to listen to the rest of the introductions. I am genuinely fascinated with the people who will determine Margot's fate alongside me. But I'm distracted by Damon. Every time he shifts in his seat, there's a waft of that saddle scent and it draws me back in. Why didn't I share Gen with him? In all our notes, all our conversations, I never told him. I can't help but think it's because I knew it would make me feel sick, like I do now. That sharing the sister I feel little connection to, knowing he lost his, would fill me with shame.

I shake my head, sit up straight, and demand my brain recenter on what is happening in the room. I've missed a couple of introductions. Tamra, juror number seven, stands. "Hello, everyone, I'm Tamra. I'm in my sixties, a mother of four — three boys and a girl — and I have six beautiful grandbabies. I'm a retired schoolteacher. I taught seventh grade math, but now I mostly help my kids with the babies. Lovely to have gotten to know you all over these last few weeks," she offers, smiling warmly.

Gray Man is juror number eight. He stands swiftly, his fingertips pressed against the top of the table as he leans forward, knees bent, and it's an oddly aggressive stance. "Stanley," he says, then sits back down. I've never heard anyone say their own name with such venom.

Pauley, a Hispanic man in his late thirties, is next, and then it is juror number ten's turn. Cam. I immediately blush, thinking of Damon knocking quietly on his door last night. I didn't hear their conversation, but I imagine it went something like, *Cam, buddy, can you spare one more?*

Dude, I could hear her begging for it through the wall. Nice work, followed by a bro hug. I want to crawl under the table, through the concrete slab of this building, and out the sewer system.

Cam stands. He somehow has his sweatshirt back on, hood up, despite the rest of us still dressed in our courtroom attire. "I'm Cam. I go to UCLA. Majoring in social sciences. Uh, fun facts, I have forty-six tattoos, and I once shattered my pelvis falling off a cliff at the Grand Canyon while trying to get the perfect selfie." He repeats nearly verbatim what he told Tamra, Damon, and me at that first dinner.

Juror number eleven, the blond man, informs us he is thirty-six and an overnight cashier at an ampm. Juror number twelve is Kate, the young housewife from Torrance with four kids. I've overheard her chitchatting enough over the last two weeks to know she has listened to one too many sensationalized true crime podcasts and believes that, here, she's part of the cast of *Only Murders in the Building.*

And this, ladies and gentlemen, is the jury of Margot Kitsch's peers.

"Great," Xavier says, clapping his hands together once we've all gone. "Now that intros are out of the way, is there anyone who would like to be foreperson?" Before anyone can speak, he adds, "I am happy to take the role, if nobody else is interested."

"I would," I say, darting up from my seat. All eyes shoot to me, and I can't miss the spattering of annoyed looks. They want to deliberate and move on with their lives, and I'm delaying it.

"Oh, well then," Xavier says, standing to join me. When no one else expresses interest, he says, "Shall we vote on it?"

I nod, though wondering if I should insist on some kind of speech to provide my reasoning for why I want the job.

Before I can speak up, Xavier has taken charge. "Raise your hand if you would like Sydney to serve as foreperson," he says.

Well, this is as in-your-face a popularity contest as I've ever been a part of. I try not to sulk as Damon's, Cam's, and Tamra's hands are the only three to raise.

Xavier records the result on the legal pad before him, though there's really no need. "And how many votes for yours truly?" he says, fingertips pressed to his chest. The remainder of the hands in the room shoot up with the exception of Stanley's, who, to no one's surprise, abstains.

Xavier becomes our foreperson, and rightfully so. He's done the work I haven't, of course. While I've been engrossed by Damon, he's been getting to know the individuals who make up the jury. I never had a shot.

I plop back into my seat, adding this to my long list of recent failures.

"Now that that's settled, the next suggestion on the instructions is to set some ground rules for discussing the case. I do have one, if you're willing to hear me out. My daughter does cheer, and they have this thing called a spirit stick. A room full of young girls trying to agree on outfits and choreography and such, well, it can get loud. So, they have this spirit stick they use. You have to hold the spirit stick to talk. They pass it around to whoever has something to say. That way, they don't all talk over each other and everyone has a chance to be heard. What d'you all think of implementing something like that here?"

I wonder how many of them now wish they had voted differently for foreperson.

My mom was a cheerleader in high school. There's a picture of her in a purple-and-white uniform, sequined to the point of being, I assume, difficult to touch without getting scraped. Her cheeks and lips are a vivid, obtrusive red, and her hair is pulled back so tight her eyebrows are straight lines. She got pregnant with me shortly thereafter. That framed photo sat on the end table of my childhood home and now sits on the mantel above the fireplace in her home with Caleb and Gen. That picture has lived with her far longer than my father or I ever did. In it, she looks happy. I think of that picture now, realizing how much of her life she missed because of my father. Because of me.

I think to tell Xavier that, based on my mother's descriptions of her team's spirit stick, what he is describing is not at all the appropriate use. Ultimately, I let Xavier have his moment.

Tamra leans toward the fruit basket at the center of the table and pulls a banana from the pile. "We could use this?" she offers, and my annoyance wanes at Tamra's good nature.

Xavier reaches around Stanley and takes the banana. "As good as anything else!" he says, clearly more pleased that nobody is objecting to his idea than he is about the choice of spirit stick. "Okay, so, from this point forward, if you want to express an opinion or thought on the case, please hold the banana."

"That was a strange sentence," Cam muses.

Forty-five minutes into deliberations, and

all we've done is make introductions and anoint a spirit stick.

"Another idea," Xavier says, and it's clear Xavier has a running list of ideas he will be sharing. "Why don't we take a preliminary vote, just to see how things are shaking out right now. Who knows, perhaps we are all already on the same page and deliberation won't even be needed. I say kick things off with a quick show of hands vote. What do you say?"

I wiggle in my seat. Yes. Finally, we're getting to it. I am eager to vote. I've been questioning for the last several days what I would do once we got to this stage. But now that we're here, my fortitude kicks in. I will do what I came here to do. I will ensure Margot is judged fairly.

I expected an anonymous vote first — for anonymity, yes, but also for the dramatics of watching Xavier pull pieces of paper out of a bag or dish, all of us evaluating one another, attempting to determine whose vote is whose while keeping our faces neutral — like the parchment reveals on *Survivor.* But, alas, it makes more sense this way. We should all know where everyone stands. And if we are willing to vote a certain way, we should also be willing to share it outright.

Once again, nobody objects, and once again, Xavier is thrilled. "So, let's just do it then." He rubs his hands together excitedly. The anticipation in the room is palpable. It's like we've been staring at the back of a bundle of cards for two weeks, making assumptions about each person's situation. And now, we finally get to see one another's hands. Xavier clears his throat deliberately. "Put your hand up if, right now, you believe the verdict should be innocent."

I shoot my hand into the air. So do Tamra and two others — juror number two, Amir, and juror eleven, the ampm cashier. I take note that Xavier's, Cam's, and Stanley's hands remain firmly planted in their laps.

Xavier does a quick count and records the number on his notepad. "Okay, and how many votes for guilty?"

I feel Damon willing me to look at him. I don't. In fact, I turn away completely so I can't see his vote. It's not that I'm trying to be intentionally cold. I've been dying to know where he stands on this case. But now that the time has come, I don't want to know. I don't want there to be a reason to be out of sync with him. I can't bear being on opposite sides of something so monumental again.

So, I don't look at him. But I do watch in

dejection as several of the hands in the room shoot skyward.

42.

Hung Jury (n., phrase)

1. a jury that is unable to reach a verdict by the required voting margin
2. insert "well-hung" joke here

I see the arm to my left rise slowly in my peripheral vision, though I don't want to believe it. I tell myself I've got to be wrong. But I turn to find Damon's hand in the air, his eyes locked on mine. My breathing goes shallow and my stomach takes flight. Damon — the man who's been distracting me from this case, the best friend I've ever had, the one who kissed my forehead after we went two rounds last night, the one who has given me hope that ten years is enough to wash away the sins of our parents — wants to convict Margot.

Damon continues to watch me after the

hands in the room go down. Xavier asks for undecided votes, and a few hands go up, though I've lost count of the room.

How could I feel like I have so much connection to someone only to find we've been sitting side by side in a courtroom for two weeks, listening to the exact same testimony, hearing the exact same deluge of words, only to reach such differing conclusions? I've sensed throughout that he's leaned this way, but I've tried to ignore it. I've tried to ignore so much when it comes to Damon to preserve our delicate balance, to preserve my feelings. I ignored the hints he's left about his feelings on the case. I've ignored his warnings about being bad at relationships. I've ignored the nagging feeling that I can't fully trust him after everything.

Xavier clears his throat and pulls my attention from Damon. "So, there it is," he says, holding up his notepad. "Five guilty, four innocent, and three undecided."

The room is quiet after the vote. I'd expected everyone to be chomping at the bit, talking all at once now that we are unleashed after being silenced for so long. Instead, we stare at one another. Perhaps everyone is equally surprised by the outcome of the initial vote, for their own reasons. Perhaps no one wants to be the first to speak up. Perhaps nobody wants to hold the banana.

Xavier takes charge. "Right, so good to know where we all stand. Would have been far too easy if we all agreed right off the bat. The deliberation instructions didn't give specific directions for *how* to deliberate, they simply state to deliberate as we wish. So, anyone want to kick things off?" Xavier clenches the banana in his fist and adds, "Remember, there are no bad ideas in brainstorming."

"I'm not really sure that saying applies here," juror number six says.

Xavier ignores the comment. I get the impression he wants to start, but Cam speaks up first. "How 'bout that Tenley Storms?" he says, and the male juror beside him huffs in some semblance of a laugh.

Ignoring Cam, Xavier says, "Okay then, happy to do it. I voted guilty." He cups the banana tightly in his left hand. "There was certainly motive established, what with all of Joe's affairs and ownership of her business. And she had opportunity. The empty eye-drop bottles. Her relationship to Ms. Pembrooke. Even if Margot didn't do it directly herself, she certainly could've gotten that house manager to."

"Lots of people use eye drops," Tamra

states. We make eye contact across the table, and the look we exchange says it all. *Allies.*

"Right, next time." Xavier says, thrusting the banana into the air, then gesturing it toward her. "Certainly true about eye drops. And we don't have any indication that's what actually happened. It's simply the prosecution's theory. But the correlation here cannot be ignored. Even for someone who uses eye drops daily, it would be hard to use three full bottles. That's a lot."

A few heads nod. I have a moment of panic. How many people around this table are willing to follow Xavier to a guilty verdict simply because he's the most vocal and they want to get this over with?

In my daily life as a mediator, I am meant to be neutral, to make decisions based on the cases presented by both parties. But this time, I get to argue a side.

"But she had a solid alibi," I say. "And there was no clear evidence that Margot got Ms. Pembrooke to do it. And Emblem was a little hoarder. Who knows when she found those bottles. And," I continue, "Alizay knows Margot. She would have spotted if something was off." Though some of the evidence presented made me see the prosecutors' theory, it simply wasn't damning enough to declare her guilty.

I can't help but think of the times in my life I've wished I had been more vocal. That I had communicated to Damon how much he meant to me. That I had told my father how much his actions impacted me. Who knows whether any of it would have mattered, but at least I would have spoken up.

The eyes of the room descend on me.

"Sydney, would you like the banana?" Xavier asks, holding it out toward me. I shake my head.

"But there's too much there for it to be coincidence," Cam says.

"Cam, banana?" Xavier tries.

Damon clears his throat. "We know from the toxicology report," he begins, "that Joe Kitsch was otherwise healthy. People don't just die suddenly like that without previous health issues or some kind of forewarning. He got regular checkups. Was in pristine health."

"Here, banana!" Xavier says, exasperated, tossing the banana in front of Damon.

I stare across the table, attempting to keep the judgment from reaching my face. He's allowed. Damon is entitled to his opinion. I should not think differently of him because his views differ from mine. Admittedly, my own views have fluctuated throughout the case. But the ramifications of his views, they could cost Margot her life.

It's a reminder that, despite the tender moments we've shared — how Damon makes me feel and how he looks at me as though I'm his only weakness — we hardly know each other in these new versions of us. After all, are we really, at sixteen, who we will be? And if it weren't for the forced proximity of this trial, we likely never would have crossed paths again. This notion makes my chest ache.

His eyes lock on the side of my head, willing me to look at him. I can't. My own eyes might give me away.

"Joe Kitsch died of cardiac arrest. That much is clear. If we are playing the odds, this is far more likely a result of natural causes than foul play," I say.

A few heads around the table nod, reminding me that Damon and I are not alone.

"But don't forget," Cam interjects, grounding me again as one of twelve in this room. "Her mom was violent. Threw things!" He flings his hand in the air in the motion of a throw. "So, Margot could have inherited some of that rage."

"No," I say firmly. "That is completely unreasonable and unfair. We are more than the sum of our parents' worst offenses."

Damon's head whips to face me, and it is

just him and me again in the room, in the whole damn world.

I don't speak again for the remainder of the day's deliberations.

43.

Perspective (n.)

1. the viewpoint from which judgment of a communication is administered
2. worth gaining

We break for the day, having not achieved much beyond appointing Xavier as foreperson, taking a preliminary vote to determine we disagree, and choosing a banana as our spirit/talking stick.

I plan to avoid Damon at dinner. It's not that I'm mad at him. How could I be? That would be childish and unreasonable. I'm just trying to wrap my mind around all of this. And I need space, to ensure nothing clouds my judgment about the case. That is, until he doesn't show up. Then I can do nothing but question his whereabouts and the reason for his absence. I glance at the empty chair beside me when I sit at "our" table with Tamra and Cam, pondering how quickly something can become habit, and how quickly we can grow to miss something we've just barely had.

I eat quickly and head to my room, his absence tugging at the hairs on the back of my neck. I lie in my bed, staring up at the popcorn ceiling. Do Damon's views on the case change how I feel about him? I know they shouldn't, but that doesn't mean they don't. Being on opposite sides of something again, something so massive — it triggers all the remnants of disappointment I've carried all these years.

It's not yet curfew, so technically I can roam. And I can't help but think, despite our scolding from Judge Gillespy, that the fraternization rules are not as imperative now that we have reached deliberations. I let out a weary breath and push myself up out of bed. I throw on a cream zip-up hoodie and painstakingly open my hotel room door. I peek my head out, looking right, then left. It's empty. Most of the jury is still at dinner, and I'm not even sure there's a bailiff at the post around the corner by the elevators yet.

I plod carefully to Damon's door and put my ear to it. Silence. I knock gently, then instinctively look to the right to see if

George peeks his head around the corner. Nope. I tap my knuckles against it again, slightly stronger. Still nothing. Dejected, I turn and lean against his door.

Eventually, I give up. But I can't seem to go back to my room. I stare at my door, envisioning another night of rolling around restlessly, of staring at the inoperative TV. Instead, I take a chance and head to the stairwell.

On the second floor, the door to the presidential suite is slightly ajar. I step inside, closing the door behind me. The lights are off, though there is still a bit of daylight insisting its way in through the sheer curtains. My eyes catch on the patio door, also open. Shit. What if the maid is on her break again? My hand instinctively curls around the door handle, ready to make a stealthy escape. But then I realize there is no maid cart to be found and there is no smoke billowing across the glass. I take a cautious step forward, then another, then another, until I'm squeezing through the opening of the sliding door and onto the terrace. There sits Damon, staring out at the strip mall below. He looks incredibly sexy and invitingly cozy in his black sweatshirt and dark jeans.

He looks up at me, as if my eventual appearance were inevitable. "Hey," he says.

We silently stare at each other, neither inviting nor retreating.

"Sit," he says, finally. It's not a demand, rather a calm invitation.

I sink into the Adirondack chair beside him, attempt to find a comfortable position in the too-low seat, the cold of the splintered wood further jolting my adrenaline. We both watch as two employees exit the back of the Verizon store, laughing over something on one of their phones.

The silence lingers, and I recognize that just last night, less than twenty-four hours ago, we were one. The thought sends my heart racing in an emotion I can't quite decipher.

"You didn't eat," I say finally.

He shrugs. "Wasn't hungry."

We are quiet again, our attention on the alleyway below as if immersed in a theater show.

I have things to say. Of course I do. But part of me feels too deflated to try.

"Two things can be true, you know." His words break into my thoughts as he stares steadfastly in the direction of the alleyway. "She — Margot — she can be who you think she is, who you needed her to be. She can be the strong, independent woman, the symbol of the healthy relationship you needed over the years. And she can also be guilty."

I look at Damon. I don't know if he's talking about his mom or Margot, but I have to believe it's both. He is not reckless with his emotions or words. I know this to be true. As true as how he makes me feel.

Two things can be true.

We can have summer rain, the smell of jasmine, Kara's laugh, him and me. But, perhaps, only in the suspended state of our memories.

I can crave him more than anything I've ever wanted but also know too much complication exists between us to work.

"There's a lot I regret about us, Syd." He exhales as if he can no longer hold any of it in. He shifts to face me, and his elbow unintentionally bumps mine. I feel its friction run through me. His blue-green eyes look more green than blue, the way they do when he grows more intense or worried. "I wish we had more time back then. Leaving town, starting over, and never seeing you again was the hardest thing that had happened to me up until that point."

The pressure in my chest grows as he speaks.

"And even now, I wish . . ." He looks from

me to the alleyway and back. "I wish I knew how this all ends."

We stare forward again. The Verizon workers head back inside, and there's no longer any activity to focus our attention on. His statement is cryptic at best. How what ends? How the case ends? How we end? Does there have to be an end? Do I want there to be more? Is more even possible? When I went to his room last night, he tried to tell me. *I can't give you . . .* I hadn't let him finish. But I know what he intended to say. *I can't give you more than right now.*

We watch the final splinters of sunlight disappear behind the strip mall's tile roof.

"You abandoned me," I say, releasing my full feelings on him. He shifts his body to face me. "When everything happened you just . . . abandoned me. We were best friends." I thought when we had this conversation it would require several minutes of explanation and unloading. Turns out it's pretty straightforward.

He hangs his head, then forces himself to look at me again.

"I get we were young and there weren't many other options than for you to go, but . . . you could have stayed in touch. You could have called. You could have . . ." I stop myself because this list of things he could have done to show me he cared back then and over the last ten years is too long to be impactful.

"It's one of my biggest regrets, Syd," he says, rubbing at the back of his neck.

I can't help but catch on his choice of words. *One* of his biggest regrets. I egotistically want it to be his sole, biggest regret.

"I've thought about you every day for the last ten years. There are so many times when . . ." He pauses, looks out to the alley again as if it's the corridor to his memories. "When I wanted to reach out. When I got so close. But I figured the more time that went by, the more you hated me. And by the time I felt strong enough after Kara, so much time had passed." His eyes look so pained I have to force myself to stay focused on him.

"I understand," I tell him, because I do. I don't like any of it, but now that I know what happened after, I understand it. Two things can be true after all.

"No, you don't," he says, and I'm surprised by his response. "If I'm being completely honest, I couldn't separate you from your dad. As much as I wanted to, as much as I knew his actions had nothing to do with you, I . . . I just couldn't separate it. What happened, it robbed my family of so much.

That last year of Kara's life was so consumed by it. I was afraid I'd look at you and only feel anger. And I couldn't bear that. I was a coward."

"I suppose I was, too," I say, because I'm ashamed to admit that I've rarely claimed my own responsibility in all of it. "I could have reached out, I could have told you how I felt at any point, but I put it all on you."

He shakes his head, and I can see he's about to tell me I have no reason to blame myself, or something similar, so I speak again before he can.

"What was it like?" I ask, my voice coming out like a delicate vibration.

We face each other.

"What was it like, having parents who cared about you so much?" I feel silly for even asking. I'm in my mid-twenties, it shouldn't matter. But, being back with him, I know it does.

His lips part, and I see my brokenness reflected in his face. He swallows hard and doesn't break eye contact. "I'm grateful for it. But also, I took it for granted. The way we do when things are good, I suppose. And then after what happened with your dad, it all felt fake. Punitive. And after Kara, none of it mattered anymore. I had to forgive my mom. It took a long time before I saw it for what it was, a mistake she will regret for the rest of her life."

He turns to the strip mall again, and I continue to evaluate his face. Something has shifted. Something subtle. Like one candle in a sea of a hundred flickered out. It's all too clear. The last year of Kara's life was marred by the remnants of our parents' affair. And I am a biological reminder of that fact, no matter how many years later, for him and his family.

"How come you never mentioned your baby sister before today?" The anguish in his face makes me see how betrayed he feels as a result of my omission.

"I don't know," I say. I bite the inside of my lip when he turns to me. We've shared so much. *He's* shared so much about his life with me. Any time I'm not fully honest with him, it feels unfair. "I guess because I don't view her as my sister fully. I mean, she's my mother's daughter, but the life my mom has now is so far removed from me and the life we once had together. I guess I just don't feel particularly close to her."

Even as the words emerge, I hate myself for saying them. They are honest, yes. But I am complaining about my sister, a baby, when Damon beside me would give anything to have his back. I try to tell Damon all my regrets through a look of wide-eyed sadness. That I'm sorry for what happened to him and his family, and that I regret my own separation from the family I still have.

"We can't seem to stop hurting each other," he says. It's not a statement or a plea. It's a realization that I can see him mentally calculating — a supporting argument for why we can't be together.

I desperately want to argue the point, but the lingering thought that we are on opposing sides of this jury, it nags at me like a persistent itch I can't quite reach. He's right. We do keep hurting each other. And after ten years, there's no room left on my body for the scar tissue of him.

Even if we can't be together, in this moment I care only about his heart and our now connected hands atop the arm of his burgundy Adirondack chair.

"All the lonely Starbucks lovers," I say quietly, and he huffs in some semblance of a quiet laugh. I squeeze his hand.

We sit in silence, watching the day fade, our fingers firmly intertwined. I came to find him today, largely to ask about the trial, to try to understand how he could believe Margot is guilty.

But now, I can't seem to make any of it matter.

44.

Burden of Proof (n., phrase)

1. the responsibility of a party to present sufficient evidence to support their claims or assertions beyond a reasonable doubt
2. my best friend

Day two of deliberations kick off unexpectedly. Gray Man — Stanley — stands as soon as we have settled into the deliberation room, proclaiming he has something to say. We all look on, awaiting an insightful monologue.

Xavier holds out today's banana, still green at its base, and when Gray Man ignores him, he leans across the table and pointedly tosses it in front of him.

Stanley's fingertips press against the table, palms raised, forming his hands into cones as he leans. The front sides of his suit jacket flop loosely in front of him. His face holds the same grimace it has since the first time I saw him.

"This case has dragged on for two damn weeks," he gripes. "Reach a decision. Do it soon. I've got elsewhere to be." He drums his fingertips against the table, then sits back down with an actual Scrooge-like *humph,* looking between Xavier and the banana. After contemplating a moment, he shifts and reaches forward. Then, in an act of pure defiance, he picks up the banana, peels it, and takes a long bite, staring down Xavier as he does.

Not exactly what I was expecting.

"What if it was you?" Tamra says, her voice hard but kind.

"Excuse me?" Stanley says, turning to face her, still chewing.

"What if it was you," she repeats, holding his eye contact. "On trial for murder. Your life on the line."

Stanley rolls his eyes.

Tamra continues in the face of his flippancy. "Those two kids, they lost their father. And, depending on what *we* decide, they could lose their mother, too. If we are going to possibly orphan those children, you can be inconvenienced enough to take it seriously."

A spike of pride invades my chest. Tamra's motherly demeanor is somehow firm but nonthreatening, an uncommon mix that makes the jurors pay attention, whether out of outright respect, or fear of looking like an ass if they don't, unclear.

It takes fifteen minutes but, undeterred, Xavier finds a new banana. Despite it, we volley between respectfully taking turns speaking and talking over one another heatedly, the unsure quiet of day one deliberations expeditiously replaced by heated anarchy. We've all felt it — the trapped pressure that needs release. I am momentarily grateful for the blown top two nights ago, then immediately try to shove all remnants of my night with Damon from my brain.

Midday, we take a new vote, and I'm surprised to find two previously undecided jurors are now voting not guilty. I imagine Tamra's verbal lashing of Stanley has something to do with it. We are now five guilty, six not, and one undecided.

Today, I once again remain quiet, though my discomfort grows at the direction of deliberations as day two wears on.

"Margot one thousand percent got that house manager, Gloria, to do it," Cam says defiantly as we circle the drain again. Somehow, the conversation always leads back to this point. "That woman would do anything for Margot. Did you see the way she looked at her?"

Damon, for his part, is also largely quiet today. I wonder if it's because of some unspoken truce we've come to about not wanting to argue about this case or if he's simply no longer interested in advocating his point.

After three more hours of back and forth over the same points and two additional votes, I feel a bit hopeful as Gray Man shifts his vote to not guilty. It may just be that he's voting with the new majority, but I'll take it. Now, Xavier, Cam, Kate, and Damon remain the last guilty strongholds.

The room grows quiet, weariness setting in within the group. We have sat on the cusp of the end for so long now but have ceased any forward motion just shy of the finish line. And with evening fast approaching, the notion of having to spend another night sequestered hovers ominously.

Tamra, to my delight, is not only vocal, but both her demeanor and points are compelling. "Is the most salacious thing true?" she asks, her voice sharp. "Or is it that we want the most salacious thing to be true because it's more interesting? And we've grown accustomed to the entertainment of it all. We are not writing the most interesting plot for the future Lifetime movie about Margot and Joe Kitsch. We are determining the future of this woman's life. As the saying goes, the simplest thing is usually true. So, what is the simplest thing here? Is it that Margot somehow convinced an employee of hers to *murder her husband* for her, planned this whole thing out, and went about the morning with such carefree abandon that even her *best friend* couldn't detect a change in her? Or is it that Joe died of natural causes? A simple, unfortunate death."

I nod appreciatively.

"Think about it," Kate (the *Only Murders in the Building* one) states when Tamra is done speaking, completely disregarding her comments. "Margot finally got sick of him cheating on her, holding her business over her head, and figured it was her only way out after she had built a proper name for herself. She didn't need him anymore. And knowing the eyes of the media would be on her, she convinced that Gloria to do it, so she would have a solid alibi."

A few heads around the table nod. My throat constricts. This is far harder than I imagined. I think about my time at work, negotiating settlements between two angry parties, both of whom feel deeply wronged by the time they are seated in front of me. I've always thought I am good at my job because I am the opposite of threatening or intimidating. I don't try to strong-arm anyone into something they don't want. I *know* I've got negotiating skills, and that's what this deliberation needs now.

"I think we're losing sight of what's important here," I say, fingers gripping the table's edge.

"What was that, Sydney?" Xavier asks. He hands me the banana.

I have the room's full attention.

I better deliver.

I look around at each of the faces in the room. What does it say about them if they change their minds from what they've believed up to this point? That if they could be wrong about this, they could be wrong about other things, and *that* is perhaps the scariest of realizations.

There isn't enough time, nor do I have enough influence, to cause them to question themselves in this way. But I don't need them to question themselves. I need them to question the prosecution's case.

Looking at their weary faces, I think trial fatigue has pushed everyone so far that they mostly care about being done. About leaving this room and this case and moving on with their lives. About having an interesting story to tell about an experience others will never have access to. I can't blame them, either.

"We have one charge, and that's to determine if D.A. Stern has proven *beyond a reasonable doubt* that Margot murdered her husband. It is not to determine if it is *possible* or even if it is *probable,* but to determine that there is enough evidence to prove beyond a reasonable doubt that she has done it." I walk them through the case again, point by point. Is there a world where the theories of her guilt could be accurate? Sure. Of course. But I remind them again of Durrant Hammerstead's words, knowing it's the crux of our deliberations. *Beyond a reasonable doubt.* That is the standard that must be reached. And there is simply too much to doubt.

Cam interjects, "Yeah, but there's too much evidence to simply ignore."

"Nobody is saying to ignore it," Tamra chimes in. "But we have to weigh that evidence against what we have been tasked with here."

I nod as Cam seems at least momentarily mollified. "From the beginning of this trial," I continue, riding the wave of adrenaline coursing through me, "we've been asked to see Margot as this . . . this insignificant simpleton plucked from obscurity, who had no capabilities beyond securing a wealthy husband to support her. But then we're asked to believe that once she gained some prominence of her own and decided she didn't need him anymore, she masterminded a plan to murder him without leaving any solid evidence behind." A few heads nod around the table. "But which is it? Is she a naive, incapable woman who relied on Joe? Or is she a cunning manipulator capable of persuading an employee to murder her husband? How can she be both?"

Damon's words from last night infiltrate my brain. *Two things can be true.* I shake the thought loose.

The eyes of the room still on me, I continue. "We have been repeatedly fed this archetype of the 'black widow,' a scandalous woman who leverages her sexual prowess to lure men in and then uses them to get what she wants. It's tired, quite frankly. Which scenario is more plausible? And while much has been made of Joe choosing Margot, let's not forget that *she* also chose *him.* And when she did, she gave up a lot. She deferred to his career, his ambitions. She did all those things because she loved him. And the only thing she loved more than him are those kids."

I reflect on my own mother, our complicated relationship. Her missteps and my lack of grace when it comes to her. What all of it might mean for Genevieve. "I can't imagine a mother murdering her kids' father, unless she believes that father will do them significant harm. Margot herself testified that Joe was a good father. Her face lit up when she said those things." I shake my head. "There's no way she would do that to her children. *Especially* given her estrangement from her own parents." I swallow hard. "And despite D.A. Stern's unfounded insinuations, we've been given no actual indication of mental health concerns or extreme narcissism in this case, which would be the only logical reasons to commit such an act."

Tamra nods, her eyes heavy but attentive.

Cam leans forward, elbows pressed against the table, hands clasped with sincere concentration. Even Stanley is focused on me, the most engagement he has shown the entire trial.

"But, even so, everything I have just stated is instinct. Opinion. If we intend to take a person's freedom, we cannot simply rely on our gut instincts. There must be *no reason-*

able doubt in our minds.

"Sure, it's more interesting, exciting even, to think of her as this mastermind, as Tamra said. But the notion that we would destroy this woman's life and further traumatize her children because some part of us desires the more salacious version of events, well, I know I couldn't live with that. There is insufficient evidence to support the 'more dramatic' version of events. What we personally believe happened is irrelevant. The only question that matters," I reiterate, "is did D.A. Stern *prove* that Margot was directly responsible for Joe's death, *beyond a reasonable doubt*?"

There's weighted silence for a good two minutes, everyone avoiding eye contact with one another — except for the eye contact I force between myself and each juror, attempting to, through my unforgiving stare, imbue them each with the question I hope they are asking themselves. Was the case adequately made that Margot is responsible for Joe's death, or is that what I want to believe happened because it's more interesting?

People stare at the wall, at the table, at their notes, contemplating. I've done what I can to eliminate a near-impossible self-evaluation, placing the emphasis on D.A.

Stern and the prosecution instead. My only hope here is that, while they may not be willing to admit to their own biases, they *can* admit a poor showing on D.A. Stern's end.

There is one connection in the room — between Damon and me. It's sharp and cutting. We stare at each other, his blue-green eyes stabbing at me with an intensity that creates a rush of instant heat along every inch of my skin. A lot is swirling in him. I break our connection first.

Xavier clears his throat after a long silence. "Should we . . . take another vote?"

There's a line of nods around the room, some more confident than others. One by one, we voice our votes. Some hesitate, some don't.

I am perhaps the most shocked person in the room as the vote proceeds.

Xavier raises his willful eyebrows as the room awaits the last vote. Damon gives his response, and I don't know if his vote means he is confident or just done.

After it comes, Xavier clears his throat again, and I instinctively swallow. The weight of it all is lodged in my windpipe, too.

He rises from his seat, uncharacteristically timid. "I'll . . ." He trails off, the heft of the last few minutes pressing on him. “I’ll let the guard know.”

45.

Verdict (n.)

1. the decision given by the jury or judge at the end of a trial
2. the grand finale

Xavier stands, relishing the courtroom's full attention. For the first time, the eyes of the gallery release Margot and instead grip Xavier, then Judge Gillespy, then follow the sheet of paper the bailiff delivers back to Xavier.

"I will warn the court," Judge Gillespy states, gavel in hand, "when the decision is read, I expect the same level of order I've demanded for the entirety of the trial." Her eyes rake along each bench. When satisfied with the compliant hush, she addresses Xavier. "Please read the verdict."

Xavier takes his moment of greatness. He looks around the courtroom as if memorizing each face, finally landing on Margot standing at the defense table. He holds the paper delicately in his hands, as if it may combust if pressed against too firmly. He clears his throat, looks down, stares at the words silently for a moment as if it's the first time he's reading them.

Xavier speaks the verdict and the courtroom bursts. It's not an exclamation of cheer nor a swell of disgust. It's a burst of finality, of anticipation popping, the long-hanging question finally answered. Judge Gillespy pounds her gavel and asks for quiet.

In my peripheral vision, I see D.A. Stern throw his beloved ballpoint pen at the table and it bounces to the ground. I take in the motion, but it's inconsequential. Because I'm really only watching her. Margot opens her fists and smooths the skirt of her dress twice, a palm at each side. There's a look of approval, as though her expectation all along has been met. She doesn't smile, though. Why would she? She's still down a husband. But she is free. And I helped do it. We are — Margot and me — momentarily connected. We make brief eye contact before she turns to embrace Durrant Hammerstead.

I assess the other members of the jury as

they take in the scene. I have to believe some or all of them changed their votes just to be done, aligning with Tamra and me solely because they viewed us as the most passionate and least likely to bend. But as my eyes catch Cam's and he gives me a nod, lips pressed together in what looks like satisfaction, part of me believes they felt implored to follow the court's call to the letter of the law.

Judge Gillespy enters the verdict and thanks us for serving our civic duty. We are ushered out of the courtroom through the same back door we've used throughout the trial, just as the gallery exits through the main doors. I almost feel as though *I've* been declared not guilty, going from lock-down to suddenly free.

Now that the long-standing question about what will happen to Margot has been answered, a new one takes its place. With the trial over, will Damon and I cease to exist, too?

I head to the restroom — the one just off the judge's chambers away from the public entrances — to catch my breath before we the no-longer-jury pile into the passenger vans that will return us to the Singer Suites for the last time to pack our things.

Alone at the sink washing my hands, I

stare at this new version of myself, thinking about what comes next. Part of me wants to tell Damon I don't care if he's bad at relationships. That I know he is hesitant about us because of our history and everything he has been through. That he is terrified of hurting me. That we can figure it all out if we really want to. I don't know how we'd spend holidays or tell our parents without taking them back to those memories they'd all rather forget. I want to believe we could. But there's another, larger part of me that knows relationships end. And if Damon and I are bound to end again, I'd rather it be with longing than animosity.

I run my hands through my hair, halting when I see Margot exit the farthest stall and make her way to the sink beside me. Her heels click against the linoleum, each step hitting like a vicious stab. She doesn't make eye contact, rather goes about her business as if I am not here. I openly stare.

"Hi," I manage.

She smells like citrus and jasmine and maybe some spicy vanilla mixed in. We make eye contact through the mirror as she dabs her hands with a paper towel. I look on awkwardly as she presses that same paper towel delicately at the corner of her mouth, then at her right temple. It's silent for an uncomfortably long stretch, and I contemplate leaving before I lose all dignity gawking at her. Before I can, she says, "You were the one," and it takes me a moment to register her words. Even as I do, they don't make sense. When I continue to silently stare, she goes on. "I knew when I saw you that first day that you'd be the one who'd come through for me." She goes back to evaluating herself in the mirror. "It only takes one. That's what Hammerstead kept saying." She shrugs and huffs a sharp exhale. "I guess he was right."

Her comments should fill me with pride that our connection wasn't one-sided, that she relied on me the way I had come to once rely on her. But her words have a different effect. They make me feel used.

I continue to watch as she tosses her paper towel into the waste bin beside the sink and then turns toward the door.

"Can I ask you something?" I voice into the echoey space, the words rushing out of me like water from a faulty faucet.

She turns to face me, and though she says nothing, I take her acknowledgment as acceptance.

There are so many questions I want to ask her. *What has this trial been like for you? What will you do now? Are you happy?* Did

Joe die of natural causes? How are your kids? Did you do it? But I take this opportunity to ask the question that has pestered me since the start of the trial, the one I've assigned some bit of personal affect to. I turn to face her, pressing my backside into the sink. "Where did you go when you went missing in St. Cloud when you were sixteen?" I want to know she's far beyond this thing that happened in her formative years.

Margot observes herself in the mirror, tilting her head this way and that, taking herself in at different angles. Then she stops and makes eye contact with herself square on. Despite having answered on the stand, she humors me. "I was on a coke binge with my secret older boyfriend in Minneapolis, living on canned pinto beans and Fruit Roll-Ups. When the coke ran out, I went home and told my parents I couldn't remember what had happened." She starts toward the door again, heels spearing the floor. I note her recount here as a similar but more pernicious version of what she said on the stand.

I stare at her, unblinking. "Did you take that from Joe's movie?" I finally muster.

She looks back at me at the restroom door, eyebrow arched as she evaluates me, perhaps seeing me for the first time. Her face tells me she realizes she underestimated me. And perhaps I imagine it, but she looks a bit impressed.

"Maybe," she says with a shrug, her lips pulled into an almost haunting smirk.

I've thought about how I will explain Margot to others. To Mel, when she asks me about the trial. I anticipate it will be the first, most pressing inquiry, over and over again: *What is she like?* Throughout the trial, I haven't been able to quite figure out what I might say in response to that question. But now, here, I realize she will likely always be a layered mystery. The human equivalent of a turducken.

Regardless, I don't need to know the real answer. It doesn't matter. Whatever happened to her, whether it defined the rest of her life, it doesn't change my reality. It doesn't change that what happened to me at that age did define me in many ways.

Many, but not all.

With that, Margot Kitsch saunters out of the restroom in a perfectly straight line.

46.

Public Opinion (n., phrase)

1. the collective judgment, attitudes, and perceptions of the general public regarding a particular issue, event, individual, or organization
2. the real jury

There's a collective hum of enthusiasm as we pile into the vans and head back to the Singer Suites. They are excited it's over. Anxious to get back to their real lives. But as I ride in silence beside Damon, I can't help the sinking feeling in my gut that my time with him is ending. When he looks over and offers a small smile — big for him — it feels conciliatory. By the end of this quickly disappearing day, our . . . whatever it is . . . will be over. I almost wish we were perpetual jurors, full-time courtroom decision-makers, so I could wake up every day and sit beside him in that jury box forevermore.

Thirty minutes later, George taps at my open hotel room door. "For you," he says, holding up a freezer-sized plastic bag. "Thank you," I say, retrieving the bag, immediately pulling my phone from it and holding down the power button.

"You're the most subdued one so far. That number ten next door practically tackled me when he saw his stuff," George muses.

"It was kinda nice actually, being cut off."

George smiles, the wispy hairs of his mustache jutting out over his upper lip. "You're not the first person to tell me that," he says, before giving me a nod and heading out.

After a quick review of my text messages to determine there's nothing urgent, I open Google and type in Margot's name, where I am assaulted with pictures and stories. There are myriad articles and posts, most of which, unsurprisingly, view Margot, and now the jury, negatively. They're saying she bought her way out of it. They're saying jury members fed into the hype.

The link I click first is a video of Margot standing outside the courtroom, addressing reporters. It must have happened right after the verdict and our subsequent bathroom run-in as we were headed to the hotel.

Margot stands, razor-straight, flanked by Durrant Hammerstead and his team. People shout and clamor to take pictures. She is poised, seemingly basking in her moment. She speaks into the row of microphones, instantly silencing the crowd.

She thanks the court, talks about looking ahead to the new normal with her children, asks for privacy. Before she has finished, reporters and paparazzi are hurling more questions. "If you didn't do it, who did? Was it Gloria Pembrooke?" "Are you dating anyone?" "What will the Malibu Menace do next?" "Will you return for season eight of *Authentic Moms*?" "Who are you dating?" "Do you believe Joe died of natural causes?" "Will you comment on the affairs?" "Who do you want to date?" The barrage of questions keeps coming, even as she is ushered down the courthouse steps and whisked away in a black town car.

As I place a folded sweater into my suitcase, there's a knock at my open door. Damon leans against it, left foot crossed over his right ankle. His fingers curl over the top of the doorframe, and it's an all-too-similar stance to the one he struck the night we spent together. He's wearing a royal-blue L.A. Rams sweatshirt that makes him look both incredibly sexy and familiarly boyish at once. Just seeing him leaning in my doorway makes me wish there could be one more day — or night, specifically — in this bubble. But it's more than just the sex, of course. It's *him.* All of him.

"Hey," he says, remaining stationed against the door. He twirls an origami animal, this one a bear, I think, then sets it on the dresser.

"Hey," I say back. My first inclination is to whisper, to usher him in hurriedly and close the door behind him. But we don't have to sneak around anymore. And now that we don't have to, there's nothing we have to sneak around for. The irony of it leaves me wounded.

"Need any help?" he asks.

I shake my head. "I think I've got it." He watches as I struggle to close my suitcase and then comes over to help. He zips it easily and lifts it with one hand to the ground. There's no packing left to distract us.

"Right, well . . ." He reaches into his back pocket, pulls a folded paper from it, and holds it out in front of him. "For you."

I take the paper from his hand. When I look up at him in question, he breaks our eye contact.

"Don't read it now," he says, pressing his

fingers into his front jeans pockets. "Later. It's just a final jury duty note. Seemed like an appropriate send-off, to write one more."

I attempt to swallow the mass that has accumulated in my throat. "Thanks," I say, tucking the note and origami bear into the side pocket of my tote on the dresser. We stand at the foot of the bed, inches apart, silently staring at each other. There's so much to say, but also, nothing to say.

I want to tell him the other night was the best one of my life.

I want to tell him he's velvet as a person — textured but smooth, soft against my skin and heart —

But I don't know how to do this in the real world.

I know he doesn't, either.

I'm about to open my mouth to speak, but our past and present stop me. I know we wouldn't work anywhere but here. Not with all our baggage. *We can't seem to stop hurting each other.* His words from the presidential suite just last night shadow my desires. I don't ever want him to hurt again.

"Can I get your number?" he asks as if he's never had it before, as if we didn't exchange hundreds of thousands of texts and GIFs throughout our once friendship.

I sigh. "You don't have to do this," I say.

He squares up across me. "Do what?"

"Pretend like this is something. I get it."

"What do you get?"

"I get that this was just a temporary thing." I motion back and forth between him and me in the short distance between us. "You don't have to get my number."

"I *want* your number," he says. His blue-green eyes twitch once, and I almost believe him. I want to give it to him. Part of me says we can be friends. But I know I'd never be satisfied with that. And pretending would keep me in this unfulfilled place.

"Look, let's just call this what it was. A nice, in-the-moment distraction from the case, and an opportunity for some closure on what happened all those years ago."

His eyebrow twitches up, and if I didn't know any better, I'd say he is disappointed. He opens his mouth to respond, and I lean forward, wanting to know what he has to say. He pauses.

The conflict of us is palpable. Past versus present. Hurt versus longing. Reality versus hope. Head versus heart.

Before he can get any words out, Cam arrives at the door and steps in. "Can you believe we're finally outta here?" He taps the backside of his left hand against Damon's chest playfully.

Damon doesn't take his eyes off me, even as Cam looks back and forth between us.

"Am I interrupting?" he asks.

Damon clears his throat. "No, man, you're not," he says stiffly, breaking our stare. The grimness of his face before he looks away leaves me gutted. "Why wait? We should get going," Damon says to Cam.

"Definitely. See ya, Syd," Cam says, though we've not exchanged contact information, so I doubt it.

"See ya," I say anyway.

We are taken in the two shuttles back to the courthouse, where my car is still parked in the underground garage. For one of the only times, Damon and I don't sit together on the ride. I don't quite know whose decision it was — Damon climbed into the shuttle, and though we made brief eye contact, I moved my bag off the seat so Tamra, ahead of him in line and eyeing the open seat beside me, could take it.

We exit the shuttles in the courthouse garage to avoid any remaining bystanders or paparazzi.

"Goodbye, dear." Tamra hugs me warmly — so tight and genuine that I don't want her to let go. "Give that baby a kiss for me," she adds, cupping my wrist. I think of Gen and how much I want to see her.

"I will. I'm so glad you can get back to your grandbabies now."

She smiles, her eyes more watery than usual. I try to imagine loving something so much that the sheer mention of it brings tears to my eyes.

I think to exchange numbers with her. The reality is, I would likely never reach out. We have such different lives. And she's busy with her family. But still . . .

"Tamra," I say, "would you want to exchange numbers? Maybe grab coffee or something sometime?"

She smiles, her eyes still full. "I was going to ask you the same thing but figured you wouldn't be interested in an old lady like me."

"Let's make sure we actually do it. Get together, I mean." I enter her number in my phone and text her so she has mine.

We hug again, this one a bit fuller than the first.

I say quick goodbyes to the others, including Cam again. I thank Xavier for being a truly excellent foreperson, all the while keeping account of where Damon is, who he's talking to — ensuring he hasn't slipped out.

Soon, the group has dwindled to just a

few, and Damon and I find each other, as though it were inevitable.

47.

Jury Discharge (n., phrase)

1. when the jury is released at the completion of a trial
2. I guess I'll go home now

The courthouse garage's dim light flickers overhead, and the moldy smell reminds me of our time on the roof of the Singer Suites. Damon and I have edged closer, each waiting for the other to speak first. There are so many versions of what happens now. Maybe we offer quick goodbyes, skating over everything — past and present — with our hands up in defeat. Maybe we gaze longingly at each other for what feels like hours. Maybe we do say all the things we aren't meant to say here, the words that keep us tied to this complex and hopelessly tangled thing. No matter what though, I know this is goodbye.

"Can I ask you something?" I say finally,

taking a small step toward him. He does the same, and now there are just a few inches between us. I instinctively look around to see who might be watching, but then I realize it again. It's over. We can do whatever we want. Part of me liked it better when someone was always telling me what to do and where to go.

He nods once, and the gesture alone is like a punch to the gut as I silently say goodbye to that nod.

"Do you think that if . . . if we hadn't been stuck together these last few weeks — eating every meal together, sitting next to each other in the jury box, sequestered — do you think we would have come together the way we did?"

He moves his right hand from his front jeans pocket to the back of his neck and looks down at the ground as he contemplates. "I'd like to think we would have," he says, eyes casting back to mine. "But if I'm being honest, I don't know."

I know this is the probable answer, though still, I hoped it would be different.

"And just so you know, it's not because I wouldn't have been attracted to you or *wanted* to. It's just . . . I wouldn't trust myself not to hurt you. The fear that it might ruin one or both of us again always held me back. And then after Kara died . . . having you around, it would have brought a complication me and my family wouldn't have been able to take." He runs his right hand down his cheek to his chin.

But it's been ten years, I want to tell him. *We're adults now.* Logically, I know this. But it doesn't stop me from agreeing.

I swallow around the sharp point in my throat. He's armor and paint, just like the rest of us. Perhaps I just didn't want to see it. Perhaps I would have known if I had a little more life under my nails. As I look into his eyes, I know his feelings are much more complicated than mine. He can't think of us before without Kara. That time was her time, most of her life. I know he still holds anger toward my father. Kara died just a year later. And that last year of her life, as he told me, was largely consumed by the aftermath of the affair instead of making treasured memories with her.

"Right, well, thanks for being honest," I say, curling my hand around the handle of my bag. "Besides, relationships that start under intense circumstances never last, right?"

He smirks, perhaps the biggest semblance of a smile his face has made on its own. "Isn't that what Sandra Bullock says to

Keanu Reeves in *Speed*?"

The memory of us on his couch watching that movie together only adds to the preemptive loss I already feel about us leaving this parking garage, separately. "Yes," I say. "But there's gotta be some truth to it, right?"

He doesn't respond. Perhaps our connection *is* simply some intricate trauma bond.

"Let me," he says, outstretching his hand when I reach to lift my bag.

I release, and he follows me to my car a few feet away.

I close the trunk, and we both rest a hand on the back of my car, lingering in uncertainty. As I look from him to the cracked concrete and back, there's a strange dichotomy. I know him deeply, but also, I don't. There's so much I don't actually know. His career progression and how he ended up as a transportation engineer. If he's a fan of frozen chocolate-covered strawberries. How many kids he wants, if any.

But I do know other things about him. Intimate details.

I know how he takes his coffee, having stood next to him in the breakfast line for two weeks — a splash of creamer, no sugar. I know he makes origami animals because it reminds him of Kara. I know he cups the back of his neck when uncomfortable or thinking. I know every tattoo and its meaning. I know the one, directly over his heart, is *us.* I know that even as kids, he's always been my quiet protector. I know his forehead kisses. And I know his glorious weight on top of me.

Which are the things that matter? I suppose none of it does now, because the decision has been made for us. He doesn't know how to do this. And, I suppose, neither do I. We would have died a slow, meandering death. And that is the thought that keeps me from bringing it up again.

I tuck a pointer finger into the dent of each of his cheeks, gently pull them up as I had on the roof, this time with far less vigor. He allows his face to go limp in agreement.

"Goodbye, Damon," I say, my voice quiet yet booming in the confinement of the garage walls. I don't move right away. Instead, I stare into his eyes, wanting something from him — anything — but knowing equally I should just get in the damn car.

I let go of his face.

He looks for a moment like he may kiss me, like he's strongly considering it, then instead swoops me to his chest, arms wrapped around my back in what truly feels like a bear hug. I close my eyes and inhale his worn saddle scent once more, knowing I'll smell remnants of him in random moments in the days or perhaps even weeks to come. I have a flash of the idea of taking this sweater off and shoving it into a Ziploc bag to preserve his scent, or purchasing a bottle of his Trail cologne to spray on my pillow.

"I like big butts in a can of limes," he says, and we share a knowing smile.

"A classic," I say, arms still wrapped around his neck.

He leans back in. "Bye, Syd," he says into the crown of my head, and I feel the reverberation of his voice in my neck and stomach. He presses his lips to my forehead, and I savor it.

I release first, knowing if not now, I might make a fool of myself begging this man to fall into something potentially toxic for us both, something neither of us is quite ready for. I give him a small, pathetic attempt at a smile and climb into my car. I catch him in the rearview mirror, and he looks almost distraught. *If it's the right decision, why is it so hard?* I think on repeat as he steps aside when I start the engine. He gives the trunk two taps, and I pull backward slowly. I give him another errant half smile as I pull past him, shift, and leave him behind as I emerge into the darkening evening.

And then the tears come. I curse myself for them outright, angry at myself for allowing this level of emotion for someone I can't have, who is perhaps even more unavailable than I am.

I drive slowly, perhaps a bit overcautiously, still feeling the remnants of the caged life I just came free from. I try to enjoy it. I do. I roll down the window and place my elbow against the door. I turn up the radio and then shift to a news station, taking in the details of the world I've reentered. But, I quickly find, it's dishearteningly the same. So-and-so billionaire did such and such egomaniacal thing. Fingers pointed sideways instead of up. Two pop stars dead of overdoses. Violence. I turn the volume down, the noise rattling inside my head like a nail in a tin can. I'm still confined, just in a larger net with more potential perils.

As I exit the 101, turning onto Sunset Boulevard, now just a few miles from my apartment, my thoughts shift from Damon to Mel and how I might possibly relay any of the details of the last two weeks to her. No matter how I try, I know I won't be able to accurately describe all the emotions and details and, perhaps most unexpected and yet undefined, how it all changed me.

48.

Post-Trial Disclosure (n., phrase)

1. after the trial, parties involved in the case may communicate about the outcome of the trial, potential next steps, or other related matters
2. emotional catharsis

"Come in, tell me *everything*!" Mel squeals as she embraces me at our apartment door before I've stepped inside, nearly knocking me over with enthusiasm.

"Well, hello," I say, sliding past her when she releases, noting it's the most excited anyone has ever been at my arrival.

I peel out of my jacket and throw it over the back of the couch, looking around our little apartment. Mel has tidied up, her usual collection of shipping boxes noticeably missing from beside the door and the typically full kitchen sink bare.

"You cleaned," I say.

"Yes, I cleaned. I wanted you to have a welcoming return. Did it work?" She takes me by the wrist and leads me to the couch.

"It looks great," I tell her, truly appreciative.

She stares at me with her gummy smile and throws her hand into dizzying circles in the air when I don't immediately begin speaking. "Well?" she says, eyebrows raised, the familiar movement rumpling her forehead like that of a bulldog.

"Look," I say, smiling back at her, placing my hands on her knees in an attempt at a loving gesture. "I promise, I will tell you everything. I will."

I stand, and she follows suit, frowning.

"But first, I really, more than anything, need a bath. The hotel had a standing shower only, and I wouldn't have soaked in a tub at that hotel anyway. So give me an hour, and I'll be all yours. Deal?"

Mel presses her bottom lip into her top one, a poor attempt at hiding her dismay. I smile, having missed her face, even this particular discontented grin. I wrap myself around her before she can argue, squeezing her in both because I've missed her and in a preemptive strike. She sighs, and I know I've won this mini-battle.

Alone in the bathroom, I unpack my toiletries as the tub fills. I eye the corner of the folded note Damon handed me at my hotel room door, sticking out of the front pocket of my tote. He gave it to me only two hours ago, but already the last two weeks have begun to recede into a dreamlike memory. I'm crestfallen by its breakneck transformation.

I sit on the tub's edge, running my fingers along the warm water, finding its temperature inviting. Drying my hand on the towel I have already rolled up to place under my neck, I pick up the folded paper again. It is inevitable that I will unfold his note, that I will read whatever parting words he chose to record and subsequently feel a range of emotions that all succumb to one. Disappointment. Because no matter what he wrote, I already know how our story ends. The story of us is a ghost roaming the halls of the Singer Suites, unsuitable for the real world.

The truth is I could have been convinced. I could have been convinced that despite our parents, despite our shallowly buried feelings about the past, despite how we both have and have not fully moved on, despite our fears of hurting or being hurt by the other again, we could have found a way to be together.

I sigh, carefully unfolding the paper, bracing for the impact of his handwritten words. At first, I simply stare at the shapes on the page, not yet interpreting any meaning. The too-sharp curves of his *S*'s and the barely there tail of his *y*'s that dip well below the line. Each letter, each word, slanted slightly backward, as if afraid to offend if upright. Eventually, I allow myself to go there.

SYD, it begins, and I immediately hear his strikingly deep voice in my head, see the peacock-feather blue green of his eyes and the vortex of his chin dimple, as if he is speaking the words — his words — directly to me.

BEFORE THE TRIAL, I HOPED FOR A QUICK END SO I COULD GET OUT AND MOVE ON. BUT SLOWLY — NO, THAT'S NOT TRUE. IT WAS QUICKLY . . . FAR TOO QUICKLY — I FOUND MYSELF WISHING FOR IT TO CONTINUE. TO DRAG ON DAY AFTER DAY SO I'D GET TO SPEND MORE TIME WITH YOU. THE FACT THAT WE WERE THROWN TOGETHER AGAIN — I HAD TO BELIEVE IT MEANT SOMETHING.

AS THE TRIAL WOUND DOWN, THERE WAS AN UNSETTLEDNESS IN ME I HADN'T FELT IN A REALLY LONG TIME. IT'S SIMILAR TO THE

FEELING I HAD AFTER KARA DIED. LIKE MY SKIN WAS MORE ALERT AND EVEN THE AIR HURT. IT'S NOT PAIN EXACTLY, BUT LIKE AN OVEREXPOSURE. I'LL BE HONEST WITH YOU, SYD. I DON'T LIKE THAT FEELING. I DON'T KNOW WHAT TO DO WITH IT.

BUT THERE'S SOMETHING ELSE I NEED TO TELL YOU. I WASN'T HONEST WITH YOU ABOUT HOW KARA DIED.

I stop reading, stare down at the now full tub. Something in me stills, instantly knowing what comes next is a threadbare glimpse at his soul. I don't know if I can handle it. I read on anyway, knowing that if he wrote these words, I owe it to him — to whatever we had — to read them.

WHEN I FIRST TOLD YOU ABOUT KARA, I DID WHAT I ALWAYS DO. I TRIED ON A DIFFERENT VERSION OF EVENTS TO SEE IF THEY FIT IN A WAY THAT MIGHT ABSOLVE ME. TO SEE IF PRETENDING HER DEATH HAPPENED UNDER DIFFERENT CIRCUMSTANCES, AWAY FROM ME, WOULD MAKE THE ACHE OF IT LESS. IT NEVER WORKS, THOUGH. THE TRUTH IS, I AM THE REASON SHE'S NOT HERE. IT'S MY FAULT.

I stop again, regard my breath, follow it down to my lungs, then back up and out.

Regardless of what admission comes next, I know he's carried this guilt around all this time. It's a burden far greater than the one I've held about our parents. He's had so much more pain, more challenge, more self-hatred.

I never knew.

And regardless of what comes next, I know it's not his fault. How could it be when he loved her so dearly?

I look down at the page, letting the words take form again.

I TOOK HER TO THE BEACH. THERE WAS THIS GIRL, LAUREN. I WANTED TO IMPRESS HER, AND I ASKED KARA TO COME ALONG, KNOWING LAUREN WOULD FIND MY RELATIONSHIP WITH MY LITTLE SISTER ENDEARING. I WAS USING KARA TO GET SOMETHING I WANTED.

I WASN'T WATCHING HER.

I wince, and a tear hits the page. I smear it away quickly, not wanting to hurt the ink.

FOR FOUR DAYS, WE DIDN'T KNOW WHAT HAD HAPPENED TO HER. WHETHER SHE HAD BEEN TAKEN, WHETHER SHE HAD DROWNED IN THE PACIFIC. FOUR DAYS, AND I COULDN'T EVEN TELL MY PARENTS ANYTHING OTHER

THAN SHE WAS JUST GONE.

I DIDN'T GO HOME FOR THREE OF THOSE DAYS. I SEARCHED. I SAT ON THE BEACH AND CRIED. MY PARENTS HELD OUT HOPE THAT THERE WAS SOME REASONABLE EXPLANATION, BUT I COULDN'T IMAGINE ONE.

FOUR DAYS LATER, WE GOT THE CALL. HER BODY WAS FOUND BY FISHERMEN NEARLY THIRTY MILES FROM WHERE WE WERE THAT DAY ON THE BEACH. SHE HAD DROWNED SO QUIETLY AND QUICKLY THAT NOT EVEN THE LIFEGUARDS SAW HER.

I KNOW I CAN NEVER MAKE IT UP TO MY PARENTS, BUT I'VE TRIED — IN BIG WAYS AND SMALL — EVERY DAY SINCE.

I'VE HAD ONE RELATIONSHIP SINCE THEN. AND, LOOKING BACK, IT WASN'T A REAL ONE. NOT BECAUSE I DIDN'T CARE ABOUT HER OR BECAUSE I WASN'T COMMITTED. BUT BECAUSE I COULDN'T LET HER IN. I DECIDED IT WAS BEST TO GO IT ALONE, TO AVOID, WELL, EVERYTHING. YOU'RE THE FIRST PERSON WHO MADE ME WANT TO ABANDON THAT WAY OF THINKING. TO JUST . . . JUMP. YOU CRACKED ME WIDE OPEN, SYD, AND IT HURTS — THAT CRACK. I DON'T KNOW HOW TO DO IT. I JUST DON'T KNOW HOW TO BE A GOOD PARTNER TO SOMEONE. LOOK AT OUR PARENTS. IT'S NOT LIKE THESE THINGS WERE MODELED FOR US.

SO, I GUESS THIS LETTER IS MOSTLY TO SAY THANK YOU. THANK YOU FOR OPENING ME UP AGAIN, EVEN IF JUST TEMPORARILY. FOR ALLOWING ME FOR THE FIRST TIME IN YEARS TO CONSIDER SOMETHING ELSE. SOMETHING MORE. I'LL ALWAYS BE GRATEFUL. AND WHO KNOWS, MAYBE EVENTUALLY, I WILL JUMP. AND WHEN I DO, I'LL MOST CERTAINLY THINK OF YOU.

DAMON

P.S. THIS LETTER IS:

☐ ☐

SWEET SAPPY

I wipe the tears from my cheeks and stare at his note, wondering where to store such a thing. If to store it at all. For now, I set it on the small shelf above the counter.

Not only has he been carrying Kara's loss but the guilt of that loss with him all these years. I can't imagine what that has done to him. Here, I thought our parents' affair was the driving force of his hesitation, of his *being bad at relationships.* But it is so much more. His hesitation about building something with me in the real world becomes even clearer. How could he devastate his parents like that again, bringing me around, when he believes he already caused so much hurt by losing Kara?

I remain on the tub's edge, regarding the URL he has handwritten on the bottom of the page, separate from the rest of the text. I grab my phone and, through tears, type it into the search bar. Up pops a page full of sugar-free gummy bear reviews. Even in heartache, tears blurring my vision, Damon manages to make me laugh.

When I exit the bathroom nearly an hour later, Mel sits up from her corner of the couch and scoots forward until her feet meet the ground. "Human again?" she asks, closing the book in her lap and tossing it to the cushion.

"Just barely," I say, plopping down beside her. I take in Mel's painting on the wall, towering evergreens transitioning to the outline of a stallion. I close my eyes. It reminds me of Damon. This notion cycles me through my multitude of emotions again. I look away so I don't break.

Mel leans forward and pushes a mug on the coffee table toward me, light steam rising from the speckled ceramic. I pick it up and take a cautious sip, the heat warming my upper lip and nostrils. "Is there rum in this?" I ask, sniffing after I've swallowed.

Mel shrugs. "It's a celebration, right? I mean, Margot is free! *You* did that!" She taps her black *AMOM* mug to mine.

"*We* did," I say, thinking of the eleven other faces around the courthouse table during deliberations.

"Then why do you seem melancholy?"

"Melancholy?" I repeat, raising an eyebrow.

"Yeah. I've been reading too much Sylvia Plath with you gone, leave me alone."

"There's this guy . . ." I state cautiously.

"Yes!" Mel cries, slapping the back of my upper arm across the sensitive under-fat.

I pull my arm forward and rub it.

I tell her everything. Well, almost. I tell her about his face, his tattoos, his brooding build. I tell her of his tender care throughout the trial, always ensuring I was okay. I tell her about his sister and how the loss of her made him both more tender and guarded. I tell her about the rooftop and the mix of euphoria and lust and connection I felt in that instance that I've never experienced before and would be hard-pressed to believe I'll ever feel again. That it was one of those rare experiences you know is defining as it happens rather than just in hindsight. I tell her about our history. That he was my best friend. In some ways, how he never stopped being my best friend. I even recount our parents and the abrupt end to our relationship back then.

"Wow," Mel says when I'm finally done, her silence having stretched longer than it perhaps ever has as I relayed it all. She looks up to the ceiling and then shakes her head vehemently. "Tell me again why you can't be together?"

I sigh, sip from my spiked mug again. "There's just too much. How would it work? If we, say, got married, are we to expect our families to come together? His mom and my dad, sitting at Christmas dinner together while Mr. Bradburn looks on?"

"That's twenty steps ahead."

"Yeah, but why start something we know can't be anything lasting? Besides, his letter makes it pretty clear he's unavailable."

"All the things you just described? The fact that life put you two together again? And under such intense circumstances? It all sounds like pretty compelling reasons *to* be together."

"I don't know. I think I just need to be alone for a bit. Process everything that just happened. With Damon. With the trial. Figure out how to be good on my own before jumping into something." I think about Margot. How she met Joe as a relative newbie in L.A., barely an adult and, in many ways, not one at all. That one decision — being with Joe — how it changed the whole course of her life.

"What the actual fuck?" Mel says, slicing into my thoughts. I look over at her and then follow her stare to her phone.

"What is it?" I ask, curling myself behind her to look at her screen. There's a picture of Margot with the word *BREAKING* across the top, spliced with someone else I recognize immediately. Below it, a caption that causes me to grip the back of the couch.

It reads: "Margot Kitsch has moved on with *Authentic Moms* cast member Tenley Storms's ex-husband Harry Tucker."

Though I can't seem to make Margot's dramatics matter after what Damon told me in that letter, I start scrolling through my own phone, reviewing the news. It's a nice distraction from the feelings I'm not ready to face.

Unsurprisingly, there's a flurry of opinions in the *Authentic Moms* world. Most of the other Moms have already commented, with opinions largely *not* in Margot's favor. "Homewrecker," reads one from Meredith Dixon. Tenley Storms goes for the jugular, posting a picture of a dumpster on fire, "No caption needed" written beneath it. Even Alizay's post is cryptic at best. A picture of the ocean with an overlaid quote: "Instead of cleaning my house, I'm just going to move to another one."

As if she didn't have enough already, Margot Kitsch's list of enemies has just grown tenfold.

49.

Settlement (n.)

1. a resolution between disputing parties
2. an opportunity to start again

The next day, I reach my mom's house a little after nine a.m., the best window between Genevieve's naps. Though I should technically be returning to work today, I called in sick. It would have been too abrupt a transition, I decided.

When I arrive, my mom is surprisingly put together — a full face of makeup, hair pulled back neatly in a banana clip, and wearing a trendy T-shirt dress. To someone who knows her less, the line of baggy blue under her eyes indicating terminal burnout and middle-aged motherhood might even go unnoticed. A quiet ache flows through me when I see her.

"Sydney," she says warmly, embracing me at the door before I've stepped inside.

I follow her into the living room, where Genevieve lies on her belly in a playpen, arms and legs flailing behind her in a Superman-esque spread. When she notices us, she raises her head and smiles through a chinful of drool. I'm struck by how different she looks. I saw her just three weeks ago, but she's noticeably plumper, her face having transitioned from uncertain newborn to chubby baby. I have the immediate sense that I need to see her more frequently — frequently enough that her daily changes have the chance to go unnoticed.

My mom and I sit on the blue-and-gray woven rug at the edge of the playpen.

"So, how was it?" she asks.

"It was . . . a lot," I say.

She taps my shoulder. "I'll bet."

Gen makes a noise, something between a hiccup and a burp, and it draws my attention.

"Do you want to hold her?" my mom asks.

"Sure," I say, recognizing that I very much do.

She leans forward and lifts Gen from her spot in the playpen. Gen coos and thrusts her arms stiffly about as my mom hands her to me. She's noticeably heavier, her body sturdier than before, like a dense pile of dough rolled tight. Gen looks up at me and smiles, then thrusts her head into the crook of my neck. I instinctively inhale against the top of her head. The tears come as swiftly as they possibly can.

"What is it?" my mom asks, placing her hand on my knee. Her eyes are wide with alarm. This is not something I do. I'm not emotional around her. I work tirelessly to not be seen as a bother of any kind, still. I shake my head, needing a moment.

"It's good to see you," she says once I've collected myself.

This time and space with her feels different. Maybe it was the time away. Maybe it's learning about Kara. Or maybe it's Gen and the need to do it all differently this time. I'm not quite sure, but what I do know is that for the first time in longer than I can remember, the unease I feel around my mother is slightly dissipated.

"Mom, I need to tell you something," I say. We've moved to the dining table, where Gen sits in Mom's lap as she attempts to spoon mushed avocado into her mouth. "Damon Bradburn was on the jury with me."

She shifts her attention from Gen to me. It's not necessarily surprise in her eyes but a remembrance. Her discomfort shows as her neck retreats into her shoulders. "Wow," she offers.

"Yeah."

"How did you feel about that?"

"It was good to see him. Really good."

"It's been a long time," she says, spooning mush into Gen's mouth.

"It has." I pick up one of Gen's burping cloths and hand it to my mom to wipe a trail of avocado from Gen's chin. "Do you remember his sister, Kara?"

"Yes, of course," she says. "Sawbayees," she adds with a smile.

I smile back. "Right. She . . ." I stop to swallow the lump in my throat so it doesn't crack my next words. "She died. Not long after they moved away."

She raises a hand over her mouth and instinctively looks at Gen. I look to her, too.

"That's awful," she says.

I tell her how — the real how — because Damon was right, people do focus on how. As I speak, I see it in my mom's face, her release of any residual anger over what happened between my father and Mallory Bradburn.

"All this time has passed, and we never knew." She shakes her head.

"I know. They cut ties with everyone

after." I've been thinking about it since Damon's last note. How did we never hear about it? An eight-year-old girl goes missing for four days from the beach and then it's confirmed she drowned? It certainly would have been reported on. How often have I seen a headline like it, not bothering to read the particulars? The thought that perhaps I did see it but hastily scrolled past the news without connecting it, without a second thought, makes my stomach roil.

"I should find Mal's number," Mom says, gently scraping excess avocado from Gen's cheeks with the side of the rubbery spoon. "Tell her how sorry I am." She looks at me. "You don't think it's too late, do you? To offer my condolences?"

I shake my head. "No, I don't think it's too late."

She gives me a smile that's more like a frown before picking up the jar of mashed avocado.

There are more conversations to be had, of course. Many more. I need her to know how much it hurt me when she left. I want her to know I felt unwanted as a child. And I want her to know how sorry I am for all my father put her through. I don't know yet if she can meet me where I am, but I am willing to try. In large part, for Gen.

I stay until Gen goes down for her second nap of the day, with the promise of a return on Sunday for lunch, when Caleb can join.

50.

Double Jeopardy (Fifth Amendment clause)

1. prohibits anyone from being prosecuted twice for substantially the same crime
2. dues have already been paid

Nearly six weeks later, I sit in traffic southbound on the I-5 on my way home from Sagebrook Farms. There, I spent nearly two hours with Athena, an all-brown Tennessee walking horse who I took to immediately. I hadn't ridden since my fall at Sagawa. After the trial, I felt the urge to do it again. And the fact that it smells like Damon there is a bonus.

Traffic comes to a full stop two miles from my exit. I sigh, accepting this route as the wrong choice, the evening rush hour creeping earlier into the afternoon each day. I can't drive anywhere without thinking of Damon thanks to the digital road signs. Sometimes they're straightforward. Sometimes they're funny. Sometimes they are so obviously Damon that my heart aches as I drive by, wishing I hadn't looked at all.

My phone beeps, and I glance at it in the cupholder. It's a text from my mom. I glance up at the line of unmoving cars and, knowing I shouldn't, pick up my phone. I can't help my smile as I take in the picture she has sent. It's Gen, who's crawling now, perched on her knees opening a kitchen cabinet. *Time for locks!* my mom's text reads. We text nearly daily now, mostly her sending pictures and videos of Gen and me reacting to them, but more and more I also share glimpses of my life with her. Speaking with a therapist these past few weeks has helped me come from a place of understanding rather than expectation with her.

. . . and baby gates and toilet clamps! I type back along with a laughing emoji.

The situation with my father has been harder. He's seemingly less capable of looking backward to understand what got us here and, moreover, that "here" is not an idyllic state. I'll be okay if it doesn't work out.

My phone pings again, and this time it's

Mel: *Margot's at it again!* she's written, with an accompanying link from BuzzFeed titled "Margot and Harry Step Out!" with a picture of the two of them, hand in hand, dressed to the nines at a Sea Save benefit. All I can do is shake my head.

I replace my phone in the cupholder and refocus on the road, still jammed.

Margot and Harry have apparently been together since well before the trial, though they managed to keep it quiet until the day it ended, when they released a joint statement about their coupling. "We did not ask for this, but love found us anyway," it read.

Internet sleuths did eventually make the same connection I did during the trial as they poured over court records and Margot's testimony in particular. It became a highly debated point online, how Margot referenced a piece of storyline from one of Joe's early movies in her testimony and what it might mean. Many, many TikToks were made of Fruit Roll-Ups and pinto beans being eaten together in the same bite.

They didn't believe her before, and they certainly didn't believe her after. But I'm inclined to believe they were never going to.

After inching forward a few hundred yards, I look up at the digital traffic sign ahead because I can't not look, wondering what it will be today. Perhaps something basic like a seat belt reminder or notification of a traffic delay. Maybe a funny pun referencing the Adele concert tonight.

I take in the digital sign overhead, the same one I've driven past hundreds, perhaps thousands of times. The same one thousands of drivers have potentially seen today. I stare at the sign for a long while, as if trying to make sense of it, though I already have.

Will you take a chance on me, or should I just keep chasing penguins? D.

Damon.

Six weeks after our last interaction, he makes this public declaration. I look around at the other drivers, unaffected. Of course they're unaffected. This sign is for me. *Only* me. He is thinking about us still.

I realize I'm not over my relationship issues. I may never be, fully. But I don't know anyone who isn't some semblance of broken. My eyes pool.

I pick up my phone to text Damon, as traffic is again at a full stop, realizing quickly we never did exchange numbers. I tap at the steering wheel, wondering how I might get to him, knowing I'm no longer willing to accept anything less than him.

■ ■ ■ ■

I arrive home twenty minutes later, eager to find him. I spent the remainder of the drive thinking of ways I might track him down, cursing myself for not exchanging numbers when he asked. I could find a directory for transportation engineers who work for the city. Maybe I could contact Tamra (as the only juror I did exchange contact details with) to see if she did the same with him. I could google him, which I have once again successfully avoided doing, this time post-trial.

But before I can do any of these things, my brain and body halt when I see the brute of a man standing at the lobby entrance of my apartment building.

He's already here.

I'm overcome with a rush of anxiety, fear, excitement . . . I'm not sure which is accurate.

I park and approach him as he leans against the lobby door.

"I thought I was the one who shows up at *your* door unannounced," I say.

He huffs. "Thought I should shake things up."

I take in every bit of him. He looks different after six weeks apart. His hair is cropped shorter, his skin a bit tanner than when I saw him last. But he's still gloriously the same, dressed for the unseasonably warm December day in dark jeans and a light blue Henley, the contrast making his eyes look more green than blue. Before me, I see the man from the trial, the boy from my past. I see all of it, like the still frames of a life where ten years didn't go missing.

He's so fucking handsome.

"I saw the sign," I say, stepping before him.

"I feel like I should have some Ace of Base song reference ready here."

I ignore his shot at levity, too taken with having him here before me. "How long has it been up?"

He shrugs. "Just today. I took a shot."

"Won't you get in trouble?"

He shakes his head. "It's worth a write-up."

I shake my head back. "Always the troublemaker, pushing boundaries, breaking rules."

"That's why I need you to keep me in line."

"Is that what I am? Your safety net for when you make questionable decisions?"

"No. You're the person who makes it more

fun when I do make questionable decisions."

We've both inched closer and now are practically touching. I take in his scent and tug at the hem of my cropped tee, attempting to loosen the wrinkles from the drive, realizing I likely smell like a horse. But then again, so does he.

I knew I missed him over these past few weeks. I've thought about him constantly. There's been a void I can never seem to fill, like a steady, unquenchable thirst or an irretrievable word on the tip of my tongue. The constant feeling that I've forgotten to grab my keys or unplug an appliance. But being next to him now, I didn't realize how much I really did miss him. How just having him standing here before me, I feel a wholeness I haven't felt, perhaps ever.

"How'd you know where I live?"

He looks down and cups the back of his neck with his palm, and I practically liquefy. I can't help but smile at how that small gesture is so distinctly him. How many times in those first few days of the trial I found myself jealous of the back of his neck, how much action it gets from his broad hand.

"Working for the government has its perks."

"You dug into government files?"

He smiles. A real one. I stare at his perfect teeth.

"No. I googled you. You weren't hard to find."

We stare at each other, our faces mirrored as they grow serious.

"I've got a shit ton of emotional baggage," I tell him, only now, for the first time, willing to admit it aloud.

"So do I," he says so matter-of-factly that I wonder if he's really heard me.

"I'm not sure I know how to do this."

"Do what?"

"Be with someone. Romantically."

He is quiet, and I wonder if I've misread the situation. Perhaps he's here with a different agenda altogether. But then he takes my hands in his. "You don't have to know. We will figure it out."

Is it really that simple? I'm sure the answer is no, but what if, through our actions, we can make it yes.

"Everything broken in me doesn't just change with the flip of a switch," he says, squeezing my hands gently in his palms. "But I want to try. With you. Having you to take care of, to worry about, to protect, it felt good."

"I don't need to be protected," I say.

"I know. Which makes me want to protect you more."

I swallow, give his words time to seep into every part of me. I want to feel them in the tips of my fingers and toes. "What changed?"

"I spoke with my mom. About Kara. You. About everything that happened between our families. We somehow stopped talking about her or anything real over the years. She told me her world stopped when Kara died, and the only thing that kept her going was the love she had for me, for my father."

His eyes swell before he adds, "And she told me it wasn't my fault."

I squeeze his hands. "I've done a lot of talking, too," I tell him. "I suppose I am lucky for the family I've got, even if it is a fucked-up version."

He smiles, and it's gone as quickly as it came. "I just want you," he says. "No matter what complications it might bring. I just want you." He repeats this last part with a grumbly whisper that awakens all the dormant winged things in my gut.

My free hand is now at his waist, fingers curled under the waistband of his jeans. I don't want to talk anymore. I want to show him how much I've missed him. "Come inside."

He grins.

I lead him into the lobby, and the heat quickly gaining intensity at my core makes walking difficult. As I usher him to the elevator, his hand behind me rubs gentle circles on the small of my back under my shirt. I swallow hard as his hand slides down, squeezes my ass over my jeans. The elevator doors open, and we are tangled together before they close. Thank God we are alone.

He presses me up against the side wall, his waist pinning mine. "I missed you," he whispers into my neck before his lips make contact. "I've always missed you."

He pulls back so our eyes can meet. *I know,* I think. *I know.*

Before there can be more, the elevator beeps and the doors open, Ms. Huger from two doors down standing before us, car keys in hand. She raises her eyebrows as she takes us in, mostly focused on me. Her chin tilts down slightly, and I can't help but think she looks pleasantly surprised. *I didn't think you had it in you,* the slight curve of her lips says as we pass each other.

I curl my fingers under the waist of his jeans and lead him to my door. He presses into my back, and I fumble with the keys as I feel his bulge against my backside. I unlock the door and turn the knob, then he kicks it shut after we step in. Finally truly alone, I fold my arms around his neck, and he lifts me to his waist until my legs are wrapped around him.

"Where's the bedroom?" he murmurs between kisses, his arms wrapped tightly around me, one against my back, the other under my butt. Just like in his room at the Singer Suites.

"To the right," I say into his mouth, and he follows the direction well, kicking the half-ajar door all the way open, collapsing me onto the bed as I say a silent thank you that Mel is at her studio for the next several hours.

"I'm sorry it took me so long to come to my senses," he whispers into my neck, then runs his teeth along its curve. "I won't make that mistake again."

Six weeks of fantasizing about his touch daily. My eyes roll shut as he licks up to my ear.

"Fuck," I groan, and I feel his lips expand into a quick grin against my jaw. I reach down and unbutton his jeans then unzip, rubbing the side of my hand against him as I do. His lips find mine, and his tongue pushes into my mouth in a gloriously forceful motion. He tastes precisely as I remember, like the man I've wanted since we were sixteen. In many ways, the one I wanted well before that, before I knew to want someone. I pull at the hem of his Henley shirt, and he sits up and removes it obediently. I look up at him, admire him, want him inside me more than I've ever wanted anything. I press my palm into the tattoo over his heart, feel it pulse.

He bends down to me and cups my face with his palms, brushing my lips tenderly with his. He whispers into my mouth, "I don't remember a me that didn't love you."

I look into his eyes. This close, they are opaque, and I can see all of him.

Him.

He is imprinted on me. He is the canon event, the core memory, the missing piece.

He is all of it.

I don't know how I lived so long without him, without this touch. But I know I wasn't doing much living in those years in between. He pins my hands over my head, reaches down and lifts my shirt, pulls it off, looks down at me with those peacock-feather-colored eyes full of loss, longing, want.

I slip out of my jeans and pull him down to me, the heat of his skin warming me from what feels like the inside out. He is down to his boxer briefs, and I tug at the waistband, letting them snap his skin upon release. Our eyes meet in mutual agreement, and we both scurry to remove our remaining layers. I reach for the bedside table, pull the drawer open, and grab a condom into my palm. We come together again, fully rid of everything but each other.

He presses his mouth to mine, and it's hungry, yearning. Just as I'm ready to grab at his hips and wrap my legs around him, he shimmies downward, his lips carving a trail down my neck to my chest. His lips play there for a few moments, his tongue flicking at my nipples, calling them forward. Then he continues down and my hands find his hair, pulling it into my fists as his lips trail down my stomach, then meander sideways to the jut of my right hip, then down again to my inner thigh. I throw my head back in anticipation, and he delivers without making me wait any longer, his tongue finding me. He grants me one long lick of his full tongue. I moan, loudly. Here, I don't have to hold back. He makes the motion again, and my body releases any remaining fragments of tension. My back falls more deeply into the bed, my legs fall open, and my head rolls to the side. I am his to do with as he pleases.

He does this a few more times, painstakingly slowly. Then, when I feel as though I may combust from the fiery sensation at my base, he takes my most sensitive part into his mouth and sucks. I arch again, all the tension in my body back, and I fight the urge to push him away from the intensity of the feeling. He presses a firm palm to my abdomen, holding me in place. My breath grows jagged as he sucks, his motion steady and consistent so my arousal grows at a breakneck pace.

When I cannot take it a moment longer, I tug firmly at his hair. He obliges, giving my clit one last long lick before rising to meet me again. "You," I huff as our noses touch. But I can't manage anything else. I can't even manage to finish the thought. The only thing I can focus on is the pulsing, empty ache between my legs. I take the opportunity and raise my hips to meet him. His breath comes more harshly, but he is solidly in control. His face still millimeters from mine, he reaches down between us and grinds his fingers against me for a moment, building more ache than I thought myself capable of. He rolls to his side to slip the condom on with his other hand. Then, finally, he is on top of me again. He aligns with me and, with his hand, inches himself inside me. I raise my hips again to meet him, and when he is fully pressed inside me, he releases his weight and pushes my hips back to the bed.

He fits so perfectly, so fully, I cannot fathom how I missed ten years of this. Before I can beg, he is pressing and pulling in and out of me, his pace quickening with each slick motion. I squeeze the curve of his backside, part urging, part steadying. He huffs into my neck, and the warmth and wetness make my skin feel as though it's melting into a puddle just below his mouth. His thrusts grow harder and more intense, which I didn't think possible, and for the next completely unknown to me number of minutes, he gives me everything.

I come undone, crying out as a flood of pleasure pools inside me. My vocalization pushes him over the edge, his warm release just seconds behind.

Summer rain.

The smell of jasmine.

Him and me.

I used to believe these things were the past. A suspended, ungraspable moment in time. But now I know they are alive in every bit of me — us — more organism than memory. They always were. They always will be.

We lie together for what seems like several hours, long enough for the sky outside to begin to dull. He holds me tight, as if afraid

I might leave. I don't ever plan to.

I roll to face him, unable to help my pointer finger as it gently traces the tattoo over his heart. "Why Prince Hamsterdinck?" I ask, the tip of my nail outlining the thin whiskers jutting from the right side of its face.

"You know why."

"I know it's *us,* which I love, but of all the things we shared back then, why this in particular?" I press my palm over the tattoo, only its furry sides visible.

Damon is momentarily thoughtful, looking to the ceiling, then lifting my chin with his thumb and forefinger. "Hiding that silly thing was the happiest I ever was in my life. Choosing the perfect spot to hide it. The anticipation of you finding it. The look on your face whenever you did *actually* find it." He huffs, the Damon version of a good-natured chuckle. "It was so . . . easy. Just fun. I wanted to bottle that."

We kiss for what feels like hours more.

"I should kick you out before Mel gets home," I say finally, eyeing my still-open bedroom door.

He groans.

"I know, I'm sorry. But if she walks in and sees this, well, trust me, it's for your own good."

He kisses my forehead, a long, deliberate press of his lips to my skin. “Okay,” he concedes.

I watch as he swings his legs over the edge of the bed, stands, and begins collecting his clothes from the ground. I watch his body as it twists, bends, flexes. He is exquisite.

“I can feel you ogling me,” he says after he’s pulled his boxer briefs into place.

“Good,” I respond.

He picks up his jeans and, as if remembering something, reaches into one of the pockets. “I have something for you,” he says. He pulls out a small piece of folded paper. He hands me the note, his face tender, jaw muscle flexing. I unfold it carefully, flicking my eyes up to smile at him as I do. A note from Damon Bradburn will always make me melt.

WILL YOU BE MY GIRLFRIEND?

☐ ☐

YES NO

☐

STILL PASSED OUT IN A CLOSET

I look up at him again, and he is smiling, just barely, holding a pen out toward me.

Epilogue

Three Months Later

We sit around the six-seater rectangular dining table with a familiar walnut finish, and I can't ignore the warmth at my center.

I don't want to.

Across the table, my mom and Caleb hold matching positions — right elbows perched atop the wood, chins cupped with open palms and loose fingers. Both wear doting smiles, their eyes positioned on the seat beside me, where Damon has Gen in his hands. He holds her just below the armpits, his hands providing more comfort than rails. She is seated on the table, facing her parents, her floral jumper puckering at her midsection where she bends. Though her body faces forward, her head is straining backward to look at Damon. She won't stop looking at Damon. Or cooing at him. Or smiling at him. He grins at her — the type of movement his typically unyielding face only rarely offers — and she comes undone, a hiccupy laugh infecting us all with giggles of our own. It has taken her decidedly less time to determine him worthy of full, heaping adoration than it did me.

It's only the second time we've all gotten together. Still, Damon fits into my family in a way that, up until the end of the trial nearly four months ago, *I* didn't even fit. My mom dotes on him like she owes him some retribution, though of course she doesn't. But I think she feels guilty that we lost each other back then.

My mom and Mallory Bradburn, while certainly not what I would deem friends, have spoken, thanks to my mom reaching out to give her condolences about Kara, which led to an apology from Mallory. She had apologized back then, but it was all still too raw for my mom to accept. She has accepted it now.

The holidays came and went, and we spent them with our separate families. And now, we have nearly a full year to decide how to handle them the next time around.

Damon jabs a thumb into Gen's side over and over again in quick succession, and she laughs, this high-pitched, breathless belly laugh that sounds like a car starter ticking. Like Kara's. My mom laughs so hard in response she has to wipe a tear from the corner of her eye.

Gen catches her breath and looks over her shoulder, anticipating when Damon might get her again. He threatens a few times, moving his hands close and then whipping them away. This gesture alone makes her body shake with giggles. Here, with Gen, is the softest I ever see him, outside of the intimate moments we share in the bedroom where his eyes are fixed on mine, his vulnerability pulsing through his touch. I watch the two of them, the warmth at my center spreading to my limbs, my face, like warm tea in my veins.

She's a powerful gift I didn't know I could give him but am so grateful I can.

We stay far too late into the evening, long after Gen is asleep, having moved to the living room with glasses of Caleb's favorite cab franc in hand. It feels more like a double date than a visit to my mother and her husband, something that would have filled me with anxiety just months ago.

Three months of dating Damon has taught me a lot, too. I have learned that I don't like other people preparing my array of breakfast beverages, even if it is a thoughtful, shirtless man. I've learned that sharing a bed with Damon means his foot will always find mine. I've learned I, too, enjoy unwinding at the end of the day to cute animal videos narrated by Morgan Freeman. And I've learned that two things can indeed be true at once. You can be broken but also come together with someone else to make something whole. It's not that he's a missing part of me, rather, he helps me see the parts of myself previously drowned in unmet expectations.

He's always on my left when we sit on the couch, just as he was in the jury box. When he knocks at my door, I still get the same rush as when we were sneaking around the Singer Suites.

He still doesn't speak a lot of words. But he says a fucking lot with his mouth. And, because he's still better on paper, I have a new shoebox full of notes from him that sits in my closet just beside the one from when we were kids, everything from a full page of words on our one-month anniversary to sticky notes that simply say hi, scrawled and left stuck to my kitchen counter.

It was only six years, I used to tell myself. We spent more time apart than actually together. But they were *the* six years. The years when we transitioned from children to young adults. The years we were carefree. The years we stretched and grew and had to duck our heads under the ceilings we no longer fit below. The years when the world first disappointed us, and we clung to anyone who made us feel less alone, less incongruent with the world. The years we learned that life can take as much as it gives. And the people beside you in those years are the ones imprinted in a way others can't be. They are the first. The deepest. Everyone after is stacked on top but with less hold.

Damon was the first.

He is, still, the deepest.

Now, a week after that last visit to my mom's, we sit with Mel at the bar around the corner from his place, sharing a basket of fries and another of lemon pepper wings. Damon has unbuttoned his dress shirt down to the white tee below. On Thursday nights, he volunteers as a guest teacher at a local after-school nonprofit giving lessons on key points in history. He loves it, and it has served us many a hot-for-teacher fantasy in the bedroom.

"Do you think Gen liked the blue owl?" he asks as he pops a fry into his mouth.

I picture how she clung to the plush bird as my mom carried her upstairs to bed last week. "You know she did," I tell him. "But you don't need to bring her a gift every time we see her."

"Sure I do."

He hasn't yet come face-to-face with my father again. It will likely be months before he does, if at all. Damon says he is willing, which, for now, is more than enough.

Mel reaches for a wing, holds it in front of her from both ends like an ear of corn. "That girl is gonna be so spoiled," she muses, grinning at Damon, then me. "So what are our plans Monday night?" she asks through a bite. "Are we going full theme party, or quiet night on the couch with wine and takeout?"

Damon looks from me to Mel. "It's season eight premiere night," I tell him. "I can't wait to see how Tenley and Margot interact now that Margot is dating Harry."

"And Margot! Post-trial. I am *dying* to know how they will handle it on the show. They were filming with the other Moms while the trial was going on," Mel adds as if I don't already know these details.

During the trial, there was an online petition demanding Margot be booted from the show; it got more than two hundred thousand signatures, but to no avail, and was started by none other than Tenley Storms.

Damon leans back in the booth. "Ah," he

says, clearly attempting to distance himself from this discussion. I'm pretty sure he will continue to avoid watching any episodes — old or new — of *Authentic Moms of Malibu.*

I, on the other hand, am pleased to say that, despite all the revelations, turbulence, and unsnarling of the trial, I am still, proudly, a superfan. I no longer hold any expectations of Margot, other than entertainment. I played a part in whatever comes next for her, helping to allow her a "next." There aren't many people who can say that.

As for Tenley Storms, leaked early shots from this new season show the moment Tenley found out about Margot's relationship with her ex, Harry. She accepted a FaceTime from Alizay, of all people, who broke the news. Tenley's face and neck turned scarlet as she dropped the hot curling iron in her hand to the bathroom tile, narrowly missing her bare toes. "I'll kill them both," she'd snapped. That small clip was enough to set the internet ablaze with hundreds of thousands of comments and shares, building expectations that this will be the biggest season in franchise history.

"Quiet night on the couch," Mel and I both affirm in unison.

"Better viewing experience," I say.

"Less distraction," she agrees.

Damon spreads his arms over the back of the booth, shakes his head amusedly. He finds a lot of things about my relationship with Mel amusing. Today, it is that we (Mel and me) share the same side of the booth instead of him and me.

I feared Damon and I would be a disappointment in the real world. That without the feeling of having been cut short all those years ago, the tension of the trial, the secrecy of our fledgling romance, or Cam's gummies, we would be just another boring couple hanging on to something that was once electrifying. But he is so far beyond the guy who sat beside me during Margot's trial. I've gotten to see so much more of him. I've seen who he is with someone to love and care for. I've seen his supple heart.

I reach across the table and place my hand in front of him. He grins, just barely, his chin dimple pursing as he leans forward and cups my hand, squeezes. We stare at each other across the booth, and it is indeed electric.

"Get a room," Mel says, dangling two fries above her mouth before reaching for them with her teeth. It effectively kills the rumble of excitement between us that made me ponder if I should pull him into a bathroom stall for some privacy.

We sip our beers in unison. Damon's eyes wander to the TV above my head and the fourth quarter of the Lakers game. We've reached a mutual agreement regarding what we watch — he gets NBA games, I get non-*AMOM* reality TV when there's no game on.

I'm taking another sip from my pint glass when his eyes widen, still staring at the screen. "Shit," he mutters.

My phone, lying on the table beside me, begins to shake and sound incessantly, ping after echoey ping. But I don't have to open any messages to know what is happening. All eyes in the restaurant are glued to the TVs above the bar as Margot Kitsch's face is plastered across them. I don't need to ask the bartender to turn it up, either. He already has.

On the screen is a live shot of Margot, dressed in lavender silk pajamas and a matching floor-length robe, being escorted out of her twelve-million-dollar sprawling Malibu mansion (formerly hers and Joe's) by police, dainty wrists cuffed behind her back. She is notably stoic as they lead her away.

Behind her, barely visible, Gloria Pembrooke sits crying on the front step.

Just as I'm about to share this revelation with Damon, something stops me — the racing byline at the bottom of the screen.

Margot Kitsch has a second dead partner.

ACKNOWLEDGEMENTS (N.)

1. an author's statement of indebtedness to others
2. thank-yous

Younger me always wanted to sit on a jury for a high-profile case. I was fascinated with the idea of a behind-the-scenes view of the justice system and the drama of it all (as Olivia Benson taught me to expect). Alas I was never selected, and now I'd be less enthusiastic, but writing this book was, in a lot of ways, my opportunity to live out that inexplicable dream.

For anyone in the legal field, it will come as no surprise that liberties were taken with courtroom proceedings, rules, and the progression of the trial. Apparently, jurors can indeed legally hook up if they choose to.

I must first thank Elisabeth Weed, Sophie Cudd, and the entire Book Group team.

You all are the absolute best and the epitome of audacious support. Thank you for everything you do and for all the ways you go above and beyond as agents.

Thank you to my team at Harper. My editors — Jackie Quaranto, Caroline Weishuhn, and early on, Emily Griffin. Thank you for every piece of feedback and advice. You each made this book exponentially better. My team at Harper extends well beyond my editors, and I'm so grateful for Doug Jones, Amy Baker, Heather Drucker, Emi Battaglia, Lisa Erickson, Daniel Duval, Michael Fierro, Milan Bozic, and so many more.

I must thank Micaela Carr, my former editor, continual champion, and most importantly, friend. I know you will catch all the Bravo easter eggs.

A few courtroom experts allowed me to ask many important and mundane questions. Thank you, Meryl Francolini and Kathy Murray, for the courtroom and trial insights. Audrey Ingram, thank you for the tremendous ideas. Many of your notes made their way into this story.

Alex Kiley, Christelle Lujan, Jill Beissel, and Madhu Messenger, thank you for your early reads and notes. I'm so lucky to have each of you in my circle.

My writing group, the Mouse Jigglers, I'm

grateful for each of you.

My daily support comes from my husband and kids. Kris, thank you for being my safe space to groan, vent, and contemplate my questionable life choices.

Sawyer and Sienna, don't worry; your names are on this one, too. Thank you for always cheering me on. And Sienna, thank you for your editorial help. Your seven-year-old perspective is unorthodox and restorative.

Thank you to the village that supports me whenever and however they can: Mom, Dad, Raj, Elizabeth Lyons, LaTrenda Lawson, Melati, Beth, Lindsie, and so many more.

For the real heroes, the road sign writers. It should be noted that the feds have banned "funny" roadway signs starting in 2026, so let's enjoy them while we can.

I also have to thank the Amazon gummy bear reviewers. This content really is Good as Gold.

The list of Real Housewives and other Bravo stars is far too long to name them all, but thank you and, of course, Andy Cohen for countless hours of entertainment over the years.

And, the best for last, thank you to the readers. Every book you buy, lend, or borrow directly supports an author in living their dream. I'm so grateful to you for helping me to live mine. You are Gone with the Wind Fabulous, each and every one of you.

ABOUT THE AUTHOR

Neely Tubati Alexander is the author of women's fiction and rom-coms you can escape into with a smile. Her books have been featured in *Cosmopolitan, Parade,* and *Elle,* with her novel *In a Not So Perfect World* chosen as a *Good Morning America* Buzz Pick. Her work has received starred reviews from *Kirkus Reviews, Publishers Weekly, Library Journal,* and *Booklist.* She lives in Arizona with her family.

For updates, visit her Instagram @neely alexanderwrites.

The employees of Thorndike Press hope you have enjoyed this Large Print book. All our Thorndike Large Print titles are designed for easy reading, and all our books are made to last. Other Thorndike Press Large Print books are available at your library, through selected bookstores, or directly from us.

For information about titles, please call:
(800) 223-1244

or visit our website at:
gale.com/thorndike